MW00856409

The Mists of Niflheim: Eschaton Cycle
Gods of the Ragnarok Era Book 2
MATT LARKIN
Editors: Clark Chamberlain, Fred Roth
Cover: Yocla Designs

Copyright © 2017 Matt Larkin.

This is a work of fiction. Names, characters, organizations, places, events and incidents either are the product of the author's imagination or are used fictitiously.
All rights reserved, including the right to reproduce this book, or portions thereof, in any form.

Incandescent Phoenix Books
mattlarkinbooks.com

MIDGARD
THULE
NIDAVELLIR
LAPPMARKEN
SVIARLAND
JAMTLA
DALAR
UPSAL
NJARAR
GANDVIK SEA
OSTERGOTLAND
NORREYYSKE
SKANE
MORIMARUSA
CIMBRIA
ARUS
SJAELLAND
BURGUNDAHOLMR
BRETLAND
REIDGOTALAND
LAALAND
RIJNLAND
MENZLIN
XANTEN
HUNALAND
BAIA
SWABIA
STYRIA
VALLAND
AQUISGRANA
IDAVOLLIR
OUTER MIKLAGARD
ANDALUS
KARJUBA
MIDDLE SEA
VANAHEIM
SERKLAND CALIPHATE

EXTRA RESOURCES

For full color, higher-res maps, character lists, location overviews, and glossaries, check out the bonus resources here:
https://tinyurl.com/y47j3gcj

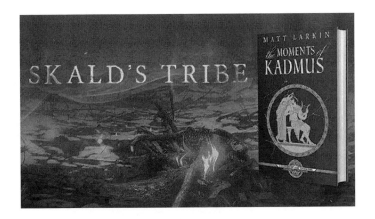

Join the Skalds' Tribe newsletter and get access to exclusive insider information and your FREE copy of *The Moments of Kadmus*.

https://www.mattlarkinbooks.com/skalds/

PROLOGUE

*I*n the throes of deep meditation, the mind was left to wander, touching Realms beyond the physical, much as beings from those Realms touched such minds in dreams. Some, practiced in the Sight, sought to harness such sojourns by deliberately projecting their consciousness and soul into the Astral Realm. Loki found such an idea abhorrent, not least because it would reveal him to the innumerable enemies and otherwise hostile forces awaiting him there, and yet, still he practiced a meditation very much akin to projection. One which allowed him to walk in a space outside of time and between any Realm, where lay darkness and a void in all directions save forward. There waited the Norns, standing before a well that itself stood nowhere and, in a sense, everywhere.

Loki had sent Odin here once, in an attempt to goad the man toward his urd—a Northern word derived from the name of one of these very Norns. Urd—Fate—demanded a great deal of Loki, but then it asked as much if not more from Odin. And if the Norns wanted to be found, one might find them in any number of liminal places separating the Mortal Realm from the Otherworlds.

Neither hurry nor hesitation guided his steps toward them. They, of all beings, had patience, if such a term might even be applied to those existing outside of time. In truth, the further one travelled from the Mortal Realm, the less meaning time held. Or, perhaps, the *more* meaning, as the tafl board became the tapestry of history itself.

"You wished to see me," he asked when he finally stood but a few feet from the hooded women.

"Who is—"

"Who was—"

"Who shall be your master?"

Loki folded his arms over his chest, scowling at the exasperating entities. "I am, as ever, a servant of history."

"Perhaps in the darkness—"

"Blinded by the light—"

"He finds himself mired in the delusions of Eros."

Loki kept his face expressionless, much as their comments made him seethe. These beings without time also existed without love or, in the sense the Aesir understood it, without even life. Thus they could not begin to understand the callings of the heart or the power it held over the living. They, in their self-superior ignorance, insinuated Sigyn was his weakness, when, in fact, she gave him the strength to face the ineffable abominations he had borne witness to in both the past and future.

Without knowing she was out there, born again to sustain him, he might have crumbled under the weight of darkness.

Such truths so far exceeded their comprehension as to not even warrant discussion. A better topic lay before them, in any event. "The Destroyer grows stronger more swiftly than we anticipated, barreling towards his destiny in great, perilous strides."

"Anticipation is—"

"Was—"

"Will be a limitation of the linear."

Loki spread his hands. "You speak of limitations, yet, as always, you still need me. It leaves one to wonder if you do not point out such supposed weaknesses to cover your own."

"We begin to believe—"

"Indeed to know and to see—"

"A man who grows too attached to the Destroyer—"

"Whose fate remains ever unchanging and bound in darkness."

"All worlds end, taking with them the one who must bring them down."

Did they suppose he would try to spare Odin his fate?

Would that he could, for Loki truly did love his blood brother. But the innumerable millennia of his life and bitter destiny had taught him that the Wheel of Fate was implacable, and history could never be denied. It plodded forward in a relentless tide, oblivious or uncaring of lives it swept under its waves.

As before, and as always, Odin was damned to his fate.

As were they all.

PART I

Year 118, Age of Vingethor
Fourth Moon, The Cusp of Winter

1
----

*W*aking or sleeping, it mattered naught. Odin could no longer tell the difference. Or perhaps he was caught between the two. His time with Gudrun and Frigg had blurred all lines while it opened his mind, until at last he could no longer say whether the things he saw were real or figments of his own tortured mind.

But he *did* see them. The Sight tormented him.

Borr. His father. Once the strongest man Odin had ever known. Head tall, the flicker of torchlight illuminating his short red beard as he wandered Unterhagen in the night. Odin had never known why his father had gone to the village that night—but he knew now whom he had met.

Jarl Arnbjorn of the Itrmanni looked up sharply at a crash from outside. He and Borr stood before a fire pit in a small house. They had been debating something Odin had not caught.

"Trolls?" Borr said.

Arnbjorn blanched and fled from the house. Borr groaned and drew his sword.

Outside, a pair of men waited for him, each staring off

nervously into the thick mist, spear in one hand, torch in the other. "Arnbjorn and his men ran off," one said.

In the mist, a man screamed. Another crash echoed.

Odin's father had gone out into the night, into the mists, to protect the villagers. Gone out ... and never returned.

"Father ..." Odin mumbled, half-aware he was talking in his sleep. On the edge of his mind he knew Frigg had placed a hand on his forehead, hoping to comfort him against visions she couldn't see. He could shut them out, leave them behind. Gudrun had taught him such things—to close his mind to the Sight. But then he would never see his father again, not while Odin walked Midgard. And, given his newfound immortality, that could mean forever. A separation so final, so absolute, keeping Odin from reuniting with his parents and his ancestors, and he had taken the apple without giving it a moment's consideration. Idunn had made him a god. But there *was* a price—solitude. He was a god doomed to walk the World without those who had shaped him.

So he could not resist the vision, the call to see what his father had seen. The temptation to understand a life that wasn't his own, but yet felt so close.

BORR and his men were greeted with more screams as they trod into the village. The people no doubt feared a raid, unable to conceive that other men would come just to help them. No. Not simply other men. Borr. Odin's father had been a hero, hadn't he? Not just to his sons, not even just to his own people. To Mankind. And Odin had failed to live up to his father's legacy.

Snow crunched under Borr's knees as he knelt to

examine a depression. In the torchlight, in the mist, maybe he couldn't see it for what it was. But Odin could see. A footprint, one so massive his father's whole body could have crouched in it. The footprint of the frost jotunn Ymir. Was any of this real? Or had Odin's mind built this vision from the bits and pieces he had learned in visiting the remains of the village, and from the tales Loki had spun of these events?

Odin's heart pounded in his chest, apt to burst through his ribs. He wanted to scream at his father, shout a warning back to that time. A warning his father would *never* hear.

Instead, the silence was broken by a crash like thunder as a house exploded, spraying splinters and thatch over Borr and his men. Through the mists, Odin could only see to the jotunn's waist as he trod forward. But he knew the thing, the blue tint of his skin, the iron plates covering his legs. Borr spun, leveling Gungnir against a foe far beyond his ken. Ymir's bellow drowned out the battle cries of Borr and his warriors.

The jotunn surged forward, smashing one warrior with his hammer. Borr never hesitated, never backed down, charging the monster. Ymir batted the spear away, and it embedded itself in the same tree Odin had found it in days later.

The jotunn snatched up Borr in one hand and hefted him to his face. From Ymir's head jutted a granite horn, stretching nigh unto five feet long. His icy breath stung Borr's face. Ymir kicked away another of Borr's warriors, remaining focused on Odin's father's face, meeting his gaze.

And then the jotunn spoke, his voice like the rumbling of a glacier. His words were foreign and unknowable, except … Odin could have sworn he made out one word—Hel. The dire goddess of Niflheim, mistress of the Niflungar.

Ymir squeezed his fist, and Odin screamed, feeling his bones snap as his father's had.

HE JOLTED UPWARD, roaring at naught, suddenly feeling stifled by the tent above them. Dimly, as though he still dreamed, he knew Frigg had thrown her arms around his chest, leaned her head against his back. Their babe cried, wakened by his outburst.

Odin shrugged free of Frigg, crawled over to Thor, and cradled him in his arms. "There's naught to fear," he mumbled.

The two werewolf babes had sat up, watching Odin with wary eyes. Geri pensive, on the edge of tears; Freki with his head cocked to one side.

Tyr stuck his head in the tent, but Frigg waved him away.

"Tell me what you're seeing," she said as soon as Odin's thegn had slipped back out.

Odin couldn't look away from Thor's eyes, from the boy's red hair. Hair the color of Odin's father's. "There is naught to fear," he repeated, unable to still the tremble in his own chest. Because there *was* something to fear. The jotunn had come specifically for Borr. He had paid no mind to the villagers or the other warriors, at least not until he had finished with Odin's father. Why? Could Odin have conjured such things in his mind, or had he witnessed the real finality of his father's last moments? They had found his body broken and no one left to tell the tale of what had destroyed that village. Only later had Loki told him about the jotunn.

"He took my father," he mumbled.

"Husband," Frigg said, gingerly taking Thor from his grasp. "You avenged him. You killed Ymir."

The jotunn had taken his father away from him ... taken him before his time. Now, thanks to the apple of Idunn, Odin might never again see his father's face. And would Borr the great, Borr the hero, be proud of all Odin had done? He had become king of the Aesir, but was that even what Borr would have wanted? Probably not. Nor had Odin wanted such a thing. Idunn had forced the role upon him, and now, responsible for all the Aesir, he could not shirk that role.

"He has my father's eyes, his hair ..." Odin said. Had his own father once comforted Odin like this? Comforted him against the horrors of the night and the mists and the cold?

Would he be proud? No. Borr would not be proud. Odin's pride had cost him his brother Ve, whom the mists had transformed into a troll. And because Odin had given Ve an apple before that, he would be more than any troll had ever been—a fresh horror Odin had now visited upon Midgard. And if they did not take Vanaheim as Idunn urged, then all he had done would amount to naught.

Odin heard Frigg nursing Thor, felt her warm hand on his bare back. But he couldn't bring himself to look at her. She was his wife, and still he dreamed of another woman. Of Gudrun, the sorceress who had ensnared him, bent him to her will, and tried to bend him to the service of Hel.

He shuddered, and Frigg removed her hand. His mind wandered too far these days. He rose and donned trousers, not bothering with a shirt. The cold no longer had so much effect on him. Still, he strapped his sword to his side—the sword Frigg had given him to protect their family. Though he always preferred to fight with Gungnir, the sword's weight was a comfort, a reminder he had not yet failed his son. "I need to find Loki."

"Again?"

Odin pretended not to hear the judgment in her voice. Yes. Again. Again he sought the council of another over his wife. But Odin's blood brother knew things beyond what even Odin's völva wife understood. And Odin could look *him* in the eye without feeling the guilt of having betrayed his wife.

He stalked into the night, among the countless tents. Thousands of them. All nine tribes of the Aesir, all marching into the unknown under his command. At Idunn's urging, Odin had uprooted an entire civilization, sent all his people trekking through field and forest and hills in the hopes of finding a better World. And if they fell, if they failed to take Vanaheim, Odin would have led his people to extinction.

Two moons since they named him King at the Althing. Two moons, and he had crushed Hunalander kingdoms beneath his march, won plunder for his people. And lost a great many lives.

"Would you be proud?" Odin whispered into the night. Was Odin a hero following in his father's footsteps, or was he drunk on his own power, entranced by his own myth? Oh, the men here worshipped him as a god. The god who had fought a jotunn, fought trolls, fought varulfur and won, time after time. Except when he didn't. His skin bore the runes of a ghost's curse, a constant reminder she had damned him, promised he would lose *everything*. As he had lost Ve. And the Aesir? They thought the runes were another indication of his mystique, of his apotheosis, as Idunn called it.

And so they had followed him across the border into Hunaland where they found little welcome. His people met skirmishes every few days—not all at once, but whenever they ventured out to hunt or forage. Thousands of bonfires lit the night, holding back the mists. Perhaps the World had never known such an army. But they were an army burdened by the young and the elderly, by those who could not well defend themselves.

And thus it fell to Odin to protect them all.

The Aesir had raided into Hunaland for generations. Small wonder the kings here did not welcome them. And through these delays, already the first snows had fallen. Winter returned and they had not yet crossed half this country if Idunn measured correctly.

Tyr had argued they ought to take only warriors, seize Vanaheim, then come back for the women, children, and elderly. It had been Idunn herself who pointed out the flaw in his plan—they would either have to leave a significant force of warriors behind to watch over those helpless people, or leave them defenseless. What she left unsaid, or perhaps was too naive to even see, was that if Odin left people behind, he risked more than their lives. He risked losing control of them. Odin's presence held these tribes together by a thread of spider silk. Old hatreds and rivalries and petty ambitions were set aside while their god-king walked among the people. But only just.

Loki sat upright as Odin entered his tent, while Sigyn burrowed deeper under the blankets, clearly naked—a sight Odin would not have minded seeing. From the look in Loki's crystal blue eyes, his brother knew exactly what Odin was thinking. Yes, Odin was a terrible husband. Frigg deserved better. Maybe … maybe Thor deserved a better father. No. By Frey's flaming sword, Odin would be worthy of his son, worthy to continue his father's line.

"I would speak with you, brother."

Loki glanced at Sigyn, then rose, pulled on his trousers, and followed Odin outside.

"I've had another vision," Odin said as they walked outside the camp. Loki always kept his tent on the outskirts, as he didn't seem to relish being too close to the company of men. Odin's blood brother held himself apart, always. Out here, in this never-ending mountain range, that meant he slept on icy slopes above the valley where the rest of the Aesir camped.

But there was no one Odin trusted more. Even despite, or perhaps because of, Loki's völva-like knowledge.

"You've opened yourself to the Otherworlds. It's not a door you can shut. The Sight carries with it many aspects, and sometimes, you see things you might rather not."

The Niflungar had said something similar, and they were sorcerers, worshippers of Hel. And still Gudrun had stolen his heart.

"Was it truth?" Odin asked.

Loki shrugged. "What is truth? Your question belies a simplistic worldview, Odin. Do you ask whether it could have been a mere dream? Of course it could have. But then, even dreams may have meaning, though not always literal ones. If what you saw was not actual reality, that does not discount that it may have held *some* reality worth gleaning."

Hel's icy trench, Odin hated when Loki spoke in such riddles. And by the gleam in his eye, the man damned well knew that. Payback for fantasizing about his brother's woman, perhaps.

"Ymir wanted my father, specifically. *Spoke* to him. Why would he do that? Why—assuming this was literal truth— would a jotunn speak to a man? Particularly a man he intended to kill."

"What did he say?"

"I couldn't understand his language. Something about Hel, I think."

The bare hint of frown. "Perhaps he merely threatened to send Borr to her."

Perhaps. But Odin's gut insisted it was something deeper. Ymir had come just for his father. He was certain of it.

Odin rubbed his face. These mountains left everyone on edge. They needed to be free of them, free of the mists and the death and the pain.

"How far to reach Vanaheim?"

Loki looked up at the night sky for a time before answering. "Several moons at least, depending on our progress. Not before summer. We have to pass through Hunaland and Valland. There will be some flatlands beyond this, then more mountains, albeit not as treacherous as these. And that is only to reach the shore at the edge of the land. We will also need to cross the sea, and decide whether to do so in Valland or press on further south, into Andalus."

"Then spread the word. We break at dawn and march hard."

The Niflungar were still out there, probably hunting him. And they would not hesitate to prey on his people in order to get to him.

To prey on his family. Odin would not allow it, not while he had breath left in his body.

2

_V_olsung's castle was a stone behemoth. Had to be built by one of the Old Kingdoms. Men didn't build like this. Not anymore. Tyr stared at it. Worked his jaw. Odin and a half dozen men and shieldmaidens waited behind him. Carefully picked by Tyr. Odin insisted on meeting this king in Hunaland. Tyr insisted on not letting him die.

Other Ás warriors held back, far off. They didn't want this to seem like an invasion. Odin thought he could make peace. If not—well, Tyr didn't fancy storming such a castle.

They had built this place to guard against the mists. Had to be. Except now, it served even better against men. A spiked iron gate opened for them, creaking on chains as it rose into the wall. Half frozen already, though the snows hadn't thickened here. Not yet.

"What a monster," Tyr mumbled.

"Smaller than Castle Niflung," Odin said behind him.

Men built _bigger_ than this? Why? He'd have half expected these walls to hold against a fucking jotunn.

A big man strode out at the head of a small army.

Scarred, bearded. Carrying a heavy axe. "You come here to die, Aesir?"

"To talk," Odin said.

The big warrior sneered. "You few walking in here, alone?"

Man thought them fools. Didn't seem to know just what Odin and Tyr had become. Hel, Tyr didn't know what he'd become. But when his pulse pounded hard enough, he was strong as a draug. Hard to control, but the apple made him a god. When it counted.

But this thegn didn't know. Thought them fools not to ask for a hostage before walking into the castle.

"Can we not trust in our safety as guests of King Volsung?" Odin asked.

The warrior grunted, then motioned them to follow. Tyr went first, Odin a step behind him. The warrior led them into a courtyard. Wide, and decorated with a dragon carved of ice. Massive horned serpent, coiling through the center yard. Linnorms, legends called these two-legged serpents. Even Hymir feared such monsters.

"Wait here," Volsung's man said and strode into the hall.

The men behind Tyr cursed, or whispered prayers to Njord, Frey, Freyja. Still praying to the Vanir. Somehow forgetting the plan to overthrow them. Tyr didn't blame them. "Who carves such monstrous things as this dragon?"

Odin drummed his fingers on Gungnir. "A sorcerer."

"What? They have a sorcerer here?" Tyr was already reaching for his sword. No good ever came from magic. Sorcerers touched powers of Hel. The mist had already begun to gather in the courtyard, held back by the torches of their men. Barely held back.

The king shook his head. "I'm not certain. This looks old."

How did Odin know such things? The man had changed much in his time with the Niflungar. Too much. He saw things, knew things he ought not. Like his damned blood brother.

"We must have peace," Odin said, softly so only Tyr could hear him. "Despite the Althing, not all the jarls love me as their king."

"Most probably don't. They don't have to love you. Respect matters more."

"They respected my father. I think they fear me."

Not without cause. Tyr grunted. "Everyone respected Borr. He was a great man."

Odin turned to him with a level gaze. "And you still think me unworthy of that legacy."

"Bah! I said naught of the sort. Unlike your new brother, I can speak plainly."

"I made Loki my blood brother, and I'll hear no ill of him, Tyr. He saved my life more than once and helped me avenge my father. What more do you *need* to know of him?"

"Where does he come from?" Arms folded over his chest, Tyr glowered at Odin. "Who are his people? What does he want from us? Why the secrets?"

Odin waved away his questions. "Worry more over the jarls, Tyr. I learned recently Father had gone to meet Jarl Arnbjorn in Unterhagen."

"What? How did you learn such a thing?"

Odin shook his head.

Hel. More secrets. Tyr groaned. The Jarl of the Itrmanni had been there, then. Had known of Borr's urd. Had shared naught of it, nor had he attended the funeral. Tyr ought to wring justice from the man's hide.

Except. Odin needed the jarls now. And Tyr had promised himself he would do things right. No more playing politics in the shadows. If he could not meet Arnbjorn in open challenge, he would not fight him at all. Even if it meant letting the past lie.

Evening approached fast. Still this king kept them waiting in the courtyard. Flaunting his power.

Odin stood very still, leaning on Gungnir. Apparently not offended. Or making of show it.

When the big thegn at last returned, he still sneered. Tyr would welcome the chance to wipe it off his face. But Odin sought peace. Like Borr. He *had* become worthy.

"The king will hear your offer," the thegn said, and motioned them into the central hall.

This hall stood flush against the rear outer wall. Inside, a twisted tree grew from the hall's heart. Its branches tangled in the rafters, reached out windows near the roof.

"Huh." Quite the sight.

The king's throne sat a step above the rest of the floor, in the back of the hall. They had to pass around the tree before they could see him. Volsung had the look of a warrior. Powerful muscles. A sword rested against his throne. Young for a king. Maybe twenty winters. Maybe less.

"So the great Ás King graces my hall." Volsung rose and gestured around his grand home. Then he turned back to them and strode off the raised step. "Odin, the man who thinks himself a god. Already two of my fellow kings of Hunaland have fallen before you, and yet you come to me and wish to talk."

"Your fellow kings tried to stop us from going where we must. I implore you not to repeat their error."

"Ah." Volsung nodded, looked to each of the many thegns and warriors standing around his hall. "Yes, I see. But you do not realize, I think, that I am not like the little men you have marched past thus far. I am the son of Rerir, and grandson of Sigi the Swift, who carved this kingdom out of the lands of his enemies." Volsung turned and pointed to the sword against his throne. "With that. So you, see, I too come from a glorious line, risen as you have done. And I do not fear you."

Fool, then.

Odin stepped forward to meet the Hunalander, hands open before him. "I don't ask for your fear. Nor have I come to take your castle. Let us pass on. That is all."

Volsung cocked his head. "Let an army march through my lands? And then? Trust to your word that none of your immense horde will take to raping and plundering every village between here and wherever you are bound? Or worse, risk that you might not intend to leave at all? Perhaps you find my lands more favorable for your people?" He chuckled to himself, and some of the other men in the hall joined him as if it were some jest. "Go back to Aujum. Your numbers are many, but so are my allies should I call a full levy. And I would trust in their honor before that of your mass of women and children."

Tyr spat. "Brazen fool! Odin offers you a chance to avoid war and you shit on it! Any one of my shieldmaidens could take any three of your warriors."

"Tyr." Odin's voice did not carry far, but it held such iron Tyr fell silent. He had spent so long representing Odin. He had let himself forget the man could speak for himself.

Odin waved his hand at the hall now, pausing to take in the great tree. "The ancient oak, Barnstokkr, has become the symbol of your house."

Volsung shrugged. "So skalds speak of it even in Aujum?"

They didn't, not that Tyr knew. How did Odin know?

"And you speak of the glories of Sigi the Swift, carving

out his kingdom. He built his riches on raids and, in the end, died to treachery from his in-laws."

Volsung gaped. "How do you—"

"Still surpassed by his son, your father, who reclaimed this great throne. But then"—Odin looked far away a moment—"then Rerir's wife had no child. And he sought guidance from a witch who bought your life at the price of your father's. Such is your glory, Volsung."

The Hunalander king backed away, holding up a hand in warding. "You cannot know such things ..."

Odin banged the butt of Gungnir on the floor. A loud crack echoed through the hall. "I know a great many things. The Aesir do not wish for your people as enemies. Believe me when I say to you, you want us for enemies even less."

The king slumped back in his throne, head in his hand. He fell silent for long enough murmurs began to spread through the hall. At last he looked up. "You wish to buy passage through my lands? Return in three days with tribute befitting such a request. Then we may bargain."

Odin spread his hands in acceptance, spun, and marched out of the hall.

Tyr's king did not speak until they had left the fortress, walking into the deepening twilight. Then he motioned the other warriors on to rejoin the camp. When they had gone, Odin turned to Tyr.

"It is unlike you to lose control, thus."

Tyr frowned. True enough, and he did not need Odin to point it out. "The man vexes me. His arrogance grates on me like a sore."

"True, perhaps. But we both know these past two moons have proved challenging in more ways than simple tests of strength in battle. You find yourself working and fighting alongside a woman you might rather not."

Tyr groaned. "You need not speak of this."

"Zisa remains a part of my court."

"My lord, please."

Odin held up his hand in surrender. He started to walk away, then called over his shoulder. "All men must accept their urd, Tyr."

Tyr scowled at Odin's back as the king trod away. Accept urd. Even when urd became sitting beside the wife who betrayed him. And the man she betrayed him with. Hel take them both.

3
------

*S*hrouded in mist, Gudrun watched as Odin and his people fled Volsung's castle. The Ás king had the Sight now, and had he thought to look, might have spied her even through her concealment. It only made her use of the Art that much more reckless. A sorceress drew such powers from the spirits bound to her and, every time she used them, those spirits gained a stronger hold over her body and soul. Many a careless sorcerer had lost themselves in the powers of Niflheim and given in to the mists. And yet, Gudrun had to see Odin off—she could not pass over an opportunity to look upon him.

So close she could almost have touched him. Could almost feel his arms around her back, feel her legs wrapped around his waist. Because she knew the truth—he might blame the love potion she'd given him, but it had only made him more pliable, allowed him to forget a woman he'd never loved at all. It had freed his heart to do what it really wanted. And Gudrun knew he wanted her just as much as she did him. He had told her he loved her, and he had meant it. And if she were to reveal herself now, to step into the light, would he take her back? Wrap her once again in his embrace and offer her the peace she had—almost—found with him?

Gudrun ground her teeth. The Ás belonged to her, had always been meant for her, whatever Grimhild may have thought. If only she could make Odin see that, make him realize how much he needed her.

Maybe soon he would see. The Sight had opened him up to knowledge she would not have expected—certainly more than Grimhild would have predicted. He'd known or intuited that Rerir, desperate for an heir, had turned to a sorceress, never imagining the price might prove his own life. Sorcery always had a price, exacted from the body, mind, or soul of both the caster and the recipient. But had Odin known that Grimhild had been that sorceress, that Volsung owed his very existence to the Niflungar? Perhaps not. Had he known such truths with any certainty, he might have struck out against Volsung more directly, instead of cowing him with tricks of the Sight.

Rerir's oath to Grimhild bound his son as well. Favors owed were sometimes the most valuable treasure one could collect. Like most Hunalanders, Volsung came from a line of the Niflungar's enemies, descended from the Siklings, a kingdom Gudrun's people had crushed centuries ago. Now, though, his once-glorious ancestry stolen by the mists of history, he had come into her service. And she would use him to drive Odin back to her side.

Gudrun slipped back inside Volsung's hall, giving a slight nod to a raven perched atop it. Father watched her. Maybe one day he would help her. Not against Grimhild, though. Never against her.

Fires inside kept the mist at bay and prevented her from relying on magical concealment. Just as well, given hiding behind an actual wall protected better against one with the Sight. Like all mortals, the Hunalanders rightly feared the mists of Niflheim blanketing Midgard. Those mists could steal away memories and transform a man from within, leaving him ripe for possession by spirits or hollowed out as a draug. Or they could bring out the darkest parts of a man, transforming him into a troll, as had happened to Odin's own brother.

But Gudrun was a Niflung, a Child of Mist, and the Mist spirit bound to her prevented such urds for her. Even if it came with its own risks and agonies. The Mist spirit—or snow maiden as mortals oft called them—was one of two vaettir she kept bound. The less loathsome of the two.

Volsung rose from his throne as she approached and inclined his head in respect. He may not have liked the oath that bound him, but he was not fool enough to deny it. Grimhild would have had Volsung destroy Odin and the Aesir in her rage over Guthorm's death. The Queen never forgave any slight, and the murder of her favored son counted as more than a slight. She might not have loved any of her children—probably was not even capable of the emotion—but she had valued Gudrun's half brother.

To save Odin from her wrath, Gudrun would have to get him to declare himself for the goddess Hel of his own free will. Only then might Grimhild be forced to stay her hand. Because Hel *did* want Odin, of that Gudrun was certain, though not why. Her father still sent his ravens to watch the Ás king. Her father wanted Odin, which meant Hel wanted Odin. And whatever Hel wanted, Hel got. Her power had swept over Midgard and given rise to the Fimbulvinter. Snow maidens and draugar, jotunnar, and even wraiths all trembled before the Queen of Death.

And Odin would be far better off as Gudrun's lover than

Hel's enemy. He had to see that—she would make him see it.

But not just yet. The time was not right. Gudrun would have to wait. Hel rewarded patience. The queen of the dead had waited for long millennia to spread her reign over Midgard. Deathless, she knew naught *but* patience. There would come a time when Odin would need Gudrun, and then she would be there. Too many horrors lurked out in the mist, dangers the Niflungar alone understood. And when Odin faced those dangers, when his people began to fall in droves, he would gladly cast aside his frail völva wife. He had to. Gudrun needed only to find a way to expedite the process.

Gudrun clucked her tongue at herself. She was not some lovesick maid to sit here fawning over a man—even one such as Odin. She was the princess of the Niflungar. This king would come to her. As Volsung's armies broke the Aesir, Odin would have nowhere left to turn.

"Princess," Volsung said. "You heard the Ás's words?"

"I heard."

"And what does the Queen wish of me?"

Gudrun struggled to keep emotion from her face. Queen Grimhild wanted every last Ás erased from the face of Midgard, wanted them left naught but frozen memories, if that. But Gudrun spoke for her here, even if she did not speak the words Grimhild would have wanted. "Let the Aesir pass—whatever they offer, accept the tribute."

"So we will not war with them?"

Gudrun ran her tongue over her teeth before shaking her head. "My dear king. Once they have crossed your borders, they will remain trapped with a strong enemy behind them and fresh enemies ahead. Trapped, they may grow desperate."

"So you would have me break faith with them?"

As Odin had broken faith with her? Perhaps. "I would have you heed my advice lest advice become commands. Let Odin and his people through your lands. And await my further ... advice."

The king sighed.

4

"All I'm saying," Fulla said, "is if you didn't take so much mind about the doings of others, you'd have more mind for the minding of yourself."

Sigyn rolled her eyes. Forests covered so much of Hunaland the Aesir had no real choice but to break up into bands. They walked in one such band, guards on all sides. Geri wiggled in Sigyn's arms, but they had no time to let the varulf girl walk about on her own. "You seem to be intimating that the mind is some finite thing, as if my having studying some small portion of Hunaland's history prevented me from learning something relevant to the Aesir. Forgetting for the moment that, as we are now in their lands, the history of Hunaland *is* relevant to us."

Fulla huffed, no doubt more exhausted from holding Freki. The maid hadn't had an apple, after all. "There now, you see that there? I'm not intimidating anyone, am I now? But you don't mind yourself, so I have to do it for you. If I left you by your ownness, you'd probably be emptying your chamber pot without warning the alfar afore you toss it.

Sure as sure, a way to vex an alf is by tossing hot piss on them."

Sigyn snorted. "I think that'd vex anyone. But that's just folk superstition. If the alfar exist at all—"

"How can you still doubt it?" Frigg asked. "After everything we've seen, after tasting the very fruit of Yggdrasil, how can you yet doubt the reality of the Otherworlds?"

Sigyn shrugged. "I've seen golden apples, and I've seen trolls. Agilaz has seen draugar with his own eyes. Not many"—she looked pointedly at Fulla—"not many reliable men claim to have seen an alf. But let us say your Alfheim exists and the alfar live in it. You think they spend their time standing about, invisible, waiting to have piss thrown on them so they might have a reason to take offense? Does that seem a likely use of a vaettr's time?"

"Oh, Sigyn," Fulla said. "Sure as sure, they're not just awaiting having the chamber pot thrown. But you can't rightly know what business they may be about. Could well be a dozen vaettir in these very woods, watching us carry on about them. All listening close-like to your non-respecting tongue." At that, the maid looked around the trees and frowned, as if she might suddenly spot these invisible watchers.

Before Sigyn could form an appropriate answer, Frigg spoke. "So these lands belong to Volsung. And you were saying Agilaz knew his father."

"Knew *of* his father, anyway, yes. Rerir's uncles murdered his father, Sigi the Swift, and stole the kingdom. A wanderer —some say a friend of his father's—came to him and helped him retake that castle we saw a few days back, all in one bloody night. But Rerir didn't sit overlong on the throne. He fell ill while campaigning against his neighbors, and he died before the birth of his son."

"Hmm." Frigg didn't seem to be truly listening. The Queen of the Aesir often remained preoccupied—hardly a surprise—but she ought to have paid attention to such details. A great many kings reigned in Hunaland, and Sigyn did not have tales of all of them, but they should use what knowledge they could.

"Something else troubles you?"

"Oh." Frigg cradled Thor in her arms, looked to his face a moment. "Naught at all."

Sigyn scoffed. If Frigg didn't want to talk, she should not have asked Sigyn to join her band. Right now, Sigyn could have walked beside Loki, who surely *would* have engaged her in interesting conversation. No matter how many hours they spent talking, Sigyn could never quite figure the man out. There was always at least one more secret. Loki never lied to her—not that she could tell—but he cultivated mysteries and half-truths, manipulating Odin and the Aesir as effortlessly as breathing. To what end? He seemed to genuinely care for all of them, to want to save them. And yet, her lover still concealed so many things.

And Loki had shown her something she could not shake from her mind. He had reached into fire and commanded it as though it were a part of him. Such sorcery would have sounded a skald's fancy, had she not seen it with her own eyes, but the man's only explanations had been evasions that revealed naught.

A sharp, brief scream rang out in the woods to her left. Followed by another.

Sigyn reacted on instinct, grabbed Frigg, and pulled her low to the ground. Fulla dropped down as well. An instant later, arrows thunked into nearby trees. Several of their guards fell the same moment. Shafts jutting from their chests, throats, legs. The whole band exploded into chaos, drawing weapons and racing off after hidden attackers.

Fulla had begun to shriek.

Sigyn glanced back at her sister. She could help, use her bow—but she couldn't do so *and* protect Frigg and the babes.

Another Ás warrior fell as an arrow pierced his eye. His blood splattered them.

Dripping with it, Frigg screamed.

Sigyn grabbed her sister's arm. "Get up! Move!"

They had been outflanked. Of course she had heard people moving about, but with a band this size she'd thought ... well she should have paid more attention. She shoved Frigg behind a tree, then went back for Fulla. The maid still knelt on the ground, her body shielding Freki, trembling like a sapling in a blizzard. Sigyn jerked the woman to her feet and ushered them away.

Footfalls, screaming, fighting. So many people, it was hard to tell who was on which side. But the Aesir had lost a lot of men already. Sigyn could run to the sound of people, but with each passing moment it grew less likely they would be *her* people. No. She had to get Frigg and the babes away from the enemy, even if that meant also getting them away from their allies.

She'd trust her own abilities over those of the Ás warriors in this forest. Agilaz had taught her well. She paused a heartbeat, filtering the sounds. The fewest people were to her right.

"Follow me and stay low!"

She rushed forward, darting between trees as swiftly as she could while running in a crouch. The Hunalanders had archers stalking these woods. She couldn't let them get a clear shot. Geri had begun to wail. Sigyn pressed the girl closer to her chest.

"Shhh. Not now. Please, please not now."

Fulla cursed and stumbled, and Sigyn glanced at her. Rising from a root she'd tripped on, hidden by snow.

"Keep moving," Sigyn said. "Walk where I walk."

The maid's breath came in ragged gasps that, to Sigyn's ears, sounded loud enough to draw every scout within a mile. They didn't have her hearing, though, thank Njord. Footfalls sounded ahead, snow crunching underfoot. Sigyn made an abrupt turn. She didn't even know which way they were heading anymore, not after the chaos, and she couldn't see the sun through the mist and tree cover.

Even if they wandered deeper into Hunaland, she could get them back to the Aesir eventually. Right now, she had to get the other women away from here. Anywhere was better than here.

She pushed on, through the forest.

❦

THEY HAD GONE another half hour before Fulla toppled over. The maid tried to rise, then slumped down again, panting and sobbing.

"I c-can't. I can't … I …"

Sigyn looked around. "I think it's all right. I haven't heard sounds of people in a good while. We should be safe."

Frigg slumped down, holding Thor even tighter against her. "Places without people are where vaettir most thrive. A forest like this might house askafroas—ash wives. They take human sacrifices, carry them back to their heart trees and consume them."

Fulla wailed.

"Without a sacrifice, an ash wife might work terrible damage upon the locals. The only way to face such a foe would be to fell her heart tree, and that is nigh unto—"

"*Frigg*," Sigyn snapped, "shut up. We're alive for now. If your völva knowledge can help us stay that way, share. Otherwise, save it for later." She looked up at the sky. "It'll be dark soon. We need to find a grove, an overhang, somewhere we can shelter for the night."

"We don't have fire," Fulla whined.

Sigyn had been worrying over just that problem for some time now. A fire might give them away. On the other hand, Fulla and Thor were mortal, and could not afford to keep breathing in the mist. "All the more reason we need a secluded place, somewhere the light won't carry as far. Now. I need you both to get up and follow me. I'm going to find a way to get us through this."

Frigg trembled as she rose, but her sister nodded. "I ... I trust you."

Sigyn hoped that trust would not prove misplaced.

5

*T*he bastard Hunalander had betrayed him! After accepting gold and silver plundered from his neighbors, Volsung had agreed to grant the Aesir safe passage through Hunaland. And then he had sent dozens of raiding parties against them, preying on the weakest groups in the back and middle lines.

"Where is my son!" Odin bellowed.

Tyr shook his head. "The queen's band seems mostly fallen, but we found no sign of her or your children."

Hel take Volsung. Odin would bring those castle walls crashing down around him. He would burn that hall and Volsung's precious tree to cinders and leave naught for their line but ash. His grip tightened around Gungnir, and the dragon's anger fed his own. Forged with a bit of the mighty beast's very soul, the spear always awoke such primal rage in him. And sometimes, as now, he welcomed it.

"I'll go," Agilaz said. "I love Sigyn as though she were my own daughter."

Odin glowered at the thegn. He'd had few enough dealings with Hadding's former hunter, though Agilaz's son

Hermod had more than proved his worth according to Tyr. And men said no finer woodsman lived among the Aesir, though Agilaz hailed from some land farther north than Aujum. "Do not fail to bring back my children. Or my wife."

"I'm going with you," Loki said.

Odin jerked. As did everyone else. None of them had even noticed the foreigner's approach. Agilaz leveled his stern gaze on Loki. If he objected to his foster daughter sleeping with Loki, he had not said so in front of Odin.

Nor did he offer any comment now, save to nod. The pair of trackers took off into the woods, their pace swift.

"I ought to be going myself."

Tyr grunted. "Can't. The men need you. Already the jarls are calling for a Thing."

A Thing. Now. While his family—his *son*, his father's grandson—remained in danger. While Volsung sat in his accursed hall, toasting the men who had slaughtered Odin's people.

Odin clenched his fist at his side. Yes, a Thing. For at a Thing, the king could declare a war. "Gather them. Call them all."

❧

EIGHT JARLS—FOR Odin still held the title of Jarl of the Wodanar in addition to being king—stood in a circle around him. They had no hall nor tent large enough to hold them all, so they had gathered in a clearing. Jarls toward the center, their thegns around them, and others—warriors, shieldmaidens, völvur, and elders—all watching, straining to hear the inane debate as grown men bickered like children. Whined over what to do when they found themselves trapped in enemy territory.

Tyr had estimated their numbers nigh to twenty thousand when they had left Aujum. In the two moons since, they had lost no few of those people, and already the numbers included the old, the very young, and others who could not fight.

Some of thegns bickered among themselves as well, men from different tribes spoiling to redress old wrongs, to revive feuds best left buried.

"You have no idea what we'll face in Vanaheim," Arnbjorn said. The jarl of the strongest tribe of the Aesir, the Itrmanni, had stopped addressing Odin with any form of honorific not long after the Thing had begun, but Odin had stayed Tyr from acting with a raised finger. Despite his own flaring temper, Odin needed these men. Though he'd have preferred to wring Arnbjorn's neck and demand to know why the man had abandoned his father. "You march us across unknown lands in a vain goal to seize the home of the gods. Now here we fall to *mortal* foes."

"There is truth to that," Odin said. "But are we to fear the unknown now? Shall we cower like babes, clutching our mother's skirts?"

The eight jarls all bristled at that. They were warriors, all, and filled with pride enough for kings themselves. Vili snorted and looked down on the others. "Fuck no. Why are we even talking of this? Let us kick down Volsung's gate, roast his stones over a fire, and hang his head from his fucking walls."

"Yes!" Jarl Lodur said. "Let us send a message to all those lands before us. Let them tell tales of the urd of those who cross us." Lodur's Didung tribe had maintained peaceable relations with the Wodanar ever since Borr's peace. That had not stopped the Diduni from seeking war elsewhere, and they excelled at it. Lodur had won many battles already in Hunaland and had grown rich off them. And Odin had more than half a mind to grant the jarl his wish. He'd have relished watching Volsung and his people burn for their treachery.

Hoenir snorted. The Godwulf jarl was probably the oldest among them, and despite his role in overthrowing Alci, favored the part of caution in nigh every situation. It would be easy to condemn him for it, but he proved in the right more oft than not. "It is not courage to rush in blindly like a snow rabbit in heat."

"You would know, old man," Jarl Bedvig said. "The talk is, you like your smith to ride *you* like his prized mare."

Odin barely stifled his groan. Bedvig and the Skalduns were also among the most powerful of the tribes. They had not taken easily to Odin's rule.

Every thegn paused at the insult, save Hoenir's men, who shouted back their own taunts. Accusing a jarl of unmanly behavior was like to start a war. If unanswered, all of the Aesir would believe Hoenir guilty of the charge, or worse, a coward. Either way, he'd lose his position and most likely be banished out into the mists.

Tyr caught Odin's eye, hand reaching for his sword. The thegn had even more reason to hate Bedvig, but if Odin let his champion silence him, doubts would linger around Hoenir. Odin could not afford to have doubts cast on one of his stoutest allies. He shook his head. Tyr scowled, but made no further move.

Hoenir sneered back at the younger jarl. "Your tongue has run away with you, boy. Now I will have satisfaction." The jarl drew his broadsword.

Now. Something he could harness, even if the timing left much to be desired. Odin rose, pounding the butt of his spear into the ground. "A holmgang is challenged. Do you accept the challenge, Jarl Bedvig?"

The younger jarl spit at Hoenir's feet, then grunted assent.

"Then the holmgang will be fought tomorrow, at dawn," Odin said, projecting his voice so all the gathered crowd could hear him. "Not here, not now. You may appoint champions or fight yourselves. For now, silence your bickering that we may actually accomplish the purpose of this Thing."

If Hoenir killed Bedvig, maybe Odin could help arrange a more pliable jarl to replace the man. Frey, he'd reward Hoenir for that.

With Hoenir and Bedvig both cowed, Arnbjorn again insisted they send a scouting party before launching an all-out attack. Jarls Jat and Lodur, in turn, disputed him, warned they would lose the element of surprise if their scouts were discovered. Lodur was correct, of course. They needed to make an example of this king if they were to avoid facing such treachery in the future. They needed to strike so hard and fast Volsung would never recover.

All of this, for Idunn's Mist-mad request that he overthrow the Vanir and claim rulership of all Midgard. As if becoming king of the Aesir was not enough. He, in his desperation and pride, had given her his oath in his father's name, without even knowing what she would ask. Not that he could have imagined such a desire from her.

And worse still, he could see himself on a throne, ruling over Vanaheim. Through the vagaries of the Sight, in his dreams, he could see such a reality. If he brought the Aesir to Vanaheim, they'd face no more mists. They would be free from the cold, free from the vaettir that preyed on them in the night, and freed at last from the threat of losing themselves, like Ve. But then, the Vanir would not give away their lands easily. They were immortal, ancient. If he trusted Idunn, then they could die—any that lived could die. But would he have the strength to kill them? What cost would a war with the Vanir impose on the Aesir? Would they fall by the hundreds, by the thousands? So many had died just to push through Hunaland. More would die now, while he claimed vengeance against Volsung.

But Lodur was right. Vengeance might preempt further resistance as they marched toward Vanaheim. Because march they would. Even had those mists not cost him his brother, Odin would never break an oath made in Borr's name. He would take Vanaheim. And if he had to crush Volsung's army to do so, he could not afford to hesitate.

Odin banged the spear on the ground once more, silencing the jarls. "I call for war against Volsung and his folk. As your king, I declare them our foes. Who will go to war with me?"

Annar, Lodur, and Vili stepped forward immediately, followed soon after by Hoenir. The older jarl preached caution, yes, but he was no coward. And other jarls could not back out now, not with half of them already pledged.

So war it would be.

6

In the predawn darkness, the campfires had dwindled. Someone always tended them, though, ensuring they never went out. Few men moved about this early, but a handful of varulfur—in wolf form— slipped in and out of the firelight. Always patrolling, searching for more of Volsung's scouts. Vili's shifters had become the salvation of the tribes, the few who stood guard in the night against the horrors of the mists. After losing so many brothers and sisters to the ambush, even the most reluctant Aesir welcomed the werewolves' presence. Not that they did not fear them. They always feared them. They were men and women possessed, given over to feral passions. One foot beyond the bounds of human civilization. Too many too easily crossed that line, grew savage and wild. Forming packs as terrible as aught they would have otherwise guarded against.

The greatest number of varulfur came from the Godwulfs. They patrolled their own camp most heavily. A pair of the wolves, a male and female, eyed Tyr as he passed. Hoenir had a large tent in the northern reaches of the camp.

The Godwulfs were not one of the most powerful tribes, but they were an old and proud line.

Hoenir himself was loyal and brave. But aging. Not a varulf like his predecessor. Bedvig, though also human, was youthful and quick. Any man wagering on the holmgang's outcome would chose him without a doubt.

Hermod, Hoenir's son-in-law, met him at the tent entrance. "Tyr."

"I'll speak with him before the holmgang."

Hermod frowned. "He's preparing."

"I will speak with him," Tyr repeated.

Hermod shrugged, then jerked his head for Tyr to follow him inside. The old jarl's wife stood near the man, helping him don a chain shirt of obviously fine quality. His daughter, Syn, scowled first at her father, then at Tyr.

Hoenir spared him a glance. "Come to wish me luck, Tyr?"

"I've come to offer to champion you, lord."

The jarl scowled now, brushing his wife away so he could stare Tyr down. "You think I cannot fight my own battles now? Maybe I've grown too old and soft? When I am too old to lift my own shield, feel free to toss me on a pyre. Until then, I can fight my own Hel-cursed fights!"

"I could have told you that," Hermod mumbled. Must have offered to champion him already. Of course he had.

Tyr worked the words in his mind. Words were not his specialty. Didn't want to offer Hoenir further offense. But Bedvig was like to kill the old man. And if not, if the Skaldun jarl beat him but let him live, Hoenir would suffer a worse urd. In the eyes of his men he would be confirmed as guilty of unmanliness. They'd oust him from his role, and Odin would lose a worthy ally.

"I owe Bedvig a debt."

"So I've heard. It's true then? This Zisa left you for him? Women can be fickle."

His wife snorted at that and cuffed the jarl on the back of his head.

Fickle was not the word Tyr would have chosen. Zisa was ambitious, and Tyr was not. She'd claimed he had the skill to become a jarl of one of the tribes himself. Tyr owed Borr everything, though, and had not been willing to leave his side. He had sworn loyalty to the man and his line. That oath would bind him for all his days. As he told Zisa. And, oh, how they had fought. And, in the end, she had taken up with a passing jarl's son. Bedvig. Now a jarl himself. It was not quite adultery, since she had divorced Tyr first. He'd had no right to stop her.

At the time, she'd been a shieldmaiden and a famed hunter. As a jarl's wife, he supposed she didn't use those skills quite as often. A greater shame then, since his fondest memories were of stalking game through snowy woods with her.

When Tyr didn't answer, Hoenir nodded. "And here I thought you came for my wellbeing. If you owe this whelp so much, you can challenge him when I'm finished with him."

Tyr shook his head. "That ... is not possible." Had Zisa not gone through the völva for her divorce, Tyr might have challenged Bedvig. Indeed, even so, he'd had every intention of hunting the man down, though the fault was Zisa's. And maybe Tyr's. But Borr had wanted to avoid war with the Skalduns and had extracted an oath from Tyr that he would do no such thing.

Tyr did not break his oaths. Especially not to Borr. But if he were to champion Hoenir, he might slay Bedvig without ever having violated his oath. It would not be his honor leading to the challenge, though he hoped seeing him defeat the man would appease his ancestors.

Now he walked close to Hoenir. "I gave my word I would not challenge him. But, if you appointed me as a champion, lord, no one would hold it against your honor. You've fought great battles in your time. All know it. You fought in the Njarar War, and you fought now in Hunaland. You and I, we know you could take that brash fool." Well, Tyr hoped it was true, though he knew no such thing. "But still, many see you and think your finest fighting days past. If you were to name me champion, I would be ... grateful my lord."

"If anyone should champion the Godwulfs, it ought to be me," Hermod said. "As your son-in-law—"

Hoenir forestalled the young man with a stern look.

"Does your gratitude, Tyr, translate into Odin's gratitude?"

Tyr nodded. Odin was not here, but Tyr suspected he'd have no objection. Whether he'd be grateful, who knew anymore? Odin was not the young man Tyr had trained. The king had spent too much time with Niflung sorcerers and strangers like Loki, and turned to cunning, sometimes even before honor. At the very least, Tyr had to believe he would understand. "I do not speak for the king. But, he does heed my counsel." If less so than he once did.

Hoenir sighed, then looked to his wife.

She snorted. "What do I know? I'm just a fickle woman."

"Right you are," Hoenir snapped at her, then turned back to Tyr. "So be it. You will carry my shield into the holmgang." The jarl retrieved it from a bench where it sat atop his broadsword. The shield was carved from ash and reinforced with iron bands. A fine arm, for certain, and its owner was obvious for the painting of the great wolf on the front.

Tyr accepted the shield and nodded his gratitude. "It's almost dawn. We should go."

ODIN HAD SELECTED a tiny rock island for the holmgang. A small stretch of land in the middle of a river. The king stood with a handful of others from the Wodanar clan. Around the island, the ranking members of the Godwulfs and Skalduns awaited their arrival. Hermod rowed Hoenir and Tyr out to the island to join the other Godwulfs.

Idunn waited there, too. Waited for him.

After clapping Hoenir on the shoulder, Tyr strode to where she stood. "So?" he asked.

"So are you doing this because of Hoenir, or because of Bedvig? Or because of her?"

Tyr spit. "Zisa has naught to do with this." It tasted like a lie even as he spoke.

Idunn offered her too-knowing smile. "Good luck."

Tyr shook his head and strode toward the heart of the island.

A sneer on his face, Bedvig stood before his Skalduns. No doubt boasting. Zisa was there, but her eyes were on Tyr. Did she suspect? She was a clever woman and might already wonder why he had arrived with the Godwulf jarl instead of with Odin.

"You know it ought to be me fighting," Hermod said again, behind him.

"I am stronger." Tyr did not look back at the man.

"You can go fuck a troll."

Hoenir snorted.

Tyr tightened his grip around his sword, suddenly filled with the urge to gut Hermod. Who did the motherless cock think he was? Tyr could and should thrash him. Maybe, when the holmgang was concluded, he would teach someone else a lesson.

Damn.

No, that was his anger at Zisa.

He drew his blade, hefting Hoenir's shield in his other hand.

Zisa scowled and said something to Bedvig, who turned to look at Tyr. The man's eyes widened for just a moment, then he spit and strode forward, toward the island's center.

Not a coward, then. Tyr smirked and met him in the middle.

"Old man can't fight his own battles?" Bedvig asked, none too quietly.

Hoenir either didn't catch it, or pretended not to for Tyr's benefit. "I come here to champion his cause, jarl." He slapped his sword against his shield.

Bedvig stood similarly armed and, after only a brief moment's hesitation, repeated the gesture.

The moment the jarl did so, Tyr launched himself forward, swinging his sword in a wide arc. Bedvig jerked his shield up to block. The impact rang out clear over the island and sent Bedvig stumbling backward. Tyr advanced at once, swinging again, drawing upon his supernatural strength. With every blow, Bedvig fell back, and Tyr's rage only grew.

A feint. A counter.

His pulse pounded.

The jarl thrust his blade, and Tyr knocked it aside with his own shield, immediately riposting. His blow splintered Bedvig's shield. The jarl grunted in pain and tossed his useless protection aside. Tyr allowed him the moment's respite while Bedvig wrung out his no doubt swollen arm.

"Tiring out already?" Tyr said. "Maybe it's you who likes to be ridden like a mare."

Bedvig snarled and lunged at him, swinging his sword overhead in an arc meant to decapitate. Tyr whipped his own sword up to parry and, at the same time, stooped forward, swinging his shield along a horizontal plane. As the swords clashed, the edge of his shield caught the jarl in the gut. Bedvig doubled over, spewing his breakfast over Hoenir's shield. Tyr slammed the vomit-caked thing into the jarl's face with a satisfying crunch of shattered cartilage.

His foe toppled backward onto the rocky ground, barely conscious. Tyr advanced and pressed the point of his sword into the man's chest. The jarl gagged, apparently unable to speak. How easy to finish him right now. He had not yielded, had not begged mercy. So Tyr was within his rights to just run the trollfucker through here and now.

Do it.

Hel, he ought to do it. His arm shook as he slowly pressed the blade further down. Blood began to well beneath Bedvig's armor. One solid thrust to the heart. A cleaner kill than what Bedvig had done to him. Do it.

"Tyr!" He turned to see Zisa shouting his name. Had she been calling it before now?

She pointed to where Bedvig had raised a hand in supplication. He mumbled something, trying to yield. What if Tyr had not heard it? The man should die. His whole fucking brood ought to die. Zisa had given him two sons, young men now glowering at Tyr.

Damn it!

Tyr raised his sword, pointing it at Bedvig's throat. "You admit you spoke falsely about Jarl Hoenir?"

"I was wrong," Bedvig managed, the words barely decipherable.

Tyr glowered. *Wrong.* Bedvig wasn't *wrong*—he was a Hel-cursed liar who had provoked Hoenir, intent on killing the old man. "You accused him of liking to take it in the arse. The most fitting atonement I see is if you kiss that arse and proclaim it clean of all wrongdoing." Bedvig's eyes widened.

Angry shouts ran out among the gathered Skalduns, especially the jarl's sons. The well-deserved shame he asked of Bedvig might be enough to make the man prefer death. If so, that suited Tyr.

Tyr did not look to Odin, lest the king try to overrule him or dissuade this course of action.

Bedvig looked to Tyr and to the blade. Tyr could have sworn the jarl ready to spit. To welcome the end, rather than bring such dishonor upon himself and his ancestors. Tyr grinned. Yes, let the wife-stealing cocksucker's blood run dry on this barren island.

Finally, Bedvig nodded.

Tyr clenched his jaw. Damn it. He couldn't well kill Bedvig *now*. Having to live with the shame would have to be enough punishment.

Hoenir chuckled, then strode forward and turned around. Tyr stepped back to allow Bedvig—blood still streaming from his shattered nose—to rise to his knees and crawl to Hoenir's arse.

Before Bedvig reached him, Hoenir untied his trousers and dropped them. "Make sure you get the spot you besmirched."

"You troll-loving son of—" the eldest of Bedvig's boys—Starkad, wasn't it?—shouted, before someone cuffed him.

Tyr glanced back to see Zisa silencing her son. His ex-wife stared at him with the icy gaze of Hel herself. Tyr turned from her, unable to bear it.

Bedvig hesitated, then moved in to kiss Hoenir's arse. As

he drew near, Hoenir farted loudly. "Had to miss my morning shit for this," the jarl commented.

Hermod and the other Godwulfs laughed.

Bedvig, looking apt to vomit, planted a swift kiss on one arse cheek then backed away.

Tyr opened his mouth to protest, to demand more.

Odin beat him to it. "The holmgang is concluded. Hoenir is held blameless, and Bedvig is forgiven for his hasty words. We depart this island as allies."

Growling, Tyr sheathed his sword. He returned Hoenir's shield to Hermod, as his father-in-law was busy retying his trousers.

"I think that was the most enjoyment I've ever had before breakfast," Hoenir said.

Tyr turned at the sound of angry footfalls behind him. Despite Zisa's shouts, her two sons—maybe fourteen and fifteen winters each—were storming over, eyes lit in challenge, one carrying a spear.

"Go home and lick your father's wounds," Tyr said. "And aught else he wants you lick."

"I do not know how, but I know you cheated. Men say you have power from the Vanir."

Hoenir shook his head and laughed. "Run home to your arse-kissing father, *boy*."

Indeed, Bedvig was chasing after his sons, shambling his way over and wailing for them to leave it be. At least that was it sounded like—so hard to tell with his hand clasped over a broken nose.

"Want to try your luck?" He spread his arms. "Go ahead, show me you even know how to use that pig-sticker."

The boy rose to the challenge, thrusting at Tyr while roaring. Like any young man, he was all passion and no control. Tyr stepped out of the way, caught the spear's haft, and twisted. His superior strength flipped the fool boy end over end and slammed him onto the rocks. Tyr yanked the spear from the boy's dazed hands then swept the haft down on his chest. The loud crack silenced everyone, the blow leaving the boy unconscious.

Tyr tossed the spear to the younger brother. "What? Want to try your luck?" The boy hesitated, then backed away when Tyr advanced a step.

A few men laughed, Hoenir among them.

Tyr shook his head and walked toward the boat, ignoring the sidelong glances some cast his way. Oh, but he should have killed all three of them. *That* would have been justice. He prayed Bedvig would give him another chance.

He grunted. "You should get back."

TYR RUBBED a whetstone over his blade. Take care of your weapons and armor, both. First rule of being a warrior. He sat alone, near a dwindling fire, some hours after breaking his fast with the Godwulfs. They had welcomed him to their table. Even if some few of them now seemed frightened of him. That was troll shit, obviously. He was their ally and meant them no harm, had fought for them. For the honor of their jarl. As he had fought for all the Aesir.

The men toasted him, offered him fresh fish and some weak ale raided from Hunaland locals.

Regardless, the Godwulfs shared freely with Tyr. But he saw the way they looked at him. With respect, yes, but always underlaid with a hint of fear. Bedvig had gotten what he fucking deserved. Less than he deserved, in fact. Of course that was what Odin wanted Tyr to do. He'd wanted Tyr to *kill* Bedvig, and Tyr had been too blind to see it. He had failed his lord, but he would find some way to make up for it, to get it done.

He looked up at the sound of someone stomping over.

"What in Hel's frozen fields was that, Tyr?" Zisa demanded.

Tyr rose, sticking his sword into the dirt before him. "Are you referring to the holmgang your ... *man* forced upon the tribes with his shameful remarks?"

"What was shameful was beating Starkad with own spear!"

"Shameful for him, yes? If his father armed him, he declared him a man. And a man challenged me. He ought to be grateful the shame visited on him was less than that visited upon his father."

Zisa shook her head, mouth slightly open like she wanted to say something. Whatever it was, she bit it off and snapped her mouth shut. She watched him with those appraising, conniving eyes far too long.

"You ought not have done either of those things, but especially not to ... Starkad." Zisa shook her head and turned away, casting him another sad glance as she left.

Tyr watched her until she was out of his sight, then slumped down by the fire. To say he should not have done as he had was nonsense, and she, a former shieldmaiden, ought to have known better.

Maybe Hoenir was right. Maybe all women were fickle. And dangerous. Idunn tempted him every time her saw her. Maybe ... but how could they have a future? How, when the Aesir marched to destroy her people?

No. Not the time.

Very soon, they would march to war. And then he'd have better things to think of than Zisa *or* Idunn.

$\mathcal{M}$ounted on Sleipnir, Odin watched the army forming up before Volsung's castle. The Hunalander king himself had ventured out for this and now walked before his lines, inspiring them. Not hiding, not a coward, Odin had to grant him that.

Odin's warriors had struck back and struck back hard, though no blow could repay Volsung's treachery. Agilaz and Loki had not returned, and thus neither had Odin's family. He tightened his grip around Gungnir's haft.

And then he raised the spear high, bellowing a war cry. As one, his warriors took up that cry, thrusting weapons skyward or beating them upon shields. Like angry thunder cresting the horizon, ready to break into the fiercest storm.

Now.

Odin kicked Sleipnir forward, and the horse took off with the speed of a diving sparrow. Volsung's line jerked apart even before he reached them, shock washing over their faces. Sleipnir crashed amongst them an instant later. Rather than risk getting his spear embedded in a foe, Odin swept it in great arcs. Its undulating dragon blade tore through armor and flesh and bone, severed limbs and heads, splintered shields.

Men charged at him, weapons high. Brave. Perhaps they would find Valhalla.

Those that did not fall to Gungnir's blade instead found Sleipnir's numerous hooves raining down upon them.

And then the other Aesir collided with Volsung's broken line. A shieldmaiden drove the edge of her shield up under a man's chin. A man—varulf, perhaps—leapt upon a foe with uncanny agility and bore him down. And there, Vili snapped a Hunalander's spine.

Where was Volsung? Where had that trollfucking oath-breaker hidden himself?

Odin turned Sleipnir about. In the chaos of such a melee, spotting a single man proved difficult.

Gungnir's blade cut down another man, and another, until Volsung's warriors ceased to charge him. They circled round him, none willing to be the next to move in. So Odin kicked Sleipnir forward, right through their midst. The horse raced straight over a man. Sickening crunches vibrated under the horse's hooves as it trampled the poor fool.

Beyond, Tyr had squared off with Volsung's champion. The big man from before. Big and strong, though not half as a strong as Tyr, Odin had no doubt. Odin's thegn ducked mighty blows, dancing aside as the Hunalander exhausted himself with wild attacks.

Odin smirked and pushed forward, riding down more of Volsung's men. A spear flew through the air, headed for Sleipnir's flank. The horse reacted on its own, dancing aside with Otherworldly grace. Odin charged at the man with the temerity to attack his mount. A wide swipe of Gungnir separated the Hunalander's head from his shoulders.

He turned back in time to see Tyr draw his blade along his foe's gut. Tyr, coated in blood, spun around and hacked into the man's back to make sure. The big warrior collapsed into the bloody slush that had become the battleground.

"Odin!" someone bellowed.

He turned.

There, Volsung advanced on him. So, the man did have courage. Courage enough to face death when it came for him. And for such courage, Odin would allow him a proper fight. He swung his leg over Sleipnir and slid down into the muck, then batted the horse away with one hand. Sleipnir could fight on his own, would continue crushing anyone fool enough to draw nigh.

Volsung beat his sword against his shield. Blood drenched both. Blood of other Aesir, fallen before the king. One more wrong Odin would need to redress.

"You betrayed us!" he spat at the other king.

Volsung grimaced. "I am beholden to others of greater authority."

"Now you are beholden to death and no other." Odin advanced, both hands on Gungnir.

Volsung circled him, not giving ground, nor charging forward. Odin turned with him, spear ready. One slow step at a time they closed. The king must have seen him cut down so many men already. He would not act rashly—not unless Odin drove him to it.

Odin feinted left then immediately whipped Gungnir back, aimed not at Volsung's body, but at the shield he had drawn up to protect himself with. His spear blade gouged the wood. His sheer strength jerked that shield out of position. Odin twisted, yanking the butt of his spear around in line with his momentum. It crashed down on the damaged shield, cracking it and driving Volsung to his knees.

The Hunalander king struggled to rise while swinging his sword. A clumsy blow, but it forced Odin back and gave his foe time to regain his feet. Volsung roared at him, all his former caution tossed aside—or crushed in desperation. He swung his blade in tight arcs. He had skill, true, but he couldn't get past Gungnir's reach. Odin gave ground rather than let the king close on him.

Other warriors nearby bellowed, rushing at him as well. A half dozen men intent to protect their king, all racing in as one. But Odin had no intention of letting that happen. He lunged at Volsung with a thrust aimed at his heart. The king twisted away and Gungnir's blade instead sheared through the mail on his sword arm. Shrieking, the king dropped his blade and fell back.

Much as Odin wanted to press his attack, a screaming man with an axe demanded his attention. He raised Gungnir to block a descending blow, then kicked the attacker, sending him stumbling away. More men raced in, interposing themselves between Odin and Volsung. The Hunalander king—clutching his arm—disappeared into a mass of bodies.

"Volsung!" Odin roared at him. "I will make you suffer for your betrayal!"

Odin blocked a sword thrust with Gungnir, dodged a descending axe, and jerked his spear around to open a man's gut. Round and round he went, slashing and impaling foes, blocking and dodging. His enemies scored several gashes on his arms and back. No one could fight so many and avoid taking a few hits. But the apple had changed him, given him endurance, strength, and an ability to fight through pain. Combined with years of hard training and the dragon spear, few men could have stood against him. Even few groups of men.

The butt of his spear shattered one man's thigh an instant before its blade severed another foe's wrist. Blood drenched his clothes, his hair, his face. Some of it his. Most of it not. But no matter how many he killed, he could not seem to get back to Volsung.

Panting, Odin broke the last of his attackers. Nigh to two dozen bodies lay around him, dead or dying, food for the ravens already circling overhead. Odin dragged his palm over his face to wipe blood from his eyes, but it too was so smeared he found little benefit in the gesture.

Many Aesir lay dead in the snow around the battlefield, but twice as many more Hunalanders.

Volsung's army had broken. Odin needed to push the attack, to storm the walls of his castle and raze his hall. But …

The hour already grew late. If his people did not make camp and get fires going … No. He would never repeat the mistake he had made with Ve. Never again.

Further vengeance must wait.

---

8

*H*igh in the boughs of a tree, Sigyn could see a long way. A very long way. Even through the mist and the growing twilight she could spot the forest's edge, and fires beyond it. Those fires might belong to either Aś camps or those of Hunalanders. Either way, they couldn't reach them before nightfall. Spending another night in the woods would not please any of them, but she could see no alternative.

Instead, she turned about, seeking any form of shelter. Thousands of ruins of the Old Kingdoms littered the North Realms—Hel, maybe even some of the South Realms—but never one when you needed it. Any shelter would do, though of course, things worse than men oft sought the very same havens. Vaettir, trolls, or savage beasts. Her improved sense of smell had let her avoid a pack of cave hyenas this morning—not something any of them wanted to stumble across by any measure.

Footfalls crunched on snow in the direction of the camps. Men or scouts, searching the forest. It could well be her own people, but she couldn't know for certain unless they drew closer. Close enough to risk discovery.

She scrambled back down the tree.

With her bow, she'd brought down a pair of squirrels. The meat helped them keep their strength up, but the longer they delayed in the forest, the more chance of one of the children falling ill. Winter was deepening, and even children could catch the thickness. Gods, Sigyn's father would have died of that had he not fallen—saving her—to the trolls. It was not a death she'd wish on anyone, least of all Frigg's children.

She tapped a finger against her lip. "There are people coming in our direction."

Frigg groaned.

"Always with the running," Fulla said. "And then the hiding and the running, both. Best thing, I tell you, is if we had some help. A few strong men to protect us."

Sigyn hefted her bow. "*I* can protect us."

"Sure as sure you can, if it be squirrels and deer come to rape and kill us dead."

Sigyn was about to point out that she'd killed trolls as well, but then again, that day had not ended well. Not well for her and Frigg's father, and even worse for Fulla.

"You're not a shieldmaiden," Frigg added.

Maybe they'd respect her more if she did start spitting and cursing and carrying a sword. Instead, glowering, she trod off in the direction she'd heard men coming from. She kept low to the ground. To her ears, she made a great deal of noise—though not half so much as Frigg or Fulla.

Sigyn waved them back. With no experience in wood-craft, they were apt to get them discovered in a heartbeat. Alone, she pressed on, until she drew up close. Peering around a tree, she spied a small party, five men—none she recognized. Probably Hunalanders.

Damn it.

This close, they'd see a fire as soon as the sun finished setting. Even torchlight might draw them. Slowly, she unshouldered her bow. She was a damned fine shot, but five men ... No one shot that fast. It took time to nock an arrow, draw it, take aim. At this range, a man with a blade could kill a woman three times over before she got a shot off.

Besides. Killing trolls was one thing. But these were just men, out scouting the woods for their enemies. She had never killed another human being, and the thought of seeing one of her arrows sprout from a person's chest, seeing his eyes go cold, it turned her stomach and left her shaking her head. And if she did naught? If she allowed these men to find her and her sister, find Fulla, then she had done worse than kill. She'd allowed harm to come to those she loved.

So she had to do something.

She nocked an arrow. Slow breaths. Steady. Let everything else fall away, just as Agilaz had taught her. Her new senses made that easier. Her vision could narrow until naught but her target even existed.

Bow drawn, she stepped around the tree trunk. Aimed at a man. He turned in her direction. Maybe he heard something. She loosed. Her arrow punched straight through his thigh, jutting out the other side. The man toppled over, clutching his wound and screaming loud enough to draw every wandering vaettir in the whole damned forest.

Rather than draw again, Sigyn took off running, dashing between trees, away from Frigg and Fulla. Without her, they might get lost in the woods, wander into a cave bear or a pack of dire wolves or Freyja knew what else. But she had to draw these men off.

On and on she ran, the shouts of pursuit ever close behind. The apple gave her stamina, so maybe—*maybe*—she could outrun them. But quite likely not.

Heart racing, she jumped upon a root, then onto another, disguising her footprints in the snow. She leapt up, caught a branch, and climbed onto the bough of an ash tree. From there, she climbed further out.

Her foot slipped, and she slammed against the branch.

An instant later, men raced by beneath her.

"Where did she go?"

"Find the bitch before one of us catches an arrow like Roelof!"

"The footprints just disappear." The speaker circled back, pausing beneath one tree over, where she had first started climbing on roots.

Damn it. She'd planned to move further, jump from one tree to the next. But any sound she made now would draw their eyes. And shooting her bow from this position was impossible.

The man knelt, inspecting the roots.

Sigyn stifled a groan. Think fast. A drop from this height would slow her for a moment, long enough for them to catch her. She could sit up, *try* to shoot one of them, but those men had bows as well.

"She must have climbed a tree."

Taking care to make no noise, Sigyn pushed herself up to a sitting position. The arrows jostling together in her quiver sounded loud to her, but none of them looked in her direction. They had, however, began scanning all the trees in a haphazard pattern. No plan or organization, but sooner or later they'd get lucky, and then she'd have nowhere to go.

So.

Slow breaths.

If she could somehow take out two of them, maybe the others would flee for cover, giving her time to get down. It was a slim hope, but better than none. She eased an arrow loose from her quiver.

More footfalls sounded from beyond the men. Sigyn grit her teeth. Last thing she needed. Reinforcements.

The twang of a bow caused her to drop flat again on pure instinct. An arrow sprouted from the chest of the one of the men. The victim fell, crashing into the snow.

"She's behind us!"

As they fumbled with their own bows, another arrow hit one of them in the face.

Sigyn gasped at the gruesome sight, drawing the gaze of one of the scouts. At the same instant, a shadow stepped from behind a tree and wrapped a hand over the man's mouth. The figure behind him—Loki! Freyja be praised—drove his victim to the ground and held him until he stopped struggling.

The last man broke and ran, but had gone only a dozen steps before another arrow caught him in the back.

Loki. Sigyn stared open-mouthed at him. He always found her, somehow. How did he do that? Not purely by tracking, it couldn't be, not the route she'd taken. So one more secret, deep and hidden as his connection to the flames.

As she climbed down, Agilaz joined them. Sigyn threw her arms first around her foster father, then around her lover. They had come to save her.

She kissed Loki.

Shame, though. Had she proved more useful, maybe she would not have needed saving.

When it came to it, she'd kept Frigg and Fulla and the babes alive, but not much else.

"Are you injured?" Agilaz asked.

No. Not injured. But she was going to have to do better in the future. She would not allow herself to become a burden. She'd had an apple, same as any of them. And that meant it was past time to start doing her part.

$\mathcal{V}$olsung stared at his convulsing hand a moment, looked up at Gudrun, then back down at his hand. At first, she thought he might ask her to ease his pain or try to heal his injury—neither of which lay within her Art —but he did naught instead. Perhaps he had not even imagined the Art could do such things. Perhaps he had simply accustomed himself to pain. Gudrun could empathize, though her wounds did not show as obviously as Volsung's.

"The stories are true," the king said at last. "Odin is a god among men."

Well, that was unfortunate. Gudrun ground her teeth a moment, before spreading her hands. "It is more complicated than that."

Volsung leaned forward, lips curled back in what almost looked like a snarl. "I count us fortunate he has not yet laid siege to this castle. It leaves me time to send word to our allies in case he does so. However, should the Aesir choose to leave us be, prudence demands we return the favor. Let them be gone from our lands, and good riddance."

"That is not your place to decide. You have an oath to the queen."

Volsung slapped his throne with his good hand and rose suddenly enough that several of his men turned on her, hands on weapons. Gudrun kept her hands at her side, careful not to further incite these people. They had lost lives and honor both, and men in such situations could act rashly.

Scowling, Volsung stalked to the great tree and stroked it. "My father's oath means naught if we lose our kingdom and still fail."

The men were still watching her. Afraid. What would such men do if they witnessed the Art? Those sensitive to it might feel unnerved, even ill, when a sorceress began to call a bound spirit. But if they actually saw her *do* something? Would they break, flee screaming about witchcraft? Perhaps not. Perhaps they would attack. She drew close to Volsung, but slowly, trying not to seem a threat.

"Queen Grimhild does not tolerate failure." She spoke softly, pitching her voice for the king alone. "And she answers to a greater power still—one for whom we can truly say there is none greater. Fail in your oath, and you may find even death offers no respite from the agonies you will suffer."

Volsung groaned, leaned heavier against the tree. "I need time. I need to gather every ally I can. If we hope to overcome them, we'll need vastly greater numbers."

"Then move quickly, before they pass beyond your lands. For if they do, Grimhild will still expect you to pursue. Even unto Valland or beyond, if need be."

Volsung raised an eyebrow at that. Maybe at learning the Aesir were bound so far, maybe at her implying she would force him to invade a foreign empire. Either way, Gudrun spun and stalked out of the hall.

She needed to gather her own information about Odin and his whereabouts, and she would not try such things here. Not surrounded by these skittish men.

Instead, she left the castle and wandered the woods. The same mist that choked and poisoned the land also offered succor and answers to those willing to bend to it.

Gudrun paused, the hairs on the back of her neck standing on end. The mist was congealing, sorcery in the air. She spun to see the vapors forming up behind her, taking the shape of a skull. Or a bone mask, as Grimhild wore when she conjured. Gudrun forced herself to stillness. If the queen wished to speak with her, there was little point in running. None of Gudrun's Art could hold a candle to Grimhild's. The queen carried a tome said to be written by Hel herself, and with it, Grimhild could summon spirits Gudrun would not dare even name.

Grimhild had been Queen of the Niflungar for centuries at the very least. And through all that time her hair had retained a luster as blonde as Gudrun's own, her face blemish free. Indeed, her mother could pass for Gudrun's older sister. What secrets she used to maintain her youth, Gudrun had never been able to uncover. And Grimhild gave naught away for free. Everything with her had a price. That was one lesson Gudrun would *never* forget.

She rubbed the spirit glyph on her arm as if to remind herself.

"Where are you?" The vapors hissed as her mother spoke.

"Near Volsung's hall. His people died in droves, and still the Aesir march on. They may reach Valland within another moon."

"It will be enough time." Though the words were but a whisper in the wind, Gudrun heard them clearly.

"Time for what?" Did Grimhild now sanction her attempt to win Odin back?

"For your army to catch them."

"*My* army?" Gudrun had many talents, but she was no general. Her brother Guthorm might have been able to lead men, but Gudrun had other ways of getting what she wanted.

"You are the closest. You will serve, directing the troops to harry Odin's warriors. Cut them off—do not let them reach Vanaheim."

Vanaheim would be beyond the Niflungar's reach, true, but Gudrun doubted she could stop the Aesir through any direct confrontation. She caught herself about to shake her head. One didn't deny Queen Grimhild. Not ever. To do so was ... Gudrun had to suppress a shiver that threatened to overcome her. Some mistakes a woman made only once. "How will an army catch them, much less get ahead of them?"

She could have sworn her mother snickered, the sound like the crunch of snow underfoot. "Because, daughter, your army need not sleep."

The mists shifted again, revealing an image of a snow-field nearby. Across it tromped the shadow of a man, its gait uneven but steady. Its flesh had turned sallow and wan, though remnants of armor concealed most of the wretched thing. But not its eyes. Eyes filled with hatred of the living, lit with a red gleam. More and more of the creatures trudged forward, never faltering, never slowing.

Draugar.

Revenants of the dead, animated by the mists. Warriors not fortunate enough to have had a funeral pyre, now bound in service and trapped in eternal hatred, become ghosts possessing their own corpses. Stronger than any man, tireless, and utterly relentless. An army of the dead that could match even the so-called Ás gods. And where had her mother gotten an army of the dead?

Deep down, Gudrun knew. A whole battlefield of fresh corpses lay strewn about, men fallen from both sides. The Aesir and Hunalanders alike would set pyres, but perhaps they had not moved quickly enough. And Hel granted Grimhild the strength to raise those fallen tainted with the most hatred. Why now? Why would the goddess grant such a thing centuries after the Niflungar were defeated and driven to islands in Reidgotaland? Was Hel herself so bent on Odin she would expend such power to see him brought to ruin? Or brought to heel.

And the very warriors he had just slain would rise against him again, more powerful than ever.

Gudrun hugged herself, for once not caring if Grimhild saw it as weakness. Even for a priestess of Hel, this seemed profane. A single draug possessing a corpse was enough to leave even most Niflungar on edge. An army of them was like the myths of old. But ... but it was an opportunity. Pushed to the brink, Odin *would* at last turn back to her. And the draugar would push him there. Odin and those who had eaten the fruit of Yggdrasil might match a draug, but his mortal warriors would fall like leaves from a tree.

And faced with the annihilation of all he knew, Odin would finally see where his true love lay. Finally embrace his destiny at her side. And if he did so before Grimhild could reach him, Gudrun could hope to save him from the queen's plans.

10

*W*ith Volsung's army broken, Odin had called another Thing. Voices filled the circle, wondering why Odin did not order them to storm the castle of those who had betrayed them. Tyr wondered the same. Odin seemed only to have a mind for his family, now returned.

Thanks to Agilaz ... and Loki. The man who always knew too much.

Tyr tried to keep his watchful eye on the crowd, but found his gaze ever drawn to Odin and Frigg. They stood in the midst of the people. Thor held tight to Frigg's breast.

Only Jarl Bedvig held silent now, no doubt yet reeling from his shame. It brought a slight smile to Tyr's face. The man deserved worse still, of course.

"Why are we not pushing forward?" Lodur demanded.

Odin held up his hand and, like that, everyone fell silent. They had seen what he'd done in the battle. Fewer and fewer of them would challenge his authority now. At least while the memory remained fresh. "We could lay siege there, yes. Spends days or moons trying to breach those walls while winter deepens and our supplies run low. Do you suppose, then, that we will find enough game and forage in one place to feed all those mouths out there?" He waved to indicate the greater portion of Aesir. "No. We will starve before they do. Believe me, I wanted to make an example of this king—and one day, perhaps I will. We do not forget the debts owed to us."

Men shouted at that, a few banging weapons on their shields.

"We cannot afford to sap our strength fighting every petty king between here and Vanaheim. Instead ..." Odin looked to Loki. Damn it. Foreigner had some other fool plan. "Instead we must push south, into the mountains no man lays claim to."

The Sudurberks. Damn it all.

"No man," Vili said. "Fucking vaettir, though. Mist so thick you'd choke on it."

Odin scowled at his brother. "We'll have torches."

Other jarls began bickering. Complaining about leaving foes behind them. Or the hardships of marching their tribes through mountains. Or who would get to go first in narrow mountain passes. Which tribe deserved the highest honors.

Agilaz wended his way among the Thing. Tyr watched him, arms folded over his chest. Nigh to twenty thousand people trying to move through mountains. Hard to say whether it would cost more lives than it saved.

Roughly a third of the people were what Tyr would consider warriors. Some others could fight if pushed to it. More important were the berserkir and varulfur who had fallen roughly under the command of Vili and Hoenir. Dozens of the shapeshifters guarded the Aesir against the night, against other vaettir.

Varulfur had always existed on the fringes of Ás society.

By adopting those two werewolf children, Odin had bestowed honor on the entire breed. Once, Tyr had heard a legend that all shapeshifters had a progenitor. An ultimate ancestor of the breed that embodied all the true, unbridled power the Moon vaettir wielded. Rage and power made flesh. Born to slaughter all in its path. What had Heidr called the ancestral varulf? Fenrir. That was it. A story the völva had used to frighten children. To keep them huddled close around the fires. Or perhaps, the stories of epic slaughter were intended to separate ordinary men from the varulfur who protected them.

Now, though, Vili seemed primed to portray all shapeshifters as the elite of the Aesir. And true, they did make astounding protectors and guardians. But it was hard to trust one who was half controlled by a vaettr. Particularly one that could be given over to animal savagery at any moment.

"The mists have worked too quickly in the night," Agilaz said. "No few of the fallen are missing."

"Missing?" Odin demanded.

A hush fell over the circle.

Agilaz scowled, took in the Aesir. "Battlefields are chaos, so it's hard to say with certainty. But I believe some of the dead rose last night."

"Draugar." Odin fairly spat the word.

"Yes. I believe so. And when the sun sets … They seem already to be trying to flank us. Hem us in."

Tyr's groan was one of many. Men feared few things more than draugar, and with good reason. Unlike trolls which were given to stupidity, draugar held the skills and cunning of men. Matched those with relentless strength and stamina and hatred for the living.

Murmurs passed among all gathered. The Ás leaders,

clan jarls, völvur, all stirred. The looks on their faces, the tremors in their voices, Tyr watched them all. Some of these men and women would break, panic. Others didn't seem to believe Agilaz.

"Are you certain?" Odin asked.

Tyr could understand his skepticism. A draug might be expected in the wilds. Indeed, perhaps even groups of them. Entire hunting parties brought down by the cold or vaettir. Brought down, and raised once again by the mists of Hel. But hundreds ... that was an army. *Their* army. Such things did not happen this quickly. Völvur stories spoke of such occurrences when the mists first covered this world. Back before men knew they must always burn their dead. But such times had since long passed into legend. Myth.

Even Tyr could not fight such an army. Some of the other warriors looked to him, so Tyr forced his gaze to remain impassive. Courage was worth a hundred spears. It was the one weapon they could not afford to ever break.

"Can we avoid them?" Frigg asked.

The scout hesitated. "They move faster than we can transplant the tribes, and they seem to know where we are bound. Their greatest numbers gather to the west, where we head."

The murmurs once again filled the crowd. A few jarls started arguing.

After several moments, Odin banged Gungnir on the ground, once again drawing silence. "Then the course is clear," Odin said, casting his voice so deep it would carry beyond the Thing to the crowd that, by now, had begun to panic. "We must take to the mountains. We cannot face human enemies and draugar both. I will gather my forces and head off those who may block the passes, clear the way. The rest of you," Odin said, looking to the jarls, "send your finest warriors to guard our flanks. We cannot allow this to slow us."

Slow us. Interesting choice of words. Odin implied there was no actual worry of the threat defeating them. Only disrupting their advance. Was that a conscious choice to instill confidence in his people, or was it his own pride in thinking none could stop him? Either way, Tyr had to approve. Courage was what these people needed to see. And courage was what Odin showed them.

Even if it was false or vain courage. Seven of Odin's people had taken the apples, but Frigg and Sigyn were not warriors. Ve was gone. That left Odin, Vili, Loki, and Tyr. Four men-become-gods to fight an army born of Niflheim. Berserkir and varulfur might match a draug. Maybe. Tyr would bet on the draug. And Men were even worse off. The truth was, many of the Aesir would die for this. Tyr could not save them all, but he could help them meet their ancestors with pride. Maybe that was all a warrior could ever do.

With the Thing dismissed, Tyr moved to begin gathering his warriors. He needed the best, the bravest. A decisive victory against this threat would ensure the Aesir morale held. And a failure ... Best not dwell on such an event.

By the time he had finished selecting, Odin stood before him, cloth-wrapped bundle in his arms.

"A moment, Tyr."

"My lord?"

"In private."

Tyr nodded and led Odin back to his own tent. Inside Odin crouched on the furs, so Tyr slunk down beside his king. The man's eyes had grown dark—darker than usual, even for these days.

"An army of draugar," Odin said. "An army of the undead ..."

Tyr folded his arms, not certain what Odin was implying.

"It's the Niflungar," Odin said at last. "The draugar are born of the mists, and the Niflungar command those mists. I killed their prince, Tyr."

Tyr nodded. Odin had told him all this some time ago.

"My family," Odin mumbled. "Tyr, I want you to do something for me. My children, my wife, I cannot lose them. Please, protect them."

Children? Odin now thought of those varulfur, Geri and Freki, as his own children. Apt, perhaps, given the king had killed their mother. Tyr placed a hand on the man's shoulder. "You know I would protect them with my life, my lord."

"No," Odin said, shaking his head. "No, I ... I lost Ve ... I lost Father ... I can't ..." Odin shook himself, then unwrapped the bundle, revealing a sword. Runes covered the length of its blade, woven steel that spoke of ancient times long forgotten. Ice-blue gems were set in its crossguard and bone-hilted pommel. "This was the blade I took from Guthorm."

The Niflung prince. Odin had said the man carried a runeblade, one supposedly forged by dvergar. Blades of power, legends now.

"Take it."

Tyr placed a hand over its hilt, but hesitated. "I have my own sword, given to me by Borr."

"Keep it, please," Odin said. "There may come a time ..." The king shook his head, clearly once again lost in his own mind.

Tyr closed his palm around the hilt. It was cold. Colder even than the bone handle ought to be on a day like this. Rather than draw the blade, he took it sheathed and set it aside.

The moment he did so, Odin nodded and rose, staring at something beyond Tyr's vision. Beyond his understanding, perhaps. The king ducked out of the tent without another word, leaving Tyr alone with this magic-wrought blade. Would wielding such a weapon fill him with the same bloodlust Gungnir did? Would it make him savage, like a berserk or varulf?

But it would grant him power—maybe the power to save lives. To protect his people. This he needed.

He was still staring at it when Idunn slipped into the tent shortly thereafter, a skinned rabbit clutched in one hand.

"The hunters caught it this morning. I thought maybe it was time for some of that famous Tyr stew."

Tyr shook himself and looked to her, but her gaze had fallen on the blade. "I have not the time," he said. "We go to battle soon."

"With that?"

Now Tyr glanced back at the blade, too. "You know it?"

Idunn knelt in front of him, setting the rabbit aside. Her red dress settled around her, shimmering in the soft light that filtered into the tent. To call Idunn the oddest woman he'd ever met would be like calling a jotunn taller than a man. Her skin was rich like it had been stained with mead. Her hair darker than was oft found among Aesir. At first, when she had taken to visiting him, he'd been as entranced with her as any other man in the camp had. But over a hundred such conversations she had eventually put him at ease. Mostly.

The Vanr goddess picked up the runeblade without any sign of fear. In truth, Tyr couldn't recall her ever showing fear. Idunn ran a slender finger over the gems in the pommel, then the runes in its sheath. "Gramr." Then she looked up at his face. "Oh! Well, I know its reputation. Weapons like this, Tyr, they have their uses. Frey carries one. But they have dangers, too."

"You can read the runes."

"Immortality gives one time to learn all *kinds* of interesting things."

Given her mischievous smile, Tyr doubted she was speaking merely of scholarly learning. He could not afford to dwell on whatever she meant, not now. Instead, he looked back at Gramr. "Is there reason not to use it?"

"Oh, yes, for certain. But you never seem too interested in hearing stories about the supernatural world, dear sweet warrior."

An understatement. Given the choice, Tyr might not have eaten the apple at all. Though it had made him stronger, faster, and more resilient than any man. He would not now be marching on Vanaheim nor waging war against draugar without it. But Tyr had sworn his oaths to Borr and his sons, and he would never turn his back on those vows. Where Odin led, he must follow. Even into the mists, into Realms man had no business treading.

"I don't know what to do," he said.

Idunn snickered. "I'm not that kind of goddess. I don't answer prayers for guidance, Tyr. Really, I'm just a woman."

"I never knew a woman afraid to tell a man what to do." The words slipped out of his mouth before he realized he'd said them, and he immediately flinched. Perhaps he was a bit *too* at ease with this woman.

But her smile grew wider for a moment, before she looked away. "You still miss her?"

Now Tyr rose, leaving the sword resting where it lay. It had been another moment of weakness, telling Idunn of his wife. "No." Did he miss Zisa? "I have preparations to make."

He slipped from the tent without another glance at Idunn. He had no desire to dredge up the past, not with the Vanr woman. Not with anyone. Practical matters were, more oft than not, a reprieve from the torments of days gone by. His only reprieve.

He needed to kill something.

11

"The pass is the shortest route, and the safest," Loki said. "They'll know that."

Snow flurries obscured Odin's view of the rocky, snow-crusted path Loki indicated. Odin hadn't wanted to do this at night. At night it was harder to see, too easy to slip on the mountain slopes. But Loki insisted their enemies would not show themselves in daylight.

"And you're certain that qualifies as a pass?" Vili asked. At Loki's appraising stare, Vili shrugged. "I mean we have children, elderly. Rough trek, that."

"It will be rougher if we don't clear the draugar before the others reach us," Odin said. He nodded at Tyr, who in turn motioned a dozen of his best men forward.

The so-called pass was a route through these ancient mountains, and one Odin prayed would offend no vaettr dwelling within such a timeless place. Jagged peaks jutted at irregular angles in all directions, each covered in ice and snow, bare hints of the rock beneath poking through. The path was barely wide enough for two men to walk abreast—or a single man in Vili's case, as Odin's brother pushed his way forward. Not to be outdone by Tyr and his warriors, of course.

And off the side, that drop had to be as tall as ten men. More, perhaps, for he could see no end through the mist. A misstep, a patch of hidden ice, and a man could know what it was to fly—for a moment, at least.

A sudden brisk wind whipped the snow flurries into Odin's eyes.

"Fuck me," one of the men ahead cursed, the lot of them throwing themselves against the rock face to avoid being blown off.

"Vaettir don't want men here," Vili mumbled, himself hugging the mountainside.

There was no getting around a man of his size, so Odin shoved his brother forward. "Keep moving."

Those things were here somewhere. Their small party was all that stood between the undead and the Aesir who had followed Odin into these mountains. All that stood between the monsters and Odin's family. If they didn't deal with these bastards before—

Metal creaked on bone from above. A shriek that sent a shudder down even Odin's spine ripped out of a black form. The creature fell upon a man in the middle of the line. The man's scream was brief. Odin tried to push forward, but through the press of bodies and the Hel-damned snow he couldn't ...

Grunting and shrieking, both man and draug tumbled over the side. Odin spun, rushing to the edge, though he knew himself too far and too late to help the fallen man. Even as he watched the forms disappear into the darkness of the gorge, the snow beneath their party erupted. The impact tripped Odin and sent him careening over the edge himself, his grip on Gungnir lost.

Rocks snared his furs and caught on his mail, tearing both as he tumbled downward. For a heartbeat he was breathless, plummeting. Then all wind blasted from his lungs as he impacted a rock outcropping some fifteen feet below the pass. Odin struggled to catch his breath, staring at the icicle-laced overhang above. Like the jaws of a dragon hovering above him.

How was he going to get back to his people?

Gods above, his people. How many of the fucking draugar had been waiting under the snow? Odin hadn't even considered it ... The draugar didn't breathe.

A dark form dropped from above. Odin rolled to one side, barely avoiding the impact and almost flinging himself off the outcropping—a ledge not much larger than he was. The creature landed in a crouch where Odin had lain, fist embedded into the ice caking the rocks. It lifted its head up, revealing a red gleam in its eyes. Black, corroded armor concealed its gaunt arms and sallow flesh. A helm hid much of its face beyond the eyes. When it smiled, it revealed a missing tooth.

With a grunt, it yanked its fist free of the ice, spiderwebbing cracks all across the ledge. The ground shifted beneath Odin's feet, and he slipped, banging his knee on the ice. It was all the time the draug needed to bear down on him. The creature moved with uncanny speed, leaping atop Odin and driving him to the ground with its sheer weight and ungodly strength.

The creature's hand on his throat was cold as hoar. Cold as the grave. The hatred of all life filled its eyes, trying to swallow up Odin's very soul. He had but to give in. To accept the rage and the curse ...

To give up.

The one thing Odin would never do.

The edges of his vision faded from lack of air. But Odin had been practicing the use of his apple-granted boons. They came at will now. Strength flooded his limbs—the strength to match even this Hel-spawned monster. Odin's grip tightened on the draug's arm, and he at last pulled it away from his throat. Gods-blessed air rushed back into his lungs in gasps that left him even more lightheaded. The draug yanked him upward with its other hand, pulling them both back to their feet.

It shoved Odin, trying to hurl him from the precipice into the gorge. Odin flung himself forward, driving them both toward the mountainside. He rained blows against the draug, heard its bones breaking even beneath the armor. Odin's knuckles split, his blood caking the undead. If the draug felt aught, it gave little indication. Instead it countered, catching Odin with blows first to the ribs, then the face. Odin struggled to get his arms up, to block blows that could challenge his own supernatural strength.

At last he caught the draug's arm and landed a mighty blow to the side of its head. The impact knocked away the thing's helm and seemed to stagger it, if only for a moment.

"Die!" Odin shouted at it. Why would the cursed thing not die?

Again the draug advanced. Odin blocked its blow with one arm and scored another uppercut to the thing's chin. Once again, it staggered for an instant. Was it vulnerable to blows to the head?

Before the draug could attack again, Odin roared and slammed shoulder-first into its chest, knocking it back against the mountainside. He leapt up and caught an icicle as long as his arm. Then he slammed it straight into the draug's eye and out the other side.

The monstrosity continued to twitch in the snow, but gave over attacking.

"Odin!" Loki shouted from above. The man's face peeked over the ledge, followed a moment later by a rope.

Odin grabbed on and half-climbed the rope as Loki pulled him upward. He crested the ledge back onto the pass, then faltered at the sight. A draug crushed one of Tyr's men's throats with his bare hand, chuckling as it did so. Another beat a man's shield to kindling with its axe, then tore into the now-exposed warrior. Tyr spun, cut off one draug's legs, then kicked another in the chest, sending it toppling over the cliff.

Vili had assumed bear form and was mauling one of the creatures, but most of Odin's soldiers had fallen. More and more of the draugar surged forward, converging from the pass ahead and the seemingly unscalable cliff above them.

Odin retrieved Gungnir from the snow where it had fallen. The moment he held it, its ancient power filled him. His pain dulled, his fear vanished. "I am Odin! Son of Borr! Come to me and die again!"

He lunged forward, his thrust punching through a draug's shield, its armor, and its flesh. Odin jerked it to the side, flinging it free of his spear and straight off the mountain. The creature did not scream as it plummeted into the gorge, leaving Odin to wonder if even such a fall would break these unholy things. Völvur said one had to burn them.

Odin turned on another draug, driving it too toward the edge. Dead or not, from the chasm below, these fucks were a lot less worry.

A sudden bellow from Vili stole Odin's attention. A draug stood atop Odin's brother, having driven a sword straight through the bear's shoulder and out the other side.

"V-Vili?" Odin stammered.

The draug Odin had engaged leapt at him. An axe soared through the air and impacted the creature, driving it over the edge. Odin barely glanced at Tyr, too distracted to even acknowledge the man who had saved him.

Gods above and below. Odin had lost one brother because of his pride, because he hadn't been strong enough. He'd lost one of Father's sons, failed both brother and father. He couldn't lose Vili. Not now. Not now!

Odin roared and charged forward. He saw naught but the draug atop his brother. He barreled into the thing and bore it down, then proceeded to beat his fist into its skull. Again and again he pounded the fiend, crunching bone and decayed brain beneath. And finally, finally it lay still.

Loki yanked him away. "We have to get him to a völva."

Vili.

Odin nodded, unable to form words over the lump in his throat.

Tyr charged another draug, now fighting with a mere dagger. He'd lost his sword somewhere. The draugar's numbers were growing, and so few of the Ás men remained. "Fall back, my lord! Your brother is beyond saving."

"No!"

Loki glanced between Vili and Odin, then knelt beside the fallen bear, who still weakly tried to crawl toward the fight. "I have to remove the sword so you can shift back. We cannot carry you in this state."

If Loki pulled that sword out, even a berserk might bleed to death. But if Vili lost consciousness and shifted back to a man with it still in him, the injuries would prove even more dire. Loki waited for no further answer. With one hand he jerked the sword free, then cast it aside.

A rumble left Vili's chest, then he collapsed into the

snow. Slowly his body began to shrink, the fur retreating back within his skin. Odin moved to carry Vili, but Loki lifted his brother before he got there.

"Clear the way," Loki said. "We must move with haste. They will pursue us until the sun rises."

"How long?" Odin asked.

"Two hours," Loki said.

Even with his apple-granted endurance, that was a long time to flee these creatures. Calling on supernatural strength and stamina gave him energy, but would drain him all the more afterwards. And would Odin lead the undead back to his people? There was no choice. He had to get Vili help now.

Odin rushed forward, batting another draug off the mountainside as he did. It didn't matter what it took or how long he must fight. He was getting his brother out of this. He was *saving* Vili.

He owed it to Ve.

He owed it to his father.

12

—————

Sigyn brought another bowl of steaming water from the fire and set it beside Frigg. Her sister still worked fervently over Vili, hands drenched in the berserk's blood. Sigyn had seen Frigg work miracles with her völva healing arts, but this wound must be beyond even her sister's skills. The look on Frigg's face told her that much. Vili was no mere man, of course, which was probably the only reason he yet lived.

"Please," Odin said, his voice nigh to breaking. "Please, Frigg ... I can't lose him too. I ... I beg you." Odin seemed to stare at something beyond Frigg, as if seeing visions in the shadows. "I won't fail you again."

Was he speaking to someone else? His eyes barely took in any of the people here. Idunn and Loki lingered on opposite ends of the tent, as always, seeming to avoid each other. Sigyn had no time for their rivalry now.

"I won't," Odin mumbled.

Sigyn swallowed as Frigg frantically applied herbal poultices. Men said a berserk could live through almost any wound that didn't kill him instantly. But even a berserk needed blood to live, and Vili couldn't have much left. Not with the rivers of it he'd lost on the way here. Perhaps the otherworldly spirit within him could save him.

"I don't know what to do," Frigg whispered, her voice clearly pitched only for Sigyn.

Sigyn bit her lip. She was no völva. Instead, she looked to Loki.

Her man shook his head, but did approach. "His life energy is depleted," Loki said. "Even the Moon spirit inside him needs more energy to recover from such a wound."

Energy? "Like seid?" Sigyn asked.

Frigg looked at her, then back at Vili, as though she'd caught the same idea. Her sister placed one hand on the berserk's head, the other on the wound. Sigyn looked to Loki, but his eyes gave away naught. Could this really work?

Frigg had begun to tremble, beads of sweat building on her forehead. She drew a ragged breath, and Sigyn heard Idunn encroach close behind her. Everyone, even Odin, now looked at Frigg.

Then Vili spasmed, his body lurching forward. On instinct, Sigyn grabbed one of his arms to hold him down. Even with both hands she could barely hold it in place, though Odin had pinned his brother's other arm with little apparent effort. Vili roared in pain.

Frigg moaned, swaying in place, her eyes locked on Vili's shoulder. Her skin had gone pale, and Sigyn wanted to touch her, to comfort her, but she dared not let Vili up. It took her full weight to hold the man's arm in place.

Frigg trembled, her breath coming in gasps. And then she screamed and fell.

Sigyn scrambled to her side, no longer caring, as Vili lurched upward, sputtering blood.

"Frigg? Frigg?"

"She's a healer," Idunn whispered.

"Obviously," Sigyn snapped. "She's a völva."

"But she managed to transfer her pneuma, her life force, into another. Even among the Vanir, such healers are rare. Freyja can do it, a few others. I can do ... more with plants than people."

Sigyn frowned. *Her* boon from the apple appeared to be superhuman perception. Tyr, Vili, and Odin *all* got enhanced strength, Frigg held power over life itself, and Sigyn was stuck with the stunningly useful ability to hear a mouse fart.

And now her half sister was nigh to as pale as Vili had been. "What does that mean for *her*?"

"That she passed some part of herself into Vili."

Sigyn's frown deepened. The bear man was clearly going to live, which was good, but she couldn't say she liked the sound of what Idunn had said. If Frigg had passed part of herself into Vili, wouldn't there be some long-term ramifications? Would Frigg's own life force recover? Would Vili forever hold part of her inside himself?

"Thank you," Odin mumbled. As if he didn't care what cost Frigg might have paid to save his brother.

Frigg nodded weakly.

"Loki," Sigyn said, "can you help her?"

Her man immediately lifted Frigg and carried her to a fur where she could rest. Sigyn knelt beside her half sister and rubbed her forehead. Frigg had grown clammy, like a woman fighting a fever or losing to deathchill. Sigyn could only pray she wouldn't be tempted to use this ability often.

Loki walked back to where Odin knelt beside his brother. "We cannot remain here. Those draugar in the pass will move on us come nightfall."

Odin sat with his head in his hands, not looking up as he

spoke. "If we retreat, we allow those behind us to box us in, trap us in the valley. There has to be another way."

Loki was silent for a moment. Sigyn knew that look on his face—he would offer them a choice of damnations. "There might be. A river flows under these mountains, through ice caves carved beneath them. It could carry us well past Volsung and the draugar, both."

"Please tell me you're not thinking of the Ylgr," Idunn said. "The river is cursed, born from the chill on the edge of the World and saturated by the mists of Hel. It is not a place for Mankind. My people, even *my* people, would not challenge its rapids."

"Your people?" Loki said. "Those same people grown complacent on the blessed isles of Vanaheim? People content to bask in five millennia of spring while the rest of Mankind freezes and scrapes by out in the mists? *Those* people, Idunn?"

Odin paced around the tent. "Last night told us we are ill-prepared to face the foes ahead. We must take whatever route we can to press forward. We have to reach Vanaheim."

"Then we need to be on the river long before dark," Loki said.

Sigyn frowned. She didn't like the sound of this. She trusted Loki to protect them, he always had, but if this river frightened even Idunn—and naught had ever had such an effect on the Vanr that Sigyn had witnessed—it was probably no place for the Aesir.

Odin sighed. "Fine. I'll tell Tyr. Loki, move Vili to his own tent. We have to give him at last half an hour to rest." The berserk had regained a hint of color, but his breaths remained shallow.

Loki nodded and lifted Vili with little apparent effort. Sigyn's mouth hung open. Son of a bitch! Did Loki have superhuman strength too? *All* the men got that? How was that fair?

As soon as they left, Idunn chuckled. "Oh, don't worry so much. You'll both probably develop another boon or two over time. The apple awakens all the potential within you. You just have to learn to harness the pneuma."

Had Idunn just read that off her face? Sigyn closed her mouth, not answering. The Vanr goddess was more perceptive than she seemed. Most of the time she played at innocence. But Sigyn had heard the way she'd spoken to Loki, a conversation laced with ancient animosity and ulterior motives. Sooner or later, Sigyn was going to unravel that puzzle too.

First, she had to tend to Frigg. If Odin thought to march soon, Sigyn's sister was going to need her strength.

Idunn left, and Fulla entered, Thor in her arms, the two varulf children scampering about her feet. "These adorable babes wanted to see their ma, they did."

"She's too weak to hold them right now," Sigyn said, cutting off Frigg's attempt to grab Thor. "Just sit down, Fulla." The maid clearly didn't want to be alone, hadn't even wanted to be left outside while Frigg tended to Vili.

The woman did as Sigyn had bid her, settling down on a fur and ushering the varulf twins over to her skirts.

"I worry for him," Frigg said a moment later, though she didn't even sit up. For Frigg to show such weakness must have been a testament to her exhaustion.

Sigyn looked back to her sister. "I'm certain he'll recover now."

"Not Vili. Odin."

Sigyn frowned. More weighed on him than draugar, that much a fool could see, but her sister spent too much time thinking of a husband who, as far as Sigyn could tell, thought little on her. "What is it you want to say?"

"I think Odin never truly mourned the loss of his father."

Sigyn folded her arms over her chest. "His time of mourning is long past."

"Rage may have carried him a long way. His desire for vengeance, his pride ..."

"Rage?" Sigyn frowned. "Odin certainly has more than his fair share of that. But then, so should we."

Frigg shook her head, then pushed herself into a sitting position. "Our father's death was not truly Odin's fault. And we, at least, took our time to grieve."

Sigyn grunted, then leaned forward. "And you, despite yourself, you truly love him." Odin might make a fine king, but Sigyn doubted he was an ideal mate.

"Should I not love my husband?" Frigg asked.

"That's not an answer."

Frigg frowned. "What answer are you seeking, then?"

Sigyn shrugged. "Same as always. The truth." Loki was right. You could help another to the truth, but you couldn't give it to them. They had to figure it out for themselves for it to hold meaning.

"The truth is ... yes. Yes, Sigyn, I think I do."

"Well, that's half the truth."

"Sometimes I think you spend too much time in Loki's company."

Sigyn laughed. Was she that obvious? "Oh, but I love him. And I know how much he loves me. I can see it in his eyes."

Frigg sighed. "Fine. Yes, Sigyn. I do fear Odin doesn't truly love me. Is that what you wish to hear? Is that—" Frigg paused, almost choking on a sob. "Is that what you've been trying to say?"

Sigyn took her sister's hand in her own. "It's half of it."

Frigg sighed. "Please. Just have out with it. I have no energy for your riddles—save them for your lover."

"Let us say you hold only half Odin's heart. What should you do? Accept reality for what it is? Be grateful for what urd has offered you? What would you do if you thought a jarl not loyal, not confident in you as a leader?"

Frigg had helped Odin win over the jarls. She'd sent Fulla among their maids to tell the tale of her rescue. She'd sent gifts of plunder Odin had recovered as a promise of future riches. She'd even called out a particularly recalcitrant jarl, forced him to openly challenge Odin. Often enough, she'd asked Sigyn how best to manipulate her opponents.

"So I should bribe or manipulate my husband into loving me?"

Fulla snorted, then immediately went back to pretending not to listen.

"No, Frigg," Sigyn said. "Those are just tactics in a larger plan. A plan to fight for what you want. If it is something worth having, isn't it worth fighting for?"

"Whom am I supposed to fight, exactly?"

Sigyn shrugged. "I guess that's what you have to figure out. Know your enemy. Either way, Frigg, eternity is a long time to spend unhappy." Sigyn paused. In truth, Frigg needed more time to rest and probably needed a bit more sisterly advice. Unfortunately, circumstances didn't allow for either. "Just try to rest."

ALREADY, the camp had begun to move, heading deeper into the mountains, toward a river even Idunn feared, one that apparently could carry them under the land itself. Had Sigyn not seen all she had, she might have dismissed such a claim as fanciful.

She woke Frigg with a hand on her shoulder. "Can you walk?"

Frigg groaned, then nodded. Sigyn helped her to her feet, then guided her outside. Even as they exited the tent Loki was already on his way over, a bit of roast rabbit in his hands.

"You need to eat," he said, pushing the rabbit into Frigg's hands.

Frigg bit right in, and Sigyn had to stifle a giggle. Gods, she'd never seen Frigg eat like that. Hel, she ate like a berserk. Where had that dainty völva gone? And maybe more to the point, how had Loki known healing would so drain her?

Sigyn's man nodded at her, as if acknowledging her unspoken question. "Odin waits for you in the front." He pointed toward the gorge, then swept up Geri and Freki in his arms.

Sigyn started down the gorge, Frigg at her side and Fulla and Loki trailing behind them. As if the mountain passes had not been bad enough, now they *descended* into misty darkness that looked much like she imagined Niflheim itself.

The Ás camp was largely packed already, everyone prepared for another march. Most probably didn't know where they were bound yet.

Frigg leaned on her shoulder while they walked, and Sigyn said naught. She'd seen the gorge when they entered this valley. The chasm was deeper than even her enhanced eyes could see the end of, but there was a path down into it. If Loki was wrong, if they went down there and there wasn't a way forward, they'd be trapped. The draugar would hem them in and pick them off, one night at a time.

But Loki never seemed to be wrong.

"It will be all right," Loki said from behind her.

"Y-you don't think there's trolls down there?" Fulla asked.

"There's no trolls," Frigg said without looking back.

Of course, there damned well could be trolls in such a place, but Sigyn supposed telling Fulla that would only make things worse. So they continued downward, entering the gorge. A steep slope led into an ice canyon, the walls covered in icicles jutting out at every possible angle like countless spears ready to impale the fools who entered. The mists wafted over the gorge, creating a near ceiling that left the canyon looking more like a cavern. Thousands of Aesir all marching to the gates of Hel? The further down they went, the colder it grew.

Idunn had spoken the truth—the curse of Hel settled upon this place. Sigyn's skin prickled and, though she saw naught, she could have sworn she felt the brush of the damned, moving invisibly beside her and welcoming the living to join in their torment. Yes, the gorge seemed exactly like a passage to Niflheim.

Her footing grew slippery. It wasn't snow down here, it was solid ice, matching the shimmering walls of this place. From the way Frigg stumbled about, Sigyn realized her sister couldn't see well enough. Ahead, other Aesir held torches, but Sigyn hadn't thought to light one. How easy to forget her own eyes could see better in the dark than the others'. She glanced back. Fulla was watching her own feet carefully, but Loki stared ahead, meeting her gaze. Could he see, or did he simply trust her to lead the way?

A long, long way down into the gorge they walked. Hundreds, thousands of footfalls sounded behind them. Frigg shivered beneath Sigyn's arm. And if they were cold after having eaten the apple, how would the mortal Aesir fare? The answer was as simple as it was abhorrent—many would fall to the deathchill. The young, the old, the sick. They would freeze tonight.

Many of the group ahead had paused. The bottom of the gorge opened into a cave, its maw like that of some enormous dragon. Stalactites and stalagmites of ice jutted all around it in a circle, the dragon's teeth, ready to swallow any foolhardy enough to pass.

At the cusp of the cave, Odin stood, watching the Aesir line collect, giving the long camp time to catch up. "You're certain?" he asked Loki when the man walked up to his side.

"Unless you can fly," Loki said, "this is the surest way to bypass the creatures that pursue us. We have a few scant hours until sunset, then they will be on us. You cannot afford to hesitate."

"We've come this far into the gorge," Sigyn said. "There's no time to turn back." Even if it did look like Hel waited for them within.

Odin nodded at her, then looked to Frigg. "Be strong."

Odin hefted his torch higher and wound his way between two stalagmites. Sigyn could have sworn a fell mist wafted off the ice as he passed. Odin led the way, followed by Loki. Sigyn grabbed a torch from one of the other Aesir, then followed with Frigg, who now seemed able to walk on her own.

The walls inside were solid ice, a blue-white hue that only reinforced the stomach-clenching sensation of passing beyond Midgard. Before they had gone far, she heard the rush of water, its rumbling echoing off the ice cave walls, growing louder with each step they took. It must have been the river, but gods above, it sounded like a waterfall. How fast was this current?

The path sloped downward, the ice slick and moist, each step threatening to send them all sprawling. Sigyn tried to move cautiously, but Odin and Loki were getting too far ahead. Rather than heft her torch high, Sigyn kept it low, watching their footing.

Exhaustion wore at Sigyn's legs when at last the ground leveled out. The sound of rushing water now filled the entire cave, drowning out conversation. She rounded a bend and saw why. The underground river cut a path through the ice cave, flowing so quickly that ice floes—some ten feet wide or more—passed out of her view in a few breaths. An endless stream of those floes poured forward, perhaps cut loose by the currents, or perhaps hurled straight out of Niflheim itself. Idunn had called this river cursed. Sigyn believed her. It swept round bends, splashing against the ice walls, the floes smacking into the sides and each other.

"How do you propose we get boats down here?" Odin asked.

Or guide any boat through that? No waterman could avoid smashing his craft to tinder in such a tumult.

"I don't," Loki said. "We'll have to ride the ice floes."

"Have you gone mad, brother?"

Sigyn was forced to agree with Odin. "There are thousands of people behind us, Loki. Some carrying children, all laden with supplies."

"Tell them to leave aught they can spare," Loki said. "If the draugar catch us, we will have no use for extra tents or food, much less golden trinkets or treasures. Some of those floes are fifty feet or more across. We can make it."

Some of them would, perhaps. Others would die. And Loki knew that, Sigyn was certain. Gods, they *all* knew that now. But he must've known before suggesting this place. Was this truly their only option? A chill settled on her heart. He'd known what this would cost and still suggested it. Perhaps it was the least of all the evils.

Others came forward, helping Vili along. The berserk gasped at the sight before him. "Not really in the mood for swimming."

"We cannot steer the ice floes," Odin said.

Loki shrugged. "You won't have to. The current will carry us past the Sudurberks, beyond Hunaland and into Valland. From there we can follow the Middle Sea toward Vanaheim."

If they survived the river Ylgr itself. Perhaps it truly flowed out of Niflheim.

Odin indicated a massive ice floe flowing quickly toward them. "All of you, on there as soon as it passes close. Do not miss this chance."

"What of Thor?" Frigg asked. Fulla still carried her babe, but Frigg would never allow her to do so in such circumstances.

"I'll ride Sleipnir and carry him myself."

Sigyn looked at Loki, who nodded. Sigyn shook her head, trying not to smile. Gods, this *was* madness. But she'd wanted more adventure in her life. Loki watched as a large floe, this one perhaps thirty feet across, slipped into view, then took off at a run and leapt for it, the twins still cradled in his arms.

Her man landed on his knees, unable to use his arms for balance, and skidded along the ice before coming to a stop.

Well, damn. If he could do it while holding two babes, she was damned well going to do it too. Sigyn sprinted for the edge before she could outthink herself and leapt.

The floe didn't tremble under her weight, but it was impossibly slick. Sigyn had to extend both arms, going with the slide as her feet skidded.

"Come on!" she shouted behind her.

But rather than Frigg, it was Vili who next jumped onto the floe. And the berserk's weight did pitch the ice to one side. Odin's brother scrambled toward the center of the floe.

Sigyn reached a hand toward Frigg. If she hesitated any longer, this floe would pass out of reach.

"Go!" Odin shouted at her. "I will guide the others. Go!"

Frigg took off running and leapt onto the ice floe. She barely caught the back edge of the floe as it passed and teetered backward. Before Sigyn could even get to her, Vili threw his arms around Frigg's legs and pulled her to the center, then wrapped his arms around her.

"You're safe," Vili said. "Thank you for what you have done, völva."

Frigg clearly tried to worm her way free, with little success. "You're welcome. It's my duty as—"

The ice floe slapped against the cave wall as it wound around a bend. The impact sent shudders ringing along the platform. Freezing water splashed over their perch. Frigg lost her footing and slid along the ice, shrieking as she fell toward the river.

Vili's massive hand clenched Frigg's wrist and yanked her back toward him. Vili once again pulled her into his embrace and guided her toward the center of the floe.

With every twist and turn, their position slid, forcing all to constantly shift. And every time they hit the side, more of the ice floe cracked off.

Maybe Hel would claim them all for coming here. But as the floe rushed around another bend, splashing up more icy water, Sigyn let out a whoop.

Frigg looked at her like she was mad, and Sigyn had to laugh.

Everyone else had crouched to keep their balance, but Sigyn remained standing, arms outstretched. She screamed with delight as the wind whipped her hair back.

PART II

Fifth Moon, Winter

13

For hours, they were at the mercy of the river Ylgr, but Sigyn didn't fear. Not much, at least. Loki knew what he was doing. In truth, Sigyn desperately wanted to know *how* Loki knew such things. Because of Idunn she had learned Loki was far older than the rest of them, that he was, perhaps, one of the Vanir himself. Though he claimed otherwise and shared no love with Idunn. The goddess spoke as though she knew *of* him, rather than knowing the man himself.

And still, Sigyn had no real explanation for his control over fire.

Sigyn crouched on the ice floe, watching the endless cave rush by, all of it like a dream. At last the floe carried them out of the cave and into the night air. Loki held her, wrapped in one arm, the other holding a torch. He had hardly moved in hours, but as sky once again covered their heads, he eased her to her feet. Others followed his lead.

On the back of Sleipnir, Odin had ridden up to check on them several times. Seeing the horse run as easily on water as ice was like an impossible dream. How did the monster manage it? What magic coursed through its veins?

"The ice will pass close to the shore," Loki said. "Jump when it does."

Well, that should be exciting. Easier than jumping onto the ice had been, at least. Sigyn tried to keep her breath slow and calm, tried to use the hunting training Agilaz had imparted to her. The icy wind stung her cheeks and the mists made it hard to see more than a few feet ahead of her.

But Sigyn could feel the shore as it neared, feel it with some sense she couldn't explain or quantify. Almost see it, through the mists.

Two deep breaths, then she took off running toward the edge.

"Sigyn!" Frigg shouted.

She dared not slow now, nor allow fear—hers or Frigg's —let her falter.

She leapt.

For a brief instant she was flying, speeding through the air. Then she slapped onto the shore, the impact stunning her. She rolled once, back toward the river, before she caught her foot against a rock. Graceful, Sigyn. Very dignified.

"I made it," she shouted to the others, grateful they probably hadn't been able to see her landing.

One by one, other Aesir made the jump, Frigg right after Sigyn. A sudden splash and brief scream was the only sign Sigyn caught of one who failed. She scrambled to the river's edge, eyes searching the rapids for whoever had fallen.

There was naught to find. Whoever it was must have gone into shock from the cold, pulled under in an instant.

"He waited too long," Frigg said beside her.

And more would do the same, as the other ice floes drew nigh. Gods, how many would be pulled under, drawn to Hel or caught in the icy net of Rán? They probably couldn't even see the shore. How could they be expected to make a jump when they could barely make out their destination? They had escaped the draugar only to find death at the bottom of the river.

"A fire," she said.

"What?" Frigg asked.

"Everyone!" Sigyn said. "Start the biggest bonfire you can! There, close to the shore. Burn aught you have, but get it going!" It would drive away the mists, give the others a chance.

The Aesir rushed to follow her command, not stopping to ask who she was to give orders. After such an ordeal, Sigyn supposed they welcomed anyone taking charge. They threw their torches in a pile, lit more, and began piling on timber, spare clothes, aught that remained of their scant supplies, just to bring the blaze higher. Only fire protected them from the mists. Only fire would save them now.

Fire is life. Loki always said so.

More Aesir jumped from floe after floe, guided by the bonfire. When it had grown into a massive blaze, Sigyn ordered the others to make another and another. Perhaps the flames would guide the draugar or even other vaettir toward their location. Would her actions bring fresh doom upon them all? But they had to survive this doom to care about the next.

For hours she watched as the Aesir piled upon the shore. Hours more as they warmed themselves beside the fires she had lit for them. Few thanked her, but she didn't need them to know what she'd done for them. Most of the tents had been lost, so men and women simply lay beside the fires, huddling together for warmth and comfort against the night.

14

Tyr rested on the shore, Gramr across his knees. They had lost a lot of people. Couldn't be sure how many until sunrise. Maybe they'd avoided the draugar —and gods, never had he heard of so many in one place. But the river. The river had claimed lives too.

Those drowned at sea fell to Rán, men said. Caught in her net, and Njord alone might know what she did with their souls. But those drowned in a river? Who knew. Maybe nixies claimed them.

Sigyn came over and sat on a log beside him. The Hasding woman wore a blue embroidered dress Tyr had seen Fulla working on for the past moon. He'd thought it meant for Frigg—certainly it was fine enough for a queen— but Frigg must have gifted it to her sister. Girl probably had to change after the river.

"The queen send you?"

"Not exactly, though she is concerned. We heard about the holmgang."

Tyr scowled. This woman always thought she knew

better than everyone else. She was intelligent yes—too much so, in fact.

"You are no warrior nor shieldmaiden. What do you know of a man's honor?"

"I know it's not worth shattering this alliance over."

"Honor is worth everything. All we have in this bitter world." He spat. "Not something I suspect you or that foreigner you bed down with to understand."

Sigyn rocked back, eyes flashing. For a moment Tyr wondered what went on in that head of hers. But he didn't really care. "I'm not your enemy, Tyr."

"Nor are you really my friend." He cracked his neck. "My loyalty is to Odin and his family."

"You mean to my brother-in-law."

Tyr paused. Damn. Sigyn, Frigg's half sister, *was* part of the royal family, more or less. Having no good response to that, he grunted.

"You have so much anger inside you. I heard about your past."

Damn it. Fool girl just had to keep digging into things that didn't concern her. "Did you now?" He spoke through clenched teeth, barely able to contain the urge to knock that knowing look from her face. Did she know about Hymir?

"Zisa ..." Sigyn began, then stopped.

Tyr looked up and followed her gaze. As if summoned, his ex-wife herself strode over, head high and back stiff.

He wanted to tell her he was glad she'd survived. Wanted to. Words wouldn't come out. Woman had betrayed him in the worst way. No words served after such as that.

Zisa stood there, hands on hips. She knew it too. Naught left to be said.

"What?" he finally demanded.

Zisa worked her jaw. "The things we've seen these past few moons ..."

War with Hunalander kings. Draugar. Now this river seeming to spew from Niflheim. Tyr grunted.

"That's it? That's all you have to say? I shouldn't be surprised."

Tyr looked at her sharply. "You came to me."

"More fool me, then." Zisa glanced at Sigyn. "Your new woman?"

"No," he said at the same time as Sigyn.

Zisa snorted, shook her head. "You ought not to make an enemy of the Skalduns. Odin's mad quest has cost him enough support already, Tyr ..."

He rose so he could look down at her instead of the other way around. "You saying your cock-loving husband might turn on his king?" His grip tightened on Gramr. His runeblade would punish such disloyalty.

"No! Gods, Tyr! You just don't ..." She waved her hand as if in dismissal, then turned and walked away.

Gramr wanted him to draw her. She wanted to right this wrong. And he could. It sounded to him like the man's wife had all but reported him for treason. Now Tyr just needed a way to challenge the man again, and this time he'd have no mercy.

"You know ..." Sigyn said after a moment.

Tyr turned to her. He'd almost managed to forget she was there.

Sigyn sat there, waiting for some acknowledgment.

"Fine. Out with it, woman."

"She wanted to talk to you."

"Didn't have much to say."

Sigyn shook her head and waved a finger. "She did, but you were not listening."

Tyr faltered. "What are you saying?"

Sigyn shrugged. "You think she hates you."

What? Didn't she? Should he even care? Zisa had betrayed him, gods, what? Sixteen winters back now. He'd been a young man then, and it had nigh to broken him. After that, he'd dedicated himself to training Odin and his brothers and to naught else.

No reason to care what she thought now.

None.

And yet ... he could not quite suppress the tiny surge of pride in his chest. To hear part of Zisa might still care. Perhaps a woman clever as Sigyn had *some* use as an ally.

Bedvig, on the other hand, did not. Man was a coward and a wife-stealer. He might prove a threat to Odin, to all the Aesir. Tyr looked at Sigyn a moment. Hard to trust her.

But her foster brother, Hermod—he had helped Tyr bring down one wicked jarl already. And maybe he'd do so again.

Tyr shook his head. "I have someone to see."

Sigyn smiled and rose herself. "Then go see her."

What? She thought he meant Zisa. No. That part of his life was gone.

Stolen by Bedvig. And thieves ought to be slain like beasts.

15

For a long time after leaving Tyr, Sigyn sat alone by a fire. She couldn't say how long it was before Loki came and sat beside her, before she could at last rest herself, his arm around her shoulder.

"Was this truly a thing done to Midgard?" she asked. These mists covering the Realm, blanketing it in chill and giving rise to draugar, trolls, and gods-alone-knew what other horrors ... Was this never the way this world was meant to be? "Does Idunn speak the truth?"

"As she sees it," Loki said at last.

"And what do you see?"

"More than I'd like, sometimes. Or perhaps, not enough."

She leaned closer to him. Would he tell her now? If she asked again, would he finally reveal his secrets? Gods, but he was one puzzle after another. Maybe she didn't even want everything revealed. Maybe it would take the fun out of figuring him out.

"Idunn said her grandmother blamed you for something, Loki. How could her grandmother have known you? Wasn't that five thousand years ago?"

"Almost."

"Who *are* you?"

"I am yours."

Sigyn smiled, despite herself. It wasn't an answer to her question, not really. But she liked the answer all the same. As she liked his mystery. Let him keep it, then. She'd unfold his secrets, one layer at a time. They had eternity together, after all.

"I have to leave soon," Loki said.

Sigyn jerked. Damn. He'd said that almost as though he'd known what she was thinking. Could that be his power? Many of the others had superhuman strength. Sigyn had uncanny senses. Had the apple granted Loki the ability to read minds? The thought left her flush, and more so when she considered all the intimate, sultry things she'd thought about him. And how would he react to those thoughts? Rather than answer, she concentrated on him.

Can you hear me?

"Sigyn?" he said. "I'm sorry, but there are things I must do."

Ignoring her direct thoughts. Fine. Sigyn drew up a mental picture of them making love.

Loki offered no reaction other than to lean in. "Don't be angry, my love."

So he was either the greatest actor in history, or he didn't actually read minds. Sigyn blew out a breath, then shook herself. "I'm not angry. Just curious."

"I have to push ahead," Loki said. "Prepare the way. We cannot afford to dawdle, not with what pursues us."

"Prepare what?"

Loki shifted, turned his gaze to the west, where they

were soon bound. "We'll need a way to cross the sea to reach Vanaheim. On the far side of Valland lairs an ancient power bound to that sea."

"Then I'll go with you."

"No. I won't risk you, Sigyn. Stay with the others and keep true the course. Idunn will be able to guide you there."

She folded her arms. Why was everyone always treating her like some delicate flower, some fawning maid? Gods above and below, her mentor Agilaz had trained her to hunt, then constantly urged her not to wander from town. She did not need it from Loki as well. Nor would she let him push her to the side the way Odin did to Frigg. She'd had a damned apple too for the gods' sakes.

He scowled. Reading her mind. No, he was reading her *face*. Sigyn looked down, then stared at the fire. Let him see her pout, then. "You don't trust me. Fine. Just go."

"Sigyn ..."

She shrugged him off then stalked away, toward the fire where she knew Frigg sat with her husband and child. But she did not sit at the fire. Instead she watched them while keeping an eye on Loki. At last he slunk off into the mists, carrying no torch.

He wanted her to stay behind. He wanted to keep her safe. Maybe she should appreciate the gesture. But Sigyn wasn't the sit-by-the-fire-and-knit type.

She stopped to grab a bow and quiver, then slipped out of the camp.

꧁

THE MISTS WERE no longer a threat to those who'd had the apples, and her eyes could see even in the darkness. Keeping to the shadows beyond the edge of the firelight, she followed Loki into the hills. A moderate wood soon surrounded them, but after so long trekking through the Sudurberks, this was a journey Sigyn could relish. So they had truly entered Valland. A place so far beyond Ás lands to become mere legend. What people called this land home? More pleasantly disposed ones than those of Hunaland, she hoped.

Beyond the camp she knelt in the snow, pausing over Loki's tracks. A long stride. He was moving quickly. The man knew exactly where he was going and was in a hurry to reach it. And he'd made no effort to conceal his tracks, which meant she could follow just as quickly.

Yes, a good night's sleep would have gone over better than a run at night, but then she might never uncover this piece of the puzzle that was Loki. One needed all the pieces to solve a puzzle.

She ran after him, trying to soften the crunching of snow under her feet. He was probably too far ahead to hear her, but she'd not take that chance. Loki's tracks passed into a valley between the hills. Without a torch Sigyn might never have been able to follow his tracks at night, at least not before the apple. Now, her eyes drank in moonlight and illuminated every footprint Loki had left.

She pressed on and on, her heart surging. She could do this. Track him no matter how far he fled. The apple had made her a hunter with no rival. Her senses were—

A low rumble echoed from the valley on the other side of the hill. Had Loki found some sort of trouble? Sigyn wouldn't let him face it alone. She nocked an arrow to her bow. A few well-placed shots and maybe he'd see just how much he needed her. However ancient he might have been, she still had a lot to offer. Gods, he knew that, it was why he'd chosen her. Leaving her behind was just fool male pride.

She crouched atop the hill, spying three shapes in the valley beyond. They hardly moved at first, then one raised its head and sniffed. The monsters were nigh to eight feet tall and covered in mossy, rock-like protrusions, oversized mouths, and ugly tusks.

Trolls.

Hel's frozen underworld! Sigyn skidded back down the hill. Speaking of foolish pride. Now was not the time to be spotted.

A bellow filled the valley, echoing off the hills. Followed by another and a third. Damn it! They'd heard her. The ground shook as the trolls charged up the hill, ice cracking and rocks tumbling down hill.

"Well, fuck," Sigyn mumbled, then took off in a mad dash. Rocks bounced along the ground as the trolls chased after her. One was so close she could feel it behind her. Sigyn dove to the side, rolled, and came up drawing the bow.

She loosed a shot, but it was too close. The arrow bounced off the troll's chest and it batted her bow away. The blow sent her tumbling along the ground. Sigyn rolled with the impact as Agilaz had taught her. Pulse pounding in her ears, she scrambled to her feet again. She tried to run, but a single shove from the beast sent her stumbling back to the ground.

The troll straddled her, grabbing at her bodice.

"No! No!" she screamed. She was not going to be a troll-wife. The other two had caught up and began letting out whoops.

Sigyn struggled against the panic as the troll ripped her

dress away. These were men, once. Men taken by the mists and transformed into things of rage and lust. And pride?

"Stop!" she screamed. "Stop, I'm only for the strongest! I belong only to the strongest male!"

At that, the troll did pause. So he did understand her.

One of the ones behind whooped and bellowed.

"Him?" Sigyn called, pointing at that troll. "Are you the best?"

The troll howled like a wolf and closed the distance to her in three strides. It reached for her, as if to yank her right out from underneath its fellow. Instead, the first troll spun and punched the challenger in the face. Sigyn scrambled backward as the two collapsed into a wrestling heap. The third troll watched her a moment, glancing at the fight.

Sigyn motioned him toward the others. Still it hesitated.

The Hel-cursed monstrosities thought with their stones. Sigyn gave over any attempt to cover herself with her rent dress, even pulled it away to reveal a breast, and winked at the troll. At that, the thing flew into a frenzy, leaping atop the others and pounding both fists down onto them.

Sigyn snatched her bow as she rose, then ran for the next valley, weaving in and out of the trees. Too much to hope the three trolls would kill each other. She had to put distance between them. With their great strides, she couldn't outrun them, but maybe she could lose them.

Ahead, the trees cleared in a circuitous route through the valley. Only a river would cause a break like that. Sigyn rushed down to its frozen banks, then gingerly stepped out onto the ice. It creaked beneath her weight.

Fall through that ice and she was a dead woman. She backed away and looked to the trees. She could climb one, but they might still smell her. Even if they couldn't climb the tree—and she wasn't sure about that—the trolls could probably knock the damned thing down.

Another bellow erupted from behind her.

"Hel take you," Sigyn cursed, and glanced back to see the third troll rushing toward her. One tusk had been broken, one eye bruised shut. It loped along the ground, using its arms like legs.

Sigyn looked back to the river, then to the troll. Freezing to death would still be better. She took off at a dead sprint across the ice. It groaned with each step she took. Faster. Faster!

Her foot slipped out from under her, and she skidded, then fell. Her shoulder slammed into the ice, sending jolts of lightning along her limbs. The ice cracked and began to spiderweb where she'd impacted it. Grunting against the pain, Sigyn crawled along the river, toward the opposite bank. More and more cracks spread beneath her.

Fuck!

She collapsed into the snow on the other side and rolled over to see the troll hesitating on the riverbank. Stupid as the beasts were, it must still realize what the cracks in the ice meant. It couldn't follow.

Sigyn rose. Was she safe? Maybe. At least until the troll found another place to cross and came hunting her again.

How long would she have? Long enough to get away? Maybe not. Nor could she take the chance—she needed to keep on Loki's trail.

Sigyn nocked an arrow to her bow. Focus. She let everything blur around her, focused only on the vulnerable flesh of the troll's throat. She loosed. The troll raised an arm to block the arrow and it clattered off the rocky protrusions on its forearm.

"I'm going to kill you," Sigyn whispered.

The troll began to howl. Had it heard her? Deep down, part of it was still a man. Men could be easily tempted.

"Come on! Come and get me!"

It howled again. Damned thing would bring a whole horde down on her. She had to silence the monster.

"You want to plow my trench? Come get it!" she shouted.

The troll leapt up and down and beat its chest. Sigyn almost laughed. Would have, if its display wasn't likely echoing across half this country.

"Fine," she mumbled. "You need some enticement, fine." She pushed her dress off both shoulders and let it fall, standing naked in the chill mist. "You *know* you want this!"

With a final bellow, the troll charged forward. Not three steps onto the river the ice shattered, pitching it into the frozen waters. The troll flailed, waving its arms and only serving to smash the ice it tried to climb up on.

Sigyn grabbed an arrow and moved to the edge of the river. "Hope you like the sight. It's the last you'll ever see."

She nocked the arrow, letting everything else slow, fall away. Her enhanced senses had one incredible side effect—her archery would now have put Agilaz to shame. She loosed, the shaft burying itself in the troll's eye. The monster disappeared beneath the river.

Sigyn paused just long enough to pull her dress back on.

16

Few among Mankind understood the truth about trolls. Few knew most of the monsters had been men, once, before the mist changed them. Gudrun knew more than she cared to. Some trolls, of course, were spawned by troll-wives, born as a new race, one cursed. But the mists took those weak of heart and filled them up. It was not meant to be breathed by the living, for the mist saturated the Realm of the dead. When a living man breathed it in long enough, it had unnatural effects, changing them, evoking primal instincts long buried. They became beasts that knew naught but eating, fucking, and killing.

Except now, Odin had changed all that, having given a troll an apple of Yggdrasil. Long had the Niflungar sought the most guarded prizes of the Vanir. And Odin, in a fool's attempt to save his doomed brother, had given an apple to a man already lost to the mists. The so-called Troll King had spread his influence outward from the Jarnvid, taking all the lands the Aesir had now vacated. They didn't know, Gudrun assumed, that most of Aujum now fell under the sway of Odin's brother. And indeed, beyond, where Ve had begun uniting the trolls throughout the mountains. They could pass beneath the peaks, relying on ancient dverg tunnels where available, or digging their own burrows when necessary, hidden from sunlight and moving faster than men could hope to.

And under the leadership of a troll with the power of gods, with some remaining semblance of human wit, they had swept across Midgard. Taken thousands of troll-wives as if they thought to outbreed Mankind. Several petty kingdoms in Hunaland and Bjarmaland too began to fall before Ve's hordes and, if left unchecked, perhaps they would soon challenge the great empires of the South Realms. Ironic, that in his own way, Odin had taken great strides toward the annihilation of the lands of men.

Her father's ravens kept the Niflungar informed as to the actions of the Troll King and his brethren, enough to know he was a danger if not curtailed, or a weapon if properly controlled. Never in history had a troll held so much power. One day, Odin would look back and see every human kingdom in Midgard fallen to the Troll King. The men who did not become trolls would become their food. The women —slaves to their lust, raped unto death, or worse, until they conceived their troll spawn. Such a birthing, oft as not, tore the woman to pieces, and left the trolls to feed her corpse to the newborn. Trolls were born of Hel, and they looked, and acted, the part.

Gudrun stepped gingerly into the cave-turned-troll-burrow. Not that she feared the trolls, so much as the troll droppings. Hel would protect her. In some primal way, trolls knew the mists of Hel had given them rise, and they knew to tread with care around the Children of the Mist.

Jagged roots sprouted from the cave ceiling, turning the place into a warped mirror of the Jarnvid itself. The trolls' power, no doubt, unconsciously shaping the land to match the twisted torments of their own existence.

Countless trolls watched her, a few looking up from fucking human women like dogs as she passed. Gudrun sympathized with the troll-wives, but she could do naught for them. And yet … Almost unbidden, ice coalesced in her palm, summoned up from the snow maiden bound to her. Before she could think better of it, Gudrun flung the chill like a bolt at one of the trolls. The creature dropped his woman and wailed, fleeing into the darkness.

Gudrun ground her teeth.

She deluded herself if she thought she did any service for the woman other than a moment's reprieve. The greater mercy would have been to kill the woman herself. She had done no good, but calling on such power had raised a chill in her heart. The Mist spirit she'd bound coiled just a little tighter about her insides like an Ethereal tapeworm.

A fool's move.

Besides which, if she sought help from these trolls, she could not deny them their prizes. And though every troll she passed looked on her with undisguised lust, none made a move on her.

Yes. Keep your mortal wives. Gudrun was no maid to be carried away—she was a princess of the Niflungar, and even these trolls could feel it. The power of Mist was deep in her soul. These sick creatures were born of it, but they were not the essence of Mist.

Gudrun cursed the trolls and cursed Grimhild and cursed herself for not being strong enough to do more. Instead, she jerked her torch in front of her, sending trolls clambering away from the flame. Like aught else born of Mist, they feared flame and daylight. As, in truth, did any Niflung.

Beyond, trolls feasted. Bile burned her throat as she realized one was gnawing on a human femur. Rather than dwell on it, she pushed past the sight, feigning indifference so as not to let the creatures see her disgust.

Deeper and deeper she stalked into the burrow, until her single torch seemed scant illumination against the prevailing darkness.

Odin had fled, deep beneath the mountains in tunnels not so unlike these. She had hardly believed the reports her draugar had made, that Odin had chanced the river Ylgr. In truth, she wondered how he even knew of the river. Had that Vanr witch told him?

His gambit might well have cost him many of his people, but it had allowed him to get far ahead of her, bypassing Hunaland and passing into Valland. A land where the Niflungar had little influence, thanks to the strange religion of the locals. Now she could no longer corner him in the mountains. Now she needed allies if she was to hem Odin in once again. And she must do so—if she let Grimhild reach him, Odin was lost to her. She had no reason to care about the deaths of the other Aesir, but Odin she could not lose.

And what better ally than the fallen brother of the man himself?

The Troll King reclined upon a throne that seemed to erupt from the ground, roots grown out in the wrong direction. Outward-facing thorns jutted from the throne's arms and base, no doubt responsible for the countless shallow scrapes covering the naked women who sat beneath the throne. Gudrun forced herself not to meet their hollow gazes. These women were already lost. Too long in the mist, too long serving the lust of the trolls, their bodies and minds and very souls broken by the torment ...

And she would not look upon the one on the left ... By

Hel, the girl couldn't be more than fifteen winters. Her eyes still pled, still begged for a savior that would never come. Gudrun could not be that savior. Despite the sudden short-ness of breath in her chest, she forced her gaze to remain locked on that of the Troll King, hunkering in the shadows against the back of his throne.

"Your brother has fled beyond these mountains, beneath them," Gudrun said.

Though the Troll King shifted on his throne, naught more than a shallow grunt escaped him. Gudrun loathed using such savage beasts to her ends, but Grimhild had insisted, demanding Gudrun turn to the trolls, who might know the deep routes beneath the mountains. Gudrun doubted Odin's quest against the Vanir would have succeeded and, given a little patience, she could have easily shown up in time to save him from his own arrogance.

But now she had to deal with trolls. And maybe Ve *could* head off his brother, leave him desperate enough he would turn back to her. Except that the Troll King was no longer Ve.

"If you move quickly, you can still reach them. Take the old roads, the hidden paths the dvergar once dug through these mountains."

A rumble like a rockslide bubbled out from the Troll King. "You ... do not give ... orders. This is my ... kingdom."

Gudrun didn't think she'd ever heard a troll speak, at least not more than an inarticulate word or two.

"Do you know who I am, troll?"

The Troll King chuckled again. "You bitch ... who will mouth ... my rod. Get on your knees." He shifted forward enough to reveal his erection. "Or first I let ... horde plow your ... trench?"

Gudrun set her jaw. She could not afford to let them see

her fear. She had to slow her heart. These disgusting beasts *were*, after all, beasts, driven by naught but primal lust. And primal fear. And they ought to fear her.

Rather than fall back as the troll might have expected, Gudrun took a step forward. "Irpa aid me," she whispered under her breath. The wraith's glyph on Gudrun's arm warmed as she called it. It was there, bound to her service through her greatest sorcery. Gudrun did not call on the ghost often—it would invariably enact a toll, and its hatred exceeded even that of the snow maiden—but sometimes a point must be made.

Almost as one all the trolls paused, looking around. They felt it. A change in the air, though for certain they didn't understand what it meant. Gudrun let her eyes shift to see the Penumbra. Numerous shades drifted about the burrow, most probably victims of the trolls, others perhaps lost souls.

But one was different.

Black, even against the oppressive vision surrounding her. A shadow, moving in the night, trailing wisps of a tattered shroud behind her. Irpa passed dangerously close to one of Ve's trolls. The troll didn't have the Sight, but he felt it and backed away toward the wall.

Others began trying to edge out of the Troll King's chamber. So quick to abandon their leader when faced with such horror. The wraith at last settled on one of the empty-eyed girls at Ve's feet. She had been so hollowed out by the abuse, perhaps there was naught left inside. And that meant Irpa had ample room to take control.

The possessed girl rose, shoulders straight, any hint of timidity gone. "You want my mouth?" the wraith asked. Its voice was low, like a whisper on the wind, but it echoed through the cavern, and Gudrun could have sworn a troll whimpered. "You want *my* mouth?"

With uncanny speed, the girl lunged forward and grabbed Ve's rapidly dwindling erection with one hand. From the sudden squeal, Gudrun imagined Irpa must have crushed it. Her other hand settled on Ve's throat and she straddled him, her mouth nearly touching his. Through her Sight, Gudrun saw the wisps of vapors seep out of the Troll King and into Irpa. He shuddered and trembled as the wraith fed upon bits and pieces of his soul.

The glyph on Gudrun's arm burned. The wraith drew strength from her, the will, the permission to feed. As Irpa grew in strength, Gudrun's control would weaken. There was always a price.

Gudrun's chest tightened. Her lungs weren't working. She clutched the golden bracelet she wore on her forearm. A talisman ... replete with ... energy to draw on ...

"Enough," Gudrun said, trying not to gasp the word.

Irpa lingered over the Troll King, her will straining against Gudrun's for just an instant, before she released him and backed away. The pressure eased on Gudrun's chest, releasing her lungs, yet Irpa's hold on her had tightened a hair more. If not for the talisman, it would have been worse.

"You may be a king here," Gudrun said, still trying to keep her voice steady, "but there are always powers greater. Believe me when I tell you, you would much rather have me as an ally than a foe. Go after Odin. Now."

The Troll King rubbed his chest with one hand, shielding his bruised genitals with the other. Both likely felt the icy chill of the grave.

"We will ... make for ... the Aesir," Ve said, his voice now reminding her more of bouncing pebbles than a landslide.

Gudrun took another step toward him. "And as your ally,

you will grant me a gift." Gudrun pointed to the girl at Ve's feet, the one troll-wife here still alive enough to shake with real terror.

Ve looked toward the girl and gnashed his tusks. "Why?"

"Maybe *I* want her mouth. If you prefer, I can leave the wraith in your other woman. I'm certain she can see to *all* your needs, my king."

The Troll King's rumble now reminded her of an angry snow bear. He nearly leapt to his feet as he shoved the girl toward Gudrun. "Take ... both!"

The girl sprawled at her feet, then Gudrun pulled her up by the shoulders.

"We ... remember ... this."

"I certainly hope so. Irpa, leave the vessel."

The possessed woman collapsed in a heap as the wraith fled her body and retreated back into the Astral Realm. Guiding the girl by the arm, Gudrun walked from the burrow, trying desperately to keep her steps slow and deliberate, despite the sickening pounding of her heart.

Hel, the trolls *would* remember her little display. Cowing others with terror might have bought her service—it would not buy her true allies. But that sick beast had thought to treat her as his whore. Her, a princess of the Niflungar, a priestess of Hel.

And as a woman willing to use terror as a weapon, did that now transform Gudrun into Grimhild's daughter in more than blood? The thought alone left her dizzy. She could not let herself vomit in front of the girl, much less the trolls.

Outside the burrow, Gudrun fell back against the mountainside, hugging herself with her free hand to still the trembling as her pent-up tension finally released itself.

Naked and shivering, the girl watched her, eyes wide.

Gudrun stripped off her fur cloak and wrapped it around the girl. She could do naught for her feet, sadly. Poor thing would likely have frostbite so bad she might lose a few toes, but it was a far better urd than letting those trolls hollow her out. How many troll babies could they plant inside her until the flower wilted and her body gave out? Gudrun didn't think she wanted to know the answer, though she'd heard many troll-wives didn't survive even the first birth. Most probably wound up in troll bellies.

"What's your name, girl?"

The girl's mouth opened, but only a whimper came out.

Gudrun shook herself, then pulled the girl into an embrace. "It will be all right," she whispered. "You are under my protection now."

"I-I'm Hljod."

Good. Gudrun held her at arm's length to look into her eyes. "You are my servant now, Hljod. I am Gudrun, princess of the Niflungar and heir to the ancient kingdom. Serve well and you will find a life unlike any you have dreamed."

The girl nodded, and Gudrun led her away from the burrow. Best if neither of them ever looked on such a place again. Gudrun would need to find and skin a rabbit or something to wrap Hljod's feet.

"C-can we have a fire?"

Gudrun shook her head, but handed the girl the torch. "We are the Children of the Mist, Hljod. We do not make fires. But you have naught more to fear in the mists. I swear it."

17

*H*eidr had commanded Borr remain outside for the birthing. Borr always listened to his völva. Always, except for now. Bestla's screams rent the night air until Borr shoved aside the warrior who tried to block his way and charged into the tent.

"Push!" Heidr urged, casting a wrathful glare Borr's way.

Borr dropped to his knees beside his wife, grasped her hand in his. It had grown clammy as a woman in deathchill.

"One more push," the völva said. "One more, Bestla."

Odin moaned. How was he seeing this? He knew what would happen, his father had told him of it, though he hadn't been old enough to understand. He didn't want to see it.

Borr rubbed Bestla's fingers, trying to massage warmth back into them. "Come on, love. Come on, you can do it."

Bestla screamed, her grip on Borr's fingers first tight, then weakening.

"I've got him," Heidr said. "It's a boy, Bestla."

"You hear, love? A third son," Borr said, trying not to

choke. Gods above and below, she had lost so much blood. The furs were drenched in it. "Are we not blessed?"

"Ve ..." Bestla said. "Call him Ve ... Y-you'll protect him?"

"With my life. Ve is our blood."

❧

ODIN SHOT awake at the sound of a bellow. His mind reeled at being jolted out of the vision and back to the waking world.

But he knew that sound. Treacherous, monstrous sound. Blood—his blood—Father's blood. Ve was here, wasn't he?

He shook himself, trying to clear his vision-addled brain, but not bothering to pull on his trousers. He snatched up Gungnir. The Aesir now slept beneath the stars, huddled under furs and cuddled close to the fire.

They had enjoyed but a few days' reprieve from the draugar, and now trolls turned on them. And could it be Ve? His father's son, the last part of his parents ... Come for Odin's son? Trolls ate children and men ... No! No, Ve was blood. If he could just get through to him ...

"Take Thor, run!" he told Frigg. Trolls, coming for the women and children of his tribes.

The ground shook as a troll charged forward, kicking dirt over the campfire. Headed straight for Odin's family. Borr's grandson.

"Never!" Odin shoulder-charged the beast and flung it backward, then whipped Gungnir around, slashing its throat.

Gurgling on its black blood, the troll tumbled to the ground. Odin rushed forward, ran it through, and kept running. More and more trolls stomped across the camp. In the distance, Odin could already see so many with women flung over their shoulders.

No! He would not allow this.

Fulla had fallen to her knees, the varulf twins forgotten before her. Eyes wide with shock, clearly frozen as a troll advanced on her.

Odin charged that troll, ducked a swipe of its meaty fist, and slashed open its legs with Gungnir. He came up spinning, drove his spear through its belly. "Go!" he shouted at Fulla.

Still the woman just whimpered.

Just beyond, a troll slammed its hands into another warrior, crunching his skull and helm into a bloody pulp.

Gods above, mortal men would not be able to fight this. Was this Ve? Was he here? Odin's blood, come for his own?

Tyr's battlecry drew Odin's gaze. His warrior leapt upon the troll's back and rained ineffective blows with his sword. As the troll reached for him, Tyr drew a dagger and slid it through the monster's eye socket. It fell with a crash. Tyr shook himself, tossed aside his own sword, and drew the runeblade Odin had given him from his back.

Odin turned at another bellow, as yet another troll killed more of his people. In a single motion Odin reversed his grip on Gungnir and flung it. The dragon spear soared through the air like an arrow from a bow and punched right through the troll's rocky chest.

The others had no magic spears to aid them. And the trolls were tearing his people apart. One troll stomped up and down on a corpse while another swung a man around like a flail. More and more of the monstrosities charged into the camp from the southwest. The same direction they had wanted to head. There were too many to fight—an army of trolls. And too many for this to be coincidence. Somehow this had to be connected to the draugar.

Could the Odling ghost's curse have meant this? Every vaettir across Midgard was converging on Odin. Or was this the Niflungar, still seeking revenge for what he'd done among them? Too much to hope killing Guthorm would have ended this. No, it would have only further incensed them against him.

Odin yanked Fulla to her feet, shoved the twins into her arms, and pushed her into a run. "Fulla! Go to Frigg. She will protect you."

He couldn't watch over her now—he had to retrieve his spear. Odin dashed for it, snatched it up, and spun to take in the carnage. The battlefield was littered with hundreds of dead—men and shieldmaidens giving their lives to protect their loved ones, and, more oft than not, to little avail.

Tyr whirled back to face another rampaging troll. He leapt into the air, sword first. It punched through the beast's hide as easily as Gungnir had. Tyr's momentum and weight bore the troll down. Before it had even finished falling, Tyr leapt off and rushed another, cutting its legs out from beneath it. Whatever price that runeblade might exact for its power—and Gungnir affected Odin, he knew it did—it would be worth it to save as many people as they could.

Odin whipped his spear around to hunt down another target. More trolls closed in on Frigg and Thor. Odin once again flung his spear, ending the fiend that would threaten his family.

He closed the distance to them at a sprint, then wrapped both in his arms. "You have to flee this."

"There is nowhere to go," Frigg said. "The trolls are ahead of us and the draugar behind."

Gods, they truly had been outmaneuvered. These trolls

were raiders, but their attacks would demoralize and weaken his people, cost lives. If Ve was here, if Odin could only stop this ... He shook himself. The visions were driving him mad, weren't they? Even if Ve was here, there was naught Odin could do now to reason with him.

"There!" Odin shouted, pointing to a hilltop where warriors had begun to form a protective ring, trying to guard the weak.

As Frigg ran off, Odin called to his jarls, shouting at the top of his lungs for a retreat. He would cover them, he and Tyr. Even if it cost his life, he'd protect his people. That was his duty.

One look at Tyr's face and Odin knew the man understood it as well. Together, they fought troll after troll as men and women and children rushed past them.

"Ve!" Odin shouted.

None of the trolls answered.

"He is not here, my lord," Tyr said. The man's sword cut down troll after troll.

For at least an hour Odin fought, his muscles burning, time blurring. Odin drew upon his supernatural stamina just to keep moving. Ás warriors fell by the dozens to the onslaught, until at long last, the rays of dawn peeked through the mists. And with those rays, the trolls began to retreat, disappearing back into the woods and burrows. No sign of Ve.

Odin slumped to the ground. As soon as he let go of his supernatural power, his exhaustion hit him tenfold. For a moment, all he could do was breathe. Try to think through the haze of fatigue and lost blood.

There were far too many of these creatures for this to be a mere raid.

Father forgive him. This had all been for naught. He'd

lost Ve, and this was his punishment. What a fool he'd been to think to challenge the gods—he couldn't even reach the damned gods! The Niflungar were hemming him in, because they knew exactly where he was going. They could not fight the seemingly endless horde of trolls.

Now he had to do whatever it took to protect his people. It's what his father would have done. Protect the tribe and protect his son.

This had to be the Niflungar. What else could have summoned an entire army of trolls?

ODIN WADED THROUGH HIS PEOPLE, laying a comforting hand on each as he passed. A shallow, empty comfort as they wept and wailed for stolen wives and slain husbands.

Gods above, he'd thought he'd learned to move past his pride. Instead, he had continued this vain quest to overthrow the Vanir, to return the Middle World to spring. Because he could not bear what had happened to Ve. No, not just Ve, but their father, and Heidr, and all the others. Lost because the Vanir had left Mankind out in the mist to suffer.

Odin shook his head. It was not vanity, and more than just his oath to Idunn bound him. It was necessity. It was urd. He *knew* that, and he had no time to doubt himself, least of all in front of his people. They needed his strength now. He had chosen to embrace his urd, and now, because of that, he had to take whatever steps urd required of him.

He worked his way forward to find Frigg, and laid a hand upon Thor's head. Frigg didn't speak, but she must have seen the decision in his eyes. He would give his son a better birthright than this. Thor was his blood, as Ve was his blood. As they were all the blood of Borr. There had to be a way to save them all. To reach Ve through the madness that had crept so deep inside his brother.

Idunn stood nearby, apparently trying to comfort Fulla.

"We cannot continue south," Odin said. "The trolls block our way."

"You have to," Idunn said. "Vanaheim is southwest of Valland, beyond the Straits of Herakles."

"Did you not see what just happened?" Odin roared. "Hundreds of our people are dead, Idunn! Is this the future you want for the Aesir? Is this the future I have brought my son to?" Before he knew what he was doing, he had her by the shoulders, shaking her. "Is this your dream, Vanr?"

"Odin!" Frigg protested.

For a heartbeat, the gravity of Odin's arrogance settled on him, accosting this goddess. But only for that heartbeat —he planned to make war on her people. Why should he not manhandle one mere Vanr woman?

"I will not lose my son! I will not lose my people!" He had started this quest to make his father proud, and continued it in some hope to save Ve. And for what? To lead all the Aesir to ruination? "We cannot defend against the trolls like this."

Idunn's face fell, and she stammered. "I ... I'm sorry, I ... I didn't expect this. Trolls don't normally act like that. But, but ... Running away to the north only takes you farther from your goal. And if these trolls and draugar truly hunt you, they will catch you. They are relentless, especially if someone is driving them forward. And that does seem to be the case. So ... so you have that hard choice that's not even really a choice at all. I think that's kind of like what my grandmother said my grandfather faced."

Odin released her at last. "What are you talking about, Idunn?"

Idunn took a step back, clearly shaken. "Well, you can fight a losing battle, or you can run from it and wait for it to find you, right? And by then, you may risk losing even more."

"Are you saying I should stand my ground against the hordes of the mists?" Fight a battle sure to claim innumerable Ás lives before they even reached Vanaheim to challenge their real opponents?

She shrugged. "Odin ... I don't think they're going to give you a choice about that. Your choice is *where* you fight, and when."

A wise warrior chooses his battleground, Tyr had taught him as a child. Hel, if only Loki and his woman had not wandered off. Odin needed his blood brother now more than ever. Loki always seemed to have options no one else saw. But Idunn was ancient and had to know Midgard as well as Loki did.

"Give me an alternative, Vanr," Odin demanded. "If we must make a stand, we must have a place to keep the defenseless safe—or safer, at the least."

Idunn shook her head, looking around, then up at the sky as though it might hold some answer. "I ... I don't ... There's Idavollir, it's northwest of here, I think. But Odin, that's in the wrong—"

"What is it?"

"An ancient castle of the jotunnar, back before the Vanir drove them from these lands. Maybe you could defend it, I suppose."

Jotunnar. The thought soured Odin's stomach, and he reached for Frigg's sword's comforting weight, though, of course, it still lay by the fire. The dwellers of Utgard. Ymir's

people, the very being that had come down from his mountain abode and destroyed Odin's World. And now a castle
built by those monsters was their only hope?

A fragile, shallow hope. But it was a hope, and that was
all they had to cling to.

And if they fled, if they turned away, it meant making a
stand against the Niflungar. But Idunn was right—they
would never reach Vanaheim without doing so. First, he had
to protect his people. Then he would hunt down Gjuki and
make the Raven Lord pay for all that had been stolen from
the Aesir, from Odin himself.

"Prepare the people," Odin told Frigg, then grabbed her
arm as she turned to go. "Wait." He placed a hand on Thor's
head. The redheaded child had Borr's hair, his eyes, his
nose. Odin's blood.

"Odin," Frigg said. "We have to use the daylight."

Yes, they did.

And there was precious little of that.

he Hunalander king had no way of knowing who Gudrun was, but he'd been kind enough to avail her and Hljod of his hall. Gudrun would have liked to think it was hospitality, but it probably had more to do with the Niflung gold she'd offered as tribute. And while Gudrun might have been just as comfortable camping in some old ruin, Hljod needed proper clothes and proper food. And Hel would likely forgive the girl for warming herself by the hearth fire. This time.

She could have returned to Volsung's lands, of course, and called upon a true ally, but she needed to head toward Valland with all swiftness—and she would not risk those troll burrows. Not alone, and certainly not with Hljod.

For certain, these locals had eyed two women traveling alone—one barely clad—with suspicion and, in some cases, undisguised lust. But no one turned away travelers. After all, no one wanted it to be their turn to be caught out alone in the mists. What would it have been like to grow up in their world? Afraid of what lurked out there?

Gudrun snorted over her rabbit stew. *She* was what

lurked out there, wasn't she? So far from the shores of the Morimarusa, these people probably didn't even remember the Niflungar. They would, though; one day soon, all the North Realms would fall under Niflung sway. Maybe with Odin's help—the man had undeniable power within, the spark of greatness that came along once in a thousand years.

And while her father seemed more than inclined to let Gudrun control that spark, Grimhild now seemed utterly bent on extinguishing it. If the queen had her way, Odin and all the Aesir would fall to the draugar or perhaps the trolls. Fall before Gudrun had even had the chance to show him the true wonders of her World. The Aesir were but children compared to the Niflungar—children staring up at the stars and thinking them mere holes in the sky.

But Odin was ... Odin. Gudrun had never known a man with such passion in his heart. Beautiful, in the way fire was both beautiful and horrifying. The Children of the Mist hated and feared the flame, enemy of Mist, but still they needed it. Odin was like that, she supposed—a flame she loved and feared and tried desperately to control, even as he burned her.

Gudrun would not dare go against Grimhild. Never again. Only her father could even think of such a thing, and he didn't seem to want Odin dead, or at least Gudrun wasn't so sure. He alone might aid her, buy her the time she needed to help Odin see the truth.

Hljod moaned, rubbing her foot. The poor child had lost her small toe to frostbite, and the only comfort Gudrun could offer—save a draught against the pain—was that she could have lost more than that. Well, one other comfort too —she had inspected the child's aura with the Sight, and Hljod did not carry any troll spawn in her belly.

Gudrun rose and clucked her tongue, then drifted over

to where Hljod sat by the fire, careful not to draw too close. She'd told Hljod they didn't build fires, but that was a bit overstated. Of course the Niflungar had to cook their food and required flame to see in the darkness. But the smaller the fire, the better. The mists were a part of them, and all fires were born of Muspelheim, the World of Fire. The flames drove off the mists. Not the best way to please her goddess.

And still they needed fire. As she needed Odin.

"Hljod, come to my room. Bring a bowl of water."

The girl jerked at her voice, but calmed quickly and nodded. Gudrun could forgive the child for being skittish after all she'd been through.

The king had given her a small chamber at the back of his hall. A fur skin served as a flimsy door, but it was enough. They'd offered Hljod a place to sleep among the other servants, but Gudrun expected she'd probably keep Hljod in her own room. The girl was prone to night terrors, and Gudrun didn't want to see any fresh abuses laden on her, not even from other serving girls.

Gudrun retired to her chamber. The tiny room housed only a straw mat covered by a bearskin—a far cry from her comforts at Castle Niflung, but still better than she'd have found in the wild. From her bag she pulled a paint of smashed berries and traced a spirit glyph on the ground before her.

Then she folded her legs beneath her and sat on the bearskin, allowing her eyes to shift into Sight, revealing the Penumbra while turning the real world hazy.

Hljod came in and set the bowl before her.

Gudrun reached a hand over the bowl, palm a hairs-breadth above the water. She could feel the flow of the water. Even in the still bowl it had motion, movement, energy. She moved her hand with the motion, tracing slow, steady circles above the bowl.

"You're a völva?" Hljod asked.

The sudden break in her concentration caused Gudrun's vision to shift back to normal, revealing the slight tremble in the girl across from her. A child, really, wrapping her arms around her legs, fearful of the night.

Gudrun smiled, hoping it came across as warm. "I am a sorceress."

Hljod nodded, so Gudrun allowed her eyes to relax again, embracing the Sight.

"What's the difference?" the girl asked after a moment.

Gudrun snorted. "The same as the difference between an apprentice and a master."

"Oh. That was illuminating."

Gudrun chuckled. The girl had a bit of a mouth, but then, so had Gudrun at her age. Hljod was so much like her —more than the girl could possibly realize. Gudrun almost wanted to look away. In Hljod's eyes, she could see so much, like looking into memories she wanted to bury in the snow. Hel, maybe she ought to just leave the girl here among the king's court. The man would likely take her in. Hljod would find work as a maid, marry some hunter, have a few brats ... And spend the rest of her life haunted by nightmares of what had been done to her. Assuming the king didn't make her a slave and force her to share his bed.

Or ... Or Gudrun could bring her to the Niflungar, make her one of them. Give her the power to never again fear. To heal, to be saved.

And if she was going to truly bring Hljod among her people, to keep her as her own, the girl would have to understand. She blew out a long breath and removed her hand from the bowl. Father could wait.

"Men call any woman who knows secrets of the Other-worlds a völva, a witch. Most of those witches know naught of the true Art, but they fake it with herbs and poultices, with knowledge that seems frightening to simple men. Others possess a hint of the Art, a control of their life force, or a semblance of the Sight. But sorcery goes beyond this— sorcery is the evocation of spirits, beings of the Spirit Realm, which we can bend to our will or bond to our bodies. A sorceress uses spirits and ghosts to enact her will."

At a price. Spirits marked their own glyphs on your body, a constant reminder of a bond not easily broken. A spirit would always require payment for its services, feeding on the life force or the very soul of a sorceress who tried to master it. Push your limits too far and you'd wind up a vessel for beings of terrible nature. Gudrun shifted, enjoying the stare of wonder—and perhaps even the fear—on Hljod's face.

"Like what you did to that ... that fucker who ..."

So more than a bit of a mouth, then. Gudrun nodded, trying not to smile. Hljod would need to learn to guard her tongue before they came among the Niflungar. "I called a wraith, a ghost—a very angry, ancient ghost. Trolls are horrors of this world, but they have naught on the horrors of the worlds beyond our own."

Hljod scooted forward a little. "Worlds?"

"Tell me what you know of the Spirit Realm."

"Like Niflheim?"

"Niflheim is one of the nine worlds of the Spirit Realm, specifically the World of Mist. It is ruled by our queen, Hel, and there is none greater than she. And do you know why?"

The girl shook her head, predictably frightened to silence at the mention of Hel. The great queen was a name of fear, a curse among the common people of Midgard. She was the darkness they—justifiably—blamed for the state of their world and the horrors they faced.

"Hel is here with us," Gudrun said. "Even though her essence remains bound in Niflheim, she is among us, out in the mist. She is the queen of death, the mistress of the cold. The Vanir, the so-called gods of your people, are naught before her."

Hljod bit her lip a moment, then cocked her head. "And the other worlds? Do they have mighty rulers?"

At that Gudrun rocked back. This girl was more perceptive than she'd given her credit for. "We do not speak of such things. Not to someone as yet uninitiated in our full ways. Now I need you to remain very still and very silent, Hljod. Remember what I just told you of sorcery? I'm going to call upon a spirit to communicate across a great distance." She pointed to the glyph she'd painted on the floor. "Trust me when I tell you this—do not ever interrupt a sorceress in the midst of evoking a spirit. To call a spirit and not bind it is to risk being taken as a vessel. Spirits do not have physical form in our Realm, but they will happily take control of our bodies."

Eyes wide, the girl fell mute. Gudrun hadn't wanted to frighten her, but, in truth, a certain amount of fear was due to the Realms beyond Midgard. A sorceress might touch minds, beings ancient beyond human imagining. And doing so was a risk equally unimaginable.

Once again, she reached her hand over the bowl and resumed her motion over it. A mist formed over the water, pulling up the moisture and wafting through their small chamber. Perhaps some would drift under the fur door and alert the mortals to what she was about, but Gudrun had to take that risk.

The glyph on Gudrun's thigh warmed as she called out

to the Mist spirit bound to her. The snow maiden would let her bridge the gap between here and Castle Niflung. "Show me my father." Her voice was barely a whisper. The mists congealed into a hazy image, borne to her across the Veil that separated Midgard from the Astral Realm.

Mighty Gjuki, the Raven Lord, stood stooped over a parchment, the room illuminated by a single candle. A whole unkindness of ravens perched around the room, all watching her. Almost as he came into view, he straightened, turned to face Gudrun.

"Daughter." His voice carried as if on the wind, far away, yet clear to her ears.

"Father. I have done as Grimhild commanded. I have set the Troll King upon the Aesir."

"I know this."

Her father's ravens watched all Midgard, offering him reports and secrets. But they didn't see everything. They didn't see into Gudrun's heart. Maybe even Father would not understand her true feelings for Odin. He'd ordered her to seduce him when Odin had first come, but somehow, somewhere along that path, she had fallen into her own trap. And if he knew she was putting her heart before the will of Hel … She wouldn't want to see her father's rage.

"Grimhild would see Odin torn to pieces by the trolls."

"Hel has reason to hate the man."

And what reason was it? That, neither Grimhild nor her father had ever revealed. "Please, Father. We both know she wants him dead because of Guthorm. If he was so easy to turn to us, he might not be so valuable. It is because he is strong-willed and powerful that he could be such a boon to us. You *know* this."

To say naught of Gudrun's own heart. With Odin, for once, she was not alone. Maybe that was what she'd wanted all along. Someone to understand her, in a way her parents never could.

Her father stared at something she couldn't see for a time before answering, perhaps reading her unspoken words off her face. "That may be true. But Grimhild will have what she wants, daughter. Have you forgotten what happened the last time you defied her?"

"I will *never* forget! Y-you should have punished her," Gudrun spat at her father. Hel take Grimhild and Father both!

"I am king, but even I am not as beloved by Hel as your mother."

"And will you *still* not choose me over her? Will you not come here and help *me*?"

Her father again stared off into darkness. "Would that earn your forgiveness, child? I am still bound to the will of Hel. Your beauty and potions and magic did not bind Odin to our will. If he is to live, he must serve. You know this. I am giving you this one more chance to win him over."

It might earn him forgiveness. There was no forgiveness for Grimhild. Not ever. Oh, Gudrun had never defied her mother again, nor would she. Some lessons could not be unlearned.

"Odin?" Hljod whispered. "I know that name ... Son of a trollfucker! You're after the Troll King's brother!"

"Who is that?" her father demanded.

"I told you to be silent!" Gudrun snapped at Hljod. "She is no one, just a servant. Please, Father. Help me."

Hljod folded her arms across her chest and opened her mouth, but Gudrun silenced her with a glare. Even in the momentary distraction, she felt the Mist spirit strain against her control. Gudrun grit her teeth, forcing her will back on the vaettr.

Her father sighed, and didn't speak for a time. "Then I will come to you, daughter."

"Good." Gudrun waved away the mists and let her vision return to normal. She let the vaettr slip back inside her, trying to slow the pounding of her heart. It strained against her will, but she could take it. She didn't want to draw more power from her talisman than she must—even such treasures oft had their limits.

"I'm no one, huh?"

Gudrun grimaced, still trying to force the snow maiden into dormancy. "The next time I tell you to—"

"I'm right, aren't I? You told the Troll King to go after his own brother! You should be killing the trolls and everyone related to them."

Gudrun's hands trembled, ice forming around them in glittering crystals. Hljod's eyes widened as she caught the sight, but she didn't apologize.

"You forget yourself, girl," Gudrun said. Gudrun had not meant to call upon the snow maiden's power again. The vaettr itself was tempting her, like a man who could not resist his drink.

Hljod leapt to her feet. "I didn't forget what that *thing* did to me! You ever been raped by a troll, Gudrun? You think you understand me?" The girl's voice broke at the end, suddenly choking on her own sobs.

The ice dissipated from Gudrun's fingers in an instant. Hljod shifted from mouse to snow bear and back in no time at all, her anger a mere cover for the fear and pain and rage. The utter aloneness. Except she wasn't alone.

Gudrun rose, opening her mouth but unable to speak. Instead she took a step toward Hljod and reached for the girl's hand, who jerked it away. "I ... do understand. Not by a troll ..."

An instant of confusion appeared on Hljod's face, to be washed away by horror as she understood. "But you were ... ? You're a princess! Who would ... ?"

Gudrun squeezed her eyes to force the water out. She was not this person who wallowed in self-pity. And she did *not* tell this story. Not ever, not to anyone.

"When I was your age ..." Gudrun began, then choked, unable to speak. She slunk back to the floor. "I had a lover. And I—Grimhild didn't approve. My mother, I mean. She demanded I break it off, and I ... I was young, and given to folly as the young so oft are. I insisted I loved him. So she told me ... Grimhild ordered me to murder him, sacrifice his soul to bind a vaettr to me."

Hljod sat down before Gudrun, eyes wide, face ashen. "And did you?"

Gudrun shook her head. "Not then. I refused. Grimhild called me ... lustful. She ordered one of her guards to sate me."

"Oh, Hel," Hljod said.

"I ... I still refused." Gudrun could no longer stop the tears. Some princess of Hel she was, weeping in front of this child. A child who had known all the same abuses. Hljod was her, wasn't she? "S-she brought in more guards. Continued to let them ... Until I ... Until I did it. I sacrificed my lover and used his soul to bind Irpa—the wraith I used on the Troll King."

Gudrun jerked at Hljod's sudden embrace. Rather than force her away, Gudrun wrapped an arm around Hljod's shoulders. This child had suffered as she had suffered, perhaps even worse. And she deserved to know she was not alone.

"I used Irpa ... I had her kill all the men who ..."

"You should have killed that Troll King, too," Hljod said, her voice cracking.

Hel, the girl was right. Gudrun *should* have done so. She'd let fear of Grimhild, of facing her wrath once more, stay her hand.

"Make me like you," Hljod said. "I want to be … strong."

Gudrun stroked the girl's hair. She'd thought to keep Hljod on as a servant, as if that was enough to make up for what had been done to both of them. But naught would ever be enough. Make her strong? Was Gudrun so strong, sitting here weeping, clutching this young girl for strength?

Naught could change the past … but …

But Gudrun would control the future. Hljod would be more than a servant, more than an apprentice. She would be like a sister. And Gudrun was going to protect her, this she swore.

19

*L*oki's tracks led Sigyn all the way to the coast. For the better part of a moon she followed, passing through a few towns here and there. Few of the locals spoke the North tongue here. Indeed, Valland was part of the South Realms. Still, she had traded rabbit pelts for supplies. Too, Sigyn had avoided draugar and trolls, wading through endless mist until she had become an expert in sneaking around dangers. This must have been how Idunn had travelled this world. What difference was there between them, really? Both were women who had eaten the apples, and if the Vanr woman could walk from one end of Midgard to the other, so too could Sigyn.

Idunn had once spoken of a lush island chain in the far southeast, one from which her ancestors had come. Sigyn would have loved to have seen that, though it must lay in Utgard, beyond the Midgard Wall. Instead, she followed Loki all the way to the great ocean, and it, too, left her breathless. The land at last gave way in a great, glacier-like cliff and dropped down to ice-topped rocks on the frosty shore she guessed waited at least sixty feet beneath. Mist poured over that shelf, obscuring much.

But not enough, not from her. She saw the spires rising so far above the mist they seemed to scrape the clouds. A castle rose up out of the sea, topped by a half dozen of the great towers. Each tower was filled with innumerable windows, each of which had to be twice as tall as she was. Other separate towers rose out of the sea as well, making it clear some portion of the architecture must actually be underwater.

Sigyn had to hug herself at the sight. Like something out of a dream, a palace of another age. And Loki had gone down into it. And if he could do it, she could too. Couldn't she? She shook herself, then set out for the edge of the cliff. Looking out over the lip of it, she swayed with dizziness and sank to her knees.

This was probably the stupidest idea she'd ever had. Of course, it was a little late to turn back now. She might not even be able to find the rest of the Aesir at this point. Forward was the only way. Loki was down there, probably getting himself in trouble and almost certainly revealing yet another mystery.

Situations like this, one just had to do it. Just one foot in front of the other. She couldn't afford to think too much—that was her weakness, of course. She swung one foot over the edge and felt around for footholds. She was a goddess, wasn't she? Just how immortal was—

The ice cracked beneath her foot and she fell, skidding down the cliff side. Ice and rocks ripped open her palms as she scrambled, desperate for any handhold to slow her descent. Mist blurred everything, but her hand caught on some rocky protrusion. The sudden stop yanked at her shoulder and sent jolts of pain throughout her body. And she felt her hand slipping, too slick with blood. Sigyn shrieked as she fell again, ice scraping her shins and what remained of her dress.

Focus. Focus!

She forced her eyes to look through the mist, to see the fall ahead of her, then twisted to land on another protrusion. The ice cracked beneath her, slowing her fall only briefly before pitching her downward again. Sigyn tumbled into the snow at the base of the cliff, rolled, and slammed into a rock. Her whole World blurred and spun. Pain shot through her entire body until she couldn't tell head from foot, nor even guess how many bones she had broken.

Immortal. And she'd still almost managed to kill herself. A feat worthy of song.

For a long time she lay where she'd fallen, unable to even consider moving. Inside, she could feel her bones knitting back together. If she'd stayed with Frigg, her sister could have used her newfound healing powers. Of course, if she'd stayed with Frigg like Loki told her, she wouldn't *need* healing. But Sigyn had never been very good at doing what she was told. Or at being left behind. Loki had shown her a new World, a new reality where she was no longer the outcast, no longer shunned for intelligence and enthusiasm. He'd showed her a World where someone would look into her eyes and see her very soul.

That was worth eternity. It was sure as Hel worth risking her life over.

When she rolled over, a fresh lance of pain shot through her arm. She screamed, or tried to, but it came out as more of a whimper. Broken arm, broken ribs. Gods, she was a fool, wasn't she? Maybe just a little sleep. Odin had said the apple allowed him to heal from almost any wound. It meant she was going to be fine ...

⁊❦

THE FEELING of herself being lifted jolted Sigyn awake. She squirmed in a man's arms, her body still aching. It wasn't Loki who had lifted her, but a blond man with a bushy beard. He was brawny and bare-chested, covered only by a cloth wrapped around his waist like a skirt.

"She thinks she is a bird," the man said.

Sigyn glowered at him. Was the man rescuing her? Abducting her? It must be someone from the sea castle. "Put me down. Who are you? What do you want?"

The man clucked his tongue. "She sings like a bird, too. I am Fimafeng, little bird."

It was a start. Sigyn had to take control of this situation, before this Fimafeng got any ideas about her. "Do you know who I am?"

"A pretty bird." The man continued carrying her, his gait steady toward a massive stone bridge that stretched out to the castle. The bridge didn't reach far above the sea, and now, with the tide in, a few inches of water lapped at his heels as he crossed.

Sigyn twisted in his arms, trying to worm her way free. "This pretty bird wants to walk on her own."

"Birds don't walk so well. I will carry you, Bird, until your wings heal."

Sigyn couldn't be sure whether the man was truly simple, or just mocking her. Either way, continuing to struggle against him in her current state was pointless. Instead, she took the opportunity to check out the castle. The archway leading inside had to be fifty feet high. Massive columns supported a vaulted ceiling carved with all manner of sea creatures—animals Sigyn had heard of only in tale. When she looked down, however, she spied things that should have only lived in myth—mermaids. And mermen, in fact. Though human from the waist up—and naked—these people had long, twisting fish tails.

The central bridge continued through the great entry hall, but to either side the floor dropped away, revealing great pools of clear water. Inside swam schools of mermaids, some passing right under the bridge and disappearing into underwater chambers.

"By the gods," she whispered. "Those are the people of Rán?"

"Yes, little Bird. The queen is with her husband."

Wait ... What? "You mean this is ... ? The sea goddess Rán actually lives here? This is her castle?"

Fimafeng chuckled. "Bird would rather be a mermaid? Maybe they will let you choose. This is the palace of Aegir the Benthic, husband to Rán."

Aegir—the name sounded familiar. Old legends had spoken of a sea jotunn by that name. Had Loki come here to barter with the jotunn? He said he wanted to prepare for the Aesir to cross the sea. Had he come to negotiate passage? Sigyn shook her head. She'd been a fool to follow, but if Loki *was* here and a guest of Aegir, then she'd be saved.

"Don't I get to meet the lord of the castle?"

Fimafeng shrugged, the movement causing Sigyn to shift uncomfortably in his arms. "That depends on what my lady wants for the Bird." He turned down a side path that connected to the bridge and descended a short staircase that left him waist deep in the waters.

Then he dropped her. Sigyn plunged into the water, and though it was only five feet deep, in her shock she sucked down a lungful of water. Strong arms hefted her upward and squeezed her abdomen, forcing the icy water out of her.

"Silly Bird. Not a mermaid yet." His legs had transformed into a fish tail. A merman? Damn, she had to be dreaming.

Except already her hands shook from the cold. Mere moments of this and she'd be taken by the deathchill. And what on a troll's stones did he mean by *not a mermaid yet*? Was that possible? Gods, did he think to put a vaettr in her?

Sigyn tried to stumble away, but her limbs would barely respond.

Fimafeng hefted her up once again, keeping her head just above the waterline, and this time swimming through an open archway. Whatever he intended, she couldn't help but cling to him if only for the fragile warmth he radiated.

Almost as soon as he entered the next chamber the waters warmed. Near-continuous bubbles burbled up from underwater, filling the chamber with such warmth that a curtain of steam rose off the surface. Fimafeng lowered her into those waters, and luxurious warmth filled her, easing her aching body. For a time she sat there, eyes closed, feeling the waters aid in her healing. She'd guess a few hours of this and she might be able to use her arm again.

What was this place? A hot spring in the middle of the ocean? Sigyn was no sailor, but it sounded impossible to her. Of course, she supposed the king and queen of this sea could do as they wished. Only when her body at last began to warm did she take the chance to open her eyes and look around.

A dozen or so young women lounged in and around the waters, all naked or garbed only in sheer dresses that concealed naught. And birds—swans—swam around the spring. One of those swans drifted toward her, then rose. As the swan did so, her feathers fell away in a cloak, seamlessly revealing a naked woman before her.

The girl brushed a hand over Sigyn's cheek and winked at her.

"More birds," Fimafeng said. "Birds have to ask Rán for their new friend. Maybe she'll be one of us. First, the bird must get warm."

Sigyn swallowed, her head swimming from the dizzying events of the last few moments. It was as if she had passed out of Midgard and into an Otherworld. Perhaps this place was indeed something on the border of two Realms. Liminal places could be thick with vaettir and dangers—or so völvur said. Sigyn was suddenly realizing she should have paid a lot more attention to Frigg's völva nonsense.

20

*T*he fortress of Idavollir watched over a seemingly endless plain Idunn called by the same name. The stones were clearly ancient. Cut from blocks so large no mortal man could have built this place. Even Hymir, the jotunn Tyr had known, would have been hard pressed to construct it, though Odin had said Ymir stood much larger. Tyr had not gone with Odin on his quest for vengeance. He'd wanted to. Instead, Odin had taken Loki. Damned foreigner always knew too much and yet was never around when needed.

As now.

This place was not for men. Chains as thick as Tyr's chest ran along the length of the drawbridge, leading up to a fortress that passed through the mist. Couldn't even see the top of the castle through it.

The gates stood mercifully open. Otherwise Tyr couldn't imagine how they would have opened a door that must have reached sixty feet into the air. He ran his fingers along Gramr's bone hilt. Touch of it gave him some small comfort. It was all that could defend him against the Otherworldly.

All he could trust in these days. He'd not ever let it leave his side. This sword could slay trolls and aught else that might come for the Aesir.

"Tyr," Odin said. "Idunn. With me. We'll scout ahead. Such places can house"—Odin ground his teeth—"vaettir."

Odin would clearly never forget the Odling ghost. Shade had driven Odin on his mad quest to the Niflungar. A people the World would have clearly been better off without.

Tyr drew Gramr and advanced at Odin's side, Idunn trailing behind. The sword weighed less than a normal blade, at least when drawn. As if it wanted to fly. Wanted to hunt, to claim the lives of foes. And Tyr had fed it well recently.

All three of them bore torches that kept the mists at bay and cast the entry hall in shadows. Dancing shadows. Torches were too meager a light to reach the ceiling or walls of Idavollir. But any light was better than none.

Odin waved him toward a hall to the left, while he headed farther down the main hall. Idunn, for her part, glanced between the two men before drifting after Tyr.

"What?" she asked. "I'm not a warrior. You don't think I should go wandering off on my own?"

"Have you not crossed this world alone?" Tyr asked, keeping his eyes forward. This hall led to a staircase which clearly led onto the battlements. Each stair, however, was nigh to three feet tall. Meaning every step climbed was awkward, tiring.

If he'd had a free hand, he'd have helped Idunn up, but she climbed with surprising agility.

"That's going to be a long way up," she mumbled, after they had crested the fifth stair.

Indeed, probably another two dozen to reach the upper

landing. But if his people could reach the battlements they could potentially fire down upon attackers. The fortress was surrounded by the great plain on all sides. Meant trolls could not approach them unawares, even at night.

"Place is a marvel," he mused.

Idunn chuckled. "If you say so. Frey mentioned it, on occasion. Mentioned what an ordeal it had been to drive them from here."

Frey? Idunn spoke so casually of the greatest warrior of the gods, but then, why not? She was one of them.

"So you ... knew him?"

"Still do."

"He—does he truly bear a flaming sword?"

"Well, yes. It's kind of his prized possession, one taken after the fall of the Lofdar. Hmm. Sort of the way you hold on to that icy blade of yours, addicted to its call. I did warn you, right? I thought I had, but sometimes I get flustered and forget what I told people, and what I just think I told people. And what I think I *should* tell people and maybe I have ... you know?"

"Idunn?" Tyr said, hefting himself up another stair. "You recall asking me to tell you if you started babbling?"

"That I do remember." She climbed up after him. "Oh! You mean now? Damn, sorry."

Comforting as the runeblade was, he needed a free hand to help him climb. Tyr sheathed Gramr, then continued up the rest of the steps to the landing. In a pair of alcoves at the top stood two great iron wheels, vertical, each with multiple spokes. A jotunn might have been able to grasp them and raise the bridge. Tyr suspected it would take a dozen or so men on each wheel to operate them. Assuming they could first be cleared of the coating of ice.

But if they could close the bridge, it would cover the

main gate. Then assailants would be forced to climb the walls while defenders rained arrows and stones down on them. Sadly, such tactics would only delay trolls. But delay might be enough. If the trolls held true to form, they would retreat with each dawn. Tyr needed only keep them busy that long.

Tyr gazed out from atop the battlements. He was deep in the mist here. Torch kept it off him, but he couldn't see far. They wouldn't have much warning, but this had to be their best option.

"Can I ask you a question?" Idunn said.

Tyr grunted in acknowledgement, then turned to look at the Vanr woman. He couldn't see the plains anyway.

"Do you … fear me?"

"What?" What need had a goddess to worry over such things?

"Well, some of the others do. Not Odin, of course, but many of the Aesir do. I can feel it."

Tyr leaned back against the battlement. He hadn't taken Idunn for someone who should care what others thought. Maybe he didn't know her as well as he had thought. She was easy to take in at a glance. To believe she was just this beautiful, intoxicating goddess. So full of life and joy. How odd that she should worry over what impression she gave.

"Should I?" he asked. "Is there reason to fear you?"

Idunn frowned, apparently unsatisfied with his answer. What did she want, then? Approval? A chill ran down his spine. That was it, wasn't it? She had come to Odin, acting certain of her mission, driving him onto this path. But she was not certain at all. Had she doubted all along? Or had the thousands of deaths at the hands of draugar and trolls and the frozen river shaken her convictions?

"You no longer think we can win," Tyr said.

"I—no! No, of course I don't think that! Of course you can." Her voice held all the confidence of a snow rabbit facing down a cave bear.

"You cannot allow the others to see your doubt, Idunn. It would break them. You set us on this path—"

"I know! Damn, but I know. There were so many Aesir, and you were such great warriors, and I thought ... I mean, I thought about it for years and years. I thought this was what she would have wanted."

"She?"

"My grandmother. I was trying to ... to honor her wishes, her memory. But now it feels like a facade and I just wanted someone I could be honest with, someone I could ... I don't know."

"Trust?" Tyr shook his head, then pushed off the wall, put a hand on her shoulder. "You have that, Idunn. But then, you must tell me everything from now on. Whatever dangers we face, I have to be prepared. I have to protect Odin and the others."

Idunn shook herself, and looked far too deeply into his eyes. Judging whether he was serious? At last she nodded.

Tyr grunted. Good. Good. "I uh ... never asked. Why are you doing this? Why would gods want men to rise against them?"

Idunn blew out a long breath and flipped her hair from her face. "That's a complicated question. It's filled with so many half-truths and misunderstandings. Where do I even start? I went over this conversation in my head so many times over the years, waiting, wondering if it was really the right thing to do. They never approved of me going out into the rest of Midgard, you know. As though I couldn't take care of myself? The real issue was, deep down, they knew they should be ashamed of what they let people like your tribe suffer. While they lounge in a land of spring, most of Midgard freezes and withers, dying in slow anguish. So I guess that's the answer—most of them *don't* want you to rise against them. Just me, mainly."

He had assumed as much. Tyr groaned, cracked his neck. "People will die. Lots more people. Frey ... he as good with a blade as legend claims?"

She shrugged as if such things mattered naught. "I think that ..." Idunn paused. Turned to the battlements. "I don't have much of the Sight ... but I have some intuitions, Tyr. I feel something moving, very nigh to here. Old dvergar tunnels may run close to this castle."

Huh. Would explain where the trolls went in daylight. Also meant they might close on the fortress very soon.

THE SETTING SUN dipped below the horizon. Still, Tyr stood on the ramparts, Gramr resting atop them. Stroked her hilt. If Idunn's intuition spoke truth, the night would be long. With help from Vili and a dozen others, they'd lowered the gates.

Wells deep under the fortress meant they'd have water. No food, though. Couldn't hold out long without food.

Archers lined the walls now, braziers burning behind them. But with the mist, they couldn't see the ground. Couldn't see even if massive forms moved out there.

He ought to be out there. Gramr hungered for the black blood of trolls. Men gone savage.

As if in answer to the thought, troll bellows echoed through the mist. Very close to the fortress. They had snuck through.

He snatched up a torch and held it over the lip of the wall. Still couldn't see a fucking thing.

Great clangs sounded against the iron gate. Trolls beating on it. He'd set men down there, with spears, to keep them off the gate. It would be a long night.

A great many long nights.

---

21

*A*fter Sigyn's body had healed, Fimafeng carried her to a mercifully dry chamber. As he rose, he shifted back into legs, and Sigyn realized the skirt-like covering he'd worn had drifted away when he first changed form.

"Oh gods," Sigyn mumbled as she caught a glimpse of his manhood. That was not something she'd needed to see.

The merman set her down, then pulled at her dress.

"No!" Sigyn shrieked.

Fimafeng just chuckled and gave over the attempt. "Little Bird," he said and clucked his tongue. "Shy like a human. Bird's dress is ruined."

He turned away and approached a wardrobe. Sigyn's heart wouldn't stop racing. Instead, he pulled out a white dress, held it up to her, then clucked his tongue again and put it back. Next, he withdrew a dress the color of the sky on those rare days when the sun broke through the mist. Fimafeng held this one against her, cocked his head to the side, then nodded.

He pressed the dress into her hands. "Wear this."

Sigyn accepted the offer. The truth was, between the

troll attack, weeks in the wild, falling down the cliff, and being dunked in the sea, her dress was *beyond* ruined. "Fine. Turn around."

Fimafeng frowned. "Bird must get over human modesty." He folded his arms.

Sigyn glowered. She should pick her battles. Gods, she'd been willing to expose herself to outsmart the damned trolls. If that was what it took to make this merman complacent, let him ogle her breasts. Oddly enough, as she let her dress fall, his face remained expressionless. Other than a quick—and blatant—appraisal of her body, he showed little interest.

Sigyn yanked the blue dress over her head. Maybe Fimafeng preferred mermaids over humans. Or other mermen. If so, she was probably safe, at least from him. Other than the fact she was pretty sure he intended to force a spirit inside her, leave her a vessel to a mermaid, or one of those swan girls, or some other vaettr. Which meant not so safe at all, considering she'd just as soon remain in control of her own body.

As soon as she had dressed, Fimafeng guided her by the shoulder into another hall. This place was massive, so easy to get lost. A left, then a right. Twenty paces, another left. She could not afford to lose her way. If this Fimafeng tried to force a mermaid into her, she was going to need to make a hasty retreat.

They passed into another chamber, this one similar to the entryway, with a central bridge Fimafeng walked along. Around it, mermaids swam in pools forming an exotic school of women—and men—with tails of every kind of fish imaginable. Some she had *never* even imagined—yellow and blue stripes, orange and white frills. A dazzling display of beauty. Once, back in Halfhaugr, she'd have given aught to see this. Once, back when such things were stories, puzzles to unravel.

About forty feet up, water poured from a groove cut in the walls in a horseshoe shape, creating a waterfall curtain on three sides of the circular chamber. As Fimafeng neared the back of the chamber, a shadow drifted forward from behind the waterfall. A woman's form stepped through, the water parting around her, seeming to *be* a part of her. Her stunning beauty left Sigyn no doubt this was the goddess Rán herself. Her hair was so blonde, so shimmering, even Sigyn might have felt jealous of it—in another circumstance.

Like most of the others in the room, she was naked save for golden jewelry, but water streamed over her in a curtain that seemed to create a kind of sheer, sparkling gown.

The woman smiled, a wild mischief in her eyes that sent Sigyn's heart racing. "What is this?" she asked. Her voice seemed to come from everywhere, from the waters all around Sigyn.

"A lost traveler, my lady, and my gift to my queen. Do you wish her for mermaid? Or for swan maiden?"

"I'm not lost!" Sigyn blurted. Maybe this queen could be reasoned with. If Rán had been with Aegir when Loki came to meet him, this could be her chance. "I am the consort of Loki, who has come to call on your husband, my queen."

Rán's smile only deepened. "I like her. Mermaid, I think."

"No! I already belong to someone."

"Indeed you do, little girl," Rán said. "You belong to me. And I have sisters in need of a vessel in this Realm. Once, long ago, this Realm housed tens of thousands of us. Did you know that? Once, our waters covered near all of your Midgard and the glory of Mu spread through endless seas.

Now it's so difficult to find willing hosts of sufficient beauty to be worthy of my kind." The goddess chuckled to herself, smiling and bobbing her head.

"Wait! You said willing hosts. I'm not willing."

Rán shrugged. "Of course you are. That's why you're here. You just don't know it yet. Fimafeng, prepare her." The goddess laughed again, and disappeared back through the waterfall.

Fimafeng's grip tightened on her shoulder and he yanked her from the room. Now Sigyn fought in earnest, straining against the merman's impressive strength. He pulled her through the hall.

"Stop! Please, I don't want to be a mermaid."

Fimafeng clucked his tongue. "Very insulting, little fish. If you wanted to be a swan maiden, you should have spoken up earlier. Now it's too late to choose. Besides, a mer spirit is a greater gift than a swan cloak."

"I don't want to be any—"

"Release her!" Loki's voice boomed through the hallway.

Sigyn turned to see her lover. She'd never heard him shout before. She'd never seen such anger in him, such darkness in his eyes. A surge of hope filled her heart like the break of dawn. She could kiss that man.

"I cannot do that. Queen Rán has given the command—this one belongs to her now."

Loki strode purposefully toward them. Sigyn's heart raced, surged with relief not only that he had come for her, but at seeing him again. Maybe she would have to start doing what she was told. One day.

"Sigyn is mine."

Loki's words made her feel surprisingly warm inside. Part of her wanted to see him beat the mermen who'd dragged her here. She had not seen Loki fight, but he often traveled with Odin's warriors, and she'd felt the incredible strength in his limbs, the fine muscles of his body.

Fimafeng shoved Sigyn and she fell into a pool of icy water, once again overcome by the sudden shock of it. She tried to put her foot down, but the water was too deep. She splashed around, flailing, trying to keep her head above water. A few short dips in the river with Agilaz had not made her an apt swimmer.

Sigyn slapped for the side of the path, missed and went under. Not like this. She wasn't going to drown like this, not after everything.

Loki splashed down beside her, then she was wrapped in his arms and hefted toward the surface. He surged upward, flinging them both onto the path. Sigyn gasped, trying to catch her breath. A few feet away, Fimafeng lay on the stone, blood pouring from his mouth and nose.

How long had she been down in the water?

"My lady," Fimafeng shouted—or rather, sputtered loudly.

Loki dashed over to him and landed with a knee on his chest. Then he punched the merman in the throat.

Sigyn choked on the sudden violence of it.

An instant later, Loki was pulling her to her feet again. "Sigyn, are you all right?"

She nodded, not trusting herself to speak.

"We have to move. Aegir will learn of this. That mer was a favorite of his. He will be displeased."

Then why did Loki have to kill the man? "What does that mean? He won't help us now?"

Loki frowned. Yes, fine. It was a foolish question. They had just murdered the sea jotunn's right-hand man. *Help* was out of the question. Just how much *harm* would they be talking about instead?

Sigyn shivered from the cold. She missed the hot spring. The spring where those swan maidens swam ... "There's women here. They have cloaks that let them turn into birds." Women or spirits or whatever they were.

Loki rocked back on his heels. "Swan maidens. Where?"

Stupid, stupid maze of a palace. It was left first, then ... Sigyn shut her eyes. She could do this. "That way."

She took off running, Loki right behind her, leading the way back to the hot spring. The girls inside shrieked in surprise as the two of them burst into the room. Before they could recover, Sigyn sprinted for one of the numerous feather cloaks lying around beside the spring.

"Stop!" one of the girls wailed. The girl ran over as Sigyn tried to don the garb.

Sigyn punched her in the face, then grimaced as the girl pitched over, grasping her bloody nose. "Sorry." She flung the cloak around her shoulders and watched Loki do the same. She pulled up the hood. "How do I—"

A wild energy rushed down from her shoulders. The cloak began encircling her of its own accord, and a shock rushed out her fingertips. She'd heard it pained varulfur and berserkir to shift, but she felt only elated. Instinct took over, and a beat of her newfound wings hefted her upward. Another beat and another, and she was flying, soaring.

Air rushed over her feathers, filling her with such a profound joy she would have wept, could she have done so in this form. Loki, a black swan now flying beside her, flew for one of the giant windows high above. Sigyn followed him outside, out above the sea and into the night sky.

Above the mists and up, up toward the clouds. Naught bound her anymore. She was free of all constraints.

A fell roar rumbled from the castle, and the waters outside it began to swirl. And then he rose out of the sea. A man's torso, stretched into the sky twenty feet, a long white beard streaming around him. His arms were thick as tree trunks and knotted with muscles, but it was the glowing runes covering them that drew Sigyn's eyes.

Loki passed in front of her then beat his wings even harder, drawing her to follow. They were racing for the cliff beyond the sea.

Almost immediately, the sky darkened and the winds picked up. A sudden gust flung Sigyn back out to sea and nearly sent her toppling out of the sky. She dove down, trying to cut under the air currents. Streaks of lightning lit the night sky. Loki circled back again, clearly seeking some way to aid her. But this was on her.

Sigyn banked in one direction, then quickly turned as the winds shifted to block her. Her maneuver allowed her to cut through the prior gust and soar above the cliff. Loki skidded onto the ground and yanked off his cloak. Sigyn did the same, another gust of wind threatening to fling her back out to sea even as she shifted.

Instead, she stumbled to the ground.

Loki leapt to her side and caught her, then pulled her to feet. "Run! We have to get as far from the sea as we can, beyond the reach of their power."

His hand wrapped around her wrist, they ran.

Lightning coursed through the sky behind them.

22

*A*t night, they weathered the barrage of trolls, hiding in the fortress and praying for daylight to send the monsters scurrying back into their holes. By day, Odin allowed his people some sleep while sending others out to forage for food. Agilaz reported local Vall farms and towns had been smashed to bits by the trolls, the animals and women taken. And night by night the Aesir's supplies dwindled, almost as quickly as their resolve.

Odin stood at the gate, beside Tyr, waiting. Another night was fast approaching. The trolls would try to climb the walls again. A few had gotten inside last night, and a score of men had died to bring them down. When would it end? Ve was out there, Odin knew he was.

And unless Odin did something, this would continue until the Aesir at last broke, having never even laid eyes upon Vanaheim. So really, only one choice remained to him now.

"Tonight, we open the gates."

Tyr grunted.

"Choose the finest warriors among us, but leave the

archers to man the walls. You and I, your chosen, we will head into the mist."

"To what end?"

Odin clenched his fists at his side. Indeed. What could he do? "Trolls don't act with such deliberateness. It means a leader drives them, and we both know who that leader must be. I have to go out and find him, face him."

"And if you do?"

Odin glowered. Ve. Son of Borr. Odin's blood.

Urd was cruel.

A FELL WIND swept through the mountains and into the hills, washing over Odin's army as they clashed with the trolls. Odin was done with hiding. He would take the fight to the trolls and end this threat, avenge the fallen, find a way to save his brother, to get through to him. They had headed out to valley between two hills, knowing the trolls would follow, thinking them easy prey.

But tonight, the Aesir were the hunters.

From atop the taller hill, Odin reared Sleipnir, fully conscious of the silhouette he created for his people. He hefted Gungnir into the night sky behind him. The trolls would not come out to fight during the day, and his people dared not chase them into their burrows. And so, now, on this night, he was going to end this.

"Tyr!" he shouted, then indicated a cluster of the trolls trying to charge up the hill.

The mists had taken his brother. They would not take his son, nor any more of his people. Tonight, these Mist-spawned trolls would be the ones to fear men. Odin leveled Gungnir like a lance.

Vili, as instructed, rampaged among the trolls, lining them up. The bear's claws could score a troll's hide, but wouldn't easily slay them. He would, however, drive them into position.

Odin's chest shook, a rumble building in it. These creatures had taken his brother from him. They had slaughtered hundreds of the Aesir, the people who looked to him for protection, for guidance, for a champion. And, by his ancestors, he would give them one. Men needed something to believe in, a symbol. And Odin ... he needed to keep his family and his people safe. Whatever the cost.

A war cry erupted from his throat, and Odin charged down the hill. Sleipnir's hooves kicked up snow and rocks as the horse flew forward, men and trolls rushing by in a blur. Odin slammed into a troll, Gungnir punching straight through its chest. His momentum lifted the troll off the ground, the beast's bellows now turned to whimpers.

The weight already threatened to yank Gungnir from his grasp, but Odin held on, and Sleipnir turned just enough. A heartbeat later another troll was impaled on Odin's dragon spear. This time, Odin didn't fight the momentum. He let it carry him off Sleipnir, then flipped over the trolls and used his own weight to yank his spear free.

Odin landed in a roll and immediately launched himself forward. He could not slow. These trolls were animals. And animals feared those more savage than themselves. He whipped the spear in a wide arc, cutting a gash through a troll's nose and another's chest. The beasts recoiled, clearly stunned by a human not only charging into their midst, but able to pierce their rocky hides.

Odin used the distraction to ram Gungnir through a third troll's face, roaring as he did so.

"I am Odin! Son of Borr! Fear me, beasts!" He didn't

know whether these creatures could understand him, but they did begin to draw back from him. He cut out a troll's leg with the undulating blade of his spear.

Other trolls buckled, at least two actually turning tail and running.

"Not ... your subjects." The voice was rough, like gravel.

Odin turned to face the speaker. The creature before him no longer resembled Ve, but Odin knew. The Troll King was much like other trolls—an elongated nose, tusks, and a hide like moss-covered rocks. Scraggly hair hung past his shoulders. But his eyes held more than animal cunning. They held wisdom and hatred beyond the capacity of a mere beast.

"Brother ..."

Ve rose up to his full height, now half again as tall as a man, and raised arms as thick as tree trunks. "You ... kneel."

Odin swallowed. That had never been an option. The trolls would like as naught eat his men and claim his women as troll wives. He just had to reach his brother, find a way to bring out his human side. Ve was still in there, he had to be.

"Are you working for the Niflungar, Ve? Why? Why betray me?" Why, after Odin had spared Ve's life in the Jarnvid? There had to be some semblance of his brother left behind the Troll King. A remnant of the young man Odin and Vili should have done better by.

"I am ... King. I ... work for ... no one. We work with ... Mist."

"Ve! *Please*, brother. Heed me."

Ve snarled, his hands balling into massive fists.

Odin leveled Gungnir at Ve. His brother knew the dragon spear, knew its power. Even through the haze that now seemed to blanket his mind, he had to know he could not win against such a weapon. "Send your ... *people* away, brother. Don't make me do this."

Indeed, how could Odin fight his own blood? Fight another son of Borr? He wouldn't—he couldn't. Ve would come back to him, Odin just had to figure out how to reach through the mist that blanketed his brother's mind.

Ve grinned, revealing the full horror of his tusks, then bellowed, beating his hands upon his chest. The sound of boulders cracking together like an avalanche. And Odin felt all the other trolls look to their leader.

The same symbol Odin had tried to be to the Aesir. A god among them. And if Odin allowed Ve to rally the trolls, the Aesir would pay the price. They would die in droves, carried off by the trolls as breeding stock or feasts.

And Odin could not allow that. He had to protect his son. His father would have done it for him. His father ... Ve's father. But if he did not fight the trolls would take them all. Father ... How could he fight his own brother? How could he kill his father's son?

"I'm sorry, Ve," Odin mumbled, shaking his head. "Father ... forgive me." He charged Ve, spear thrusting forward.

Ve leapt forward, slamming both hands straight into the ground. Odin dove to the side and rolled to avoid the blow, as it shook the earth. Odin rose quickly, but Ve was faster, flinging a giant fistful of snow at him.

The snow caught Odin in the face, blinding him. An instant later, a mountain slammed into him, flinging him back. The impact slapped Odin into the snow, and he sunk at least an arms' length beneath the surface. Odin gasped, struggling to suck air into his lungs, fighting the pain of cracked ribs. Gods, where had he dropped Gungnir?

He flailed, trying to dig himself out of the snow.

Calm, he had to be calm. He needed to call on his power within to fight the pain. If he could just focus for a moment—

A giant rocky hand yanked him out of the snowdrift and flung him through the air. Odin crashed against rocks poking out of the snow. He heard his own arm break, the sickening sound registering even over the shock of another impact.

When at last he managed to get a breath, he coughed up blood. Gasping, unable to rise from the pain, Odin tried to crawl to where Gungnir lay in the snow, ten feet away. Ve covered the distance between them in a single bound, his landing blanketing Odin in a fresh dusting of snow. Before he could even clear his vision, Ve hefted him up again.

A fist like a hammer slammed into Odin's face, and everything blacked out. Merciful unconsciousness threatened to swallow him. Ve was—his brother was going to kill him.

Odin's mind clawed at his powers, trying to pull it up and block his pain.

"Odin!" Tyr's voice sounded far away. "Where are you?"

Odin forced himself to focus, to look up. A solid wall of mist had encircled him and Ve, cutting off his view of aught else.

"Here," Odin croaked, knowing his voice would never carry.

Ve lifted him again. His grand quest ended here. And Odin had failed, had led his people to their destruction.

All you build will turn to ash, your children shall die, and your dreams shall burn.

The ghost's words echoed in his brain over and over.

His children. His child, Thor. His own blood, the blood of Odin's father and forefathers. Rage cut through his pain, and he grabbed Ve's wrist. Finally he caught his power, allowing him to match—or at least challenge—Ve's strength.

Odin tried to yank himself free of Ve's grip.

"That will be enough," a voice said. "Release Odin."

Ve snarled, then looked at the speaker.

The mists parted to reveal a man with long black hair, a raven perched on his shoulder and a golden crown upon his head.

Gjuki.

Odin tried to speak, but blood burbled out of his mouth.

The Raven Lord seemed to drift over the ground, a faint wisp of shadows trailing off him. A mere hint in this Realm of the endless shadows he cast in the Penumbra. Gjuki placed a hand on Odin's head, and Odin's vision began to dim. His power slipped from his grasp, and with it, consciousness fled.

"Worry not, Odin," Gjuki said. "You will have your chance to say all you wish."

Everything went dark.

PART III

Sixth Moon

23

*A*nother body, but still not Odin, Njord be praised. Tyr had searched the hills hours past the dawn, walking like a man in a daze. The mist itself had turned on them in the battle. Odin must have been right. Niflungar must have come for him. And now, with all the bodies laid to rest on the pyres, and still no sign of their king ...

Now what? If Tyr could not protect his king, his charge, what was left for him? The shame of his failure. Of his broken oath to Borr. Of living on.

Yes, the Aesir had taken down dozens of trolls in Odin's charge. In the sunlight their corpses looked like boulders covered in black ichor. But hundreds of warriors had been taken by valkyries this night, their bodies now burning to keep them from rising as draugar. And Odin himself captured. It was the only explanation Tyr could think of— no sign of the king or his body. And where would they take him? Halfway back across Midgard toward Reidgotaland? Or somewhere closer?

Perhaps Tyr could use the varulfur to track Odin and his captors. That was what they were best at. His legs felt numb as he trod back toward Idavollir fortress. Back toward Frigg, where he would have to recount his failure. For all the power in his sword, still he could not even *find* his foes.

INSIDE THE FORTRESS, he found Frigg's maid, fretting about.

"Where is she?"

"U-up on the battlements," Fulla mumbled. "Did you kill all the trolls full dead as dead?"

Hardly. "We killed many of them."

Fulla wrung her hands, then busied herself tending to the wounded. Of which there were many. Trolls had cost them all a great deal.

Tyr pushed on, toward the stairs. Didn't get far before shouting drew his ear.

"The trolls broke off," Jarl Arnbjorn said. "With them gone, we have a chance to retreat."

Retreat?

"We swore an oath to our king," Hoenir said. "And we must remain until he's located."

Arnbjorn's son Kory spat. "Man is troll fodder. He's not coming back, and we cannot afford to waste time here." Man might've had twenty winters. He could fight, Tyr would grant. If he kept talking such folly, Tyr would grant him a chance to prove it.

"You do not know that Odin has fallen," Hoenir said.

"Even if he had," Annar said, "we don't know what people lives here. Marching through these lands, even back to Aujum, we may face other foes."

Arnbjorn waved that away. "You suggest we simply dawdle here like frightened children awaiting our parent's return?"

Tyr pictured his hands crushing Arnbjorn's windpipe. The jarl and his son were a thorn. Always boring into him. Fucking up Odin's plans. As if Bedvig did not present enough problems. Now the jarl of the Itrmanni wanted to return to Aujum. Make all they had lost for naught.

Before he could say aught, though, Hermod drew him aside.

Hunter bore a gash on his forehead. Probably ought to see a völva. Man leaned in close, speaking into Tyr's ear. "You asked me to watch Jarl Bedvig."

"And?"

"He's been taking meetings with Moda and Arnbjorn."

Making allies. Moda, Jarl of the Bjars tribe had never been one of Odin's stoutest supporters. And Arnbjorn ... Last thing Tyr needed was those two allying themselves against Odin. Arnbjorn commanded the Itrmanni tribe, and that meant the largest group of warriors. Lose the Itrmanni, they'd all wind up supping with Hel.

"Forget Moda for now. I want to know everyone Arnbjorn or Kory meets with. And don't let them know you watch them."

Hermod nodded.

Tyr clapped him on the shoulder and left. And Bedvig Tyr would deal with himself.

First, he needed to see Frigg.

TYR LOOKED TO THE STAIRS, drew a deep breath, and began the climb.

If not for the endurance the apple granted him, he would have long since collapsed. When he figured out how to draw on its power, he grew stronger, faster, nigh immune to pain and fatigue. It all came rushing back on him in the end. The thing made him like a varulf or berserk himself, but sadly, not with their enhanced senses.

Despite his supernatural endurance, Tyr's chest heaved by the time he reached Frigg, who looked out over the battlements.

"Any sign of him?" she asked. It was truly unlike her not to look one in the eye when speaking to him. A sign of her distress, or just of her displeasure with Tyr himself?

"He is not among the fallen. Niflungar may have taken him somewhere north. In the Sudurberks, maybe."

"Can you not track him?"

Tyr swallowed. Throat was so damned dry. "We don't know these lands. That foreigner seemed to, but the gods below alone know where he got off to. Bastard is never around when we need him."

Frigg did turn to face him now, her face creased by a deep frown. "Yes. I've noticed. And he took my sister with him. What of Idunn? She seems to know all of Midgard and beyond."

True enough. Perhaps the Vanr could guess where the Niflungar were bound. And Agilaz could track almost anyone.

Though there had been no sound, Tyr had the sudden sense of being watched, and spun to find Vili approaching. Surprisingly stealthy for a man so large, but then the animal spirits made berserkir like that, if not as much as the varulfur.

"We should press our attack," Vili rumbled. "Now is our chance to hunt down the trolls. Find their burrows and slaughter the fuckers while they sleep. It worked for Odin in the Jarnvid."

Frigg shook her head. "Odin was trying to rescue our people, and was faced with only a handful of trolls."

"I am the king's brother." Vili lumbered over toward her, dwarfing her in his shadow. "The command should be mine."

His nostrils flared and eyes dilated as he stared down at her. These days, he watched her like that a little too oft. Perhaps Vili thought Tyr had not noticed. Perhaps he simply didn't care. Berserk was always too brash. Sometimes that served the Wodanar. Sometimes not.

Oft enough, Odin had to rein in his brother. And now the king was not here to control the berserk.

Frigg straightened her shoulders and met Vili's gaze with an impassive stare. "I am Queen of the Aesir, wife of Odin, and mother of his heir. My words are the words of your *king*, Vili. Do not make me repeat them."

Tyr's grip tightened around Gramr's hilt over his shoulder. Feel of it offered a sudden comfort, though he didn't recall reaching for her. Vili glanced from Frigg to Tyr, as if thinking of trying his luck.

"Vili," Tyr said. "Find me your best varulf trackers. Send them to me."

For a moment, Vili glared at him. Testing his will. Then the berserk snorted and slunk back toward the stairs.

"He is apt to be a problem," Frigg said when the man had gone.

"You handled him well."

Frigg nodded. "Tyr, I ... I can't lead the people after Odin."

Tyr released Gramr and cracked his neck. What to say to that? Frigg was queen. Odin would want her obeyed.

Frigg frowned. "If we leave the shelter of Idavollir

without defeating the Troll King, we risk losing everything, all Odin has struggled for. All our people."

"This shelter will not last us long, either way. Not enough food to sustain our numbers. Hunters can't bring in enough game while we linger here. Always have to be back before dark." And Odin had been gone less than a day, and already the jarls were vying for his throne.

Frigg's scowl only deepened. "You have my decision, Tyr. We have to remain here and continue whittling away at the trolls."

Tyr drummed his fingers against his biceps. Frigg knew the truth already, even if she wouldn't face it. Some twelve thousand Aesir were left, which meant nigh to a third of their number had already fallen on this march. The people could not take much more without breaking. But the decision was Frigg's, and Tyr did not envy her it. He could see no good choices.

Instead, he returned downstairs and to his room. A few hours' sleep before he met with the varulf trackers. Just a little rest. As if he could shut his eyes. As if he could shut out the visions of his failure. Tyr sat on the straw mat that served as his bed but did not lie down, just stared at the wall carved from blocks as large as he was tall. Further reminder they had traveled beyond lands where they belonged.

Of course, Tyr would have followed the son of Borr into Niflheim itself if he could. And what would Odin want now? Would he want Tyr to come for him? Or to remain at Idavollir and protect Frigg, follow her? Fuck, but the man *would* ask Tyr to protect his family. It was everything to him, wasn't it?

A rapping on his door shook him from his musings. He hadn't expected Vili's varulfur so soon.

"Enter."

It was not a varulf, but Idunn who slipped into the room, closing the door behind her. "I heard what happened."

Tyr couldn't think of aught to say, so he just nodded.

Idunn crooked a half smile, then slunk down right in front of him. She took one of his hands in her own, tracing its rough callouses with her soft fingers. "Men like you want to remonstrate with themselves for everything that goes wrong around them, huh? One could be forgiven for thinking the apple was to blame, that it led to delusions of grandeur. But I suspect—and you can tell me if I'm wrong—that you had this problem before. So every man and woman who died out there, that was your fault, right?"

Tyr snatched his hand away. "Who else ought I to blame?"

Idunn shrugged. "The trolls, maybe? The Niflungar? But you, Tyr, you're the one trying to make the World a better place."

"You mistake me for Odin. I'm just a warrior following his lord."

"Mmmm, no, I don't think so. You're a hero in your own right." She placed a hand on his face, and Tyr felt himself flush, his pulse pounding. "I believe in you."

"You believed in Odin, too ..." His voice seemed barely a whisper.

When she withdrew her hand, her warmth lingered on his cheek. "I still do."

"There are no heroes, Idunn. Just blood. Us and them."

Idunn smiled wanly. She rose, and, though Tyr wanted to tell her to stay, he couldn't.

lying above the mists, Sigyn looked down on the giant fortress. Loki, the black swan beside her, continued flying, making no move to land on the battlements.

Loki had tried to speed them all away from this, tried to get passage from Aegir, and if Sigyn had listened when he told her to stay behind, if she had just for once done as she was told, maybe this could have ended. Instead, she and her people remained holed up in this ancient place.

At long last, the sun rose, its warmth heating her wings. Up here, above the mists, the World was beautiful. She could see for miles, and though the mists covered the World like a blanket of clouds, the peaks of mountains stuck out above them.

Exhausted as she was from the flight, still her heart longed to remain up here. How many people would ever see such a sight? But Loki dove down through the mists, landed somewhere beyond the Ás scouts' range. He didn't want to reveal the cloaks to the others. How clever—by not letting them know about his newfound powers, he could seem even more mysterious. She followed him, beset almost immediately by the chill as she passed through the cursed vapors.

These mists locked the World in Fimbulvinter, gave rise to draugar and trolls, and gods-alone-knew what else. Odin's quest had seemed unreal, like Mist-madness—maybe because Sigyn had spent her entire life living among the mists—but now she had seen a glimpse of the World without them. The World that should have been, the World that, according to Idunn, once was. And Odin would create that World again. Sigyn had to believe he could do it.

Her whole body ached as she resumed human form. The transformation itself was as painless as removing the hood, but it served to remind her just how tired she was. Before she could falter, Loki was there, supporting her in his arms.

"Why do they linger in this place?" Sigyn asked.

"We must get back, something's wrong."

Something wrong besides that the goddess Hel had spewed her unholy mists across all of Midgard? Something besides how badly Sigyn had thwarted Loki's attempt to save them all. And how did Loki know what was wrong?

"Do you have visions like Frigg?" she asked as he guided her toward the fortress.

"Not exactly."

Despite herself, despite the guilt she'd wallowed in since leaving Aegir's castle, Sigyn smiled. This was their favorite game, after all, and Loki always seemed to find time to play, to dance with her. "You don't exactly have visions, or your visions are not exactly like Frigg's?"

"Yes."

Damn it. Sigyn shoved him a little. "Which of the two things I asked was the *yes* in answer to? And don't say both, because the questions were mutually exclusive."

"The latter."

"So you *do* have visions of the future."

At that Loki pulled up short. Sigyn slipped from his arm then turned to look back at his face, waiting. If she asked the wrong thing now, he'd be able to deflect her original question, and she was pretty certain she had him now.

"Prescience is a complex burden, Sigyn," Loki said. "Maybe the greatest burden. I've known others who bore such burdens, and it has nearly broken many of them, left them writhing in madness or despondency."

"Which men?"

"I did not say they were all men. Come, the Aesir have need of us."

Loki took off again, forcing Sigyn to follow. She frowned. So those of whom Loki spoke were not all male, or not all human? For that matter, was Loki human? Was Sigyn herself? The apples had made them immortal, given them powers. Made them, according to Idunn, exactly the same as the Vanir. Frey and Freyja, and the great king Njord, beings of myth her people had worshipped for millennia—no different than she herself. Such thoughts were a heady mead apt to go straight to one's head. Would the Aesir one day look down on ordinary Men, be worshipped themselves as the Vanir before them? If they succeeded, Sigyn didn't need prescient visions to know they *would* be worshipped, and, without proper care, they would become as apathetic as the Vanir—or worse, despotic tyrants.

But if Loki could see the future, why had he not seen that she would follow him? Or had he? But that didn't make any sense. If he'd known their whole moon-long trek was for naught, why go? So that must mean he saw glimpses of the future, but not everything. Not enough to avert every disaster Sigyn might stumble into, nor to spare the Aesir from every consequence of their folly.

SHE FOLLOWED Loki into the fortress, much to the surprise of the gate guards. After a brief bout of questions, she drifted off to find Frigg. Large as this fortress was, the Aesir seemed to fill every corner of it, people packed so tightly together that everywhere stank of human sweat and human waste. Men and women and children looked up as she passed, eyes pleading with her—for food, if their sunken faces and gaunt bellies were any indication. They were starving, yet they had not fled this place.

And Sigyn had naught to offer them, a failing that only magnified the weight upon her shoulders. Maybe, had she not gone after Loki, maybe he would have had a solution for them. Or perhaps not. The guards had told her trolls had besieged them, and trolls no doubt meant Ve had returned, pursuing them even to the farthest reaches of Midgard. The Aesir paid for Odin's failings, and Sigyn had blamed him for that, but now, they also would pay for her own.

Her sister walked in the midst of her people in the great hall, head and shoulders straight, seeming regal despite the losses. The jarls were here too, each shouting about the best possible course, some saying they must seek out Odin— where was he?—and others insisting they ought to return to Aujum. What madness had gone on in her absence?

And though Frigg barely smiled at Sigyn's appearance, Sigyn could see the relief in her eyes. And since Frigg was too damned proper to do so herself, Sigyn ran up and embraced her half sister.

"What's happened?"

"Trolls attacked us not long after you left. Odin had thought this place would offer succor but ... they took him, sister."

"The trolls?"

"The Niflungar, Idunn thinks."

Frigg spoke softly, speaking of her fears for her husband. And for her people, who were already beset by these trolls. Was Odin all these sorcerers truly wanted? If so, why? Sigyn had once spied on Idunn and Loki speaking of Odin. He'd dodged all her questions on the subject, but Sigyn had heard him call Odin the Destroyer. The Destroyer of what? The Vanir?

In the depths of Halfhaugr, Sigyn had read ancient dverg runes. They too had spoken of a Destroyer, something the dvergar feared, which, at the time, Sigyn had taken to mean Hel herself. But Loki had referred to Odin by that very term.

Like it or not, the Aesir needed Odin. He had carried them this far, and if the jarls were any indication, the whole alliance would splinter without him. So, if all of their lives rested in Odin's hands, Sigyn needed to understand as much about him as she could. Whatever this Destroyer was, Idunn seemed to know, and if Loki wouldn't tell her, maybe the Vanr woman would.

"I am losing them all," Frigg whispered.

Sigyn nodded and glanced around the hall.

Jarl Arnbjorn was at the forefront of those proposing they retreat back to Aujum. How he intended to do so—they could not well go back the way they had come—he did not say. Bedvig, meanwhile, kept carrying on about how they ought to go conquer the local Valls. In her flight here, Sigyn had seen a few cities, enough to know the rulers here must have a great levy of men to call if needs be. And the last thing the Aesir needed was more enemies.

They needed to find Odin before one of these malcontent jarls drove them all to annihilation.

Sigyn hugged Frigg again and slipped off, hunting down the goddess. She didn't have far to look. As usual, Idunn traveled among the people, hopelessly fascinated by the details of Ás lives. This time, the Vanr walked with Fulla, asking about every last duty of a midwife.

"Don't the Vanir have midwives, Idunn?" Sigyn asked.

"Oh, you're back, Sigyn. Welcome back! We do indeed. Well, sort of. They just don't find that much employment. We don't have as many babies as your people. I mean, we certainly have as much sex—or, probably more. I think maybe the apples make us less fertile, nature balancing out our immortality. We don't need as many offspring. Nevertheless, many of my people practice various forms of preventing conception. Freyja actually taught me a trick where you—"

"You don't think I actually buy this vapid waif routine, do you?"

Sigyn almost bit her tongue when she realized she'd just interrupted Idunn from telling her about some magic method of contraception. Not that Sigyn seemed to need it. Often as she and Loki warmed each other's beds, they had no child to show for it. Perhaps Idunn was correct about a side effect of the apples. The flurry of Idunn's words made her sound as simple as Fulla, and yet, this was a woman who vied with *Loki*, competing to manipulate Odin, a man all seemed to agree could change the whole of Midgard.

Idunn clucked her tongue, then spoke to Fulla. "Maybe you should give us a bit alone. Sounds like someone has something she needs to talk about. Loki not running it deep enough for you?"

The woman's smile was so innocent Sigyn almost

wondered if she really meant it. "He gets the job done. How about you?"

"Oh, I'm still looking for someone to see to my needs. I spend so much time traveling out in Midgard. I guess that's why I get lonely. It's so comforting to be able to actually talk to people, hear about their lives. Sometimes I get carried away, I guess. Which is not a reason to be rude about it. Given a long enough time frame, most things begin to seem trivial. Modesty, social customs, they're generally affectations of mortal minds, so we, at least some of the Vanir, let them slip away. Courtesy, however, never loses its value."

"So you're saying letting your mind jump around like a cluster of bunnies is not an act?"

Idunn frowned, then. "Have I done something to offend you, Sigyn?"

Now Sigyn frowned. Was she too hard on Idunn? Sigyn had to admit, she did not like that Idunn and Loki seemed to know each other from some time before, and, perhaps she had let Loki's obvious distrust of the woman affect her own judgment about the Vanr.

"You want to be my friend, Idunn?"

Idunn laughed. "Child, I've tried to be a friend to all the Aesir. I'd never turn down a friend, though I'd prefer my friends not call me vapid. I'm not vapid, I'm enthusiastic. Spend a year or two with no one to talk to and see how you feel."

"Then I apologize. I spoke too harshly. I'll watch my words"—Sigyn was *always* careful with her words—"but you won't call me or any of the others 'child.' Because we're younger than you does not make us children, least of all *your* children. But we *can* be friends, Idunn. Why don't you tell me about Odin?"

Idunn sighed and glanced off to the north. "As best I can tell, the Niflung king or one of his minions came for Odin."

Sigyn had gathered as much herself, but she didn't intend to stop Idunn until she got some real answers. "Where?"

"I don't know. I don't think they'll kill him, though."

And *now* the woman decided to drop the effusiveness? "Why not?"

"Oh. Well, I don't really know, just a feeling I guess. I mean, if they wanted him dead, they'd have killed him on the battlefield, right? His death would have broken the Aesir. But the mists came in, and they took Odin and they left. They must have wanted him alive for one reason or another."

"Yes. What reason?"

Idunn giggled. "How should I know?"

Sigyn paused as a troop of warriors passed them by. This was not for others. But she sure as Hel wasn't buying Idunn's act now. "What is the Destroyer?"

Idunn, picture of grace that she was, actually faltered a step. "Oh, Sigyn. You should not be spying on others. That's rude. Now that you're living forever, you have to think of your manners. Without trust, what is there?"

"What is the Destroyer?"

"A myth, Sigyn. A legend passed down from my grandmother to the Vanir. A primal force, like one of the Spheres of Creation. A force of ... change. Change on a grand scale, the end of one World and the beginning of the next. The end of an Era. Like ... like the coming of the mists."

The mists had come nigh unto five thousand years before Odin's birth, brought by the dire goddess, Hel. What had any of that to do with Odin? Or maybe that was the wrong question at the moment. "And who was your grand-mother, exactly?"

Idunn sighed. "She was magnificent, Sigyn. A warrior from the Skyfall Isles, a child of the moon. She guided our people to Yggdrasil, back before I was born, but she refused an apple herself. She was a hero, and she fought to save the World, giving everything she had to protect it from Hel."

Sigyn had heard most of that already—that Idunn's grandparents had tried to stop the mists, had battled Hel herself—but this morning Sigyn had seen the sun, pure and undiluted by a shroud of vapors. She'd looked down on the World and up at a sky so blue she'd wanted to cry. "It seems they failed."

"They didn't fail!"

Several other Aesir paused and stared at Idunn's outburst. Sigyn couldn't blame them—she hadn't thought Idunn even had a temper to lose.

"My grandfather *died* to send Hel back to Niflheim and keep her there, Sigyn. He died to see my grandmother—and my mother in her womb—to safety. Whatever horror you think this world faces, believe me when I tell you it would have been far worse if they hadn't closed the rift between the worlds."

Sigyn tapped her finger against her lip, uncertain how to interpret that. Things could have been worse? Somehow Hel had created a bridge between Midgard and Niflheim, and through that bridge she had unleashed the mists. And if this man, Idunn's grandfather, had not stopped her and severed the bridge ... Then what else might have come through? More mist? More vaettir?

"But why the Destroyer?"

"You haven't been listening. Grandpa Naresh saved the

World by destroying the old one. Odin can do the same— destroy the World of the Vanir to save Midgard. He has to."

Sigyn grunted, not certain what to say. Idunn really believed Odin could be some kind of savior, not just of the Aesir, but of all Mankind. She'd spoken of Odin bringing spring before, but maybe Sigyn had never truly believed it. But Idunn did. She truly thought Odin was … what? Going to finish what her grandfather started? So Idunn's grandfather had been some previous incarnation of this Destroyer, and now Idunn thought Odin was as well.

But Odin would do none of that now. He'd been taken by the Niflungar. And if he was destined to be some kind of Destroyer, what would it mean if he was made to serve them? Now Sigyn was the one hiding from the truth. She knew what it meant: it meant he would destroy the current World on behalf of the Niflungar. He would build their new World, one ruled by the Hel-worshipping sorcerers.

As expected, Loki stood atop the ramparts, staring off to the east, back toward the Sudurberks.

"They've taken him there, haven't they?"

Loki didn't turn toward her, in fact, he leaned forward a little, resting upon the battlement. "I cannot see everything, not even in the flames."

She laid a hand upon his shoulder. "But you think he's there. And we're going after him."

"Sigyn …"

"No. I won't be left behind again, not this time. We have the cloaks, we go together. I still don't have all the answers, my love, but I have enough. I can see the fracturing and dissolution of all we've worked for. Everything falls without Odin, does it not?"

Loki nodded, once, then turned to stare into her eyes.

"So I *am* going with you. And we are going to find our king and bring him home."

He kissed her then, long, passionately. And then he pulled up the hood of his cloak and became a swan.

Sigyn did the same.

25

"Odin has already set a precedent," Hermod said. "The Aesir are primed for a king—at least for the moment. Arnbjorn knows this and knows, too, that his chance at a throne will slip away as soon as a single jarl breaks from us."

Tyr ran his fingers over Gramr's scabbard, savoring the rough leather and silver inlay. Fine work. All crafts that dvergar wrought became the stuff of legends. "You think he'd dare move against the king?"

Hermod shrugged. They sat apart from prying eyes, in a —sadly empty—larder. Some few others camped in the room, true, but they gave Tyr space. "Odin is not here to meet any challenge."

"Frigg—"

"Is a strong woman, but a woman still, and not every jarl fancies bowing before her."

Tyr groaned. "You think her not fit to lead?"

The other man shook his head. "The opposite, but it doesn't matter what I think. What matters is what we convince the rest of the tribes to think. Hoenir listens to me and will support Odin's wife. Annar and Vili are family—"

Tyr spat. A few of the men and women in the room nearby looked to him, forced him to keep his voice low. "Vili is less reliable than we might have wished."

Hermod raised his eyebrow at that. "That is not ... welcome news. Last night, Arnbjorn took a meeting with three other jarls and raised doubts as to Frigg's ability."

"You know this?"

Hermod nodded. "This place is vast, thick with secret ways those adept at such things can use."

The scout was his father's son, for certain. "And who attended this treason?"

At that, Hermod held up a finger. "It's not treason yet, Tyr. Cast all those men as traitors and you'll destroy this alliance yourself."

"*Who* was *there*?"

"Who do you think?"

Tyr's grip tightened around Gramr. She knew. "Bedvig."

"Of course, Bedvig. If he wasn't an enemy before, you made him one."

"I didn't—"

Hermod held up a hand. "Peace, Tyr. Moda and Jat were there, too."

Tyr scoffed. "Odin *made* Jat Jarl of the Friallafs." By brutally killing his predecessor at the Althing, but still.

"And Jat argued against any action at this time. In fact, Jat won't do aught until Odin returns."

"Good. The others ..." Well, Tyr had something for them. Gramr would see to each, one by one. She would feast on the blood of traitors and purify the tribes. "We need to make an example of them."

"You are not listening to me." Hermod rubbed his forehead. "If you want Odin to have a kingdom to return to, you need to move with care."

Tyr lurched to his feet. Gramr begged him to draw her. To feed the unworthy to her and send them screaming down to Hel. "Each of those men deserves death."

Before he could storm out, Hermod grabbed him by the arm. "Think what you do here. The tribes, jarls too, they're in unknown lands facing strange threats from the mist, and suddenly the king vanishes. Dissent is to be expected."

"Expected." Tyr spat again. "Not tolerated."

"Listen to yourself."

"You say this? You who helped assassinate Alci?"

"To *stop* a war. Not to start one." Hermod glanced over his shoulder at the people now watching them intently. "I beg you listen to me and take this to Frigg, let her decide what course to take."

Tyr glowered. Cracked his neck. Frigg did have a right to know. Maybe Hermod spoke wisdom. Damn him for it.

A series of horn calls shattered the quiet and sent everyone in the room tensing. Tyr exchanged a brief glance with Hermod. Drew his sword. And they both rushed from the larder.

HIS BREATH CAME heavy as he crested the last step to the ramparts. Up there, braziers burned away the mist. The night had settled. Archers rained arrows upon foes far below. A shieldmaiden blew another long blast on a war horn.

Shieldmaiden—that was Olrun.

"What happened?" Tyr demanded.

Panting, she turned to him, blonde hair billowing about her face in the night wind. "Trolls are back."

The woman handed him the horn then rushed over to join her husband on the edge. Agilaz fired arrow after arrow. Sweat streamed off him despite the cold. Drawing a bow like that took a lot of strength. A man couldn't do it all night.

Tyr peered over the edge. Hard to make aught out through the mist. Massive forms moving ever closer, though. Some trying to climb the walls. Agilaz put an arrow into the eye of one such. Beast pitched over backward, tumbled end over end. Crashed into the snows below. Impossible shot, that.

Olrun had not taken up a bow. Instead, the shield-maiden gave commands to the other archers. Pointed out the most important targets. Trolls most like to reach the top. And every man up there listened to her. She knew the battlefield better than most. Rumors, camp talk really, claimed she had been a valkyrie in some other lifetime. Seemed mortal enough now, though, and Tyr had never asked Hermod. Maybe he ought to.

"East side," Olrun shouted, pointing with her sword. "Two of them drawing nigh. Move!"

Tyr raced over there, Gramr in hand. Indeed, two trolls already had scaled half the wall. Their claws dug in the ice coating the stones. More agile than they looked. Heaving themselves up great swathes all at once. Arrows clattered off their rocky hides and thick skulls. Not many archers could target a troll's very few weak spots.

"The necks," Olrun commanded. "Aim for the necks!"

One troll flung itself upward, covering a half dozen feet. Its great hands clutched the top of the rampart. Almost on her own, Gramr leapt for the beast. The icy blade severed fingers, cracked the ice beneath, and even scored the stone. Shrieking, the troll pitched over backward.

"Well done."

Tyr spun at the speaker. Arnbjorn. Food for Gramr. Before he knew what he was doing, Tyr had taken several steps toward the Jarl of the Itrmanni. Runeblade starting to rise on her own. The jarl fell back at his glower.

Tyr's hand shook.

Gramr tried to rise further. She needed to drink this man and be done with it. And he deserved it, oh how he deserved it. His blood would stain the ramparts.

Tread with care, Hermod had bid him.

Damn it.

Damn it!

Arnbjorn's men, his archers, took up positions along the wall, joining the others. Jarl had come to help defend the keep.

And still, *still* Tyr wanted to spill every last drop of Arnbjorn's blood. This bastard who conspired with Bedvig.

He deserved death ... didn't he?

No, not tonight. Hermod had spoken truth—if Tyr acted against these jarls, Odin could lose everything. And he could not trust himself in this man's presence. Instead, Tyr clenched his teeth together and raced down the stairs, almost falling over the steep drops.

He had come so close to killing a man trying to defend their people. Hymir would have been almost as proud as Borr would have been shamed. Tyr slammed his fist against the wall beside the stairs.

No matter what, he would not become what he had once been. Not again. Never again. He rammed Gramr back in her scabbard.

26

*I*ron manacles bound Odin's wrists to the obsidian altar while others held his feet. He struggled to lift his head, unable to make out much in the darkness. A few candles lined the shelves, but otherwise the stone room was thick with shadows. He was underground, he suspected, given the total lack of windows. A ruin, perhaps another place of the Niflungar.

They had removed Odin's shirt and painted a glyph on his chest, covering many of the runes that marked his flesh. Or maybe it wasn't paint—it looked an awful lot like blood. Odin strained against his bindings, but they did not flex, even when he flooded his limbs with supernatural strength.

No mere iron, no matter how well wrought, was that strong. Was this some new metal, or had the Niflungar placed magic in the chains? Either way, Odin suspected he couldn't escape by brute strength alone.

Which meant he ought to save what strength he had. He embraced the Sight, and, though the World grew hazy, it also filled with a pale luminescence. Shadows twisted and writhed about the room, the place filled with far too many ghosts. Unsent victims of the Niflungar, most like, trapped here in torment.

The door creaked open, and Odin's vision shot back to normal, though he found it hard to focus on the shadowy figure that drifted in.

"Release me," Odin demanded.

"No." Gjuki's voice, though soft, carried the utmost command, a surety that brooked no further discussion. "Not until you are ready to serve your true mistress."

Odin snorted. "Serve Hel? Not in this lifetime."

Gjuki drifted over to the altar so Odin could finally make out his face, lit by the candlelight. As always, a raven perched on his shoulder. "Perhaps, Odin. But you have many lifetimes now, don't you? Our mistress will wait as long as needs be."

Odin set his jaw, refusing to let this man see him squirm. The Raven Lord spoke with complete certainty, and he might just be right. Given a long enough time frame, anyone would break. How long could Odin hold out against Gjuki? A moon? A year? A century? But then, maybe that was exactly what Gjuki wanted him to think. The moment Odin began to see his failure as inevitable, he had already lost.

"I'll watch the stones crumble in this place before I serve you."

Gjuki laid a hand over Odin's biceps and squeezed. "Your body is strong, Ás. It helps feed the strength of your mind, of your soul. But all three can falter, given time and appropriate techniques." The Raven Lord drew an unseen knife along Odin's arm, opening a long shallow cut from elbow to shoulder.

Odin clenched his teeth, refusing to cry out. Sick fuck

wasn't getting the satisfaction. Odin had been mauled by a snow bear. If Gjuki thought this was pain, he would be sadly disappointed.

The Raven Lord repeated the cut on Odin's other arm. "Pain, blood loss, hunger, thirst, fatigue—they will sap your body. Eventually, your will, too, must begin to waver. A weakened mind and body lead to a vulnerable soul, and that is when the denizens of the Spirit Realm can truly find a way in." He drew both hands along Odin's bleeding arms, then slapped his bloody palms against Odin's cheeks. When the Raven Lord next spoke, Odin could not make out many of the words—an incantation. Sorcery.

Whispers built from the shadows, sounds that plucked at Odin's nerves, seeming to dig at the strands of his mind. He tried to focus, tried to shift his vision back to the Penumbra, but the pounding of his heart drowned out his concentration. A burning built along his arms, like Gjuki had poured acid into his cuts. It spread, like a thousand sharp claws digging into his flesh.

It was all in his mind. Through gritted teeth, Odin glared at Gjuki.

The Raven Lord smiled. "Shall I give you some time alone with your guests?"

Small cuts began to appear on Odin's chest and arms, tiny tears ripping through his trousers. Like a swarm of rats crawling all over him. Despite himself, Odin grunted in pain.

The Raven Lord chuckled and left. And still the clawing and biting went on and on. Most of it left no visible mark, but Odin could feel himself covered in sweat and blood. Unable to bear it, he shifted his eyes again, embracing the Sight. A blanket of shadows clung to him, eyes in the darkness, invisible to normal sight. Tearing at his body, siphoning away his blood and life force. And as he looked at them, he swore a dozen sets of eyes met his gaze, laughed at him. Driven to fresh frenzy by the thought he could see them?

Odin moaned, then cried out. Did they feast on his very soul? What had Gjuki said? That as his mind and body weakened, so too would his soul? Why? Did Gjuki plan to …? Odin shook his head. The Raven Lord was right; it was already growing hard to think clearly. Possession. They'd weaken him until a vaettr could enter him, take him over. Hadn't Gudrun said something about vaettir only being able to take those with weak, damaged souls? Or was it more complicated than that?

Odin shut his eyes, unable to bear seeing the creatures feasting on him anymore. Think of aught else, anywhere else. He was falling, letting his visions take him, offering him blessed relief as they drew him back to times forgotten. To a snowfield somewhere in southern Aujum, where three boys trained with wooden swords. Odin had not remembered this, but then, these weren't his memories—they were Borr's.

⁊

TYR BESIDE HIM, Borr watched as Odin bested Vili once again. Though Vili was larger than his older brother, he was all fury and no control. Sometimes it allowed him to get the upper hand and simply overpower Odin. Mostly, though, Odin outthought his brother, leading him into traps, feints, and poor footing that oft as not ended with Vili sprawled on his arse.

Borr beamed with pride. They would all be great

warriors one day, even little Ve, chasing his older brothers around and waving his wooden sword in the air.

"Give Vili a new target, would you?" he asked Tyr.

Tyr, now seventeen winters, had been with them long enough, and Borr trusted him to teach his sons well. Tyr was a natural, as though born with a blade in his hand. Considering the way Tyr had come to the Wodanar tribe, that was probably not far from the truth. Besides, after losing Zisa, Tyr needed something to focus on. Borr could give him that.

Tyr did as Borr asked, and Borr motioned for Odin to come to him.

"You're the eldest, son. One day you'll be jarl. You have to protect your brothers. But you'll need them too, for all your cunning. Family is everything, Odin."

"I will protect them," Odin said. His son, a mere nine winters old, said it with such conviction that Borr didn't dare laugh.

He just smiled and nodded. "Then show me how." Borr picked up a stick and allowed Odin to demonstrate all he'd been practicing.

Back and forth he and Odin danced, Borr unable to keep the smile from his face. Odin had Bestla's spirit, more than any of them. The boy overextended and Borr tripped him into the snow.

"That might have worked against an opponent your size, Odin. But from time to time you may face foes larger than yourself."

Borr offered his son a hand up, pulling the boy to his feet.

At once Odin felt both his father's strong hand grasping his own and the feel of his own weak grasp. Pride moved his father, so much Odin almost choked on it. He'd been there every moment of their lives, teaching, guiding, helping. A hero to his own family as much as his people.

Odin wailed, not at the pain in his body as much as the loss of the vision. He replayed it over and over in his mind, desperate to dive back into his father's memories. But he couldn't reach them.

※

"ODIN." Gudrun's voice drew Odin's consciousness back to the surface, and with a start he realized the vaettir had withdrawn when she had entered the room. "Oh, my love. It doesn't have to be this way." Gudrun. Odin hadn't seen her since he'd leapt from her window. It seemed so long ago now. Her smile was like a breath of spring, her features soft, golden hair hanging down and brushing his cheeks as she leaned in to kiss him. Smiling, though he swore he saw unshed tears in her eyes.

Her lips were soft and warm on his own cracked and parched ones, but their touch was almost painful.

"Oh." Gudrun clucked her tongue and drew a wineskin from her belt. "Come, drink."

Odin turned his head away. "Another potion?"

"It's just water."

Water. Gods above and below, he'd kill for water. But how could he believe aught Gudrun offered him now? She'd enchanted him, tried to control him, made him believe he loved her. It was her Art—that's all it had ever been. He was married to Frigg. He had no need for …

Odin didn't resist as Gudrun drew his face back to her and poured a slow trickle of water over his lips. He almost choked on the sudden moisture.

"You're lucky it was my father who found you."

Odin snorted. "Yes. I feel very lucky at this moment, Gudrun."

"It would have been worse if Grimhild had found you."

The sorceress queen of the Niflungar. "And you think she could do worse than Gjuki."

"She can do worse. Much worse." Gudrun climbed onto the altar and straddled him. She poured water over her hands, the excess dribbling onto his chest, then wiped her palms over his cheeks.

Odin couldn't bring himself to speak as she cleaned the blood off his face and shoulders. No more than he could bring himself to hate Gudrun. It was just the lingering effects of her potion. He didn't have real feelings for this woman. Did he? He couldn't. She worshipped Hel. She was a princess of these corrupt sorcerers. The enemy. He *should* hate her. He should have killed them all.

Gudrun planted a gentle kiss on each of his eyes. "My king, please listen to me. There are much easier, much more enjoyable ways to the same end. Things will be better if you choose of your own will, and before Grimhild returns."

"You call your mother by her name."

"She gave birth to me. Since then, she's lost the right to the title *mother*."

Odin frowned and shut his eyes. Of all the horrors he'd seen and heard, that one should not bother him so. His own mother had died giving birth to Ve—the brother Odin had failed—but what Odin remembered of her was a warm embrace, an easy smile, a quick laugh. She had loved his father, and she had loved her children. Odin could only picture her face when he thought of her laugh. Except he'd seen her in his visions ... He could almost hold on to his parents ... They were gone, and now Thor would know the same emptiness. Odin's son would never know his father.

"I don't want to talk of Grimhild."

Odin opened his eyes, glowering at the woman atop him, then had to look away. He was drunk on her beauty, and the warmth of her eyes threatened to swallow him. "Let me go, Gudrun. Release me from these chains."

"I-I can't do that. But I can help you." She turned his face back to hers again and leaned in, then planted another kiss on his lips. He tried to look away again, but her eyes trapped him. Again and again she kissed his face, her hands tracing down his abdomen and over his hips.

Odin wanted to tell her to stop as she unfastened his trousers, desperately tried to, but his voice wouldn't work. It caught in his throat and wouldn't let go. This was wrong. He was wrong. What kind of man would let this sorceress seduce him again?

But his body responded to her every touch, to her delectable warmth as she pulled him inside her. Her gentle motion drove all other thoughts from his mind, until he strained against his chains in an attempt to wrap her in his arms.

And when she shuddered her release, it drove him to his. Vital energy slammed against his soul, settling in his mind. Bits of her power lodged itself inside him, as part of him, too, passed into her. A cascade of confusing images flooded across his vision. A woman in a bone mask, the feared queen of the Niflungar. She spoke to Gudrun through the mists, as Gudrun spied on the Aesir. And Gudrun hated the woman—an icy loathing that would have made Hel herself proud.

It all flashed over him in an instant, most of it making no sense. Gudrun's sorcerous nature meant she shared so much of herself. As Odin no doubt shared pieces of his own soul with each woman he took. With Gudrun.

And the one thing that burned clear through the haze of pain and confusion, through the blurred memories of the woman atop him, was that she *did* love him. In spite of all that had passed, in spite of what she'd done to him, she had true feelings for him.

And that only made it worse. It meant that, one day, even if Gjuki failed to turn him, Gudrun would succeed.

27

*A*t nightfall, Tyr would go out to face the trolls. Try to fight them off the wall until one more dawn. Then a few hours' sleep so he could repeat it all again the next day. Days of it, and every warrior seemed nigh to breaking. Exhaustion touched even him, even after the apple. The others would have it worse.

They had missed any chance to escape. All knew it. Now, in the great hall, they debated only who to blame. Eight jarls and the queen, plus their gathered thegns and völvur.

And more and more, those thegns and the weaker jarls, they looked to Arnbjorn instead of Frigg.

"We must flee from here at the next break of day," Arnbjorn said. "We cannot hold this place forever."

Still trying to return to Aujum, the fool. Tyr ran his fingers over Gramr's bone hilt.

Frigg rose from her throne, regal. Looking each jarl in the eyes. "We would not make it more than a few miles from here, and then find ourselves facing trolls in the open, once again. Besides which, I will not abandon Idavollir while Odin remains missing."

"Odin is dead," Kory said.

Several jarls and thegns murmured agreement.

Tyr glowered, tightening his grip on Gramr. Bastards. All of them. Especially Arnbjorn and his son.

"Loki thinks otherwise," Frigg said, "and has gone to find him."

Arnbjorn scoffed. "Forgive me, my queen, but you place your trust in the foreigner? Besides which, how does he, how *could* he know that which he claims?"

Much as he hated agreeing with Arnbjorn, Tyr found it hard to argue with that.

Frigg fixed him with a level gaze. "He is the blood brother of your king. He says he would know if Odin had fallen."

"And still you'd have us trust him?"

"I would have you trust me, Jarl Arnbjorn. Indeed, as your queen, I rather insist upon your trust."

More murmurs. Silent accusations that, had they fled sooner, they might not now be in such dire times. As if the tribes could agree on the color of troll shit.

Arnbjorn looked around at his fellow jarls, shared an overlong look with Bedvig. Bastards. Trollfuckers. Gramr would have their blood one day. "My lady—"

"Queen," Frigg said.

"My *queen*, the Althing chose Odin. And if he has fallen, we must hold another to determine who should speak for us."

Implying the role would not fall to Frigg in Odin's absence. "What makes you so certain he has fallen?" Tyr demanded. "Did you see it happen? You speak oft enough of the event, jarl. Perhaps you *aided* in his fall?"

That settled many of those in the hall, all now looking to Arnbjorn.

Tyr had all but accused him of treason—which was true enough, if not likely for actually moving against Odin. Arnbjorn's honor would demand he meet such a challenge, or send a champion to do so. Either way, Tyr would kill one of them, and the Itrmanni tribe would lose honor.

Arnbjorn nodded solemnly. "Indeed, Tyr. We all did."

What? Had he just admitted to betraying his king? Tyr shook himself. This must be some trick.

"We all aided in Odin's fall, for none of us did aught to save our king, who, in his valor, challenged trolls alone. Not a man among us stood beside him in the end. Not even his own champion walked by his side."

Tyr recoiled, unable to quite form a response. No. He had not been by Odin's side, though not by choice. And Arnbjorn had turned Tyr's challenge into a rebuke against everyone. Who could question his loyalty now? Trollfucker.

"There may be truth in that," Annar said. "But the gods gave Odin uncommon valor, and we could not have easily followed where he went. Either way, we do not even know what peoples live in these lands. Our best course may be to send a few scouts, men who could pass unnoticed by the trolls."

"And if we find such locals?" Bedvig demanded. "What then, jarl? Should we beg their assistance against the trolls?"

"Beg? I beg of no one. It does not mean—"

"If people dwell in these lands, we ought to raid them for supplies." A rumble of agreement ran through the great hall. Men agreeing with Bedvig of all people. The mead had run dry. It made men fools. Already they had begun to ration their food, but that too would dwindle soon enough.

Several jarls began shouting at the same time, some arguing for raids, for retreat, even for advancing without Odin. Continuing this Mist-mad march on Vanaheim without their leader. Frigg tried to speak twice, but men talked right over her. Over their queen, Odin's wife.

"Enough!" Tyr bellowed. He looked to Frigg.

She nodded at him, then turned to each jarl. "We will send a few scouts. Whatever course we decide on, it still behooves to us to know our surroundings. But we will also remain here, in Idavollir, until Loki returns with Odin. Such is the command of your queen." With that, she strode out of the hall, effectively denying them any further chance to argue with her.

Not, however, stopping them from bickering among themselves.

TORCHLIGHT REFLECTED off Idunn's eyes and hair as she sat crouched in the corner of Tyr's room. She'd taken to sitting there, claimed the spot as her own, as they so often passed the evenings here. In the hour or so before twilight, they could take the night meal together. He no longer ate with the others. So often, anger gripped him there.

Here, perhaps he could pretend he was not down to some thirty berserkir and varulfur to guard against the trolls. The shapeshifters were his greatest asset against the rocky monsters, and the trolls seemed to know it. Every night Tyr lost at least one of his shifters. The trolls tore them to pieces, or a few just vanished into the mists, which worried him more than the deaths. Were they being deserted by their allies? When the march had begun, there had been nigh unto six score of the shifters. If so many had fallen because of his and Odin's decisions, could he blame them for leaving?

"You're stroking the sword again," Idunn said.

Tyr looked down to realize he indeed had begun running his fingers over Gramr's hilt.

"Do I need to make any phallic references, or does the action speak for itself?"

Tyr groaned and pushed the sword aside.

Idunn rose and came to sit beside him, pulling the runeblade away. Sent it skittering across the floor, to the far side of the room.

Tyr had to restrain himself from chasing after it, unable to take his eyes away from the sword.

"You need it."

"I-I have to have it. I have to protect my people, only the sword can—"

"Hmm. I understand, of course. I knew what Gungnir was when I gave it to Odin's ancestors too. Weapons like that, they're made from the essence of living beings. Freyja calls it soul forging, though she refuses to practice such aspects of the Art. A soul is literally bound into the weapon —I think it's the only place these magical weapons really come from. The spear, or its point rather, belonged to a friend of my grandmother. A dragon-souled blade. She called it cursed, gave it up, despite the dangers of the World around her, because she thought it her best chance at a peaceful life. Later, my people had that blade affixed as a spear point. It proved very effective, even against the jotunnar."

Tyr shook himself. The jarl of Wodanar had long held Gungnir as a symbol of the tribe. He had given little thought to it. "Why are you telling me this?"

"Because I care about you. Because you cling to Gramr like a woman."

Tyr supposed that was better than her claiming he was stroking his own phallus. Besides, Gramr was his woman.

Wasn't she? Nor did he truly wish to spend their last few moments this evening talking of weapons or war.

"Idunn, I ... These times mean a great deal to me. The chance for us to talk and ..."

"I *love* talking, Tyr. You have no idea how lonely it gets sometimes. Try not talking to anyone for a year or so and see. Or, I mean, don't do that, because it makes anyone miserable."

He grunted, eyes locked on hers. Her beauty was truly entrancing. Often, she told stories handed down to her from her grandmother. Stories of far-off places, of lands of sunshine and warm waters. As he imagined Vanaheim itself must be. If they ever reached it.

"You did not hear him tonight ..."

"Who, Arnbjorn? Why are you so concerned with this jarl, anyway? I thought it was Bedvig you hated."

The mere mention of the name filled him a fresh desire to go reclaim Gramr. Idunn's hand on his arm restrained him. "I do. But Arnbjorn may be more dangerous. He wouldn't rise to my challenge ... I don't know. Maybe Hermod and I ..."

"You want to assassinate him, the way you did with Alci."

He nodded, not trusting himself to speak.

"This is not you, Tyr."

"Are you not the one who drove us to act against Alci?"

The Vanr chewed her lip a moment. "An altogether different situation—Alci had to fall to secure Odin's throne, and moving against him, from within his own tribe no less, it also stopped him from pillaging the other tribes. Here you plan to kill a man because you dislike him or disagree with him. But he has not actually betrayed Odin, as yet."

"So I should wait until he has the chance to *actually* move against us?"

Idunn shrugged. "If not, you give up any pretense of justice. If you begin to execute men for what they might do in the future, you darken Odin's reign with a shroud of tyranny. Even were that not unfair to your king, still we could not afford such a course now. We have already reached Valland. If we can just push on to the south, we could reach the Middle Sea. From there we have a shot at Vanaheim."

Tyranny. Probably some truth lay in her claims, much as it shamed him. Before, he'd have gone to Borr with such moral questions. You could trust Borr to take the right path. Or even Odin—Tyr could trust him to ... win. Here, neither victory nor morality seemed clear.

And as he contemplated murder, he shamed both Borr and his son.

And still he could not quite set aside his desire for blood.

28

*G*udrun's father always liked to sit in the dark, the walls of his private chamber lined with candles whose light barely reached his face. The candles were a nod to what remained of their humanity. Fire might be an enemy of Mist, but even the Children of the Mist needed light by which to see and read. Her father probably liked the tension between the two, the darkness and the shadows broken by hints of light.

Before the Niflungar were driven from these lands, this Hunalander fortress had belonged to them. Had her father been here back then, so many centuries ago? No one had come here in a great many winters. Lost in the mountains, the men had forgotten this place. Men, but not her father.

Countless ravens perched up in the rafters, watching Gudrun as she sat before her father.

He glanced at her, then turned back to the decaying tome in front of him. If it had been her, she'd have lit a few more candles. Straining her eyes to make out faded glyphs was not her idea of an enjoyable evening.

"What troubles you, daughter?" he asked at last. Unlike

Grimhild, her father never tried to conceal his spell tomes from her. He had once told her she alone could decide what knowledge she was ready for, as she alone would pay the price for it. Ironically, that had proved a more effective deterrent to keep her from delving through his secrets than any threat would have.

Gudrun opened her mouth, shut it, opened it again, then sighed. A hundred times she'd run this conversation over in her mind, and now she couldn't get a damned word out. "Father," she began, then sighed again.

"I have never known you to stumble for words, Gudrun."

"Is what you're doing to Odin really necessary?" she blurted. True, the steps he took were naught compared to what Grimhild would do to break the man. She'd done worse to her own daughter, so Gudrun didn't want to imagine what the woman would do to an enemy. She couldn't cross Grimhild, but there had to be some way to help Odin. Seeing him on that altar ripped her heart out.

Her father's face remained impassive, but he arched a brow—which invariably meant she had uttered some folly. "You'd rather we wait until your mother arrives? I imagine she will be here very soon."

"I don't want Grimhild anywhere near him!" The queen's methods probably would have been more effective, but all the more destructive to his soul—assuming she didn't simply kill him. "I can still turn him myself. These tortures weaken him, make him less useful."

Her father shook his head. "You tried that already."

That wasn't fair. She'd done as he commanded, using her potions and spells to enchant Odin. This time it was *real*. She had so much she could teach the man, and he had so much power within. With her brother gone, she was heir to the Niflungar kingdom. What finer husband could she hope for than the immortal warrior? He was her perfect match, her destiny.

"I have a connection to him," she said.

"That may be true, but we underestimated him once before, and it cost us Guthorm. Your brother died because you and I failed to properly contain that man. And if he is not contained before your mother returns from the east, that is a failure she will exact terrible payment for—out of him and ..."

Out of Gudrun, more than likely. "You could always stand up to her."

"She is the chosen of Hel, daughter. Do not forget that."

Gudrun never forgot. Through the blessings of Hel, Grimhild had destroyed the Odling kingdom and left their queen as the ghost who had cursed Odin. Another irony, since her curse might actually make it easier for the Niflungar to sway him.

The things her mother would do to Odin would make her father's techniques pale in comparison. Nevertheless, what her father was doing to Odin set her stomach roiling. He didn't deserve such tortures. If they broke him at all, they would do so by leaving him an empty shell, one ripe for possession by a spirit. And then, he wouldn't really be Odin anymore at all. The thought of that opened a hole in Gudrun's stomach as deep as the bottomless pit beneath Castle Niflung. She felt like vomiting.

"Does torture so vex you?"

Gudrun sighed. "There must be a better way to turn him."

Her father looked back at his book. "Then try it. I have never denied you an opportunity to test your limits."

Maybe not, but Grimhild had made her pay for pushing those limits. And her father offered no promise to cease torturing Odin. Gudrun rose and slipped out of the room, then slumped against the wall.

"Are you all right?" Hljod asked. The girl had waited outside, no doubt shifting nervously in the dark and chilly hall. And, indeed, she wrapped her arms around herself despite the fur cloak Gudrun had given her.

"Yes," she said. "I will be fine." Gudrun took Hljod's arm and led her away, back down the stairs from the tower her father had claimed here.

"So?" the girl demanded. "Is he going to help you?"

"No."

"Your parents are charming people, aren't they?"

Gudrun glowered. "I only have one parent. And he's ... complex."

Hljod snickered, then laughed loudly, the sound echoing through the halls. "Complex? Gudrun, what about your life is not complex? You've got a man chained up in the dungeons—a man you fucked, if I'm not wrong—who is being tortured by your father. Your mother is like the goddess of thunder cunts, and you're in love with a man who probably hates you."

Gudrun couldn't quite suppress her snort, but she shook her head. "Keep talking like that, and someone will hear you and have your tongue out, girl. Do you remember the potions I showed you this morning? Go to my chambers and bring them down to the dungeons."

"Wait, me?" Her voice came out as a bare squeak. The girl was all bravado one moment and timidity the next. It was to be expected, Gudrun supposed.

She allowed herself a smile. Under other circumstances, a girl Hljod's age could be inducted into the mysteries by letting her lie with one of the male sorcerers. But given what Hljod had suffered at the hands of the Troll King, Gudrun wouldn't send her for that until she was ready, and Hel alone knew how long that might take.

Nevertheless, with a mouth like Hljod's, the girl deserved a little shock now and then. "You can trust me, Hljod. You have naught to fear in this place. You are under my protection."

"You're afraid of your mother." From the way Hljod's eyes widened, the girl regretted the words the moment she said them.

As well she should. Gudrun forfeited any attempt to hide her irritation. There *were* lines, after all. "Go and bring me the potions, Hljod. Now."

Her new protégé scampered off to do as Gudrun bid.

GUDRUN TROD back down to the dungeon alone. Odin was no longer bound to the altar, but chained to the wall. He squinted as she opened the door. Her father had put out the candles, leaving Odin in darkness. A minor torment, compared to the others. Servants had allowed him to use the chamber pot and had cleaned him up after his ordeal.

"What now?" he demanded. "Here to fuck me or flay me?"

Gudrun knelt before him, hiding her disgust at the grime and filth that covered the dungeon floor. "Neither, my love. I don't want to hurt you."

"You have."

Gudrun recoiled from the venom in his words. Had she not just made love to him a day before? "I'm sorry." The words just slipped out. Grimhild had told her a princess of the Niflungar apologized to no one. "How long has he kept you in the dark?"

Odin snorted. "Has your father forgotten I too have the Sight? There's starlight in the Penumbra, enough to sustain me. Or is that part of his plan? Force me to look there, to see the ghosts that flit about this place? Are they meant to be a vision of my own future? I do see them, Gudrun. The vaettir, waiting in the wings, so eager to slip inside me if my guard should drop."

"He'll put you back on the altar at midnight," she said. "Please, Odin. If you choose me of your own free will, I can stop all this. He's desperate to bring you to our side before Grimhild returns."

"Even your father fears your mother, then?"

"He's trying to save you, for my sake."

"Save me?" Odin spat at her. "Save me! If you want to save me, take off the fucking chains! Release me, Gudrun, and I will spare you. I will ..." He shook his head, and his voice softened. "Please, Gudrun. You have to know this is wrong. However much Hel has corrupted your heart and soul, surely there is *some* humanity left in there."

Corrupted her heart? Was that what he thought of her? Her stomach burned with an empty fire, and she rose and backed away. Her heart wasn't corrupted. She and her people had made their choices, that was all. They had done what was necessary to survive the Fimbulvinter and the chaos that it brought with it.

"I am a descendant of Halfdan the Old!" she said, thumping a finger against her own breast. "I am a princess of the Niflungar, greatest of the kingdoms born of Halfdan. My people built an empire while the Aesir hid in caves! We built the castles and monuments spread across Midgard. Do not speak to me as though you understand our ancient lineage."

"And where is this empire?" Odin spoke through gritted

teeth, his anger still driving her backward, making it hard to hold on to her own. "If Hel is so great a patron, why did your people fall?"

The fire-worshipping Lofdar and their priest, Loge. Gudrun shook her head. She wasn't about to admit that to him. Even among the Niflungar, no one liked to speak of the fall of the old kingdom.

Hel, this man was difficult. But if he wanted to open old wounds, she could do the same. "Do you know why Ymir came down off that mountain and slew your father?" Gudrun asked.

"What?" Odin now jerked forward, straining against his chains. "What do you mean why? What are you saying?"

Gudrun shook her head. She hadn't wanted to reveal it, had been a fool to even let that slip out, but maybe the truth alone would get through his thick skull. "Hel sent him."

"What the fuck? Why would Hel send a jotunn? What did she want with my father?"

Gudrun blew out a slow breath. This had been a mistake. She should never have mentioned this. All it would do was inflame Odin's rage. But he'd never stop without an answer now. "It ... was never about Borr, Odin. It was about you. She wanted to make certain you were who she thought you were."

Odin's mouth hung agape, his eyes begging her to admit it was a lie. "You took my father from me as ... a test?" For a moment, she thought he might actually weep. "A test?" His voice sounded so frail.

"She hates you, Odin."

"Why?"

Gudrun shook her head. "I don't know. But she will have you serve her, or she *will* destroy you. She will take everything from you."

Odin launched himself forward, straining against the chains. "You took my father! You took my *father!*"

Gudrun fell back, nearly tripping over her own feet.

"Who is that?" Odin demanded before she could even recover. "Now you've brought another whore to tempt me?"

She followed his gaze to see Hljod trembling in the doorway. Gudrun snatched a ceramic vial from the girl's hand, then stalked back over to Odin who still strained against the manacles. "Take this. Or don't; it's your choice. It will ease your pain and protect you from the ravages of the spirits when Father begins again." She leaned closer. "And do not *ever* call Hljod a whore again, Odin."

"Nice to see you care about something."

"I care about *you*! You stupid, arrogant man. *I* didn't take your father away from you—I didn't even know who you were back then. You think my soul is corrupt, but you don't want to see what my parents will do to yours. Think about that before you slap my hand away again."

29

*I*ron rent with an ear-shattering cry. From atop the battlements, Tyr could barely make out what was happening below. One of the trolls was directing the others at the gate. Ve. Had to be. And he was coordinating *trolls*. Not a threat a man usually had to worry over.

Bunches of them had gathered at the main gate. From the sound, they were actually bending the iron.

Damn it.

"Shoot them! Shoot the ones at the gate!" he ordered.

"They have no clear shot up here," Olrun said. "And more are scaling the walls. We cannot—"

Tyr didn't bother listening to the rest of her objection. Gramr in hand, he dashed down the stairs, leaping several at time until he could jump to the ground floor.

More shrieking iron.

And then trolls crashed through the ranks of men at the gate. A troll grabbed a man, wedged its fingers in his mouth. One hand up, one low, and the troll tore the man's jaw off in a shower of gore. The bastard laughed, a sound like grinding boulders.

A backhand swing sent another warrior colliding with the gate. The man impaled himself on one of the now bent iron spikes. More trolls kept pushing their way inside.

Screaming a war cry, Tyr charged forward. Gramr cleaved through a troll's arm, severing it at the elbow. Black ichor splattered over the gathered men and women. They rained ineffective blows on rocky troll hides. Another troll caught a spear in its hand, snapped it in half.

Tyr slashed his runeblade through the monster's throat.

Some of the breachers had pushed inward. Past the warriors. Toward the civilians.

"Hold the gate!" Tyr bellowed. "Let no more inside." He knew better, knew they could do little without him. But the civilians inside would die in droves.

He raced after the trolls, following the sound of screams.

He darted down a hallway strewn with bodies. Men and women's guts and blood splattered the walls, even the twelve-foot-high ceiling. Gore was so thick his foot slipped. Banged his knee on the stone floor. Tyr raised a hand to his mouth to keep from gagging. Whole corridor stank of blood and shit. Had to be a score of dead in here. Arms and legs ripped right out of their sockets. Skulls splattered on walls. On the floor in front of him rested a head with its nose bitten off.

Further down, a troll had bit through a man's crotch, severing the legs.

Tyr rose. "Gramr ..."

She felt his anger. Or he felt hers.

These foul creatures of Mist had come into a place of men, a place far too thick with people.

More screams rang out from ahead. He raced on, fast as he could without falling. A troll had blundered right through an ash wood door without bothering to open it.

More bodies. A shieldmaiden swung a sword at him. Troll ignored it. Caught her by the legs and drove her to the ground. It yanked apart her legs with such force Tyr heard bones break. Shieldmaiden screamed.

So did Tyr, charging. Troll didn't turn in the chaos. Didn't even look before Gramr bored through the back of his neck while he tore at the shieldmaiden's trousers. Tyr jerked the blade free, half severing the head. Body fell atop the shieldmaiden. It took all of Tyr's now significant might to pull the beast off her. One look told him she might never walk again.

He shook his head in sorrow.

But too many others needed his help for him to remain here. He kicked the woman's sword over to a boy—maybe ten winters old. The oldest and largest person still standing in this room. "Defend these people as best you can!"

In the next room, a pair of trolls feasted on the dead. No living men or women here. Tyr raced in and leapt at one. It tried to stand. Gramr slid through its heart before it gained its feet. Tyr rolled off it, twisted around and came up even as the second troll stumbled to its feet. Still holding a man's half-eaten foot in one hand.

Tyr scrubbed black ichor from his face, trying to clear his eyes.

The troll seemed to at last realize how much blood of his kind drenched Tyr. It tossed aside the foot and loped forward, swinging its great arms. Tyr surged forward at the last instant, a swipe of Gramr tearing long gouges into each of the troll's forearms. It shrieked, as if somehow still surprised a blade could hurt it. Tyr pressed his advantage and swung low, opening the troll's guts. Oily, serpent-like intestines spilled out over the floor. The troll stared down at that in sheer shock.

For the barest instant, Tyr considered leaving it to die slowly. But it could do more damage between now and then. He swung up, cleaving through the skull.

A great many more trolls might still lurk inside. And every instant he delayed, more Aesir died.

❦

"THE GATE MUST BE REPAIRED," Hoenir said. "We must reinforce it before nightfall."

Indeed, the rising sun had spared them further casualties, but Tyr could not begin to guess how many had died last night. And if they could not fix the gate, tonight would be worse.

"You want to waste time on such tasks," Jarl Jat said, "then you do it. I am taking my people and leaving this cursed place with as much daylight as we can. I aim to be miles away before they come seeking us again."

They all stood before the mangled gate now, taking in the newly risen sun, and the carnage it cast to light. Tyr had almost gotten used to the stench of corpses. No one had had time to burn the dead yet, but it had to become a priority.

"You cannot leave," Annar said. "We are stronger together."

Jarl Moda spat. "As last night clearly attested. Was your tribe not in charge of holding the damned gate, Annar?"

"You think you might have done better?"

"I *know* the Bjars would have done better."

Arnbjorn scoffed. "They could hardly have done any worse."

"All of you, silence," Frigg commanded. "We must work together. Hoenir is right, we have to repair the gate as best we can. Tribe Bjar can begin digging a trench in front—"

"We're not digging a damned thing," Moda said. "I'll say this much for Jarl Jat, he has the right idea. If we break apart and each go in different directions, they cannot pursue us all."

"So instead they pick off a few tribes at a time?" Hoenir asked. "Don't be a fool, boy."

"Please," Frigg insisted. "We have no time for this. Hoenir, send your varulfur out to patrol. Moda, get your people digging *now*."

"I'm not going to—"

Vili's roar cut him off. The berserk hefted the jarl of the Bjars off his feet and drove him against the broken gate with one hand. "Dig the fucking trench before I shove a spear up yours." With that, he pitched the man through the breach.

Tyr cringed. As if Moda had not wanted to leave before.

He moved to Frigg's side, hand on Gramr's hilt.

She waved him back. "Once the trench is dug, line it with oil. We'll use flame as a barrier to hold the trolls back."

"We'll burn through half our oil in one night," Arnbjorn said. "Then what do we burn against the mists?"

"Use the troll corpses," Lodur said. Odin's childhood friend had rarely joined in any of the arguments. Hard to judge his mind most of the time. "Coat them with just a little oil to get a blaze going. Should prove doubly effective in driving back their kin."

"Do it," Frigg said. "Jarl Lodur, have your men help Moda."

"Maybe Lodur should be king," Bedvig mumbled.

Gramr growled at that. Begged Tyr to draw her. Idunn had counseled him otherwise but ... Idunn. He had not even checked to make certain she was unharmed.

Damn it.

Tyr rushed away from the jarls.

٭

HE FOUND Idunn tending to the wounded and mercifully uninjured herself. Blood soaked her arms up to the elbows as she rose from a man with his guts exposed. He'd not see sunset, no matter what she did.

"I feared for your safety," Tyr said.

Idunn murmured something under her breath, then shook her head. "Our defense does not go well."

"To say the least."

He moved closer so none of the wounded would hear him. "I no longer know what to do. The jarls question Frigg at every turn. I could strike them down, but ..."

"But you don't want to be a murderer."

Oh, he already was, whether he wished so or not.

Kill them all.

He would not.

Coward. Weakling.

Could Gramr truly speak to him? No, it was just fatigue that made him hear her voice so clearly. Ever since Idunn had told him someone's soul had been forged into the blade. That didn't mean it actually had a mind.

Craven.

No!

"Tell me what to do."

"I wish I knew, Tyr."

"You are a Vanr!" Several others looked at them at his harsh outburst.

"I am a woman made immortal, but I'm neither warrior nor general, Tyr. I looked to Odin for both roles, and now he is lost to us—at least at present. I am as adrift as the rest of you. But you, at least, *are* a warrior. Men will follow your command if you but take up the mantle of leadership."

Tyr groaned. Gods, Zisa had said something similar so many winters ago. He could not. Not then, not now. He was no leader of men. But Arnbjorn was ... and he was going to lead them away from Odin's wife. If Idunn could offer him no other course, then maybe the only course was Gramr's.

Tonight, the trolls would come again. If they breached, there would be chaos, melee. And in such chaos, a man could fall, even to a friendly blade.

With Arnbjorn dead, the other jarls would *have* to look to Frigg for guidance. They'd have to.

30

---

*S*igyn loved flying. The air currents washing over her, lifting her skyward, the sun warming her feathers. Every breath an exhilaration. Soaring above the mists was like a living dream. Like making love and being carried away to new worlds.

On and on they flew, and though exhaustion slowed the beat of her wings and strained her shoulders, she didn't want to stop. She didn't ever want to stop. And yet, Loki descended toward the mountaintop. Its peak was covered in snow, but it still rose above the mists. From up here the World was pure. Sigyn settled on the mountain beside him and removed her cloak's hood as he pulled off his. She tossed her pack aside. In truth, she hadn't expected it to take so long to find their king.

The moment she retook her human form the cold set her shivering. Loki wrapped her in an embrace and pulled her down with him. From the rapid rise and fall of his chest, even he was drained from the long flight over the Sudurberks. They sank down in the snow, and it began to soak through her dress. Damn, but sometimes she wished for leather trousers like the men favored.

"How much farther is it?" she asked, leaning against Loki's shoulder.

"It depends on which ruin they've taken up in. I doubt they've brought him all the way back to their castle in the islands."

"Samsey, right? In Reidgotaland?"

Loki grunted in acknowledgement. He wouldn't answer a question she already knew the answer to. But then, there were plenty of other questions to ask anyway.

"What are they doing out there?"

"Plotting, most likely."

"Do you know that's vexing?"

"Do you think it should be?"

Sigyn laughed. "Don't you think?"

"I don't think you're terribly irked."

In answer, she pulled away so she could look into his eyes—startlingly crystal blue, and deep as the sky. How much had they seen through the centuries? How old was Loki, really? He *had* to be one of the Vanir if he'd known Idunn's grandparents. The only other explanation would be if he'd become immortal in some other way. And what other way could there be?

"You may never again have such a pristine landscape to ask your questions."

"Is that a prescient vision?"

Loki waved a hand as if to take in all the Sudurberks and the blue sky above. "Do I need a vision to recognize beauty?" He brushed a hand across her cheek and ran his fingers through her hair, the motion leaving her warm despite the chill wind atop the mountain.

"If you can see the future, why don't you just know which ruin they're in?"

"Do your sister's visions work with such acuity?"

No—even Frigg herself rarely seemed to understand what she saw. Not that Sigyn missed that Loki had, once again, evaded the damned question. Maybe she needed a different approach. Loki made her work for every answer, but then, that only made the uncovering of those answers that much more satisfying. If he wasn't so inclined to reveal details about himself, he *did* seem to understand their opponents, and approaching a puzzle from a new angle often yielded better results than staring at the thing endlessly.

"The Niflungar are an ancient people, older than the Aesir."

Technically it wasn't a question, but still he shook his head. "People are people, and people have been around a long, long time. So many times humanity has faltered like a dying flame, only to be once again rekindled. The Aesir, at least as you are now, didn't really arise until after the fall of the Old Kingdoms eight centuries ago."

"What happened? How did the Niflungar fall?"

"Why does any kingdom fall? War, corruption, enemies within and without."

Sigyn fell back and stared up at the clouds. Before gaining the swan cloak, she'd never really seen clouds, not clearly. Loki still hadn't really given an answer, but she was willing to work for it. "War with who?"

"Everyone."

Everyone? "What, all of Mankind? The Vanir? Themselves?"

"Yes."

All right, fine. Bastard. "They fought the Vanir? So the Vanir were the ones who defeated them?"

"The Niflungar skirmishes with the Vanir were minor compared to their wars with the other descendants of Halfdan."

Now they were getting somewhere. Sigyn rolled over, trying to ignore the growing shivers building across her body. Her wet clothes were going to bring her to deathchill, but she could *not* let this opportunity pass. "Who was Halfdan?"

Loki pointed down at the mists. "What do you see?"

Sigyn shrugged. "The World? Midgard?"

"And the World was changed. All people across the World feared that change. Some turned to any source of succor against the mist, no matter the cost. Halfdan the Old bought three hundred years of life through a pact with a vaettr. In those three hundred years, he sired nine sons. As the Vanir withdrew more and more from Middle World, each of those nine sons used the treasures of his father to build a kingdom. Among them, Naefil, whom his father had named for Niflheim. Little surprise, then, that Naefil himself made a pact with the queen of Niflheim."

The man had founded the Niflungar, given rise to the Children of the Mist. By embracing Hel herself, by making all his descendants sorcerers. "Are they immortal too?"

"No. But using their sorcery, the heirs of Naefil have lived even longer than Halfdan himself. And now Naefil's great-great-grandson rules the Niflungar."

"And he wants Odin because he is the Destroyer?"

Loki shook his head. "You do not understand."

"Then help me to."

"We've tarried too long here already. We have to find Odin."

Dammit. She was getting somewhere. She wanted answers to the questions, and even knowing she had all eternity didn't bide her over. She was going to understand their World, and he was going to reveal it. One way or another.

Loki started to rise, and Sigyn threw herself on top of him, bearing him down.

"Ever made love on a mountaintop?" She kissed his neck.

"Romance, Sigyn? Or do you think you'll get your answers like this? Isn't it cheating?"

She continued kissing his face, fumbling with his trousers. "Stop me if you want to."

Despite the freezing cold air, she was probably warmer without her wet dress. She yanked it off in a jumble and settled down onto him, clinging to him for warmth.

"Show me," she mumbled between kisses. "Show me everything."

With one hand he clutched her shoulders, pulling her closer, the other clenched on her arse. "It doesn't work like that."

Sigyn cried out as he rolled atop her. Freezing snow crunched under her back. Gods, she was making love on top of a mountain. Her voice echoed off the peaks, driving her to further excitement. She had never, never felt so alive.

"Show me!"

His release hit her like a wave, the mix of visions as confusing as always. Bits and pieces she was forced to string together through countless nights of lovemaking. Islands covered in greenery, a battle against the undead, creatures like draugar but somehow different. A war against Hel. And the coming of the mists. Loki had watched it all, and visions from long before that.

She clung to his shoulders to keep from sliding down in the snow, weakened by the impact of so much information.

She had seen some of these things before, but maybe it was enough to begin to understand. Loki had been there when the mists came, had tried to help Idunn's grandparents stop it. And he had been there long before that. Long, long before that, in flying cities.

"You don't know what you're digging into," he mumbled, panting.

There was no way Loki was a Vanr. The Vanir had become immortal when Idunn's grandmother had led them to Yggdrasil, years after her battle with Hel. And Loki had been immortal before that. But he had eaten an apple, she had felt that the first time they made love. A lifetime ago, it seemed now, though it had been just about a year.

"Who are you?"

"I am yours."

The same answer as before. Sigyn trembled in his arms. She had been wrong. That answer was not enough after all.

31

"You should have taken my daughter's offer," Gjuki said.

Odin once again lay bound to the gods-damned altar, again painted by spirit glyphs. "I thought this would be more enjoyable."

Gjuki slashed a knife over Odin's stomach, opening a shallow cut. Then he dug a finger in that wound.

Odin grunted against the pain, keeping his gaze locked on Gjuki's face. Maybe he should have taken the potion Gudrun had given him, but he could not trust her, much as his heart longed to. He could never trust her. She had seduced him with her tonics once already, and he would not willingly drink another.

The Raven Lord next traced blood across Odin's forehead, marking some unseen symbol there too. "You are a fool, King of the Aesir."

"I've heard that before. Do your worst, troll-spawn. When it's done, I'll be the one standing over your corpse."

Gjuki's hand tightened around his throat. "There will be no mercy, Odin Borrson."

Odin gasped for air, sucking down none. His vision blurred at the edges and began to seep into the Sight. Shadows shifted around him. Shadows that waited for Gjuki to break him, to open him up to them. The Penumbra was home to unfathomable horrors, all eager to use mortals as a vessel. Most men never saw the liminal place, never saw the other side and the terrors that lurked just out of sight. Most men were lucky.

At last, Gjuki released his grip.

Odin coughed, trying to fill his lungs. They burned like fire, every breath stinging his swollen throat. "No need ... for mercy ..." he said, a clear rasp in his voice.

Gjuki chuckled. "I admire your tenacity. I can see why the goddess wants you. The choice is yours, whether you find yourself under her thumb or under her heel." Once again, he dug a finger into Odin's cut, then painted more glyphs in blood.

From what Odin could remember of his lessons with Gudrun, there was no actual need to paint the glyphs in blood. Any rendition of a spirit's name would draw its attention. The Niflungar no doubt favored these blood glyphs as a means of intimidating their foes. Or perhaps some of the darkest vaettir fed on pain, on suffering. As Odin bled out, they'd be drawn to him. He probably should have taken that potion after all. It wouldn't be the first time pride had cost him.

"Your ... mistress ... took my father. Took my brother. I'm going ... to kill you. And then I'm ... going to fucking kill her, too."

"You're going to kill the goddess Hel?" Gjuki rolled his eyes and shook his head. "I was wrong, Odin. You're not a fool. You're a madman."

"Madmen are dangerous," Odin spat, then jerked against his chains.

Sadly, Gjuki didn't even recoil. Bastard had faith in these fetters, Odin had to give him that.

"You are correct, Ás," Gjuki said. "Madmen *are* dangerous. Most of all to themselves." The Raven Lord drew a long, black dagger and held it before Odin's eyes.

Was that supposed to intimidate him? What was he going to do, cut him some more? Odin would heal. Pain was just pain. These bastards served Hel, and Hel had taken everything from him already. She had taken his father, his brother. They were all he had. She had taken nigh unto all he loved. Odin gritted his teeth. He was going to enjoy returning the favor. He was going to burn the Niflungar to the ground and—

Gjuki slammed the dagger through Odin's palm and embedded it into the obsidian altar.

Odin screamed, wailed at the pain. Almost immediately lances of ice began to jolt outward from the dagger, shooting through his veins. Odin couldn't make out Gjuki's chant over the sound of his own agonized cries.

His confinement had given Odin ample chance to practice slipping back into his father's memories. Odin dove in, seeking any solace, any chance to escape the pain. Any reprieve from agony, no matter how temporary.

§♣

"I CAN'T GET him to stop crying," Bestla said, offering the newborn babe to Borr. "What kind of mother can't comfort her son?"

"Hush now," Borr said. "You have done naught wrong.

Boy just needs some time with his father. Isn't that right, Odin? I'll just take him for a little walk."

Borr stepped out into the afternoon sun as, for once, it seemed to cut through the mist and offer a clear view of the woods. The moment he began to stroll the babe quieted, slept. Borr smiled. He walked out of the Wodanar camp and through the woods, walked for an hour before sitting on a rock by the river.

As soon as he stopped walking, little Odin woke and began wailing again.

"Oh, really?" Borr asked, chuckling. "You think I have the stamina of a berserk, it appears." And still he rose and walked again, walked for hours and hours, until at last twilight forced him to return to the safety of the bonfires.

It was just the motion lulling the babe to peace, of course. Borr knew that. Still, he liked to think it was something about him, some connection he had with his son.

ODIN JERKED as pain snatched him back to his own mind and body. He moaned, not caring if Gjuki thought it for the torture. His father had loved him so much, had walked for hours and hours and ... And Odin just wanted to go back there.

Chilling claws snatched at Odin's neck, his arms, his legs. His vision flickered between Sight and normal vision, revealing glimpses of the Penumbra, of the unutterable monstrosities answering Gjuki's call. A shade lingered over him, its black-gray form hazy in the starlight of the Penumbra. Though roughly humanoid, its fingers ended in claws reaching out from a tattered shroud within which all light vanished, like the fathomless expanse of a starless night.

No mere ancestor shade, this, but a wraith, the vilest and direst of all ghosts, festering in hatred for uncounted centuries. Gudrun had bound one such vaettr, though she admitted she feared it and feared to call upon its power as it slowly consumed her from the inside out.

The wraith straddled Odin, and pressure built in his chest. It sank a claw into his left shoulder, then another into his right. He shrieked, squirming in a futile attempt to dislodge the ghastly presence now writhing atop him like some perverse lover in the throes of forbidden passions. The figure pulled itself forward, crawling up his body until its face—or lack thereof—rested inches above his own. Forcing him to look into the absolute blackness of its eyes, of its broken soul. And the deeper he looked, the more he realized beyond the blackness lurked a glow, though not one born of light, but rather an opalescence spawned from hatred in its most undiluted form.

The entity wailed and dove into Odin, seeping through his eyes and mouth and nose and ears. Odin jerked at the awful pressure spreading through his body. He tried to scream but only managed a choking gasp. An alien presence built in his mind, like another person's thoughts, a whispered conversation where he could make out intent, but not words. And it was growing louder. Became a cacophony of madness and despair.

Bucking against his chains, Odin slammed all his will at the vaettr. *I am Odin, son of Borr!* He tried to shout at the abomination inside him. *I am Odin!*

He would not let this thing take him. Not now, not ever. His people needed him. His wife needed him. His *son* needed him. No one should take a father from his son. Never.

It was about will.

Gudrun had said that, back when she tried to teach him sorcery.

They can be bargained with, cajoled, or dominated, whence comes the power of a sorcerer.

The strongest will survived. And even an ancient font of power such as this might find itself cowed by an implacable human will. And Odin trembled, flinging his will at the vaettr. It felt like trying to wrestle a waterfall, a torrent that swept him up and threatened to drown him.

"You are mine," he said, his words broken.

The current bound his limbs, choked him, slithered down his throat to steal his words.

"What are you doing?" Gjuki said, his words blurred and sucked away by the shadows clogging Odin's senses.

Odin spoke ancient, eldritch words Gudrun had taught him, a language from beyond the Realms of men. Words that a vaettr could not ignore.

His hands clasped around the wraith's wrists as though they were solid, flesh writhing under his grip. Everything had gone dim, even dimmer than using Sight to pierce the Penumbra brought about. And he had slipped free of his fetters, even as the vaettr had leapt into twisted clarity. Beneath a tattered shroud drifting off into oblivion lay eyes, gleaming with fell light. Odin tumbled off the altar and head-butted the creature in his arms.

It was in him still, but it had begun to recoil, as if seeking to vanish into the dark prevailing all around them.

Gudrun had made him learn the words of binding. And, free of her potion and sorcery, Odin had sworn never to use such things. But now, on the edge of oblivion, what choice remained? Surrender, or fight. Bargain. And Odin began to speak the words.

He could draw no glyph no warding circle, call upon no

talisman for aid, nor otherwise fortify his body or will against the wraith. But he would not surrender, not ever.

The wraith hissed back at him in the same vile language, though he could not understand it. The words set his stomach quivering and his head trembling. He tightened his grip on the wraith's wrists. His life force was bleeding out as he did so, feeding this thing.

"Serve me," he said, barely able to form the words.

No ...

He repeated the binding words in the vaettr language, each ringing in his head, each threatening to be his last as his breath gave out.

A sudden burning arose on his forearm, his skin sizzling as the wraith's glyph seared itself onto his flesh. And Odin pitched forward, the vaettr suddenly gone. No. Not gone. Drawn within him. Darkness enveloped him.

---

32

*H*e had to make sure everyone was in position. Couldn't afford another breach like last night. If it happened, if he had to strike down Arnbjorn, he would. But if he could stop a breach, he had to do everything in his power to do so.

That meant Tyr had to be on the wall. Had to check everything. Fool jarls were going get them all killed if he let them. Everyone wanted to take the lead now.

No one knew how.

As he crested the top of the stairs, Tyr heard Vili speaking to Frigg. "Odin is lost."

"Loki and Sigyn have gone to rescue him."

Vili snorted. "The foreigner and his woman? They can't help him."

Tyr hated to trust in Loki, but what other choice did he have? The foreigner had returned, learned of Odin's urd, and insisted on going after him. And since the varulfur he'd sent to track Odin never came back, how could Tyr argue with that?

"You underestimate both Loki and Sigyn," Frigg said.

Tyr paused, waiting in the shadows. What was this now? The sun would set in an hour at most. And they were still arguing. Other jarls, thegns, they also walked the battlements. No one did aught about this.

Vili grunted. "They're all lost. You will need a new husband by your side."

Now she glowered at him. "Was there someone you had in mind?"

"Me."

Tyr's hand tightened around Gramr's hilt. How dare the man dishonor his brother thus? He advanced slowly. Frigg was Odin's wife. His *wife*! And Vili thought to claim her while Odin may yet live?

"I am the king's brother. I am strong." As if to emphasize his point, he grabbed her upper arms and squeezed, pulling her even closer.

"Release me," she demanded.

Son of a troll! Tyr jerked Gramr free of its sheath.

Vili spun at the sound, dropping Frigg, then turned to face him. "This does not concern you."

"You shame your family. That is my concern. Draw your weapon!"

Vili's smug grin faltered for just a moment.

"Tyr," Frigg said, "your sword is not needed here."

"My lady—"

"*I* am the queen. You will both heed me." She turned to the berserk. "Strength alone is not enough to rule, Vili. One needs wisdom." She shook her head. "And it is *not* wise to proposition a völva, especially a married völva who is not yet a widow. Odin will return. But if you behave yourself between now and then, he need not hear of this conversation."

Vili growled. Fucking bear.

"You have not learned!" Tyr spat at Vili.

Vili reeled back as if not quite certain what was happening. Tyr was nearly upon him before the werebear even bothered to pull the broad axe from off his back.

"Tyr!" Frigg demanded. "Cease this immediately."

"What is—" Arnbjorn started to say.

Tyr didn't look at the approaching jarl. He'd be next.

Tyr lunged, swinging with a vicious overhead arc. The berserk flung his axe up, blocking Tyr's sword with the blade. A chip of metal flew from the axe, spinning wide. The iron barb slashed Frigg's jaw, and she shrieked.

Her scream drew Vili's eyes, but Tyr didn't slow down. Needed every edge against a berserk. He twisted his sword, bending Vili's axe out of position, then rammed his fist into Vili's face. The berserk fell back. And Tyr was on him, punching again and again.

Vili roared, shrugging off the blows, and tackled Tyr. They fell to the ground. Rolling, wrestling. In a moment, he pinned the berserk and rained more blows on him, smashing him with Gramr's pommel.

Arnbjorn grabbed Tyr's arm. With one hand, Tyr flung him to the ground. He snarled at Arnbjorn.

"Tyr!" Frigg shouted, now having risen. "Tyr, I command you to stop immediately. In Odin's name!"

Odin.

Son of Borr. Like Vili.

Kill him. Kill the bastard berserk.

The son of *Borr*.

Tyr hesitated.

Vili shoved him upward and then bodily flung him to the ground. The impact dazed him. Gramr scattered away from him. Werebear dove on top of him. Some else kicked him in the face.

Beating, pounding, smashing.
Tyr's skull cracked on stone.
Everything went dark.

33

The wraith seethed beneath his skin, coiling about his heart and mind, probing against his will. It —*he*—pushed against Odin's consciousness before Odin even realized he had woken.

"Audr," Odin groaned. The wraith was inside him, and now he knew its name.

Odin tried to sit, but as he did so, a clawed, spectral hand jutted up from his own, breaking away from his flesh until his elbow. It rent his soul and threatened to shatter his body. Screaming, Odin threw his will against the wraith until he at last receded back inside Odin's flesh.

He could hardly breathe. Everywhere, darkness pressed in on him. The Penumbra ought to have been suffused with more starlight than this, or so he had thought. But now, Odin was no longer looking through the Veil at the Penumbra—he had somehow fallen through that Veil, projected himself into the Astral Realm entirely. Unless he was dead.

If he was dead, where were the damned valkyries? Shouldn't they have carried him off to meet his ancestors?

To meet his father … And what would he tell him? Would his father be proud of what he'd tried to do? Tried and failed. He'd lost Ve. He brought the Aesir halfway around this world but never even made it to Vanaheim. What had Odin done with his immortality? Naught. He'd squandered his gift. And he could not face his father with only that answer. Maybe that was why there were no valkyries. Maybe he didn't deserve the glorious afterlife. Maybe Gjuki had damned Odin to join Hel and the unworthy dead in Niflheim.

And if so? Then he would spend the last of his strength storming her gates.

A lump formed in his stomach as he rose. Gjuki still stood beside the altar, watching it. Watching Odin's body on it.

Not yet dead, though his body lay dying and … aged. He looked down at himself, at hands that grown withered well past the twenty-five winters he had seen. Binding the wraith had eaten through so much of his life force it had ravaged his body. Perhaps the apple would prevent further aging, but already pain had begun to form in his joints. What was he now, a man of forty winters—at least physically speaking?

Odin groaned. The wraith inside laughed, the sound filled more with a loathing of all good in life than with any mirth.

"Silence," Odin commanded. Uselessly. He reached for Gjuki, but his hand passed right through the Raven Lord. His action did draw the man's attention, who smiled at Odin. He spoke, the sound echoing wildly. A spirit's name, perhaps? Had Gjuki called upon another of the cursed—

A hand grabbed his wrist and pulled, the motion causing the World around him to twist, blur. Odin fell, tumbling for what seemed far too long before he collapsed on a ground of shadows. The impact of such a fall should have broken bones, but it merely stunned him for an instant. Perhaps his spirit body had no bones to break.

He rose once again, to find himself no longer within the Niflungar ruin. Indeed, his surroundings had warped beyond all recognition. The starlight had dimmed, and the darkness suffused the horizon in all directions, blocking his view of much beyond his immediate surroundings. And those surroundings! Something like glimmering black rocks rose from the ground, twisting into unnatural shapes that ought not have supported their own weight. Those shapes slowly moved, as though writhing in pain, as though this entire World was formed of agony and nightmare.

Yessss ...

Audr's voice echoed in his mind.

The Astral Roil ...

Oh, dear gods above and below. Gudrun had told him the Astral Realm extended beyond the mirror of Midgard, into deep Realms where even a sorcerer dare not tread. He had passed beyond all known reality into some alien depth, some darkness apt to drive men to derangement. The very air pulsed with such despondency he almost choked on it, though he could not say for certain how much came from this Realm and how much from the wraith he had bound inside himself.

All power ... is darkness ... is despair ...

"No." Odin spat. "I refuse to believe that."

Again, the mirthless laugh that withered his soul. Odin had bound to himself a ghost filled with deathless hatred, a loathing of all the World it meant to share with him.

Yes ... as you lose yourself ... as you lose ... everything ...

And the wraith spoke with such absolute certainty, Odin

could not deny his claim. His body had a little life left in it—for now. But this place would erode his soul until so little remained Audr would win, would take him over. Or until ... until Odin had become a wraith himself, lost in darkness and preying on the World he had once known.

THE ROIL STRETCHED out in all directions, an expanse of shadows with neither beginning nor end. Darkness spread like blood, staining snows, revealing at long last the underpinnings of reality in all its empty horror. Odin had once thought the glimpse of the Penumbra he saw through the Sight was dire, that it represented the sum of the nightmares in which the dead dwelt. Back then, he had seen less than naught.

Oblivion is eternity ...

Audr's taunts had become his inescapable companion on this sojourn, offering yet another torment upon his senses. This Realm stank of the ancient dead. Audr's words grated on his mind. Fell winds chilled his flesh. But these visions, they held the greatest horrors of this place.

What you cannot see is worse ...

Worse than what he could.

With every step, you tread deeper into shadow ...

Odin pressed a palm against his forehead as if he could somehow silence the wraith inside him. But he could no more quiet the mad ghost than he could his own mind.

All the dead are mad ... or perhaps finally bereft of the madness of the living ... the illusion of light that so befuddles your senses that you can imagine ... the ultimate lie might hold some sliver of truth ...

What lie?

Hope ...

"Go to Hel, Audr."

What know you of Hel ...?

As much as any man, he supposed, and more than he wished.

The ground beneath his boots felt too pliant here, like walking on the surface of mud. A fog rose up around his legs—not with the thickness of the mists clogging Midgard, but the vapors seemed fell, nevertheless. He could turn, head back the way he had come, but one direction seemed as true as any other.

Besides which, he could hardly be certain of traveling in a straight line, what with shadows stretching out into the horizon. He could make out so little beyond his immediate surroundings.

As he pushed on, the sound of rushing water reached him, drawing closer, even as the mud grew thicker. "What is this?"

You wished to find Hel ... You need find but the bridge ...

What bridge? What was this place?

Gjöll, the river of Hel ...

Indeed, the fog was rising off a freezing river. Odin could see little beneath its surface, save that the swift current swept what looked like blades along. Daggers, perhaps of ice, perhaps of iron, but they would shred anyone attempting to wade the river. No wonder they needed a bridge.

But then again, why would he want to reach the gates of Hel? If beyond this river lay Niflheim and the inescapable fortress of Hel, no man would willingly tread there.

Odin backed away. What he wanted was to find a way to return to Midgard, to his body, to his people. His hand brushed over something, but when he turned, he saw naught but a mass of shadows.

A sudden wooziness seized his gut, and the desire to sleep.

Audr's laughter mocked him.

I expected you to last longer ...

What?

Odin turned about but saw no sign of a threat. What was the wraith trying to say?

Sleep now ... weak mortal ... sleep and lose it all ... let all you know fade to dust and let your light finally dwindle ...

What was he saying? Odin just needed to rest for a few moments. This journey, Gjuki's tortures, they had both taken their tolls upon him. But what did Audr mean, lose it all? What had he lost?

A fleeting image graced his mind, an instant of him training with a sword, under his father's careful instruction. And then that image evaporated. Even as Odin tried to replay it in his mind, he found naught there. A memory of his father, and he couldn't ... he had just seen something. It was on the edge of his mind. In fact, he had just relived it not long ago, through Borr's eyes. But now he couldn't remember.

"Gods? How did this happen? What's happening?"

You have already forgotten what I told you ... The dead lose ... everything. All that makes you who you are ... fades ...

His memories? No. No, no. He would not lose those. Never! Not those.

Soon, you will not even know ... what has been lost ...

The mud suddenly grew hard, grasping. Hands reached up out of it and clasped his legs, dragging him down. Arms slurped out of the darkness, wrapped around his feet, ankles, shins, knees. All trying to carrying him under the surface into the oblivion.

Odin surged forward, calling upon all his strength. Arms broke away and returned to mud, but others took their place which each faltering step he took. The World itself tried to consume him now, as if this place devouring his memories were not enough.

He broke free of the mud and tumbled to the ground from the sudden removal of resistance. He came up in a roll, panting. As he rose, a bank of shadows like a cloud of darkness spread out before him. He thought he had come this way, but now it blocked his path even as it seemed to block out the sparser and sparser starlight overhead.

More slurping noises rang out behind him. Odin glanced over his shoulder. From the mud rose a pulsating wave, edging toward him.

He scrambled away, around the cloud of darkness, almost tripping over his own feet.

"Audr! Unless you want to spend eternity dragged down into whatever depths—"

The darkness erupted.

Three tentacles jutted toward him, converging on his position, each many times longer than he was tall. Odin rolled to the side, reaching for any weapon. He had none. The tentacles writhed like living shadows, attached to some unfathomable monstrosity dwelling within the shadow cloud. Each bore countless spines, and worse still, tiny maws lined with shark-like fangs.

The tentacles surged for him once again. Odin jumped one, but another enwrapped his legs in midair. A third coiled itself around his arm. It tightened around him until he felt his muscles would burst. The maw raised up in front of his face and hissed at him like a serpent. Each of those fangs had a tiny, opalescent eye, blacker than black and weeping some foulness.

Odin's mind seemed unable to latch on or accept the existence of such a being, such an indescribable abomination dwelling just beyond the sight of men. The tentacle snapped forward, and those numerous fangs tore through his shoulder sending waves of burning agony coursing through him. And then it began to suck, drawing out his blood, his life force, even his very soul. With each pulsation of the tentacle, he felt more of himself eaten away, even as it drew his body toward the greater cloud of shadow. Within that cloud writhed something even larger—the body these tentacles belonged to. A body Odin did not want see.

"Audr!"

More of his memories seemed to slip away, not evaporating as before, but sucked down by the monster in great, voracious gulps. All the years of his childhood, vanishing one by one, every treasured moment devoured.

No! He knew he was screaming in pain. But not his memories. Not those.

Odin beat at the tentacle with his free hand, having no more effect than he would raging against the ocean.

Not like this. No ...

His mind flailed even as his body began to give out. Flailed, and caught hold of the wisp of a shrouded wraith, tethered to his soul. Odin seized that shroud and pulled it about himself. The monstrosity that held him recoiled for the barest instant.

Odin's form became as shadow, and he melted into the darkness, reforming a hundred feet away. He lay on his knees gasping. A shadowy claw breached from his elbow once again, as Audr tightened his hold on Odin's soul. Trails of shroud dangled from his body, as though tapering out of his own legs and back. The wraith climbed out of the place where he'd buried it, crawling up his throat and struggling to sink its claws into his mind.

Indeed, the claw began to reach for his head.

Odin clenched his fist, throwing all his will against Audr.

At last the wraith receded back within, though Odin's astral form continued to trail wafts of vaporous shroud. And his hands ... They had grown freshly wrinkled even as the ache in his bones deepened. He had burned away another decade off his life, he could feel it.

"What was that thing?"

Hungry ...

Odin groaned. That much he could have guessed. He slumped down on his arse and rubbed his temples. The Roil devoured his memories, when it didn't try to consume his body. And now this nameless predator stalked him. He had wandered into someplace worse than even the Realm of Hel.

You nearly crossed into there ... beyond the river ...

"Is that what you want?"

No answer.

Perhaps Audr did not want to fall into Hel's domain. But they both would—or, failing that, would fall prey to one of the other apparently numerous horrors lurking in the Roil.

"I don't think that's what you want at all."

Audr said naught.

"I know you hate me, as you hate all the living. Believe me, Audr, I loathe you just as much."

No ... You do not ... You cannot begin to fathom the odium of the damned. Not yet ...

"Be that as it may, I suspect you would rather return to Midgard to sate that wrath than linger here until we both wither away."

The wraith slithered beneath his skin, but did not answer immediately.

Odin waited.

Were I to guide you ... still you could not cross the Veil ...

"Maybe. But we'd be that much closer to the Mortal Realm."

And still you cling to hope ... I will enjoy watching it crumble through your fingers ...

Odin rose. Whatever the wraith thought, he was not about to surrender hope. Not hope, and not memory. Most else, a man could live without. But those two, they meant everything.

---

34

*T*hey had survived the night, at least. No one would tell him much more.

Tyr's sword rested against Frigg's throne, a mere five feet away. They had taken her from him. Taken Gramr, his legacy, his right. The law may have called for such practice during the Thing, true, but ... In a single heartbeat Tyr could cross the distance, claim the blade and fight his way free.

All eight jarls stood around him in a wide circle, eyeing him, judging him. By Frigg's command, Tyr had not been bound. The queen knew he was innocent. The other jarls, they were to blame. Bedvig and Vili and Arnbjorn, all of them. Tyr turned slowly, forcing each of the vile traitors to meet his gaze.

Finally, he looked to Frigg. A small cut marred her jaw. Hermod had claimed a piece of Vili's axe had done that in the fight. That meant the werebear had harmed his queen. For that he should pay with his life.

"So," Bedvig said, "the man's savagery is now known to all. Only one course of action presents itself."

Thegns of the gathered jarls hung behind them, crowding the great hall in here. If only the king were here. He would put all of these rank trollfuckers in their places.

"This criminal has assaulted two jarls and his own queen," Bedvig said.

Tyr spit at the jarl's feet. Who in Hel's frozen wasteland did he think he was? Assaulted the queen! "Frey's flaming sword, that was Vili's doing, you cocksucking boy-lover!"

"You fucking jest," Vili said. "You attacked me. You, who swore to serve my family until your dying breath. We took you in despite where you came from, and my father gave you a home, a purpose."

Tyr took a step toward the werebear. "Shut your mouth, berserk. Shut it now."

Vili snorted. Faint bruises were the only remaining sign of injuries Tyr had inflicted on him the night before. Damned shifters healed too fast. "*Oh.* Still don't want everyone to know who you really are? But I know. Father told *me.* How you grew up in that jotunn's castle, how he raised you like a son. Or was it like a daughter? Did daddy bend you over the fence now and again?"

Tyr trembled with rage as everyone in the hall stood with mouths agape. No, Hymir had never done such a thing. But he had raised Tyr as a killer. A raider sent out to plunder villages and bring back whatever the jotunn fancied. A life Borr had saved him from when Tyr had had the misfortune to raid the Wodanar. And a secret the jarl had kept in their family for the sake of Tyr's honor.

"Were you not your father's son I would kill you where you stand," Tyr said. His fingers twitched. He needed Gramr. She was calling him, wailing for him. Could the others not hear how the sword wept at the separation from her master?

"No wonder the man is a monster now," Bedvig said.

"No ..." Hoenir stepped forward. "No. Tyr has saved all of our lives many times over. Why should we care where he ... where he was raised? That was no choice of his. His choice was to stand with us against every danger we have faced. We'd all be troll food or troll wives now, were it not for his courage and prowess."

Frigg's head fell to her hands, her normal composure broken.

"His choice," Bedvig snapped, "was to strike his betters." The Skaldun jarl pointed at Frigg. "Look at the scar on the queen's once-pure face."

Tyr opened his mouth to protest that Frigg, immortal, would be healed in a day or so. Bedvig, however, kept right on talking.

"This jotunn-spawned bastard has struck two jarls and a queen. How many more crimes shall we permit him? Shall we wait until he commits murder before we act? The punishment for his actions is clear—he must pay with his life. Bind him, sacrifice him to the gods this very day!"

"Two jarls?" Hoenir protested. "Are you counting yourself, in a holmgang legally fought?"

Bedvig waved the comment away. "So be it—forget his needless savagery back then."

Hoenir chuckled. "I'm sure you'd like to."

The infuriating jarl just kept talking. He had taken Tyr's wife. His *wife*, granted to Tyr with Borr's blessing, for the services he had done. And Bedvig had taken Zisa. Now he besmirched Tyr's good name. He deserved a terrible death. Tyr's whole body was shaking now. Gramr begged him to heft her, not to leave her alone like this. She needed him. Was he truly going to abandon her, leave her be taken up by someone like Bedvig?

Indeed, the jarl, advanced on the blade. Or moved to speak to Frigg? No! He was after the blade!

Tyr surged forward, shoved Bedvig aside, and grabbed Gramr up into his hands. She was safe. Safe, with him. No one would take her from him. Not *her*. Roaring, he rammed her through Bedvig's side.

"Feel like a daughter?" he asked him.

Blood exploded from the man's mouth as he looked down on the blade.

A roar of shouts filled the hall, and men throughout drew their weapons. Tyr spun, frantic. They all wanted to take her away from him. Just like the dead trollfucker had taken Zisa. He would not let that to happen.

"Tyr!" Frigg shouted, the sound just reaching over the roar of the crowd.

Jarls and thegns all ringed him now, blades and axes and spears pointed in his direction. He'd kill them all if he had to. No one was taking his Gramr from him.

"He must die," Arnbjorn shouted.

"No!" Frigg said. "No! Tyr is the favored of Odin, and I will not allow his death."

Arnbjorn scoffed, the numerous men obviously siding with him. Even Hoenir was shaking his head sadly at Tyr. "You cannot plan to spare him after this murder."

Frigg shut her eyes a moment, then shook her head. "No. Tyr ... I ..." As Tyr turned to Frigg, she drew herself up, regal once again. "Your crimes cannot go unpunished, either. For the deeds done this day ... I take from you all the titles Borr once bestowed upon you. You are no longer thegn, nor of the Wodanar tribe, nor of any Ás tribe." She swallowed, as if barely able to speak. "I banish you to the mists."

A few of the jarls nodded at what was, effectively, a death sentence. Or had been seen as such in times past. Those left alone in the wild became prey to trolls or vaettir or varulfur. Or, as they now knew, became trolls themselves. But Tyr was no mere mortal.

He growled. Cracked his neck.

"Tyr," Frigg said. "You must go out, leave this place, and be far gone before the sun sets."

"Before the trolls return and kill you all?" Tyr spat. So even the queen betrayed him. Well, the legacy of Borr had fallen far without Odin. "I will go. But any man who tries to take Gramr from me shall die."

Frigg held up a hand. "A man banished is always given a weapon. Keep yours, Tyr. But know you are a stranger to all Aesir now, and ... and a foe. Be gone from this fortress immediately. You may take a skin a of mead, your arms and armor, and naught more."

Tyr held the blade close. Wise. He'd have killed every man here if they thought to take her away from him. The crowd parted slowly, allowing him escape from the hall.

Zisa spat on him as he passed. "Hel curse your soul and take from you whatever you hold most dear."

His hand shook with the urge to run her through as well. Her. The woman who betrayed him. But the thought of seeing her dead tasted foul.

Instead, he dashed out of the hall and began to run.

These were no longer his people. He had all he needed with Gramr. And long as she stayed with him, he would be a king in the wilds. Laughter poured from his mouth even as a tear stung his eye.

35

The stronger your will, the more satiating breaking it becomes ...

Unless the wraith came up against a will he could not break, one upon which he could only be broken upon.

Audr laughed in Odin's mind, as ever, a sound of wretchedness rather than humor. The laugh of a being that hated everyone and everything—most of all himself.

That thought drew a hiss from Audr, but no other response.

For days he had wandered, on and on, his body not giving out. Audr refused to answer most questions and, Odin suspected, probably did not know all the answers himself. The consumptive force that stole memories must have stolen most of the wraith's, as well. Still, the vaettr had hinted that time flowed somewhat differently the further out from the Mortal Realm one travelled. That could be a lie —Gudrun had told him vaettir delighted in misleading mortals—but it might mean he couldn't know how much time had passed on Midgard.

He had a slight sense his body yet lived, but he knew naught more of its condition.

And then, without real warning, the ground in front of him dropped away into a chasm of unending night. He could not hope to judge distance into such an abyss, but he saw no end to it. Perhaps none existed. Were he to fall here, maybe he would continue to fall for all eternity.

Then again, Audr had also implied even worse Realms lay beyond the Roil.

He followed the chasm for a time before coming to a bridge that spanned the gap, disappearing out into the horizon. The bridge shimmered like an iridescent rainbow, glittering in the starlight of this place. In the distance, a blue-green mist concealed all else. Did this bridge connect the Penumbra to the Roil?

With no better choice, he stepped onto the bridge. It felt like solid stone beneath his feet, and indeed, despite the shimmering, had the texture and heft of rock. But it gleamed, and what stone did that?

He followed the bridge for a long time, assuming time meant aught here. His bones ached, but he did not grow fatigued. Rather, it was a dull, constant ache he suspected would become his companion for the rest of his life. In the space of but a few hours, he had lost all youth and approached what, to a mortal, would have been the twilight of life.

On and on he walked, Audr leaving him in blissful silence. The silence gave him time to think on all his failures —to his father, to Ve, to their memories as even those faded away from him. He had to do better.

AT LAST HE reached a figure standing in his path.

The man was broad of shoulder and well-muscled, towering over Odin. Long auburn hair hung past his shoulders. He wore a suit of golden mail, with solid plates guarding his forearms and shins. Never had Odin seen such armor. A gilded horn hung from the man's belt. The man's hand rested easily on a sword stuck in the bridge.

"Who are you?" Odin asked.

"I am the Guardian of the Bridge. I am the sword in the night, the last watcher between worlds. None may pass but through me." The man's voice boomed, echoing into eternity.

A vaettr—a god, in fact. Odin had heard völvur speak of the bridge between worlds. Its guardian was Heimdall. According to the legend, Heimdall warded Midgard against further invasion by those who dwelt beyond the Veil.

Did that make him a foe of Hel? Could this being help Odin? "I need to get back to Midgard."

Heimdall stared at Odin intently a moment, watching something far distant, then pointed past himself. "There is yet life in your body, should you wish to embrace pain."

Embrace pain. Heimdall seemed to know only too well the cruel urd that lay before Odin. Were he to return to Midgard, he would sacrifice more. Already, he had paid with his father, his brother, his memories of them, even his own youth. And it would never, ever end. Maybe something more waited beyond the Roil, and, if he could have just pushed past it, maybe he would have found Valhalla and there found his father waiting for him. And instead he had turned back toward his eternal life and unending struggle and sacrifice. To save the Aesir he would make war against the Vanir and lose more—more than any man ought to bear.

But ... through his eternal suffering he might save

others, save them from sharing Ve's urd. Spare them the pain he embraced on their behalf.

"I have no choice." When he came before his father again, he would have a tale to make the man proud. And between now and then, Odin would keep fighting. He would protect his son and give him a better World than the one he'd been born to. "My work is not yet done."

"Then go. However long your tasks last, I will be waiting here for you, human. But know that you have drunk in much of this Realm. It is inside you now and will forever try to call you back."

Odin hesitated. He could feel the call even now. Some force drawing him, not back to Midgard, but back into the Roil. Maybe that was the most insidious trap of all. Audr had claimed it devoured light, but maybe, deep down, men wanted their light consumed and taken from them, their burdens finally lifted. With the fading of memory, a man might at last cast aside his burdens, not absolved of them, but in simple ignorance.

Oblivion ...

36

*T*he breath that issued from Odin's still body was so faint one might mistake him for a corpse. The thought chilled Gudrun's heart. Fool man hadn't taken the potion she'd given him, and now, Father considered the matter settled. Like as not, Odin's soul would never return to his body, at least, not without aid, not without a guide.

And his body had been ravaged by the process. Though his muscles remained strong, his skin had weathered and his face wrinkled. His hair had gone gray, almost white, making him look ancient. Gudrun ran her hand lightly over his arm. How anyone could have survived such a change she didn't know. Perhaps the apple allowed it—it seemed to have already healed the actual damage—but it would not reverse the aging.

"What are you going to do?" Hljod asked. The girl sat with her arms wrapped around her knees, eyes wide as she stared at Odin's body resting on Gudrun's bed.

Gudrun's father had made no objection when she'd had servants carry him up here. He always allowed her enough freedom to pursue her own ends—and the consequences that came with them. Nevertheless, she doubted he realized what she intended. If he had, she suspected even Father would have intervened.

"Shutter the window," Gudrun said, then resumed pacing around her chamber. "And light a few candles—just a few, mind."

Hljod did as Gudrun ordered, making a clear effort to hide her fear. Gudrun hated depriving the girl of her innocence, forcing her to look at the dark truths underlying the reality of the World, but Hljod had lost aught resembling innocence at the hands of the trolls, and if she was to have a place among the Niflungar she would have to learn. Gudrun had sworn to make the girl not only her apprentice, but a sister, and that meant teaching her everything.

"Our world is but a shadow," Gudrun said when Hljod had finished lighting the candles. "Like the shadows cast upon the wall by those small flames. A deeper reality underlies our Realm."

"The Penumbra."

Gudrun nodded. "Odin's soul is adrift in the Astral Realm, prey to the inhabitants that dwell in the Ether."

"Shades?"

"Hmm. Shades and other ... *older* things. Things that were already ancient before the mists came to our world."

"L-like Hel?"

Gudrun laughed at that, and shook her head. "I seriously doubt Lady Hel herself is gallivanting around the Penumbra looking for amusement." She clucked her tongue at the ridiculous thought. But there were dangers out there. Vaettir had their own worlds out in the Spirit Realm, but many *could* pass into the Astral Realm. Beings so far beyond Odin's understanding as to be gods in his eyes—gods all too eager to feed off a wandering soul and leave Odin an empty husk.

"You're going to call him back?"

"I've tried that. He's too far gone to hear me from ... wherever he has wandered. I have to go after him." It was the only way to save her love, the only way to bring him back to her. Then, finally, he would have to see what he meant to her, and seeing that, would acknowledge where he belonged.

Hljod looked around the room for a moment before frowning and turning back to Gudrun. "That sounds like a royally stupid idea."

Gudrun chuckled again. Indeed, the plan was one born of desperation more than wit. With the Sight, she could look into the Penumbra to see and speak with spirits and shades there. Doing so opened oneself to their attentions, and often, their ire. What Gudrun planned was something deeper ... to project her own consciousness into the Astral Realm. Spirits lacked substance in the Mortal Realm—it was why they could only interact on Earth by possessing a mortal host. Astral projection would change the rules. The spirits would be as real to her as any being in the Mortal Realm.

"So this is sorcery."

"Yes."

"And you're going to teach me? That doesn't sound nearly as useful as learning to do that ice thing you do with your fingers."

Gudrun paused. Ice thing? She sighed. "You mean the Art of Mist. We call such things manifest Arts because it's literally manifesting a spirit inside me—one of two I previously bound using sorcery."

"Um ... I have no idea what all that means."

Gudrun blew out a breath. For all the girl's brave face, she *was* just a girl. Alone and afraid, having suffered so much. So much that was too much the same. Gudrun shook herself. She'd promised not to push Hljod away, nor to let her be alone, but now was not the time for a lesson.

"Ask me another time," she said. "I have to concentrate."

"Have you ever done this before?"

"No." Not successfully. "I'm going to need you to be very quiet, Hljod. You can watch, but whatever happens, do not distract me." Gudrun sat on the floor in the middle of the chamber and folded her legs beneath her. Her heart was pounding. Not a good sign. The spirits would sense her fear, be drawn to it like sharks to blood, and like a wounded animal, they'd tear her to pieces—or take her. She risked that every time she evoked a spirit or used her manifest Arts, and yet, no other recourse lay open to her. "Hljod ... if I ... if I wake up, and it doesn't seem like me, you need to leave. Find my father and tell him what's happened, but do not stay and check on me."

The girl's face paled, but she nodded.

Gudrun shut her eyes. Astral projection was beyond her ability with the Sight—meaning Odin had surpassed her in at least some aspect—so for this, she needed the aid of a vaettr who could help pull her through the Veil. Neither the journey, nor the vaettr she had to call would prove pleasant. She could have turned to the Mist spirit, Snegurka, but a wraith had a more inherent connection to the Astral Realm.

"Irpa," she called. "Irpa, I need you."

She opened her eyes, now embracing the Sight. Even after so many years, seeing the wraith appear sent shivers down Gudrun's spine. Irpa drifted in and out of shadows, the darkness clinging to her and wafting off in a haze at the same time. Wraiths were shades of the dead, twisted beyond all recognition by their rage and warped by eons spent wandering the spaces between life and death. The wraith's glyph on Gudrun's arm warmed as the shade drew nigh.

Gudrun reached a hand toward the wraith, trying to hide her hesitation and knowing, deep down, Irpa saw it. She was not fool enough to think this thing she had bound was her friend or even her ally. Grimhild had forced Gudrun to bind a wraith, and one day she'd pay a price for such temerity. "I need to cross over."

Then die ...

Gudrun was grateful Hljod couldn't hear the vile whisper that was Irpa's voice. Gudrun pressed her will into the wraith, the glyph on her arm going from warm to hot to actually burning her. A trickle of blood ran down her nose and over her mouth. Gudrun gritted her teeth. If she backed down, Irpa might be strong enough to overtake her body.

The wraith appeared beside her, pressing a shadowy hand against Gudrun's temple.

A tendril began to worm its way through her mind. A worm of rage, one that hated her, hated all life with unfathomable wrath. Uncontrollable shudders racked her body as she strained against the wraith's implacable will. It was feeding off her pain, her anger, her fear, and inevitably soaking up the contents of her mind, while growing ever stronger within her.

You pretend to hate her ... your mother ... but you liked it. You liked having those big strong guards inside you, you whore ...

"Irpa!" Gudrun spat through her clenched teeth.

Hljod jerked at the sound, then fretted about with a cloth, clearly uncertain whether to come and clean up her mistress. Gudrun waved her away, trying to divert as little of her own attention as possible.

Don't worry, whore ... When I get inside you ... I'll fill you up good. And I'll call them in ... every soldier in the army ... I'll fuck their brains out with your ... trench ... your arse ... your mouth ...

"You serve me!"

The pressure in her mind eased, Irpa's grip releasing her. And yet ... her hands shook. Within the perspective of her Sight, her form had become tattered, as if her arms and legs had given way to Irpa's shroud. Ice built in her heart even as it slowed, even as her breath came in ragged pants of exhaustion and fear. The wraith had taken too much of her this time, and its hatred pervaded her consciousness such that the barest glimpse of Hljod made her want to snuff out the girl's pale existence. And, oh, Irpa had such power within her—through the wraith, Gudrun could reach over and draw out the child's life force, feast on her soul and grow strong.

And much as she told herself it was Irpa's desires speaking, Hel, it felt like her own. Sputtering, Gudrun wiped the blood from her face. "I need to cross over."

The wraith now took her extended hand without argument. Either way, her touch chilled Gudrun to the core, though it felt like no more than a breeze brushing her fingertips. At least at first.

With each passing heartbeat, though, the grip solidified, clenched around Gudrun's fingers until she thought they would break. She'd taken every precaution to protect herself from Irpa—the wraith could not physically harm Gudrun while she remained bound to her, and yet, she could do worse. Gudrun was losing herself, one gesture of the Art at a time.

A tightness built in her chest, like Irpa was yanking her heart out. Gudrun's eyes glazed over, and she fell—she felt herself falling, though she remained on solid ground. The starlight of the Penumbra snapped into sudden clarity—not the haze through which she could look through the Veil, but a barrage of brilliant colors. The Mortal Realm now seemed a mere shadow. Hljod, still crouched on the floor, was like a ghost herself—ethereal, cast in silhouette, and radiating a very faint silvery light.

Irpa, meanwhile, had snapped into startlingly clear relief. Though her features remained obscured by the shroud that rustled gently, despite the lack of wind, that shroud was no longer a blended haze with the World around her. And Gudrun would be a fool to think being able to clearly see the wraith made her less dangerous.

She stumbled, fell to her knees, and gasped, staring at her hands. Here, in this place—this state of consciousness— the changes wrought in her soul were laid bare. The hints of the wraith—the tattered shroud, the skeletal, claw-like hands—those features she had perceived with the Sight here took on gut-wrenching verity. Irpa, despite standing before her, was also inside her and had nigh to clawed her way to the surface.

"Soon you will be mine ..." Her voice still sounded as a fell whisper and yet now came from both outside Gudrun and within her.

Gudrun shut her eyes, as if she could shut out the fear.

37

This place—if *place* was even the right word—was something else, not quite the Penumbra nor the Roil. The sky here resembled the nebulous sky of the Penumbra, but there was no sight of the real world. Naught but this damnable bridge going on and on.

And much like the bridge's color seemed impossible to pinpoint, its destination, if there was one, seemed to shift before Odin's eyes. Heimdall had told him—more or less—that following the bridge this way would lead him back to Midgard. Could the guardian have lied to him?

To occupy his mind, Odin dove again and again into Borr's memories. So many of those memories were gone now—he had to hold fast to those he could still claim. He saw himself tugging at his father's big red beard, felt his father laughing at his actions. Watching his own first step with a father's pride. And every time his mind slipped back into his own body—or his spirit body—the rush of endless melancholy deepened. So many things he'd not even remembered, not savored, not understood. Time lost with people gone forever now.

But each time it was easier and easier to slip away. Maybe the Astral Realm itself made the visions more accessible.

Something drew Odin's eyes skyward—a shadow in the ever-present night of this place, like the flickering of stars. Odin's fingers itched to hold Gungnir. Alone, weaponless, he felt surprisingly naked.

In the sky, red lightning crackled along the shimmering aquamarine clouds. His eyes scanned upward, searching for the shadow and finding naught. How many vaettir dwelt here? Beyond this Realm lay the Spirit Realm, home of the greater vaettir.

A winged form surged out of the cloud cover, diving toward the bridge in front of him. The figure, a woman, landed in a crouch, her impact sending a shudder through the bridge. Feathered wings, deep brown in color, stretched out from her back an enormous distance. Her hair was an almost luminous blonde, her armor elaborately engraved gold with wing-like protrusions extending from her shoulder plates and vambraces. The armor left her thighs bare, covered only by a slitted skirt. Full freedom of movement to allow the battle maiden to fight or fly with complete agility.

The valkyrie carried a spear, a faint energy pulsating off its blade. She rose slowly, arching her back and spreading her wings in a gesture no doubt intended to impress. Successfully so, in fact.

Odin wanted to speak, but no words came from his open mouth. Not long ago he'd wondered why no valkyries came to take him to his ancestors. He supposed he ought to have been more careful what he wished for.

"Odin Borrson," the woman said. "You are traveling in the wrong direction."

Odin swallowed, uncertain if he dared approach such a being. The vaettr radiated equal parts sensuality and terrible violence. "I-I have to get back to Midgard."

The woman shook her head, once. "Your soul is strong. The soul of a warrior, exuding power—of which we have more need than the Mortal Realm."

She wanted to recruit him. Recruit him for what? He'd thought valkyries would take souls to be with their ancestors in Valhalla. But she wanted him for some kind of battle. Perhaps even death was no reprieve from war.

"I am not dead."

The valkyrie cocked her head to the side, staring intently at him. "Nigh enough to bring you to this place, to let it seep into your soul and alter your body. I am sent to retrieve you." She advanced toward him, hand outstretched. A blue energy began to waft off her fingertips.

It would be so easy to go along with her. To leave behind the troubles of the Mortal Realm. To leave his people behind. To reunite with his father and mother ... To abandon his family on Midgard? Leave Ve to his urd? Forget about Thor? No, not so easy. Impossible.

"My purpose is in Midgard." The words tasted of acid in his mouth. He had but to take this valkyrie's hand, and he might see once again the people he'd lost. And in doing so, he would have failed his father. Odin fell back, raising his hands to fend off the warrior woman.

A sly smile spread over her face. She slipped into a fighting crouch, grasping her spear with both hands. "It has been long since a man challenged me. Come. Give me sport, mortal."

The battle maiden wanted him to fight. Odin stretched and clenched his fists. He hated to disappoint a woman.

Bellowing a battle cry, Odin charged forward, fist raised.

A single beat of her wings flung the valkyrie forward. She whipped the butt of her spear upward with her momentum, her speed impossible. The shaft collided with Odin's chest and sent him sprawling to the ground, tumbling end over end. Even when he stopped rolling, the valkyrie's momentum, the wind of her wings, left Odin skidding backward. He tried to arrest his movement, but the bridge was slick and without handholds. By the time he slowed, his head hung off the edge, hair dangling over the void.

"Fuck me," he mumbled.

The valkyrie laughed, her voice high and clear. "Had enough already? I expected a man like you to have more stamina than that."

Odin rolled away from the edge and pushed himself back to his feet. "This is just foreplay." He spread his stance. Charging her had been a fool's maneuver. If the valkyrie wanted him, let her come and get him.

The woman surged forward, a beat of her wings carrying her across the twenty feet between them. Odin sidestepped her violent downward thrust and grabbed her spear. He flooded strength into his limbs, embracing his powers and forcing her downward. With his superior size and strength, he'd bring her to her knees.

The valkyrie roared in effort, flipped her spear around, taking Odin with it, then slammed him onto the ground. Stunned from the impact, he couldn't begin to dodge when she kicked him. The force of it lifted him off the ground and sent him tumbling away, toward the opposite side of the bridge.

Odin skidded. Sputtered and gasped.

Gods above, she was strong.

Blood trickled down his lips as he struggled to his feet. Before he'd even regained them, she leapt forward again, thrusting the spear down at him. With those wings, she could cover distance at maddening speeds. Rather than try to get away, Odin flung himself straight up at her, coming in under the reach of her spear.

He wrapped his arms around her waist and shoved her onto the ground, then stomped on one of her wings. The valkyrie shrieked in pain, flailing at him with her spear. Let her try to fly with a broken wing.

Rather than keep trying to dodge that spear, Odin rolled away to the side.

"Foreplay is done, valkyrie. Let me pass, or things will go ill."

The valkyrie reclaimed her feet, stripping off her helm and tossing it aside. Ash blonde hair sprawled free, hanging down almost to her waist. "My name is Svanhit. And it is not that easy, mortal."

"Who says I'm mortal?" Odin charged in again.

Svanhit leveled her spear against him. Her rapid thrusts brought his charge up short, but he caught her spear by the shaft and yanked her forward. Wrestling her for the spear would like as not end with him on his arse again. So he simply released it and smacked his fist into her jaw. He didn't enjoy beating a woman, but she was at least as strong as him and determined to keep him from his family. And if he gave her any reprieve ...

Odin smashed his fist into her face again. And again. Blood splattered out of her mouth and she tumbled to the ground. She raised an arm to ward him off. Odin snatched it and twisted, thinking to break it. It wouldn't bend. He drew upon every drop of his supernatural strength.

Svanhit screamed, but still he didn't feel bones snap. What was she made of? Svanhit slammed her other palm into Odin's chest, sending him stumbling backward, gasping for air. She beat her wings, but with one broken, they carried her only a few feet before she collapsed to the bridge.

Odin bent to retrieve her fallen spear and advanced on the valkyrie.

"I don't want to kill you, Svanhit."

She held up a hand. "Enough. Never has any man provided such a challenge. You have earned the right to choose your own path."

Odin nodded, then wiped blood from his face with the back of his hand. If that was what it took to win a valkyrie's respect, he was glad only one had come for him. He tossed the spear at her feet.

"Help me get back to Midgard."

Svanhit chuckled. "I cannot take you anywhere with a broken wing. Besides which, I will answer for releasing you —but not to you, Odin Borrson." She bent to retrieve her spear. "And there may come a day when you wish you had taken my hand and left your world behind."

"Not this day." If she wasn't going to help him, then he had no further use for the valkyrie. Except ... "I have seen many things beyond my Realm, things I would rather not have. I spare you now, valkyrie. There may come a day I seek recompense."

Svanhit rose, looking ill. Slowly, she tugged a ring from her finger. "I am bound by ancient laws, Odin Borrson. As I am at your mercy ... I am bound to grant your wish." She offered him the ring. "I will find you, when you come seeking your recompense."

He looked down at the bauble. Its crafter had wrought the likeness of a swan, twisted around itself, from some rosy gold. Svanhit shivered, as though parting with it cost her more than he could know. Perhaps this ring bound her to her lord even as an arm ring bound an Ás to his.

He nodded, then resumed his trek down the bridge, his steps now pained and slower than before. He tried to keep his head high, proud, little able to afford any sign of weakness. Despite the valkyrie's words, he did trust her.

And when she had gone, finally, he could once again dive into memories of happier times, to embrace his loved ones where they yet lived.

---

38

*O*din's soul did not appear beside his body, nor anywhere within these ruins. Gudrun had wandered the fortress, passed among the shadows of the living and the ghosts of the dead, and found no sign of her lover. The Penumbra encompassed the Mortal Realm, and thus was vaster than it, perhaps immeasurably so, if vaettir spoke truth about the Astral Roil. She might walk this shadowy place for untold days, moons even, and still discover naught of Odin. Worse, the longer she remained here, beholden to Irpa's power, the greater the risk of losing herself. To say naught of the *other* dangers inherent in this Realm, the countless ghosts and spirits eager to prey upon a mortal fool enough to project herself beyond the Veil.

"Where is Odin?" Gudrun demanded. When the wraith said naught, Gudrun sighed. "Do not test me, Irpa." The wraith's threats had unnerved Gudrun far more than she wanted to let on, though of course, from inside her, the wraith knew all her fears.

"How badly ... do you want him?"

"Where is he?"

"Would you ... give me ... the girl?"

Hljod? Gudrun had let Irpa possess one troll wife. Did the wraith think Hljod hollow enough to overtake her? And if she was? The shade *would* exact a price from Gudrun, of that she had no doubt. If she could be satisfied with simply a body ... but not Hljod—never her. That girl had suffered enough, and Gudrun had promised herself she would take care of her, give her a better life. Grimhild would have taken the deal—taken it and counted herself fortunate, but Gudrun was not Grimhild, and there were some lines she would not cross so long as she retained the least part of her true self.

Yet, she would have to give Irpa something. She could not afford another contest of wills so soon, not if she was to survive this place and bring Odin home.

"I won't give you Hljod," Gudrun said, "but I will give you your freedom."

The slow way the wraith turned her head sent a fresh chill over Gudrun. Irpa laughed. "Freedom ... Why? Soon I will have you ..."

Gudrun shuddered, then clenched her teeth against it. "Fine. You want another soul to feast upon, I will arrange that."

"Two ... On your blood oath ..."

And now she made a bargain much as Grimhild would have, offering up souls to this vile shade, allowing it to grow stronger by trading away what she had no right to give. And while part of her still remembered that this ought to horrify her, another part found the deal almost tantalizing, giving testament to just how much of herself she had lost to the Art. And oh, what she had gained to replace it.

Gudrun reached for the dagger at her side. Or, the one that should have been there, but this form was a projection and the dagger was a physical object, one locked in the Mortal Realm. Before Gudrun could even think, Irpa wrapped her wrist in an iron grip, and she drew one long, claw-like nail along Gudrun's palm. She had to bite her tongue to keep from crying out.

When the wraith released her, Gudrun held her palm up. "I swear, by my own blood, that if you help me find Odin and help us both return to our Realm safely, I will offer you two souls to feast upon."

At that, the wraith turned, silently beckoning Gudrun follow. She did so, passing out of her chamber and out of the ruins. Some of the Niflungar seemed more real than Hljod had—those looking into this Realm with the Sight. But none seemed to recognize her. And why would they? None looked for their princess in this place, and even if they had, they would not have expected her to have changed so much in such a short time.

She passed beyond the ruins, following the wraith. Other shades watched them, but none drew close. They knew the wraith for what it was and wanted no part of it. Once, long ago, Irpa must have been a living woman. Now, she was hatred made manifest.

Irpa paused, looking around as though lost. Then the wraith held up a hand for Gudrun to wait, and melted into shadows. Searching the darkness for Odin?

Gudrun shifted idly from one foot to another, instantly feeling the weight of many eyes upon her. Without Irpa here, she was suddenly very, very alone in the Penumbra. She could see the fortress in the distance, could run for it, but she would never make it. Even if she did, she'd still be in the Astral Realm. Prey to whatever ...

The hairs on the back of her neck rose, and Gudrun

turned slowly, to look at the being that had risen behind her.

A woman, her skin like ice, long platinum-blonde hair wafting around her like a cloak. The woman wore a plain white dress, that in tatters. The snow maiden's hand suddenly appeared on Gudrun's cheek, chilling her.

"Gudrun." Her voice was sickly sweet, almost childlike.

And the sound of it sent shards of ice coursing through Gudrun's veins. And the Mist spirit knew her. Probably the same one she had used to carry her will through the mists. How many spirits had Gudrun enslaved to her will? How many would gladly rend her soul to shreds for it?

"Is it worse?" the vaettr asked. "Seeing it coming?"

"Get back, Mist spirit. I serve the goddess."

"Fear not, little sorceress ... she can have what's left of you."

"I ..." Gudrun couldn't swallow over the lump in her throat. She drew frost along her own hand, calling upon Snegurka's power to manifest it.

The Mist spirit laughed at her. "You would chill me, human?"

The air around Gudrun turned ice cold, and she toppled to the ground, gasping, unable to breathe. She tried to crawl away, but the cold drained her strength until she couldn't even move.

And then the cold broke in an instant. Gudrun dared to look up. Irpa stood behind the Mist spirit, her hand plunged into its back. The wraith yanked her hand free, pulling out the spirit's icy heart. The spirit before Gudrun crumpled to the ground and began to dissipate. Irpa bit into the heart, sucking at the Mist spirit's soul.

Gudrun shut her eyes against the horror, then shook herself and rose.

"I ... found ... him," Irpa whispered. The wraith beckoned, giving no further glance or comment to the spirit she had just devoured.

Bile scorched Gudrun's throat. What fell creatures these were, feeding on each other's souls, killing and torturing without thought or conscience. What ancient hatreds drove them? The Niflung sorcerers pretended to know the secrets of the Otherworlds, but to stand here was to know the truth —they had barely scratched the surface.

Part of her longed to delve the deeper mysteries, while that faltering part of her that remained human knew such knowledge would prove her undoing.

Gudrun had started down a path from which she could not escape.

39

*N*o Aesir had ever called Valland home. Not before Odin's march across Midgard. As such, Tyr had no knowledge of who might have built the ruin down by the half-frozen river. More of the Old Kingdoms, maybe. Its single tower had crumbled such that Tyr could only assume the snow mounds nearby housed the fallen stonework. Despite the tower's state, the wall stood nearly intact. At least where he could see. Certainly offering some shelter from the cold.

Of greater import, a thin plume of smoke rose from somewhere within. Smoke meant fire, and fire meant Mankind. Few beings of mist welcomed flame. After three days in the wilds, any sign of civilization was a boon. Yesterday he'd stumbled upon some roots to eat, but since then he'd had naught. Tyr was a good hunter, true. But with no bow or snares, catching aught seemed unlikely.

He had lost count of how many times he had cursed himself for a fool for not searching for the coast. The coast would have led to villages. Local Vall places might have welcomed a warrior. He could have worked for food. Maybe even had a warm place to sleep. In his wrath, however, he had fled through the forests, headed inland.

Blind luck or the sheer kindness of some vaettir of this land had led him to find this refuge. But now, weakness slowed his legs even as he made his way down toward the river. Too long without food. Even the apple would not keep him from starving to death. Snow crunched under his feet as he gracelessly stumbled onward. The ruin's wall stood twice his height, the entire complex no larger than a jarl's great hall. A small fort to guard against rival tribes. Probably one risen after the Old Kingdoms. Few such nations lasted long—the trek across Midgard had brought them past dozens of them. Faded into memory, if even that much remained. Idunn knew of many, spoke of how their petty kings fell to trolls or bickering among their own kin. Some kingdoms had so weakened each other with their wars they could not stand against marauding packs of varulfur. These had grown more numerous in recent years, Idunn claimed. Other towns, entire kingdoms had vanished into the mist. Even the Vanr woman didn't know what had happened to their people.

Such events grew in frequency down through the centuries, ever increasing Idunn's sorrow for the urd of Mankind. The Aesir had only ever known the harsh realities of Fimbulvinter. But through Idunn, they had learned Mankind's numbers had begun to dwindle. She said that, back when the mists first came, most of Mankind, most of the Mortal Realm perished. Some few persisted and rebuilt, humanity's numbers allowed to grow once the Vanir had driven out the jotunnar. But the Vanir had left the Middle World. Grown tired of struggling against the mists. And since then, Mankind's descent into oblivion had resumed. The saga spoke of the end of time, of the return of chaos.

And Tyr knew of chaos. Hymir had introduced him to it from his earliest memories. Chaos burned. It froze. It ruined all it touched.

Tyr grunted. Frey! When did he become given to such musings? His time with Idunn had driven him to introspections he had neither desire nor wit to undertake. Leave mulling over the future and the urd of the World to Odin or Loki or even Sigyn. Tyr was the sword guarding against that chaos, he and Gramr standing together. And Frigg—though he could not truly blame her decision—would regret casting aside such a great pair as Tyr and the sword. At least *she* would not abandon him.

A fell wind chilled his ears and eyes before the gate. Growing out his beard more might help. Usually he kept it short enough no foe could grab on, but the added warmth might count for more than such things on most days. The ash wood gate hung half off one hinge, blocking the interior against large creatures, though something like a snow fox could have easily slipped beneath it. Maybe he ought to knock here, but the gesture seemed pointless given that such a door would not keep out a determined foe.

He grasped it and pulled. Frost had crusted over the entire frame, freezing it to the hinges and holding it in place. As Tyr strained, cracks spread along the ice. Finally, the door snapped free, flapping on its one remaining hinge. Tyr slipped inside.

Most of the roof remained, keeping the inner fort cast in shadow. From the darkness, something stirred, skittering away from his approach. Gramr leapt to his hand of her own accord. She was always eager to protect him. The one woman who would never betray him.

"I know you lurk there," he warned. "Do not make me chase you through the darkness."

Again, something moved, shifting around in the deep shadows before him.

Tyr edged around the sound. A warrior could not well fight a foe he could not see. Nor, for that matter, a foe without form. The thought raised the hairs on the back of his neck. "If you are living, show yourself," he said. "And if dead and you wish me gone, speak the word, and I will leave you to your slumber." Maybe such vaettir could be bargained with. Maybe not. But Tyr didn't see that he had aught to lose.

Though he heard naught, the setting sun reflected off twin eyes that had drawn closer. Those eyes watched him a long moment as he held Gramr out before him. She would protect him. She was all he had.

Finally, the figure crawled forward to reveal itself—a waif of a girl. Probably not yet twenty winters, clad in a ragged blue dress, its hems soaked as though she'd gone running through the snow or wading in the river. Her golden hair hung around her face in messy clumps. Spent so long in the wilds she had forgotten to care for it.

Tyr lowered Gramr and relaxed his shoulder. "Forgive me, girl. I meant you no harm."

"You made a lot of noise."

He glanced back at the door, then nodded. "It was stuck." Girl must have come and gone by crawling under the gap, but Tyr would never have fit through so small an opening. "You have a fire here? Food?"

"I have fish." She rose, looking around and peering out through the door. "You shouldn't have made so much noise."

Tyr frowned. "Who are you, girl?"

"You should not have done it. It will have heard you."

That did not sound auspicious. "*What* will have heard?"

Girl hugged herself and stepped into the light. Stood

under a crack in the roof, staring up at the sky. "The sun will set soon. It comes out beneath the moon."

Tyr strode toward the girl and grasped her arm with his free hand. "Tell me what you fear."

"I … I don't know. I hide when it roams."

Scowling, he cast a look outside. Damn. Hadn't meant to expose the girl to danger. He returned to the door and shoved it back in place. Making more noise in the process, though perhaps it was too late for that.

He turned to the girl. "Show me your fire."

She nodded and scampered off, running in the direction of the river. He had to run to keep up. Twice she disappeared around corners, forcing him to search her out. Finally, he spied her waiting in a doorway. She darted through when he approached. The wall on this side had crumbled more fully. Aught approaching from the water's edge could easily climb over mounds no more than a foot tall. It made the door a rather pointless worry against anyone who circled the fort. A room adjacent to one such gap housed a kiln issuing a thin stream of smoke from a cooking fire above which hung an iron cauldron. The smell of roasting fish set Tyr's stomach grumbling.

"May I?"

The girl hesitated, but looked to clay bowls nearby. "It could be here soon. We have to hide."

Tyr shook his head. "Whatever stalks you, we will kill it for you."

"We?"

"Gramr and I. First, though …" He grabbed the bowl and scooped out a helping of the stew. A few roots and herbs graced it, and perhaps algae. None of that mattered. The fish was succulent and hot and tasted like it ought to be served on the tables of Valhalla. Tyr scarfed the meal down so quickly his stomach rumbled in protest.

He belched, trying to ignore the ache in his gut. He needed his strength after all. Maybe he even ought to have another serving. "Tell me your name, girl."

"Flosshilde." She stared at her knees as she spoke.

Tyr scooped more stew into his bowl.

A long, cruel howl erupted. He glanced out to the river. The sun had just set.

❦

FRESH SNOW CAKED THE RIVERBANKS, spreading out onto the frozen waters. Gramr held low out before him, Tyr stalked forward. The moon was bright but only half full, and with the cloud cover, it provided little illumination. A wise man would have stoked the fire and holed up inside that ruin, waited for dawn. Tyr had always had more courage than wisdom. Flosshilde was in danger because Tyr had drawn the attention of this beast lurking in the night. Through his carelessness, she might become a victim. That he would not allow. Gramr agreed. A powerful need to kill something thrummed through this gut and left an anxious tingling in his arms.

Indeed, even the river seemed to shift and spin before him in his lust for the kill.

"Don't worry," he whispered to her. "You will feast on twisted flesh tonight."

As he crept forward, he kept his eyes near the ground, searching for any sign of tracks. There was naught. Naught save the snows that must have filled in any indication of his prey.

More howls rang out in the night. Wolf pack must hunt

these lands. Could that be what she feared? Wolves, even dire wolves, they didn't usually close in on a fire. She'd be safe. Except ... Varulf might slip into the ruin in his absence, though.

Flosshilde could be in danger.

Tyr growled. Back to the same choice—wait in the ruins or take the hunt outside. He did not care much for waiting for an enemy to ambush him. But perhaps he might have more luck near the fort.

Footprints in the snow before the tower. Large footprints, but human. Not wolves. Varulfur would have kept to beast form under a moon like this. Something else. Something the wolves had reacted to.

Had to keep low, now. Something would be hunting him, too.

Gramr sung to him, her voice a faraway aria of glory before the eyes of the gods. A battle in darkness with a fell beast, one worthy of such songs.

"You're not worthy of songs," Zisa said.

Tyr shook his head. His wife ought not be here. She stood, hands on hips, scowling at him. He didn't need her now. He had Gramr. She was his, and he was hers. Zisa meant less than naught. He waved the sword at her, and she vanished.

Fool woman should run back to the tribes.

Tyr's stomach clenched. Why should he miss Zisa? The bitch had betrayed him. Spread her legs for the first man who might have elevated her position. Gods, were all women formed of spite and ambition? No, not Gramr, of course. He hadn't meant that. No need for her to get her hackles up too. No, of course not. Gramr he could believe in, always. She would never turn from him, never betray him with another man. Not like the others.

"I trust you," he whispered.

He rolled over, wiping blood and vomit from his mouth. How had he fallen to the snow?

"Fool," Zisa said, and kicked him in the gut.

Her blow was strong, too strong, and he spewed up all he had eaten. Finally, gasping for air, he rolled over. Gramr ... Where was she? He had dropped her! He pushed himself to his knees. What had he done?

"I'm sorry, I—"

Out in the darkness, moonlight gleamed off a pair of eyes. A figure crouched in the snow, but it rose. Sharp, angular features. Corded muscles covered in coarse hair. And half again as tall as Tyr. A jotunn. A jotunn here, in the heart of Midgard, well over a thousand miles from the fabled Midgard Wall.

Man-eaters, spawn of chaos. This one bore the horns of a reindeer and the eyes of a wolf. Gone more savage than most.

Tyr locked eyes with the monstrous being. Gramr must lie buried in the snow now, but she had to be close. He hadn't moved much from the edge of the ruin.

Unless Zisa had stolen her. The jealous bitch could have done aught to spite him, to trap him alone forever. Tyr began to shift his weight to his legs with agonizing slowness. Had to have his hands free.

The jotunn hefted a club that looked like he'd ripped a large branch off an ash tree. Flexed its arm. Jotunnar liked men to be afraid.

But Tyr was not afraid. "I'm will send your soul down to Hel that she might feast upon it."

The jotunn chuckled, patting its club upon one hand. Then it lurched forward with surprising speed. A great sweep of that club almost took Tyr's head off. He rolled under the attack and came up, flinging all his strength against the jotunn's waist. Apple made him strong. Maybe not strong as a jotunn, but strong enough he drove the monster back several steps. Off balance.

Tyr jerked free a dagger from around his neck. Jammed it into the jotunn's side.

Creature bellowed. Caught him with a backhand that hefted him off his feet and sent him tumbling end over end. Tyr crashed down into the snow, and the World kept rolling. Eyes wouldn't focus. Ears ringing.

Had to focus. Apple would let him block out pain, too. Just had to remember how.

He rolled over, stumbling to his feet—nigh fell face forward. But the jotunn faltered. Shocked Tyr lived at all? The jotunn yanked the dagger free of its ribs, tossed it aside.

"Your flesh will ... heal ... mine ..."

Jotunnar ate their strongest foes, thought to take their power like that. Probably could take a lot from Tyr. But Tyr wasn't going to let that happen.

Gramr. If only he had the sword. He could feel her begging him not to leave her. He couldn't leave her. Never, not her. Not her. No, no, no. He would not leave her. He dove at the spot he felt her presence. Dug through the snow, flinging it about until something sharp sliced his fingers.

There!

The snows had turned to crimson slush with all his lost blood. No matter. He dug through the mess to claim his woman.

"I won't leave you. I won't leave you."

A heartbeat later the jotunn surged forward, swinging the club. Tyr jerked Gramr up again. Impact nigh sent her tumbling from his hands. Numbed his arms. But the runeblade sliced right through the club. One end of it flew off and smacked against a tree.

Jotunn stared at his broken weapon, mouth open.

His arm still shaking, Tyr thrust Gramr up into the beast's gut. Hot blood gushed out over him. Fed his woman. She'd grown so hungry.

Jotunn trembled. Even his limbs would go numb from Gramr's icy embrace. Monster reached for him. Tyr jerked Gramr upward, slicing flesh until it snared on a rib. Then he yanked it free, and the jotunn fell to his knees.

"No one separates us."

Another swing cut the jotunn's head from its shoulders.

40

*J*rpa led her around another mountain and into a valley. There, Odin fought with a group of shades. Ghosts of a long-past battle, eager for another soul to feed off of, desperate to sustain their own existence just a little longer. Despite their phantom arms and armor and superior numbers, Odin beat the trio into the ground. He stomped on one ghost's helm, dissipating its form beneath him. The others fled at her approach.

And Odin ... a tattered shroud extended from him as well, evidence of a wraith taking over *his* soul. How had he bound a ghost on his own, and *why* would he start with a wraith?

"Odin!"

He spun toward her, face a mask of confusion. As she drew near, she pulled up short. His astral form had aged just as his physical body had, giving the appearance of a man more than twice his actual age.

"Odin? I've come to bring you home."

Other ghosts had gathered, but none dared approach

them now, no doubt driven back by the wraith hovering behind Gudrun.

Odin snarled at her like a varulf and fell into a fighting crouch.

"Odin?"

Mere hours in the Penumbra had nigh to broken Gudrun, and Odin had lingered here for days. Combined with the ravages wrought unto his body, had his mind been shattered? Or worse still, had that wraith overtaken him?

"Please, my love," she said.

Odin's eyes widened, like he couldn't quite believe what he saw. Gudrun approached slowly, pausing after each halting step, hand outstretched. At last, when he did not back away, she took his hand in her own.

"Let me take you home."

He did not resist as she pulled him along behind her, though he walked like a man in a daze, or perhaps one not sure if he was dreaming. It was well—she didn't have the energy left to explain all that had gone on, nor to explain this place to him. She needed time to think, and now that he was back safe with her, they should have it. Perhaps in a few days, once they were rested, they could return to Castle Niflung. Gudrun did miss her old room, and the pleasant days they had passed there.

Odin walked in silence so long that when he spoke, Gudrun jumped at the sound. "Am I so different?" he asked, as they climbed the stairs to her chamber in the ruin, or to the Penumbra version of it.

Gudrun shook her head. "It looks good on you. You might be able to disguise it with a glamour ..." But doing so would mean drawing upon that wraith's energy.

"Gudrun, I—"

"Shh." She placed a finger on his lips and led him back

into her room here. She guided him by the hand to his body and pressed him against it. "I can guide you back. Focus on our world—it's right there, just out of reach, Odin. You're just on the other side of the window you've so often looked through."

His form grew hazy as his consciousness slipped back to the other side.

"Your ... oath ..." Irpa said.

Gudrun settled back against her body. "I promise. First thing when I return." Even if she wanted to break her oath, she knew better. Violate a blood oath, and *things* would punish you for it. Many spirits in Hel's world lived for such opportunities.

※

SLIPPING BACK into her own form was like falling in a dream: a volatile, bile-inducing disturbance to her inner balance, and a sudden jolt awake. She sat upright, and Hljod immediately rushed from Odin's side—who now had also sat up —to throw her arms around Gudrun.

"Oh, thank the gods!"

Gudrun patted the girl on the shoulder, then rose, stretching her back. She needed to speak to Odin, but first and foremost, she had an oath to keep.

Odin collapsed back upon the bed.

"Rest, my love." Gudrun had a promise to keep, much as it pained her. "Watch him," she told Hljod.

She wobbled as she rose, drained from her own journey through the Astral Realm.

Outside her room, a pair of guards waited, standing vigil over her as Father had no doubt commanded. These men sought only to do their duties, and she would repay them with agony beyond the scope of human measuring, and yet, how could she not? She had made a blood oath to a wraith already writhing and crawling beneath her skin, seeking to take control of her.

"Come with me," she commanded. It wouldn't do to let Hljod hear them, or see what would happen. Instead, she led them down the stairs into an abandoned smithy.

"Princess?" one them asked as she shut the door.

"I'm very sorry about this." And she let Irpa out. The wraith seized each man's throat with Gudrun's hands, hands that became swirling shadows. Both men immediately fell to their knees, eyes wide, mouths agape, gagging, trying to scream when no sound would escape them.

Gudrun's mouth opened of its own accord, and vapor seeped from her victims into it as the wraith sucked out their souls.

Their flesh withered and desiccated before her eyes, turning sallow. A stench of decay filled the smithy. Both men trembled, flailing weakly at her arms. Fragments of their lives flashed in her mind for the instant before Irpa consumed them. One had a daughter he loved. The other had hoped to marry soon. All they were or ever could have been fell away, granting strength to the monstrous shade within her.

When naught more remained of those men, Irpa released them. Their cracked, ancient looking corpses crashed down to the floor.

And Irpa's hands—Gudrun's hands—wrapped around her own neck. Gudrun wailed at the wraith, flung her will against it. The wraith beat her down, driving her into a dungeon within her own mind. It rose, using her body.

And it laughed.

No.

This was not the deal.

Gudrun threw all she was at Irpa, burned through every last bit of life force she could without dying. It gave her enough strength to clasp the talisman bracelet she wore upon her arm, to draw upon its power to fortify her will. So much she drew that the gold lost its luster and crumbled to dust.

And Irpa at last retreated to the recesses of her mind.

Soon, now ... Soon you will seek power again ... No one resists the temptation forever ...

Gudrun slumped to the floor, trying not to look at the corpses of the men she had betrayed.

WALKING BACK up those steps took nigh to all she had. The energy she had spent in her contest with Irpa would recover, but until it did, she could barely move, much less call upon any of her powers. And the talisman ... Losing that would cost her. It had been the one place she could turn when vying wills against shades and spirits, and without it, any use of the Art might be her last. The Singasteinn might have served longer, maybe forever, had Odin not taken it from her.

Still, she had saved Odin, and things would be better now. At last he would join her, and Grimhild would be forced to acknowledge the truth—Gudrun had won. Then, perhaps, Odin would tell her what he had done with her amulet.

"Stop!" Hljod shrieked from behind the door.

A moment later, it crashed open, and Odin rushed out of it. He raced down several stairs before pausing in front of her. "Thank you for ... Thank you for coming for me, Gudrun. I don't know why you did."

Gudrun faltered and had to lean against the wall to remain standing. What was he saying? "I did it because I love you." Talking hurt, it took so much out of her.

"Maybe you do, and I'm sorry for that. But naught has changed, Gudrun."

She sputtered, unable to believe what she was hearing. "Do you have *any* idea what I just went through to find you? Have you ever imagined anyone would care enough to cross Realms to reach you? I broke the laws of reality to bring you back to my side, and you say it changes naught?"

He reached for her, as if to wipe away the blood she knew had crusted on her face. She slapped his hand away, or tried, but lacking the strength to do so, the gesture lost its impact.

"I am sorry. I am so sorry, Gudrun. I wish ... in another lifetime I would ... I have a wife. I have a son. My people need me. My father, his legacy." Odin continued shaking his head, backing away from her.

Gudrun took a shaky step toward him, then her legs gave out beneath her, and she sank to the floor. She reached for him, willing him to take her hand. He did so, and kissed it.

Then he stepped past her.

He kicked in a door behind which her father had stored his spear. How did he know where to find it? The Sight?

He emerged a moment later. Guards came rushing up the stairs—only a three now, as she had just murdered the others. Odin tore through them like a whirlwind, his age apparently not slowing him.

Gudrun had no strength to rise, but she knew he would escape.

He had betrayed her. After all she had done, all she had sacrificed, still he rejected her.

Not even enough of her humanity remained for her to weep over it.

But somewhere, deep inside, the wraith's hatred kindled.

41

*S*lumped against the wall beside the kiln, Gramr resting on his thighs, Tyr watched as Flosshilde bound his head. She had torn the still-wet hem of her dress for a bandage. Gesture left him nigh to speechless with gratitude. Girl worked in silence save for the occasional grunt. Her ministrations complete, she leaned back and shifted to examine the bindings.

"Does it hurt?"

"No," he lied. Jotunn had probably cracked his skull. Lots of blood. Lucky his brains didn't spill out. But at least the creature hadn't harmed Gramr.

"I ... can't believe you killed it."

Tyr grunted. A jotunn, out here. First Hymir, then Ymir, now this one. Jotunnar were supposed to be cast out of Midgard. Now they seemed keen to return. And somehow this one had bemused his mind with false visions of Zisa. She could not have been here, not tonight. No, his wife—ex-wife—was among the tribes. They'd abandoned him to the cold and the mist. He had Gramr and now Flosshilde.

"Did this place belong to your people?"

"No, no. People say it was built by the Bragnings, but it's been empty for a long time."

"Where did they go?"

She shrugged. "Maybe the ruined fort didn't provide enough shelter for a large group. It was a safe enough place for one person to hide in." Flosshilde held her hands before her, as if uncertain what she wanted to say next. She said naught, however, instead, grasping the edge of her dress and slowly raising it to expose her thighs.

"What are you doing?"

"You saved me ..."

Tyr swallowed, his pulse pounding hard. Despite his injuries, his body began to respond, rising. A flush built at his neck and spread quickly. Flosshilde was pretty, young. So willing. And he ... he longed for a woman's touch. But ... Idunn ... or Zisa? Gods help him. He didn't even know what he wanted.

Flosshilde was atop him now, pulling at his trousers with one hand, shifting Gramr away from him with the other.

Tyr shoved her away. The girl pitched backward with a yelp. Her mouth hung open. Might have pushed her harder than he'd meant to. He snatched Gramr up. She was the only woman he needed. But Flosshilde looked genuinely hurt, and not just from her arse colliding with the floor.

"I'm sorry," he mumbled. "I can't, I can't. It's not right."

The girl rose, backing away with a strange look on her face. "Are you married? And so loyal to your wife ... That's admirable."

Married. Not anymore. It was complicated. More complicated than he had any desire to discuss with this girl.

He leaned back against the wall. "Just need to rest." His wound would heal best while he slept.

Flosshilde sighed, then shrugged and slipped out of the room. He'd offended her. Obviously.

No, wisdom had never been his greatest strength.

❦

HE DREAMED OF FLOSSHILDE. She walked along the river-bank, now completely unclad, her golden hair no longer looking clumped but glorious. As glorious as her perfect arse, her too perfect breasts. And he went to her, uncertain why he had ever resisted.

Her wet lips tasted of salt and moonlight. She drew him down, pulling him onto the ice. Its chill stung his bare knees. He had no memory of doffing his trousers, but he too was naked. Unable to contain himself, he was inside her now, relishing her warmth. The ice cracked beneath her. Her hair was streaming out in the current.

With fervent kisses, she drew him closer and closer.

Cold. He was so cold.

He opened his eyes. He was under the river. Flosshilde had her arms around him, kissing him, biting his lip. Blood filled the water—his blood. He struggled against her, flailed. Suddenly he was no longer inside her, and her legs had become rough, cold. A fish tail, a single beat of which flung them both against the riverbed.

She spun over him, driving him down into the silt. It stung his eyes. Couldn't see! Everything blurred.

Her mouth seemed filled with razor-like teeth. Flosshilde pushed him down, choking him. He grabbed her arms, trying to keep those jaws from closing over his face. Trying to break her inhumanely strong grip.

His limbs ached, growing numb. His lungs wanted to explode. Water filled his mouth and nostrils.

Gramr. Oh gods, where was she? He had left her on the shore. This was his punishment for such infidelity. To die, drown and be forgotten.

So Flosshilde could claim Gramr and give her to some other man. No!

Righteous anger granted him the barest moment of clarity, and in it, he seized his power. He pried her arms away then pinned them to her side. She thrashed within his grasp. Tyr wrapped an arm around her throat then kicked off the silt, flinging them both upward.

His head and shoulders burst through the surface for an instant, before a beat of her tail sent them both colliding with the ice. It tore through Tyr's shoulders and filled the river with fresh blood. Girl thrashed in his grasp. Drove them back underwater.

Tyr slammed his fist down atop her skull. And then she fell still. He swam upward, pulling her after him. Once again, he crested the surface, panting, gasping for breath. Flosshilde hung limp in his arm. Had he killed her?

Ice crunched and broke away as he tried to climb on it. He slipped back under the river, only to come up again, sputtering. With no other choice, he broke through the ice, driving himself toward shore. Finally, it grew so thick it bore his weight. With one arm he heaved himself out of the river, dragging Flosshilde out behind him.

Her tail remained, making her heavy and awkward. He wanted to collapse. To lie there, shivering. But he needed warmth, needed shelter. He got to his knees, panting. A man who had not eaten an apple of Yggdrasil would have died of deathchill already. Or drowned, more likely.

Flosshilde's chest rose and fell slowly. Tyr groaned. Maybe he would have been better off to just kill her. But she might have answers. With thumb and forefinger, he pried her jaws open. Hel. Two rows of shark-like fangs lined her mouth. A mouth that had grown unnaturally wide.

Finally, he hefted her in his arms, her tail flopping around limply as he rose and made his way back toward the kiln. His feet had grown numb, and he stumbled with every step. It ought to have hurt more. When it didn't hurt, that was a bad sign.

Chill night air stung his bare skin, feeling like a flame with every breeze. He toppled forward over the breach in the wall. He dropped the mermaid on the floor, taking no heed of how hard she fell. Rising, Tyr grabbed Flosshilde by the arm. Dragged her toward the kiln.

Its stinging warmth was almost too much after the chill outside, but Tyr forced himself closer. Not too close. You have to warm yourself gradually after exposure to deathchill. Too much heat too quickly could make things worse.

Only after warming himself a moment did he look around. Gramr still lay here, abandoned, as was Flosshilde's dress. Tyr crawled over to his sword and stroked it gently.

"I'm so sorry. I didn't mean it."

He glanced back at the foul temptress who had led him to betray his woman. She would pay for that.

With his dagger, he cut her dress into strips, then used those to bind her arms behind her back. Finally, he shoved her up against the wall.

No sign of his own clothes. That meant he must have discarded them outside.

With a last glance at Flosshilde, he headed for the breach. When she woke, he would greet her clad, armed, and ready to punish all she had done.

THE WOMAN STIRRED SOMETIME LATER, well before dawn. As she did, her tail gave way to legs once again. Despite himself, Tyr felt himself rise at the sight of her spread legs and the heavenly trench between them. To avoid temptation, he flung the remains of her dress over her.

Then he leaned close and grabbed her by the hair, knocking her head against the wall with just enough force to startle her. Didn't want her falling unconscious again, after all.

"I had a lot of time to think while you were away," he said. "The stew had some foul potion in it, yes? Something to make me take leave of my senses?"

The girl groaned, blinked. Her eyes widened in what seemed genuine fear.

"I asked you a question."

"Uh ... hallucinogenic algae, yes."

"And in my delirium, you thought the jotunn would find me easy prey."

"I had to." Her voice was barely a squeak.

"Had to?" Tyr scoffed. "Who, exactly, forced you to try to murder a stranger who happened by?"

The girl looked away, or tried, though he still had a grip on her hair.

Tyr growled and pulled, lifting her slightly up off the ground by her hair. She shrieked. "Answer me."

"The queen!"

Queen? The mermaid queen. "Queen Rán ordered you to kill humans? Or Aesir, specifically?"

Flosshilde swallowed, eyes darting one way or another, as if seeking some escape. But her hands were bound, and the river was far. "Not Rán. Grimhild."

"The Niflungar sent you after us?"

"A backup plan. I was ..."

"Supposed to kill me and steal Gramr. Of course you were." He thrashed her against the wall, drawing another yelp from her. "So is that how a mermaid comes this far up a river?"

"I'm a nixie—a river mermaid. We don't serve Rán. But still, I had no choice. The sorceress compels obedience from spirits."

Tyr frowned. Spirits ... vaettir. So Grimhild had used her sorcery to summon, or at least dominate, this nixie. And if the Niflungar queen had sent vaettir after him like this, she must know he had left the Aesir. She wanted to reclaim Gramr, take her from him.

But if she knew so much of his whereabouts, she was watching the tribes. Watching and, like as not, planning to strike them again soon. Probably sent the trolls, too.

And now his people had lost their greatest defender.

"Please don't kill me," Flosshilde said. The way she trembled might have been for show, might have been another trick. Her fear *seemed* genuine, but he could never be certain. Either way, she deserved death.

He released her hair and let her slump down, then leaned close to her face.

"Please! I don't want to die."

Tyr nodded and rose. He ran his thumb over Gramr's bone hilt. Yes, she wanted the girl's blood. She needed blood. She demanded it.

He pressed the point against Flosshilde's neck.

"Please ..."

Blood welled there. Feeding Gramr. She needed it.

Tyr growled at the nixie. "You should *die*."

She shut her eyes. Shaking.

His arm trembled. He didn't want to do this, did he? He wanted to ... to be ...

Borr had told him he could be a better man. That he was not bound by his past with Hymir. And Tyr had sworn an oath.

He cast the sword aside.

Clutched his face. "Borr ..." Man ought not have died. Ought not have left Tyr like this. Now there was Odin, and ... Odin was missing. Odin's people were dying. And Grimhild would have more plans than just killing Tyr.

Don't leave me.

Before he knew what he was doing, he'd reclaimed Gramr, stroking her. "I didn't mean it. I'm sorry."

He stumbled toward the doorway.

"Wait!"

He glanced back over his shoulder at Flosshilde.

"You're not just going to leave me bound like this?"

Tyr scoffed. "Maybe next time someone happens along and wants to help you, you won't try to *eat* them."

The girl's mouth fell open. "I ... I wasn't going to eat you. I was supposed to drown you so a nix could slip inside you and ..."

That thought made him recoil. Slip inside him and take him over, possess him and use him up. So there was a human girl underneath, one controlled by the nixie. Killing her would free her from the vaettr. Maybe even be a mercy. Gramr raised, he took another step toward the girl. Blade was hungry for more blood. Was Flosshilde the girl's name or the nixie's? Was there even a difference, anymore?

Icy, cold rage crawled out from his gut and seized his limbs. More blood.

No. He should let her go. She was so scared.

More blood.

He ought to slay her. She deserved death. She was their foe. Gramr needed her blood.

BLOOD!

Gasping, he dropped to one knee. Hand on her shoulder, he spun her around. A single swipe of Gramr severed the bindings and drew a cut along her arms.

He leaned in close to her ear. "I see you again, you will answer for your crimes."

Gramr was screaming in his ear. She had to die. She had to die.

BLOOD!

Tyr rose, shaking his head, and stumbled away. He needed to be gone from this place.

Grimhild had wrought this, and she would not stop with sending one nixie.

The Niflung queen would never stop.

And neither would Tyr. He would claim the blood of every Niflungar on Midgard.

42

*N*ever had Odin missed Sleipnir more. The cold cut through even his supernatural stamina, making every step up the snowy slope an effort. His feet had gone numb, and his joints ached, as seemed his eternal urd in his now aged body. Though Odin had slain several Niflung warriors, the Raven Lord himself would no doubt follow, and Odin held no illusions about his ability to fight the sorcerer king, at least not until he had rested.

For days he had walked, even as Audr slithered around in the back of his mind. The wraith had fallen more silent here in the Mortal Realm, but his presence was a constant weight upon Odin's soul, forcing him to spend every waking and even sleeping moment in an unconscious war for control of his own flesh.

Perhaps the wraith could be exorcised, but such was beyond Odin's meager command of the Art. All he could do, for now, was focus on getting as far away from Gjuki as possible.

Clearly, he was somewhere in the Sudurberks, and if he

continued west he would reach the sea, sooner or later. But days of walking, fleeing the Niflungar, days without food or rest, had drained him. He needed more strength, more ...

And Audr had strength, power that suffused his very being. Odin had only to reach for it and then ...

Fresh energy flooded through his limbs, giving him stamina, dulling his aches, and settling his empty stomach. Even as it tasted foul and toxic, like bathing in tar. And yet ... such power felt so good. How could something feel sickening and intoxicating all at once?

The wraith wakened within him as he called upon that power, growing more active, tightening its hold around Odin's body. Every time he used Audr, he would lose more of himself, until finally the wraith grew strong enough—or himself weak enough—to completely seize control.

The very power that sustained him would kill him, or nigh enough to, as Audr consumed his life and his soul. And still he took the more difficult route forward. He could have tried to stick to the valleys, maybe found game there, but that was exactly where Gjuki's people—and ravens—would look for him.

He'd rather fall to the mountain than let the Raven Lord drag him back to that dungeon. Whatever Gudrun might have wanted, her father would not relent. The truth was, part of him longed for Gudrun's warm embrace, longed to sleep in her soft bed, her legs entwined with his, his belly full. It would have meant an end to this torturous journey, to his endless quest. And an end to his people, to his family, to his dreams. Maybe that was what the Odling ghost's curse meant. She said his dreams would burn—maybe through Odin's own weakness.

And he couldn't let that happen. He had not fought his

way back from the Astral Roil and given up his youth just to die on this mountain or give in to the Niflungar.

Except ... still he wondered. If he burned out his own life, would he find his parents waiting for him on the other side? Was that the one escape from the immortality the apple had granted him?

He might feed Audr more of his life rather than surrender control of his body, let age ravage him beyond all recognition. Even if he could control such things, though, it offered no guarantee the wraith could not claim him as he aged beyond the limits of men, or in fact, that death would come either, given the apple's effects.

Fresh snow flurries stung his eyes. He needed shelter. The storm would stop him from making much progress, but with any luck, it would also hide his passage, even from the ravens. These mountains were littered with caves—Loki had shown him that. Ancient tunnels dug through the ice, cut by rivers or trolls or aught else.

Odin shielded his face with his arm, a futile effort to keep the ice crystals from his eyes. His stubble had grown into a thick beard, providing some scant warmth to his cheeks, but a hood would have been nice. Caves ... if they were dug into the ice, they would likely be lower in the mountain. But how to find one in this storm?

Altering his course back down the slope, Odin racked his brain. Even an immortal would likely perish if buried in a blizzard. His Sight had allowed him to see through mist and darkness, because neither extended into the Penumbra. It meant, like as not, neither would the snowstorm. He knelt in the snow, forcing his eyes to relax, allowing himself to see beyond the Mortal Realm. When he opened his eyes, the snow was just a dance of shadows across the sky. There, down the slope, waited an overhang crusted with icicles. If not a cave, perhaps it would at least shelter his body from the storm.

His own body flickered, strands of the wraith dancing around the edges of his flesh, always threatening to take over. This was what he had seen in Gjuki, how the man's astral form seemed so twisted and shadowy. The gods alone might know how many vaettir Gjuki had bound to himself. And here Odin felt apt to die with but one such entity squirming under his skin.

Vision locked in the Sight, Odin trudged for the overhang, feet skidding along the ice as quickly as he dared. As he drew closer, he saw the overhang did extend deep into the mountain. An ice cave, much like Loki had shown him. Which probably meant he owed his blood brother his life once again.

SHADES MOVED ABOUT THE CAVE, watching him with hateful eyes. They knew he saw them, but Odin needed the Sight to see through the darkness. He leveled Gungnir before him, working his way deeper. After all he'd been through, he'd not fear a few ghosts. A more terrible and ancient shade dwelt within him now. Farther he delved into the cave, but something made him stop. An uneasiness rose in his stomach, one not born of ghosts nor snow.

There was something *behind* the ice. Odin moved closer, pressing a hand against the ice crusting the cave wall. Beyond, frozen in the wall, a man stooped in clear agony. Hel's crotch. How could a man wind up inside the ice wall? Should he cut the man free and burn him, send his soul properly? But it was impossible to tell how deep in the ice the man was, and Odin's strength was fleeting. From the look of it, this man must have died an age ago. Already, his soul must be one of the shades wandering this place.

One of them?

Odin pressed on, spotting another body in the wall not far along. A mother, holding a child in her arms.

"Fuck me," Odin mumbled, the sound reverberating through the ice cave. What in the gates of Hel had happened here? Or maybe that was just it—were these more victims of Hel? Victims of Niflung sorcery. Another of the Old Kingdoms, maybe.

Odin looked down. Hard to tell through the ripples of ice, but the stone beneath him looked worked, carved by men. A lump built in his throat, and he pressed on, his step quickening—much as he feared what might lie ahead, he could not stop himself. He had to know. Deeper and deeper he delved until, around a bend, he saw it. Far below, off a fifty-foot drop, stood a fortress on the shores of a frozen lake. A winding path led around the outside of the cavern, down to the old ruin, a place now covered in frost. Countless abandoned outbuildings surrounded the fortress, and Odin could only guess more would lie in its courtyard.

This place had been an outpost, a guard station to some fallen land, much like Idavollir, where Odin's own people must still linger. He dreamed of them from time to time, dreamed of the trolls plaguing them, of the deaths that tore them apart. But his son lived, that much he could feel, and it gave him some small hope.

More shades flitted about the outskirts of the ruins, though fewer seemed to enter the fortress proper. Perhaps they lamented their fallen home. The Niflungar had destroyed this kingdom as they had the Odlingar. Unable to take his eyes from the giant fortress below, Odin made his way down to it. What lost knowledge would be buried here?

Ancient secrets? Mystical weapons like Gungnir or the runeblade Tyr now wielded? Any such weapon would make a world of difference to his people now. Or might he find answers about the Niflungar themselves, or even the Vanir?

It was not luck he'd found this place, but urd. This was his chance to learn what he needed to know to save the Aesir—to save all Midgard. Save them from Hel and the Niflungar and the indifference of the Vanir. Save them from the mists of Niflheim, once and for all.

As he reached the bottom of the cavern, he caught himself almost running. Easy. The ghosts here could still be a danger—much like the Odling ghost had proved. And this place had waited here for centuries, perhaps longer. He could afford to side with caution.

But as he approached the gates, the ghosts fled from him rather than try to bar his way. They were mere whispers of their former selves, trapped here through the horrors visited upon them. Perhaps they sensed the wraith in him and feared it. Would burning their corpses free some of their souls? Odin hoped so. He didn't have time to dig those bodies from the ice now, but one day he'd return with his people and put the fallen to rest. They deserved no less.

An iron portcullis blocked his entrance to the courtyard, this too caked in a thick layer of rime. Odin glowered. The ice-slicked wall would make a difficult climb, so this gate was likely his best chance. Maybe the ice had weakened the metal within? He grasped Gungnir in both hands and swung it like a club. A cacophonous clang echoed through the cavern. Ice cracked over the gate, but the metal didn't break. Odin swung again, dislodging icicles above him. To avoid the falling things—some thick as spears—Odin leapt backward.

Only then did he notice the massive shadow now

lurking overhead. The serpent had crawled over the lip of the fortress, the bulk of the creature's body still on the other side. Its forelegs, larger and thicker around than Vili, held it aloft at an angle at which its massive eyes could meet Odin's own. Eyes filled with primeval hatred and hunger. Gray-green scales covered the monstrosity, with spurs rising from its spine and enormous horns jutting from either side of its head. It opened its mouth to reveal snake-like fangs dripping with venom.

Odin had seen the linnorm carved in ice in Hunaland, a monster not unlike the dragons engraved along Gungnir's shaft and blade. Though he tightened his grip on Gungnir, Odin dared not move. His heart beat so fast he felt he could choke on his own pulse.

The linnorm reared back. Odin flung himself away in a roll an instant before it crashed into the space he had stood. Its massive form dragged over the portcullis, crushing it and bringing down the wall around it. It didn't slow for an instant, lunging again. Odin dashed wildly, rapidly changing directions, then rolled to the side again as it crashed past him.

It had no hind legs, but it used its forelegs to heave itself forward with ungodly speed, if not much control. When it lunged for him again, Odin rolled toward it, swiping Gungnir up in an arc. The spear tore through the linnorm's scales, scoring a gash Odin had no time to congratulate himself on. Before he could even move, the linnorm twisted its mighty form, encircling him like the walls of a courtyard.

Odin spun, seeking any escape. This thing had to be eighty feet long, its bulk a solid wall around him. It reared its head above him, jaw impossibly wide, baring fangs that themselves must reach as long as he was tall. Rapid gasps escaped Odin. He made no effort to control his breathing, sucking in every bit of air he could while lowering Gungnir to his side.

Draw the beast in.

And the linnorm struck, surging forward like a bolt of lightning. Odin jumped forward and to the side, swiping with his spear. It slashed upon the serpent's neck. The linnorm immediately slapped its head into Odin, the sheer size and momentum sending him flying backward, his grip on Gungnir lost. Odin slammed into the monster's coils, stunned.

The serpent shook its head, flinging blood around the cavern, then hissed at him.

"You think *you're* vexed?" Odin mumbled. He regained his feet and drew his sword. "I am the son of Borr! I am no one's prey!"

The serpent gave no indication it understood. Sword before him, Odin stalked ever closer to where he had dropped Gungnir. He needed that spear. Its magic gave him strength, fury, stamina. It could cut through the dragon's scales. Some said Volund himself had forged the sword Frigg granted him, but would it pierce dragon hide?

The linnorm glanced at the fallen spear. It knew. Did it sense the dragon soul bound to the spear? Odin could use that. He feinted toward the spear. Predictably, the serpent surged forward to cut him off. Instead of continuing forward, Odin jumped onto its face, roaring. The linnorm jerked, trying to dislodge him, forcing Odin to wrap his arms around one of its horns. The serpent thrashed wildly.

This had been a madman's plan.

It slowed for an instant, perhaps even dizzier than Odin now felt—and he was apt to vomit. Which he had no time to think on. He slashed his sword down on the linnorm's skull with one hand, but the scales reflected it.

He didn't have the strength to pierce it with one hand. Odin released his grip on the horn and grasped his sword with both hands as he fell, slamming it straight down. The blade embedded itself in the linnorm's snout, and Odin found himself hanging on only by that blade, his face now close enough to the linnorm's maw to feel its foul, acrid breath.

It shrieked and jerked its head. Odin's sword snapped in half, and he flew free, crashing back down on the ice. He felt ribs break from the impact. Pain blurred his vision, and he desperately clung to the magic in him, trying to drown it out.

His sword—Frigg's sword. It was supposed to protect his family, and he'd broken it. Gods, that boded ill. The sword meant to defend his children, his wife ...

Strength. He needed more strength. More than even the apple could grant. What was another year of his life if he was eaten? Odin pulled more power from Audr, fueling himself. While the linnorm flailed, Odin scrambled over to Gungnir.

More energy filled him the moment he touched it. The power of his own dragon. Power to replace that of the wraith. The linnorm coiled around, preparing to strike again. Odin thrust Gungnir right into its throat, embedding the spear three feet into the dragon.

The creature's blood gushed over him, burning like acid. It toppled to the ground, flailing and flopping around, its movements stripping Gungnir from his grasp once again. Odin tried to crawl away. Something slammed into his back and sent him sprawling. The dragon was apt to crush him in its death throes.

Odin yanked himself over the ice, desperate to put as much distance between himself and the dragon as possible.

Icicles rained down from the cavern ceiling as the linnorm thrashed.

Odin covered his head and screamed. His Sight slipped from him, leaving him in utter darkness. Darkness, and the earthquakes caused by a dying dragon, and a collapsing cave.

PART IV

Seventh Moon

43

*I*n the snows ahead of her, draugar followed Odin's trail. Gudrun did not favor using them. They were ghosts almost as vile as wraiths—indeed, some draugar became wraiths once their corpses were finally destroyed. But few options remained open to her now. Few, or none.

No choice.

None.

Not when she must find Odin.

Must she find Odin?

Indeed she must.

Unlike the draugar, she could not see well at night, but the dead refused to walk in even the hint of sunlight that pierced the mist. To use them, she had to travel in darkness.

"I don't understand why you don't just kill the troll shit," Hljod said.

Death is no mercy ...

As if she had thought it was. Had she ... just thought that? Her mind swirled, not quite able to separate Irpa's thoughts from her own. What a fool she had been to rely on the wraith that, like a parasite, now fed off her.

Oh, but she could deny Irpa in the simplest of ways ... by using her Art of Mist so much that Snegurka would take her instead.

You would not ...

Wouldn't she? Had not she already fractured her body and mind in pursuit of a man who no longer loved her?

Never loved her. No one loved her.

Wretched girl ...

Perhaps Irpa spoke of herself now.

"Gudrun?" Hljod asked. "What's happened to you?"

Gudrun actually giggled. "I'm losing my mind, body, and soul."

"Then for the gods' sakes—"

Gudrun held up a finger to silence that blasphemy.

Hljod cleared her throat. "For Hel's sake, let the damned man go."

Perhaps the girl was correct. Odin might never truly love her. If he did not turn to her after all she had sacrificed, she could no longer expect him to ever do so.

Surrender to despair ...

Would that not be so easy?

"I think," Hljod said, "you want him more to spite your mother than out of any true love for the man."

Gudrun paused, watching the restless dead march across the snows. An army of draugar meant Gudrun could track a man across any terrain. She needed merely to send her scouts along every possible route, and sooner or later one would return with word of its prey. As one had. Odin had chanced the mountain slopes, avoiding the more obvious route. The valleys might have provided him succor, but such was his desperation he would turn away from it.

Not that Gudrun truly blamed him. Her father would visit further horrors upon the man for his escape, for the lives Odin had taken in making that escape. He'd blamed her—and rightly so—for those losses, but Gudrun did not fear her father. Who she feared was Grimhild. If she didn't return Odin to the Niflungar before Grimhild reached them, the queen would make her regret it.

But did Hljod have the right of it? Gudrun *did* want to spite Grimhild in any way she could, true enough, but Gudrun had just braved the Penumbra for Odin.

And then had seen that sacrifice scorned.

Maybe she *should* let Grimhild at Odin.

Hel, she hated that Ás King. And loved him?

No. She would not allow herself that, not anymore. Not after this.

It was Odin's fault what was happening to her. Because of him, Gudrun was losing herself to the vaettir within her. She had pushed her powers beyond their limits, and now any further use of the Art would only accelerate the process.

Because of Odin, she had become a monstrosity walking in human form, and yet, part of her still wanted him to accept her. Such was her twisted urd that she could not even answer Hljod.

44

The Niflung scout's corpse tumbled down the hillside before lodging in a snow drift. Tyr spat, then cleaned the blood off Gramr by wiping her in the fresh snow. Blade like her didn't rust, but still. Had to treat her right.

For days he'd tracked and hunted every Niflung he could find. They passed around the local towns, avoiding them mostly. And they watched. Watched as trolls besieged Idavollir. Worse than when Tyr had left it.

No Niflung would watch tonight. Tyr had cut down four already.

He swept his torch in front of him, banishing mist. Ahead, trolls scaled the fortress walls. Others tore at the weakened gate. They'd break through it tonight.

Blood.

Troll blood was foul, black ichor, but it seemed to satisfy Gramr.

And she would feast well tonight.

Tyr raced down the hill, toward the fortress, blade hungry.

٨

THE TROLLS CLIMBED atop one another, each trying to get a hand on the gate. A great lumbering pile of beasts, slavering over prey. None even looked at Tyr as he bellowed. So caught up in their own roars and grunts.

Gramr cleaved through a troll skull, into another's arm, and into the back of another. Tyr reversed his momentum and swung back, cutting the back of yet another troll. He had their attention now.

They fell atop of each other, trying to turn. To face him. He spun in rapid whirls, Gramr gorging herself on black troll blood. Great arcs and tight swings combined to fell nigh to a dozen of the beasts before they even managed to disentangle themselves.

Their foul ichor stung his eyes and soaked his clothes. Glorious!

A troll swiped at him with a heavy claw. Tyr danced back, and Gramr claimed fingers in response. The beast wailed, shaking its mangled hand in disbelief. Trolls knew naught of defense, trusting their nigh-impenetrable hides to protect them. But no armor seemed able to stop a runeblade, and these creatures had no idea how to fight a man so armed.

Two more charged him in a wild gait. Other men tried to block such blows on shields. Got broken arms for their trouble. Rather than retreat, Tyr raced forward, rolling between the two trolls. Came up swinging, severing a leg at the kneecap.

The other jumped like a beast, trying to angle him in. Tyr drove Gramr through the troll's chest. Screamed fury at it. It caught his arm and tried to draw him in to bite him. Tyr's strength surged through his limbs, and he flung the beast backward. They didn't expect a man to match their strength, either.

By Frey's flaming sword, he could do this all night! No troll could stand against him. How had he ever thought he needed caution against such beasts?

Again and again, Gramr drank troll blood.

Yes, they landed a few blows that sent him for a tumble. But he blocked the pain. Same power that granted him strength and speed let him do that. And a man without pain? It was a man who could not fail.

By the time the trolls broke and fled, a score of them led dead or dying before the gates.

Tyr bellowed after them.

He took a few steps to pursue, but as the battle-fever faded, his legs wobbled, and he sank to one knee. For a moment he stared at Gramr. Then at the mass of troll corpses. Men were watching him through the gates, mouths open, eyes wide. Unbelieving.

How could they believe?

He could not himself fathom what he had just done. Such a feat would have sounded absurd even in a skald's tale.

And yet, the corpses did not lie.

STILL AN HOUR BEFORE DAWN, but the siege had broken for the night.

Tyr almost dared hope he'd broken it for good, but perhaps not. Ve was still out there. Unlike his brethren, the Troll King had some measure of cunning. He'd come at them more carefully next time.

The gate creaked as the men up on the ramparts opened it. Tyr cracked his neck, waiting.

Jarl Arnbjorn's thegns were first out, followed by the man himself, Kory, Hoenir, and several others. Men stared at him with awe.

How could they not? Here before them, on a pile of corpses, stood a man soaked in troll blood. Tyr would not have believed it either. He had sheathed Gramr over his shoulder, but she stirred at the sight of Arnbjorn. Begged him to draw her.

The jarls and thegns parted for Frigg. The queen looked both relieved and somehow sad, hands at her sides. "Tyr."

"Queen Frigg."

"You broke the siege."

He shrugged. "Temporary reprieve. Ve will be back."

Frigg looked to the jarls, her frown only deepening. "Nevertheless, you proved a hero today. It makes things … harder." What was she on about now? "You violate the terms of your banishment, Tyr, and leave me with no choice but to order your arrest."

He worked his jaw, words failing.

"I ask you to surrender your arms willingly."

Tyr spat. "I just fucking saved you all." His hand closed over Gramr's bone hilt.

Frigg raised an eyebrow. "And now you plan to assault us for following the law?"

"The law?"

"You broke our laws by returning from exile, Tyr, and …" Again she glanced at the jarls. Afraid to lose their support. And maybe they would turn on her. "And that is not something we can simply let pass. When the king returns, he may decide your urd. Until then, I have no choice but to place you under arrest."

Kill her.

Kill Frigg? Kill Odin's wife ... No. That he would never do. Not that, not to the son of Borr. His hand shook as he unslung the sword from his shoulder.

And he tossed her aside.

he cavern branched, and branched again, leaving Sigyn shifting the torch from side to side for any sign of which way to go. In the snow, they could easily follow Odin's tracks and, of course, the tracks of whoever pursued him. In the ice cave, though, the passage of even so many boots left no clear indication which path the others had taken, assuming they had all even followed the same tunnel.

"Which way?" she asked.

Loki knelt on the floor, examining the ice as if it might offer up some clue she had missed, though she knew better.

"Can you not use the Sight?"

He sighed. "It doesn't work like that, exactly." Still, he raised his torch in front of his face, staring at so intently she'd have almost thought him lost in some somnambulistic trance, especially as he rose, drifting from one exit to another, before finally heading down one.

Perhaps the flame had offered him some vision or insight to guide his steps, or perhaps he could not bear to admit they wandered alone in the darkness without even starlight to illuminate their course. Either way, she trailed after him, putting just enough haste into her steps to catch up to him and look into his eyes.

He blinked—likely a side effect of staring too long into fire—and shook himself, before staring at her.

"What do you fear ahead?" she asked.

Loki didn't answer, but rather pushed on until they came to another branch in the tunnel, where he hesitated once again, looking down either end of the ice cave.

Sigyn's breath frosted the air. Down here, despite the lack of wind, it had grown even colder than on the surface, as if the ice itself saturated the cave with the unnatural chill of Niflheim. "So we know that the Niflungar took him to that ruin and that he escaped them. And we know many men pursued him."

"Not men."

"Yes, true, and my point exactly. The Niflungar used draugar once already against us, and who better to pursue Odin through these mountains than the dead? We have to suppose we'll face them ahead, and I am not exactly a warrior."

Loki chose a tunnel and took off. "You are what you need to be."

It was hard not to smile at that. Even so, between them they had two torches and cloaks that let them turn into swans. Such supplies did not leave them well endowed to face even a single draug, much less substantial numbers of them. If Loki had a plan to overcome such foes, he had said naught of it, and they were like to need his plan soon enough.

With a sigh, she unshouldered her bow. "In your past I saw the coming of the mists, and vibrant islands, and before all that, flying cities, and I am left to try to piece together a tapestry of history stretching farther than even the wisest of völvur begins to imagine."

"And do you imagine völvur so very wise in all things?"

The Aesir imagined them wise and looked to them with trust, though as Loki correctly surmised, Sigyn had never taken their words as any sort of ultimate truth. "How does a city fly?"

"With a terrible hubris within man, an insidious and inviolable pride that drives Mankind ever toward darkness even while reaching for the skies."

No doubt he spoke the truth, while avoiding the question, but then, she had not expected even that much of an answer. Always, it was their game, and to learn aught, she had to approach it at angle he would not foresee. "With everything I've learned about the Destroyer, it almost seems like Hel actually fears him. Why else would she have sent the Niflungar so fervently against any particular man?"

"You may find delving deep into the motives of Hel uncover more truth than you wish or are yet ready for."

"Did you find that?"

Loki paused the barest instant, shutting his eyes, before turning toward her. "I think they went this way. We have to hurry, or the minions of Hel will reach Odin before we do."

Sigyn frowned, but followed where he led. As usual, he did not seem overly inclined to explain himself, but sooner or later, she would uncover the truths he hid. Loki knew far more of Hel and of the Destroyer and the urd binding them than he had divulged.

46

*G*udrun shook her head, following the draugar deeper into the ice cave. Much as the idea tempted, she could not set Grimhild on anyone, least of all Odin. No one deserved such torment as the queen would wreak upon him. No one. And Odin had suffered too much—she just had to make him see the truth in her heart, in his own.

As if Gudrun herself might yet know what truth that was.

There is only one truth ... the withering of hope ...

Hljod trudged behind her, grumbling about the cold as she had every damned day they'd tracked Odin. Much as looking at the girl sometimes reminded Gudrun of her own worst pains, she couldn't, wouldn't leave her behind. By Gudrun's side, the girl was brash, but Gudrun could see the fear that masked, for she knew what to look for all too well.

"When am I going to get magic powers?" Hljod asked.

Gudrun bit back a response about when the girl was ready to take a man to her bed. Telling her that would drive the girl into a frenzy of doubt and anxiety and do her no good. Instead, she spoke to the more practical reality. "Sorcery is not a magic power, Hljod, and it's not to be taken lightly. Spirits will exact a cost for their services, especially if you're not strong enough to master them."

"Like what? What's the worst they can do?"

Exactly what Irpa was doing to Gudrun. Or, in her weakened state, what the other spirit bound to her might do if she drew upon her.

Mine ...

Yes. Irpa was the stronger and more terrifying of the two.

Gudrun swallowed, then ground her teeth trying to drive the wraith down. "Possession, take your body away from you, make you watch as they use it for whatever end amuses them. You can feel everything but you are completely, utterly powerless to stop any of it. Does that sound familiar, girl?"

Hljod fell silent, and when Gudrun glanced back, she was staring at her footing. Damn. Why had she done that? Hadn't Hljod suffered enough?

Focus. She had to focus on the task at hand.

You are ... mine ...

Though Gudrun had never been to these caves, they looked familiar. She had read of this place. These were outposts of the Bragnings, weren't they? Like most of the other kingdoms descended from Halfdan, the Bragnings had turned on the Niflungar. Or, the other way around might be more precise. Some claimed their legendary founder had joined the Vanir, that he would return and save them. He had not. The Bragnings fell, as did the Odlingar and all the others. Their ruins were places inhabited by vaettir now, frozen and rendered lifeless by Niflung sorcery.

Gudrun's steps faltered at the sight before her, though her draugar scouts continued on. The beast, a linnorm, lay sprawled across the cavern, its body still. In its thrashings it had brought down most of the front wall of the ruin. Such creatures were apt to take over old places, true, but she hadn't thought ...

Hel, where was Odin? Had he actually slain a linnorm? Wasn't that impossible?

Hljod shrieked, the sound echoing through the cavern and causing Gudrun to cringe. "Fuck a jotunn!"

"Find him," Gudrun ordered her undead soldiers, trying not to smile at Hljod's colorful language and, too, trying not to falter at the sight of the battle before her. She forced herself to stillness. No sign of his body, so unless the linnorm had swallowed him ... No! Hel, no. Gudrun would not allow that to be true. Maybe part of her wanted to see him suffer for betraying her, pay for turning his back on her after all she had just done for him. But not like this.

She hadn't wanted him harmed, not really.

You did ...

No.

You still do ...

She nearly tripped over her own feet, rushing down the path. At the base, the dragon's hot blood had melted the ice, though a thin layer had refrozen over the stone. For a moment, Gudrun considered questioning one of the shades here as to what had gone on, but she had neither the time nor energy to waste getting answers to obvious questions— Odin had blundered into this place and, in his folly, quite literally woken the dragon.

And then he'd *killed* the dragon.

Even the draugar gave the corpse a wide berth. The dead did not fear much, but clearly the dragon still awed them. Dragons were among the most ancient creatures in Midgard, beings even the Niflungar avoided when possible.

Linnorms were generally little more than cunning beasts, but legends spoke of some dragons grown so far beyond their progenitor as to understand human tongues.

The draugar spread out over the ruins, combing it for sign of Odin. It did not take them long before one of the creatures shouted for her, its voice hollow as ever. Odin lay in a corner of the courtyard, trying to push himself up, though clearly his arm and maybe one of his legs were broken. Acid burns had eaten through his shirt and now marred his chest. With one hand, he held Gungnir pointed at the three draugar who surrounded him.

"Another step and I send you to Hel."

Gudrun approached, trying to keep her face stern. What a battle this must have been. She almost wanted to call upon a ghost's memories just to look back, to see it for herself. This man had slain a dragon and lived to walk away—or at least crawl away. But then, the desire to do so was yet another temptation to call upon the wraith's power, to let Irpa finally claw her way from the depths of her soul and seize control of her body.

Gudrun kept her jaw set. Her concern for Odin's suffering had let him escape once, and she could not afford to repeat that mistake. Grimhild would ... She didn't even want to consider what Grimhild would do. Besides, Odin was *hers*. She knew he loved her. She knew it.

Consume his soul ...

No!

"You betrayed me," she said, standing over him, out of reach of his spear. Not that she thought he'd hurt her, but ... The man was unpredictable. Jumping out eight-story windows, fighting through Niflung fortresses. Slaying jotunnar and dragons. The thought gave her pause. Was that why Hel wanted him? No matter how impossible the odds seemed, this man consistently brought down foes that should have been unstoppable. He was a weapon. Or, more than that. The World was filled with powerful warriors, and Hel cared little for them, but it was as if Fate turned about Odin. And the goddess would see the weapon that was the man wielded by her own hand, or destroyed so it could not be turned against her. And though Gudrun had known that, she hadn't understood, not until now, not until she'd walked through dragon blood to find her lover still alive. If Hel controlled Odin, could she use him to take all of Midgard back for the Niflungar? Would it stop there? Vanaheim might fall next. Gudrun knew it should be what she wanted, but somehow the whole prospect tasted sour in her mouth. Mostly.

Odin shook his head, the motion clearly paining him. "I didn't betray you. You never had my loyalty, Gudrun. You truly think I will ever, *ever* join the Niflungar? Abandon my people, my family, my duty?"

"I can give you so much—an end to your suffering, the chance at real power."

"There is no end to suffering. Not even in death. There is only the struggle, Gudrun. Come with me, come to the Aesir and struggle with us. Or struggle against us—and you will fall."

Gudrun crooked a wan smile at the thought. Go with him? Join the Aesir, a sorceress, nigh to a god among them? She could join them in their mad march on Vanaheim, perhaps even claim an apple for herself. With such a gift, she need not uncover Grimhild's secret to eternal youth. Her name would be feared and worshipped throughout Midgard.

But then, Odin spoke of family. He had a wife, and if he returned to her, where would that leave Gudrun? As the mistress to the king? No. Gudrun had a family of her own. A father, at least, himself a king more ancient and powerful than Odin. And Gudrun was a princess, heir to her own kingdom, with her own destiny before her, one she would not and could not walk away from. She would not abandon her family's legacy to become a woman others would call Odin's whore. She was better than that.

Kill him ...

She turned away, unwilling to let him see the decision war on her face. She had to appear strong, or he would seize the upper hand again. "Take his spear. Bring him, but don't harm him any more than you absolutely must."

47

*C*rouched atop the sloping path, Sigyn stared in wonder at the ruins below. Even given her immortality, she had never expected to see a dragon, dead or otherwise. How much would a creature like that weigh? How much would it eat? Did it truly sleep for years, as legends claimed? Völvur stories said the dragons were the spawn of Jörmungandr, the great World Serpent, who slept in the depths of the ocean. If Jörmungandr woke, it would herald the end of the World. Sigyn had never believed such stories, but looking at the corpse of a massive linnorm, she had to wonder.

"Keep the torch low," Loki said. "You'll reveal our position."

They'd seen those draugar go into the ruins. Loki had guessed the woman must be Gudrun, the Niflung princess Odin had spoken of—not to Sigyn, of course, but he told Loki things he told no other. And Loki, on occasions when she was clever enough to pry them loose, told secrets to Sigyn.

"How many are there?" Sigyn asked.

"A half dozen here, more out on the slopes."

Wonderful. A single draug was nigh to unstoppable. The dead were, unfortunately, already dead, and it made killing them rather difficult. Sigyn had her bow, but she wasn't certain she could do much against the undead with it. Loki didn't even carry a weapon. They were hopelessly outmatched, and sneaking past the undead when she and Loki needed light to see, and the draugar did not, seemed unlikely to end well.

"What are we going to do?"

"Go back."

What? They wouldn't abandon Odin after coming this far. So ... Loki didn't think Gudrun would kill Odin. That seemed a fair guess—after all, the woman appeared to have some sort of connection to their king, maybe one they could use. Besides, if she meant to kill Odin, she would have done so the instant she found him. But if they left here, Gudrun would just gather her forces and take Odin back to that Niflung ruin. Did Loki think they could sneak in there and save him? Then they might not face the undead, but gods-alone-knew how many sorcerers would stand in their way.

Loki pushed her back the way they'd come, drawing her out of her musings.

She lifted her torch higher once they'd made it around the bend. "You're going to leave him behind."

Loki shut his eyes a moment, then shook his head. "No, I cannot risk that. I can't lose him, especially not to the Niflungar."

"You really think they might turn him to serve Hel."

Instead of answering, Loki pointed to a level cavern up the slope. "Build a fire. The biggest fire you can. Burn aught you have to." He stripped off his shirt and tossed it to her. "All the tinder, spare clothes, supplies, everything."

Sigyn frowned, but did as Loki asked. Lighting a fire in an ice cave was not an easy task, particularly knowing a small army of the undead was headed her way any moment. No pressure, Sigyn.

She climbed up to the wider cavern and piled everything she could think of, aught they might possibly live without. It wasn't exactly going to be a bonfire; they just didn't have enough to burn. And why did Loki want this, anyway? Did he think more light would give them an advantage? Couldn't he have just lit another torch?

She had once seen him draw flame from a fire and hold it in his hand. Could he use that as a weapon against the dead?

She used her torch to start the blaze. Loki had tossed her even the shirt he'd been wearing, though he set his swan cloak aside. Freyja! Her man was going to catch deathchill like that. Still, she threw the shirt on the fire.

They were lucky the ceiling here was high enough they needn't worry about choking on the smoke.

The sound of heavy footfalls crunching ice drew her attention. The draugar already advanced up the slope, followed by two women. The regal blonde woman must be Gudrun, the Niflung princess. The other walked behind, not nearly as imposing. A servant, maybe? A slave?

Shirtless, arms down at his side but spread wide, Loki stood in the entrance to this cavern, barring the way. Sigyn rose and nocked an arrow to her bow. What was he thinking? Did he intend to fight the undead with his bare hands? An arrow between the eyes would do more than any amount of flame.

She advanced slowly toward her lover, watching the tunnel beyond.

Draugar moved forward, spreading out to either side

around Loki. He made no move on them, though, his gaze locked on Gudrun.

"Leave Odin and be gone, Niflung."

The woman was startlingly beautiful, Sigyn realized, with a poise that would have shamed Frigg and sensuality she suspected Freyja herself would approve of. She fairly glided across the floor, meeting Loki's gaze. "Who are you?"

"The one you fear." Loki's voice was soft, barely a whisper, but Gudrun drew up short as he spoke.

Behind her, a pair of draugar held Odin up by the arms.

"I am the Firebringer, the first Firewalker, the teacher of men, who brought the first flame to the Lofdar."

Loki's words sent a shiver through Sigyn. What on Midgard was he even talking about? Lofdar?

Gudrun took a step back, her poise falling away, shaking her head as she pushed the younger girl behind her. "Nonsense. Loge is a myth." The tremor in her voice betrayed the hint of fear, of doubt, despite her denial. Loge—certainly a name reminiscent of Loki. If not for everything else Sigyn knew of him, she might think it a trick, a play on words.

But Loki was ancient, more ancient than even the Vanir.

So why couldn't he—

Flames surged past Sigyn, and she screamed as a vortex leapt out of the fire she had lit and surrounded Loki's hands. They swirled up his arms in spirals that encircled his chest and leapt from one hand to the other.

Sigyn's arrow slipped from her fingers and flew wide, clattering off the ice. She paid it no mind, transfixed by her lover. He spun, whipping the fire around him in wide arcs that trailed flame behind him. He flung both arms wide, and a sheet of fire launched forward, engulfing a draug and exploding along the ice wall behind in a curtain of steam.

The undead fell back from the blaze, but Loki didn't

pause. He continued his arc, and those same flames leapt back to his arms and surged forward, catching two more draugar. They detonated in an explosion that hurled Sigyn off her feet and immolated the undead creatures. Their flaming corpses flailed wildly before falling to the ground.

The flames had filled the cave with a wall of steam, thick as the mist outside. Sigyn pushed herself up, her enhanced senses allowing her to see through the vapors.

Gudrun rose to her feet, ice crystals forming in her hand. And she hesitated, as if afraid to even try to stand against Loki. She looked back at her servant, then grabbed the girl by the hand. Together, they fled past Sigyn. The Niflung princess spared a glance over her shoulder at Loki as she ran, paying Sigyn no mind.

Sigyn retrieved her bow and nocked an arrow. She could easily down the woman before she reached the bend in the cavern. More explosions detonated behind her, but Sigyn shut them out. Shut out everything but the sight of her enemy.

A human woman. And this woman, though one of the Niflungar, was still human. At least as human as Sigyn herself. Human enough to care for Odin? Was that their connection? A woman with a heart and a family and goals that were just ... different.

"They are not our concern," Loki said.

She lowered her bow to turn back to her lover, who now lifted Odin's unconscious form in his arms.

Sigyn tried to form a question but wasn't even certain where to start. She had seen him hold fire, but this went so far beyond that. Why had he not drawn upon such a power before? Was he so determined to keep the extent of his abilities secret? Why? The only thing she could think of was, by keeping his true potential hidden, he held power even over his allies.

She rushed after him, leaving the cave. Soot smeared his bare chest, but the flames seemed to have caused no harm to Loki whatsoever. She trotted beside him as he trod down the mountain, taking time to admire the tight muscles of his back and abdomen. The rapid rise and fall of his chest was the only indication his exertions *had* drained him.

"How did you do that, with the fire?"

"Loki is not the only name I have ever used."

Sigyn rolled her eyes. If she wanted answers, she'd most likely have to approach them at an angle.

"Who were the Lofdar?"

"One of the nine kingdoms descended from Halfdan the Old." Loki spoke slowly. "They warred with the Niflungar for control of Midgard, warred and won, driving out the Niflungar."

Sigyn grunted. So Loki had come to them as this ... Loge ... and taught them fire magic? Was that it? Was that how they defeated the Children of the Mist?

"You were a myth to her."

"One day, Sigyn, your name will be a myth to others. Your deeds recalled in legend, their truths warped as a dream."

She hugged herself. He was right, of course. By eating the apple, by making herself immortal, she had cast herself as a figure others would look to for ages yet to come. They would look to her, to little Sigyn, as a goddess. Her actions would inspire generations. And her mistakes? History would judge her for those forever.

In such a light, she couldn't blame Loki for choosing what to reveal with extreme care.

48

*B*eneath Idavollir lay freezing cells. Icicles dangled from the ceiling near iron bars. Thick around as Tyr's forearm. He'd tried to break them, but the jotunnar must have used it house their own dishonored. As if they knew aught of honor.

Borr had given Tyr his honor.

Frigg had taken it from him.

Just like she'd taken Gramr. Why, why, why? Why had he let the queen claim the blade? She was not meant for her. She was only for Tyr. As Tyr was only meant for her.

He beat his fists against the granite floor.

"Where are you?" he mumbled. "I need you. You know that, you *know* that. I would not abandon you."

You did.

"No! Never."

You let her take me.

"I will find you, I swear it."

Zisa stood, hands on her hips, scowling at him. "Now I am left hungry, left to wither."

Tyr crawled over to her and threw his arms around her

knees. "I'm going to take care of you, I'll always, always take care."

"Tyr?"

He looked up. Idunn stood on the other side of the bars, eyebrow raised.

Zisa. Gramr. Both vanished.

He shook himself.

Idunn sighed and sat down. Tyr crawled over to where she sat, and she reached a hand through the bars to stroke his knee. "I tried to warn you."

"They took her away from me."

"Her?"

"Give her back!" He seized Idunn's wrist and squeezed until she shrieked in pain.

Her terror hit him like icy water, and he released her. Idunn scooted away from the bars.

"I-I ..." he mumbled. "Ugh. Where is she?"

You left me. I'm hungry. You left me to starve.

Idunn rubbed her wrist and shook her head. "The dverg princes forged nine runeblades at the height of the Old Kingdoms. One blade for each of those kingdoms, one given to a prince to bind them to a pact of mutual benefit. But dvergar are greedy in their craft and prone to wretchedness, eager to punish any they feel have forced their hands. And they cursed so those blades, Tyr. I mean it was subtle at first, as long as the princes held them. All weapons of power are made by forging soul energy, and so they are, all of them ... angry, over it. But those runeblades, they affected each bearer differently. This one seems to bring out the worst in any who carry it."

"She's hungry!" He lunged forward and grabbed the bars, though his grip did not quite encompass them.

Idunn shook her head. "You're not listening to me. I

know the blade makes you feel powerful ... I mean it does make you powerful. But if you can't let it go, it will cost you everything you still value in your life. Can you not see what it's doing to you?"

Lies. Lies. She wants me for herself.

Tyr growled at Idunn. "She is ... helping me. Unlike others."

The Vanr groaned. "I am trying to help you, Tyr. I've spoken to Frigg on your behalf, tried to explain the curse. But she sees that as all the more reason to keep you bound. She won't kill you, but neither will she let you go. Still there, is hope. In time, I think might be able to—"

"Get me Gramr."

"No, Tyr, I can't do that. I would not, even if Frigg would allow it. Having that blade will only—"

He roared at her, and she backed further away, shook her head. "Tyr."

"Please ... Give her to me. I cannot lose her. Not *her*!"

Kill her.

No! Not Idunn. Never Idunn.

You love her more than me.

"That's not true!" he shouted.

Idunn opened her mouth. "What's not—"

"I love you more than anyone!"

The Vanr worked her mouth into a crooked smile. Sad smile. "You mean that?"

"Of course. Gramr, I *need* you. Come back to me."

Idunn sighed, a shudder taking her. Then she shook her head and walked away. Twice, she turned to look over her shoulder.

"Come back!" Tyr roared at her. "Come back! Bring her to me!"

I am so hungry.

Tyr beat his fists against the bars. Again and again. Until they bled. Until his bones cracked.

The bars did not break.

I am ... hungry ...

49

Though Gudrun did not fear to travel alone—what Niflung would?—she called several more draugar to her as escorts. It was just a precaution. She had no reason to fear that man. Clearly he was a sorcerer, but Loge? No. That was impossible. The fire priest would have died centuries ago. Wouldn't he?

But then, how old was her father, really? How old was Grimhild?

The ways through the mountains were long and tedious, even to one who knew the secret tunnels beneath them. Gudrun felt she'd been walking through such ice caves for an age. Odin had rejected her—again—and worse still, she had lost him. Thanks to his unexpected ally, he'd escaped. Gudrun had failed, and miserably so. One advantage to keeping to the ice caves, though, was the mist didn't seep far into the underground tunnels. Maybe Grimhild couldn't find her and Hljod down here.

She'd have to do something to appease the woman, something to make up for her failure. Certainly she couldn't let Grimhild kill Odin, but something else, aught that might avert the queen's wrath, because if Grimhild returned, and Gudrun gave her naught, Irpa would become the least of Gudrun's worries.

Fool child ... afraid of her mother ...

Her breath had grown out of control, turning into such gasps that a draug turned to look at her. She had to get hold of herself.

"How much farther?" she snapped at an undead warrior.

"At your pace ... an hour."

Hel, Gudrun hated the hollow, raspy voices of these things. Why had she even bothered to ask? Trying to distract herself by talking to the dead?

We are all dead ... here ...

"Are you all right?" Hljod whispered, as if the draug wouldn't hear the echoes off the ice walls.

Gudrun patted the girl on the shoulder. "A minor setback." Actually, it was a fairly major one. Gudrun had never given much consideration to Odin's allies, other than that thrice-damned wife of his. But he had a Vanr among his people, and now this man claiming to be Loge.

She needed to get this over with. Ve had become her only remaining asset. The Troll King had done well enough, so far, and his people could move about the mountains freely, even as they still laid siege to Idavollir. All she needed was to break the Ás fortress before Odin reached it, and thus ensure he had nowhere left to turn save her. Or did she yet fool herself?

Yes ...

No. If she could but drive away his allies, then she could have Odin, and Grimhild would have no need to punish her. That was all it would take.

Of course, controlling Ve would prove more difficult without calling upon Irpa. But he only needed to *think* she could still rely on the wraith. The Troll King might be half-witted, but he must still fear the shade. Hel, Gudrun feared Irpa.

You need me ...

She pushed herself harder, quickening her steps. The draugar had told her the Troll King had made a burrow in the next mountain. Unfortunately, there were no direct tunnels between the two, which meant traveling out into the sunlight—which the undead hated—and into the mist.

But then, mist seeped into the cave long before she reached its end. Maybe Grimhild would know where she was the moment she passed into it, or maybe it only worked if the queen was actually scrying for her. Either way, she had no time to waste.

"I don't ..." Hljod said. "I don't want to go in the troll burrow."

Gudrun pulled up short. She should have thought of that the moment she settled on this plan. One day, perhaps, the girl would have to face her fears.

Not today, though—Gudrun was not Grimhild, and she would not make her charge strong by traumatizing her.

Instead, she hugged the girl. "You're not going to. You'll wait outside, of course. Trolls won't come out into the sunlight."

"Oh."

Gudrun released the girl and continued on. She had to do this quickly, before Grimhild could interfere. It was her only chance to save Odin. Somewhere along the line—she couldn't even say when—she'd begun to fantasize about carrying his child, about what kind of mother she would be.

Better.

Since doing better as a mother than Grimhild was about as big an accomplishment as managing to wake up in the morning, she would do better than she'd done so far with Hljod.

Petty dreams ...

Predictably, the draugar grumbled about passing through daylight, even daylight obscured by the mist. It drained them of their supernatural powers, probably left them feeling strangely mortal. The fears of the undead were not her problems, though, and Gudrun demanded they follow her into the wooded vale.

The trees here had begun to warp, to twist in on themselves. Perhaps the trolls had made this a burrow for some time.

"Wait here," she told one of the draugar. "Protect Hljod at any cost." She placed a hand on her apprentice's cheek. "Don't worry. I'll be back soon."

Hljod did an admirable job of hiding her fear, though Gudrun could see it, bundled just under the surface. She patted the girl again and entered the burrow.

The moment she descended into the next cave, her draugar perked up. Odd, to think of dead men's spirits being lifted, to think of fresh confidence in their steps. Everyone had something they feared, she supposed.

In the tunnel she passed trolls, most alert, watching her with wary eyes. Were they expecting her? Didn't trolls usually sleep during daylight? And though she spied troll-wives off in the corners, naked and shivering, none of the trolls paid them any mind.

If her presence now inspired such fear in these beasts, maybe Gudrun could use it. Deeper she delved, draugar soldiers at her side. And then she entered the Troll King's new throne room, and she realized it wasn't her presence at all that inspired fear.

Grimhild stood before the Troll King, the pair of them watching Gudrun. The Niflung queen wore a mask of bone, half its jaw cracked away. A troll skull, in fact, though Gudrun had no opportunity to savor the obvious discomfort it must have brought to the trolls.

"Daughter."

"Grimhild."

Her mother frowned, her lips shadowed by the mask she wore. "I fear you have let Odin escape you a second time, daughter."

Gudrun held herself still, trying to give naught away in her visage, to reveal naught Grimhild could read, naught she could use against her.

"Imagine my surprise to learn you had made such a careless mistake. You can be a slow learner, daughter, but even you must eventually learn, yes?"

"Yes." Gudrun walked forward simply because it was far too late to back away. Maybe bravado might ... Maybe if she could just ... Just do something to keep Grimhild from punishing her again, whatever it might take.

Once, Grimhild had let a snow maiden overtake Gudrun's body for weeks, forcing her to watch her own actions without control. And even that was better than ... She couldn't let this show on her face. Every step was like walking through fire. Trying to still her trembles was like holding back an avalanche. "It seems you speak with one of my servants now."

Bold, perhaps, claiming Ve as her servant, but she had to be bold. Grimhild liked bold. Didn't she? Fuck, she was going to cry. She couldn't cry. These trolls would eat her alive at a sign of weakness. Her heart kept trying to beat its way out of her chest. Hel save her.

I will save you ...

All she had to do was let Irpa devour Ve's soul. And surrender her own body in the process. "I ... Ve! You are to move in on the Aesir. Your brother marches to meet them as we speak. Before he returns, you must break his people and destroy Idavollir. Kill them—kill Frigg." Without his wife holding him back, Odin would surely turn to her, and then maybe they would *both* be spared by Grimhild. "Kill Frigg and your other brother, the berserk." Remove both from the board and Gudrun's play for his heart would be made simpler.

The Troll King chuckled, a sound that grated on her ears like someone striking rocks together. "You want me ... to kill my brother ... and my sister-in-law."

"Do you still harbor them such love?"

"I need ... payment."

"The Niflungar are rich in gold," Grimhild said. "Rich beyond your dreams, Troll King. Follow us and you will have all the payment you desire."

"Gold is ... good. But a king ... needs a royal ... wife."

Son of a bitch thought to try that again. Hadn't he learned his lesson the first time?

Grimhild looked from Ve to Gudrun and back, her lips pursed. Gudrun's own mouth dropped open. No. Even Grimhild could not ... Not that. Not *that*. She *would* let Irpa possess her fully before she allowed that to happen.

"M-mother?"

Could her own mother sell her as a troll-wife? It was impossible. She was heir to the Niflung throne, and Grimhild could never tolerate the such a stain upon her own honor.

Grimhild raised an eyebrow. "Mother now, is it, daughter?" Then she turned back to Ve. "You will do as my daughter commands, Troll King. When the Ás queen is dead, you will have your reward." At that, Grimhild turned and strode from the burrow.

Gudrun chased after her, not willing to be left alone down there. "You cannot be serious."

"I told you long ago, daughter. Your sex is a weapon. Wield it, or have it wielded against you."

"And for that lesson you'd have your own daughter left as a troll-wife?"

Grimhild shrugged. "If your trench were half so precious and unique as you seem to think it, Odin would still be in your bed, and we would not be having this conversation. A sorceress must do whatever it takes to garner power, Gudrun. Lying down with a troll is not like to be the worst thing you ever do, if you live long enough." Her mother gave a passing glance to Hljod, then motioned to the draugar. "Come. It is past time I took care of things myself."

Gudrun's warriors abandoned her without a second look.

That was the lesson. Now, as soon as the sun set, she would be at the mercy of the trolls. Without calling on Irpa or the draugar, she could not protect herself, much less Hljod, from an army of trolls. True, she might use the Art of Mist to hide herself and hide from them, but she could not maintain that over Hljod for long, and, in any event, she would then find herself possessed by Snegurka. Which meant unless she threw herself upon Grimhild's mercy, clung to her skirts for protection, she would lead Hljod back to the very urd she'd tried to save the girl from.

But Grimhild was right about something else. Even if Ve had taken her—and she doubted Grimhild would truly let her family be so dishonored—it would not have been the worst thing Gudrun had ever lived through.

"I hate you," she whispered into the mist.

And then she took Hljod by the hand and followed after Grimhild.

50

When Odin asked how they had reached him, Loki had told him about the swan cloaks. Sigyn had thought her lover wanted to keep these magic tools a secret, but part of her was glad he revealed the truth.

Now Odin slumped against the mountainside, cradling the shards of his broken sword like he held a babe in his arms. Considering the sword had helped slay a dragon, Sigyn suspected Frigg would forgive Odin for breaking it, but the man didn't seem to see it that way. According to the story, the blade had been a gift to Sigyn and Frigg's father during the Njarar War, granted by King Nidud of Njarar, and strong enough to last generations. Neither her father, nor the long dead king probably ever expected it would find as much glory as it had.

Either way, they needed to pass these mountains with as much haste as possible. Terrifying as the ice river had been, at least it had offered a swift route through the Sudurberks. Even if Odin was not so weakened by his ordeal, it would have been a long trek. And Odin's injuries were far from the only change wrought in him, and had he claimed to be a man twice his true age, Sigyn suspected most would believe him. His blond hair had gone white, his face creased. Whatever those sorcerers had done to him, it had taken his youth from him, though he might yet live forever, thanks to the apple.

"I have had more visions," Odin said. The king turned a rosy gold ring over and over in his fingers. The thing was carved in the likeness of a swan, strange and beautiful.

Loki nodded, not taking his eyes off the fire. "I once told Sigyn that prescience is a complex burden. I'd offer the same advice to you."

"When I was a child, I used to dream of dragons. Mighty serpents, consuming the World. Dragons of flame and sea and terrible, terrible rage. I thought it ... prophecy. A foreboding that one day I would inherit Gungnir. It makes me wonder if I had some bare hint of the Sight even back then."

Loki shrugged. "Perhaps you did. And perhaps you dreamed of dragons for other reasons ..."

"I killed that linnorm. It is done." The king tucked the ring inside a pouch.

"Perhaps. Or maybe what you think the culmination of prophecy is merely a step on the path. Some would say a man's whole life is woven at the moment he is born, maybe even before. Your parents made choices, but those choices were based on the reality given them by the choices of their parents and so on and so on. Such that, every decision, perhaps, becomes one of necessity. Of Fate—urd. Or so some believe."

"I refuse to believe our choices amount to naught."

"That's not exactly what Loki implied," Sigyn said.

"Your man claims our urds are already decided. I will make my own future, and Hel take the plans of any who think to spin my urd. I want to understand what I see so I can control it, change it."

Loki chuckled, though the sound was empty of any humor. "I know that feeling all too well."

Sigyn frowned, unsure what to make of that. Loki felt trapped by his own prescience?

"Can you bring me back to our people?" Odin asked.

Loki shook his head. "A swan is not equipped to carry a man."

Now she had to hide a smile at the mental image. No, they couldn't carry Odin, and at this rate, whatever battle the Aesir faced would be long finished before their return. That left a single, obvious answer, much as she detested the idea. "I can go and send Sleipnir for you."

Loki looked up at the sky above them, though what he saw she couldn't say. He didn't seem surprised by her offer. Prescient insight? Perhaps he had seen this in the flames, back in the cave, or even before that. "Sigyn, I cannot leave Odin alone in his condition. The Niflungar are still in these mountains, hunting him."

"I know. That's why it has to be me."

Odin swallowed. "Brother. I hate to separate you from your woman, but she is right. With Sleipnir, I could reach our people in days. Just enough time for me to heal. We have to look to the rest of the Aesir. I-I've seen things, battles with trolls, constant battles every night. I see our people dying in droves, dying and wondering where I am."

Sigyn shifted, uncertain what to say. Odin had inherited the Sight from Frigg, but he seemed to be seeing the present rather than past or future. All she could say for certain was he was right—the Aesir needed their king. By Freyja, they needed a miracle. But then, had she not witnessed a miracle down in those ice caves the day before? Her lover had wielded fire as a weapon unlike aught she had seen or imagined or even ever heard tale of.

Loki shook his head slowly. "What you see is true enough, brother. But ... be careful with the Sight. It is so easy to lose yourself in dreams and visions. Life is right now, wherever you stand that at very moment."

Odin grunted, but Sigyn couldn't tell if it was in acknowledgement of Loki's point, or refusal of it. Either way, he gave no other answer.

"I need to say goodbye alone," she said, and dragged Loki away by the hand.

"I know you can do this," he said once they were out of earshot. "Still I fear to send you alone."

"What you can do with fire would stagger skalds and put völvur to shame. Why haven't you stopped the draugar and the trolls yourself? Why not go and take the fight to the Niflungar?"

Loki shook his head sadly. "My power has its limits too, Sigyn. All power does. And part of the power you saw me wield yesterday was in the fear the Niflungar felt toward me and toward the unknown. If I were to step into the open and use all I know, all I can do, I might win us a day, yes, but after that day, they would know my limits and account for them. Had the Niflung woman known of me before, maybe I would not have been able to overcome her. We have to choose our actions with care."

"To get to the future we have to live through the present."

"The sorceress you saw in the ruins—her power was but a shadow of that wielded by Grimhild, the Niflung queen. And now she will know I am among the Aesir and will take countermeasures."

Sigyn pressed her hands to Loki's chest, still bare since

she had burned his shirt. Was he saying this Grimhild was a threat even to him? The other day Loki had seemed invincible, like some ancient fire god. But then, he had just admitted his power had limits. "What countermeasures?"

"I cannot say, and until her course is clear, I dare not act directly. I must know her moves before I make mine. She has a tome, an unspeakably ancient book written in blood and marked with the glyphs of countless spirits. Her ancestors used that tome to wreak havoc across the World, and despite all efforts many made to destroy it, the unholy book remains. And with it, she can lay down curses you cannot imagine, Sigyn."

"Where did this book come from, then?"

He shook his head and clasped her hands in his own. "An Era long past. What matters is this—with the secrets therein she can raise and command the draugar, even across great distances. And, if she grows desperate enough, there are yet worse denizens she could call forth from Niflheim or elsewhere."

The warmth of his hands was a comfort, if a small one. Impossible though it seemed, Loki appeared afraid of this woman. She withdrew her hands and pulled his face down to hers, then kissed him on the lips. "Don't worry. I'll send Sleipnir to Odin. Then you fly back to me."

She tried to pull away, but he yanked her back to face him. "Sigyn! Do not take risks, not now. I can't lose you, not … Just be careful."

Sigyn winked at him. Always nice to hear he needed her as much as she needed him. She slipped from his grasp, then pulled on the swan cloak.

The moment she took to the skies, she reveled in it. So free.

❧

HIGH ABOVE THE mountains she flew, her enhanced eyes cutting through the mist and revealing her way. Revealing also the camp of draugar hiding in the hills just beyond the Sudurberks. Her people had no idea how close those things had drawn to them.

At nightfall, Sigyn had to stop and rest, at least for a time. She dared not rest long, with time grown so short. On she flew, until she spotted the fortress, beset once again by trolls.

Sigyn landed beside Frigg, who stood on the ramparts, vainly trying to comfort her people. Her sister spun as she landed, clearly shocked to see a swan here. There was a time to hide powers, and a time to act swiftly. Sigyn removed her hood and rose in human form.

All around her, women gasped. Frigg herself stood, mouth agape, eyes wide.

Sigyn rushed over to her half sister and embraced her.

"Odin?" Frigg mumbled.

"He lives. Loki is with him, out in the mountains, and I've come back to send Sleipnir to him."

Sigyn spoke softly, her words only for Frigg's ears. At them, her sister nearly collapsed in her arms, trembling. Hot moisture rolled down Sigyn's cheek. Gods above, Frigg was crying. Frigg!

Sigyn looked around the fortress without releasing her sister. Far fewer men remained than when she had left. Too few.

"We cannot hold out much longer," Frigg whispered. "I don't know what to do. The trolls have renewed their press."

Strong as Frigg was, Sigyn still shouldn't have been surprised. For far too long her sister had had to be the font of strength for all the Aesir, unable to share her fears. And in this situation, anyone would have been pushed near the breaking point. If Sigyn didn't do something soon, Frigg and the rest of her people would be pushed *beyond* that point.

"All will be well," Sigyn whispered. "Tell the people Odin rides to their aid." She gave Frigg a final squeeze, then raised her hood and flew down the stairs, seeking the horse.

The eight-legged monster steed had joined the warriors standing against the trolls just beyond the main gate, his many hooves trampling the monsters, able to crack even their thick skulls.

Sigyn once again resumed human form and shouted for the horse. "Sleipnir!"

She had not truly thought her voice would carry over the chaos of the battle, but the horse turned and ran toward her. She caught his muzzle in her hands and stroked it. It was not so long ago her greatest ambition had been to understand the nature of this creature. How much had changed in the past moons.

"Can you understand me?"

The horse snorted.

"Good." She pointed to the mountains. Human eyes could not have seen so far, certainly not through the mists and darkness, but Sigyn could see. "Odin is there, wounded. Keep a straight course and you'll find him. Loki is with him, waiting for you. Will you help them?"

Sleipnir snorted again, then took off at a full gallop, blanketing Sigyn in a dusting of snow. His form blurred past the battle. Snow churned under his hooves in a curtain that marked his passing. He covered ground even faster than Sigyn could fly.

Off to save his beloved Odin. Odin would ride into this chaos, risking everything to save his people. And it would not be enough. Grimly, Sigyn watched trolls kill more of her people.

They were going to fail.

Odin's return might rally them against the trolls, but an army of the undead approached, led by Grimhild, the sorceress even Loki feared. Powers far beyond the ken of the Aesir converged on them, and Frigg's fragile calm was a window into the shape of her people as a whole, apt to break on the next charge.

Sigyn had told Frigg that all would be well, but that was a lie. It was not going to be well. Not while the sorceress queen led her forces against them. Not while she wielded the curses Loki so feared.

But when Sigyn had been afraid, Loki had come to save her. Now it was her turn. In her flight, Sigyn had seen the Niflung camp. Their queen would be among that army.

Sigyn had destroyed any hope of a quick retreat across the sea. In refusing to do as Loki had bid, she had cost the Aesir an alliance with the sea jotunn. But she could do better than that, could be worthy of Loki and the others' trust. She could save them all.

She donned the swan cloak and took back to the air. Tired as she was, still she had one more thing to see to.

If Grimhild's power came from some dark tome, it was time to deprive the sorceress queen of that book.

51

*W*ind whipped against Odin's cheeks as Sleipnir charged through the hills. Miles swept by in moments, but he dared not slow his mount. Not now, not when every passing instant brought his people closer to destruction. Never had he pressed the eight-legged horse so hard. But Sleipnir understood the need, of that Odin was certain.

Loki had all but called Odin's need for visions of his father's life a weakness. How had the man known what Odin was doing? Visions of his own? It didn't matter. Odin had to see, had to feel. It was all he had left. All there was …

And as Borr, he was connected, still whole.

⁂

BORR KNELT BESIDE HIS FATHER, Buri, whose blood seeped into the snow. Raiders in the night and a spear to the gut would lead to a long, painful passing, even a glance told Borr that much. And he could have sworn the spear had ripped out his own heart.

"You'll be fine, Father," he mumbled, clutching the man's hand. It had already grown clammy.

"I'm ... not daft, Borr."

Borr choked on his words, unable to speak, unable to even think. This couldn't happen. Not now, not so soon. Bestla was due in a moon. Father would be a grandfather, would hold Borr's own child in his arms as he must have held Borr long ago.

"A-are you ...?" Borr tried to ask, then shook himself. He couldn't waste these last moments, but he had to know. "Do I make you proud?"

"Always," his father said. "Do I, you?"

"What?"

His father sputtered, choking. "It is ... our children we must ... do right by, boy. Do I ...?"

Borr could no longer hold back a sob. "Beyond words."

❧

ODIN BLINKED AWAY his own tears. His father had watched his grandfather die. Had felt all the same things as Odin. Had lamented never letting his father hold his firstborn. It was all the same. All a circle, all for naught ... All for ... for children. *It is our children we must do right by.*

And those words had guided every day of Borr's life.

At last he had no choice but to slow, as Sleipnir passed into the forests. Odin charged past a troll, lopping its head off with a slash of Gungnir, never breaking his stride. On and on Odin rode, until he brushed through the lines of his own people.

The Aesir paused mid-battle, all looking to him as he rode through. They had taken the fight out to the trolls, knowing the fortress would be breached in any event. They needed him. Odin turned, rearing Sleipnir up and thrusting Gungnir into the air. Almost as one, the Aesir joined his war cry.

"Fight! Brothers and sisters, fight as you have never fought before! Tonight trolls shall fear men!"

They could not afford to break now. To prove his point, Odin charged forward, impaling another of the rocky monsters. His people followed his charge, pressing against the trolls that beset them, though the creatures probably took a score of warriors down for each monster that fell.

The valkyries would be busy this night.

But Odin had seen glimpses of these battles in his dreams, in his nightly terrors while he'd waited for Sleipnir. His people were losing, breaking. He'd seen the gates of Idavollir torn down, the chains broken. Tonight or the next night or the night after, the trolls would overcome the Aesir. Fear, hopelessness, they had worn away at the once proud warriors, draining them of the will to fight. Odin had to return that will to his people, or they were lost.

It is our children we must do right by.

And had Borr?

Beyond words. Odin could only dream of making Thor as proud of him, of being the hero to his own child his father had been to him.

"There!" Odin shouted, pointing to a pair of trolls smashing through his people in the distance. "Your brothers need you! Will you abandon them in their hour of desperation? Will you let them fall alone?"

Another war cry was his answer, and the Aesir charged forward, rushing to defend the others. No longer were they loosely held together tribes, ready to break over old hatreds. Now they were men, men clinging together against the horrors of the mists.

That was what Odin needed them to be. And the Aesir needed him to be a symbol. They needed a victory, and they needed it now. Odin did not join the renewed charge, instead kicking Sleipnir forward through the forest. Trolls did not fight as a united front, not like this. Their godlike leader was all that held them together, and, without the Troll King, without ... Ve ... they would not hold their kingdom together.

And that meant Odin had no choices left to him. For an age he had held on, unable to let go. He'd marched on Vanaheim convinced he could save Ve.

But Ve was lost.

Round the forces he charged, cutting into trolls as he passed them, letting all his people see he had returned, but ever searching. Hunting for the one foe that could put an end to this.

The Troll King advanced on Odin's people in a slow, determined gait.

Ve, a son of Borr. Odin's brother. His true *brother*. And because of the Niflungar, Odin no longer had the choice to honor that legacy. He kicked Sleipnir into a gallop, cutting Ve off.

Now Ve leapt forward, slamming both hands downward. Sleipnir's sheer speed alone saved the horse. Ve's fists beat into the snow, flinging up a blinding curtain of it. Odin jumped down from his horse and slapped it away.

This was between him and his brother.

He set Gungnir. Twice before Odin had fought Ve and been unable to kill him, unable to harm his brother. "Come to me! Finish this."

Ve snarled at him. Then he bounded forward, snatching up a fallen tree trunk nigh to ten feet long.

"Oh, fuck," Odin mumbled.

Ve swung the tree with both hands. Odin dropped to the ground and slid under the club. Ve's weapon slammed into another tree, not only snapping the end off the club, but splintering the tree itself. The impact barely slowed the Troll King. He immediately reversed his swing, slapping at the ground repeatedly.

Odin rolled to one side and then the other, desperately trying to regain his feet, but unable to do so under the onslaught. Ve bellowed at him, snarling like an animal. Odin scrambled away, ducking behind another tree.

His hiding place exploded into shards of wood the next instant. It gave Odin just enough time to regain his footing and back away. Through the shattered trunk, Ve grinned at him. He grasped one hand on each end of his club and heaved, snapping it into two pieces. Then he advanced on Odin wielding two four-feet-long clubs.

Odin leveled Gungnir. This was not going to be good.

"Odin!" Hermod shouted, the warrior charging toward him.

"No!" Odin held up a hand to forestall Hermod. "I have to do this myself."

Ve had hesitated at Hermod's approach—or the warriors the man led—then grinned when the man slowed.

"Is this what you want, little brother?" Odin demanded.

Ve was gone. Gone forever. As Borr was gone. As long as Odin clung to them, he would never truly be able to live, never truly be what those who were left needed. Hope had died a long, slow death. And from the ashes of its pyre ... Odin had hope still, hope for Thor, hope for the future. *It is our children we must do right by.*

Because Buri lived on in Borr and in Odin and in Thor. As Odin would live on in Thor's children one day.

Ve leapt forward, swinging both clubs together, intent on

crushing Odin between them. Odin dove into a roll and came up just behind Ve, jerking Gungnir up in an arc. The dragon spear's blade bit through Ve's calf and the troll toppled forward, wailing.

As part of Ve would live on, for he was the blood of Odin and Odin's children.

"I am sorry, brother." The Niflungar had left him no choice. None. More than aught he had wanted to save his little brother. He would have given his own life for it—but not the life of his son. Not the lives of his people.

Odin *must* be the hero to his son.

The Niflungar had tried to sway him, to corrupt him, to destroy his very soul. They had proved they would do aught to break him, to sway him to their vile goddess. But Odin had seen through their ways. And still, he could not even begin to quantify the many secrets Gudrun had taught him. Or the things he had learned from watching the Niflungar.

Odin thought himself above them, beyond their corruption. But the truth was, he'd do *aught* to save his son.

The Troll King rose, eyes narrowed, and turned on Odin.

So many times, Odin had seen the Niflungar surround themselves with the mist, reach out and call it upon them like a cloak. He did not have a Mist spirit bound to him, but Audr might hold similar powers.

Yes ...

And Odin stepped into shadow, calling it around him like a shroud that settled on his shoulders with the chill of the grave. The wraith inside clawed its way to the surface, strengthening its hold on his heart, even as its power drew him across the Veil for the barest instant.

Ve suddenly pulled up short.

To his eyes, Odin would have vanished into the mist, becoming all but invisible. Odin's brother spun, wildly swinging at the vapors. Random blows, easy to avoid. Odin strode forward, crossing back into the Mortal Realm behind Ve while swinging Gungnir. His attack tore open a vicious gash along his brother's back. The troll tried to turn, and Odin swept his spear up again, tearing an even deeper gouge along Ve's chest.

Maybe he should end it. A solid thrust to a vital spot, and this fight would be finished. One solid thrust to neck or chest, and the battle would be done. Ve would be gone.

Ve was *already* gone.

Without their king, the trolls might have no kingdom, but they would still rampage and wreak havoc among the Aesir and the natives of Valland both.

Instead, Odin slammed the butt of his spear into the troll's nose, breaking it. The Troll King stumbled backward, clutching his broken face and whimpering. Black blood poured out from between his rocky fingers. Odin's chest clenched at seeing his brother thus, but he needed to be absolutely certain his point was made.

Rather than go for a vital spot, Odin rammed Gungnir into Ve's shoulder. His brother flailed in pain, nearly yanking the spear from Odin's grasp.

"Enough!" Odin roared at him, jerking his spear away. "Take your people and be gone, Troll King. You cannot win." He needed to do more than kill the Troll King. He needed their leader to send them away, drive them away for good.

The Troll King bellowed into the mist. Still not broken, and that meant the trolls would remain a threat to the Aesir, to Thor.

Odin needed to send a message to all trolls that something much more powerful than themselves guarded the Realms of man. He needed to make a statement that would not be forgotten.

He set his jaw. With a single, swift swipe of Gungnir, he severed the Troll King's nose and cut out his right eye. Ve was gone. Ve was *gone*, forever lost. Odin advanced on the Troll King, who had fallen to his knees, clutching his face and wailing.

Maybe the other trolls would turn on their king, kill him in his weakness. Odin could do naught about that. He had to make his point. "Go back to the Jarnvid and do not venture forth again. Midgard is claimed for Mankind from this day forth. Trespass at your peril. You are banished from these lands, troll!"

The Troll King actually whimpered, then looked up. His eyes held defiance or desperation. "No," he said in a rocky grumble.

"Do not force me to kill you, brother."

Ve stumbled to his feet, staring down at Odin. "Do … Release me …"

Odin faltered. Ve wanted to die? The Troll King spread his arms as if inviting the final stroke, or reminding Odin to acknowledge the monster he had become.

"Release …"

Odin gripped Gungnir so tightly his hands hurt. "Brother."

Ve reached out a rocky claw. "Live forever … No release …"

It is our children we must do right by.

Urd. Odin screamed defiance at the urd he saw before him.

Every decision, perhaps, becomes one of necessity. Of Fate—urd.

Roaring, Odin thrust Gungnir through Ve's heart.

❧

THE TROLLS BROKE with the death of their king, and Odin suspected they would not return to trouble the Aesir again. Through dark tunnels, they would disperse in small groups, some returning to the Jarnvid, other packs preying on the men of Valland and Hunaland. Given the choice, he might have hunted every last one of them down and put an end to their vile, foul race, but no such choice lay before him.

He had broken the trolls, yes, but their Niflung masters remained. Ve's blood stained Odin's hands, but Grimhild and Gjuki had forced him into making that final blow. For that, Odin would never forgive them. For that, he would tear down their ancient halls and ensure a final, tragic end to the last of the Old Kingdoms.

He fair trembled with wordless rage.

Now you begin to fathom ... hate ...

Yes. So he had. Grimhild and Gjuki had made of him a kinslayer. No forgiveness existed for such a crime, so much worse the urd of those who necessitated it.

Odin stalked back to the fortress to find Frigg. She stood in the great hall, clutching Thor to her breast. Odin placed a hand on Frigg's cheek, then slipped Thor into his arms. How long had he been gone? Already the boy seemed to have grown. One day, Thor would be a mighty warrior, tall and strong. Odin could see it already. Given the chance to grow up, the chance to reach maturity. Thor had Borr's red hair. Blood bound them, generation after generation, a connection that extended beyond time, beyond life, beyond death ... and beyond words.

Odin would do right by his son. He would make Thor proud, as proud as Borr had made him.

And Odin would see his son grow up in the light and warmth of spring, free of these cursed mists.

The only way he was going to be able to do that, the only

way he could be free to turn his gaze on Vanaheim, was to face the Niflungar. Gjuki and Grimhild and, if need be, Gudrun. They would die for all they had done.

For if he did not strike down Grimhild, the Niflungar would regroup and come after the Aesir again. And again. Ever pressing Hel's relentless agenda. Unless Odin took the fight to them.

Odin rocked Thor in his arms. Blood from his hands trickled onto the babe, but Thor just cooed.

Odin kissed his son on the forehead then handed him to Frigg.

"Where are you going?" she demanded.

They were out there, plotting, watching. He could feel them now.

"To war."

52

*G*rimhild led Gudrun back to a tent guarded by her Bone Guard, a squad of four draugar decked in carved bone armor. Grimhild's elite, most trusted servants. Once, centuries ago, these draugar had been a prince and his elite warriors among the Bragnings. Grimhild had used the mists to bind their corpses, bind their souls. She had built her personal guard out of the remnants of her enemies, forcing them into the ultimate blasphemy of betrayal. But then, Grimhild probably thought it poetic justice for those foolish enough to oppose her, now damned, denied peace even in death.

The lead draug, Prince Álf—so named for his once-fair complexion like the liosalfar—glowered at them as they entered. He always glowered, eyes glimmering red despite the lack of any fire to reflect. In life, she had been told, his hair had been like silken gold. Now what remained of it was a clumped mass of gray and white. Did Álf hate Grimhild as much as Gudrun did? Or had his hatred of all life—his very nature as draug—so altered his perceptions he no longer cared for his fallen brethren or former existence?

Hljod followed behind Gudrun and, on entering the tent, actually clutched her wrist, as if expecting her to protect her from the draugar or Grimhild. As if Gudrun could protect herself.

"The draugar are finally gathered," Grimhild said. "I did not truly expect the Aesir to overcome the trolls, but no matter. When the sun sets, Álf will lead a renewed siege. Those barbarians are accustomed to fighting brainless trolls and will not be prepared for foes who can use tactics, bows, or shields."

"And you think that will be enough?"

Grimhild offered her about the cruelest smile Gudrun had ever seen. "With Odin returned? Perhaps not. But then again, I have a surprise for his people and a special one for him. Your father saved a great deal of his blood, more than enough to establish a sympathetic link."

A link for a curse. Hel. Grimhild would make Odin suffer beyond endurance. And maybe he deserved it. Hljod was right about everything. He would never love her, and Gudrun's desire to keep him probably had much to do with spite toward Grimhild.

Kill him ...

"Álf," Grimhild said. "The tome."

The draug removed Grimhild's book from a satchel, placing it on the fur mat before her. Gudrun sat in front of Grimhild. Much as she wanted to be away from the queen—to say naught of her Bone Guard—if Grimhild wasn't going to send her away, she could hardly pass a chance to look at this tome. The grimoire was said to contain the secrets of Hel, the truths of the Otherworlds, and all the power at Grimhild's command. The queen rarely allowed anyone, save herself or Álf, access to the book. Even Gudrun's father said he had never read it.

Grimhild paused over the book, flipped a few pages, paused again. Gudrun tried to read it without making it obvious, even as Álf stared at her.

Kill them all ... Take the book ...

Gudrun almost snorted at Irpa's absurd suggestion. Grimhild would have her flayed for even thinking such folly.

It was hard to make aught of the writing and diagrams in the tome, not least because it seemed written in several hands, with annotations made by numerous sorceresses over the centuries, some probably from Grimhild herself. Other parts seemed recorded in Supernal itself, the language of spirits, which to the uninitiated, seemed little more than unnerving gibberish. A sorceress might uncover meanings therein, but she could also destroy her own mind in so trying.

"Hmmm. We will need a sacrifice to fuel such a curse." The queen peered around Gudrun's shoulder. At Hljod.

The girl started to back away, releasing Gudrun's wrist.

Before Gudrun could say aught, another of the Bone Guard snared the girl's shoulder and drove her forward.

"Wait!" Gudrun said. "Wait, this is my apprentice."

Grimhild scoffed. "An unworthy peasant bitch?"

"I have already begun inducting her into the mysteries."

The queen waved her comment away as it meant naught.

Gudrun's mind raced. By feeding her soul to some vile spirit to power her curse, Grimhild would condemn Hljod to a urd even worse than she had endured at Ve's hands. As a troll wife, she'd have suffered the abuses to her body, true, but death would have ended that. Nevertheless, the trolls had heaped more anguish upon the girl than anyone ought to bear, and Gudrun would have killed them for it, could she have done so.

"The trolls …"

"What?"

"The trolls failed the goddess and broke away like cowards."

"They are beasts."

Gudrun nodded. "Beasts—with the souls of men. Punish them even as you achieve your ends."

Grimhild smirked. "Clever." She looked to the other Bone Guard. "Take your brethren and bring me a living troll. Several, if you can."

The draug released Hljod—who grabbed Gudrun's wrist again—then ducked out of the tent.

She had spared her apprentice—for now—but Odin would still suffer, maybe more than he deserved. And in the end, much as Gudrun hated it, Grimhild would win. She would accomplish all she had set out to do and make the Aesir suffer for ever daring to stand in her way. The Aesir who had, in their own way, made Gudrun suffer.

Kill them …

No, Gudrun would not kill them.

But maybe it would be better if they were all dead, wiped from Midgard, their souls cast down into the Roil. And, knowing Grimhild, that would very soon come to pass.

53

*S*omewhere, far away, Gramr called for him. Her voice had grown dim, weary. A weak echo in Tyr's mind. Because of the others, Tyr had abandoned her.

He had betrayed her.

Or the Aesir had betrayed him.

Someone was coming now, but they didn't have her. He'd have felt if she was with them. He knew her song.

A great many men trailed down the stairs into this dungeon.

Tyr rose to his feet. Maybe Frigg had come to decide his urd. If so, he'd meet that urd with pride. With what little honor remained of all Borr had granted him.

The procession stepped into the torchlight, and Frigg was there, an old man beside her. A man somehow familiar but ... Impossible!

"Son of Borr," Tyr said. Alive, and finally returned. Unless Tyr's waking visions had grown into full Mist-madness.

Odin took in the cell, then looked to Frigg, then Jarl

Arnbjorn beyond. "Why is my champion bound here in times of war and desperation?"

Frigg frowned. "You know why."

"I know he broke through a line of trolls and saved all your lives."

"He also broke numerous laws," Arnbjorn said. "A valorous deed does not excuse a criminal one, especially not in a thegn. No one doubts Tyr's valor, my king, but he lacks respect for authority or law."

Odin scowled, turned back to Tyr. "Is this true?"

"My loyalty has always been to the line of Borr."

Now Odin looked to Arnbjorn, then Frigg. "I have seen a great many things, beyond aught any of you suspect, and other things, other places, which not even the völvur would dare to look. Therein lies madness and clarity both, and the road to understanding sacrifice. Now we stand at war with an ancient people that has seen as far as I have and holds power beyond your imagining. Should we overcome them, still we must face down the gods themselves. I will *not* face such battles without my greatest warrior at my side." He waved to a soldier. "Release Tyr immediately."

The soldier rushed to fumble with the lock to the cell.

"Odin," Frigg said. "You truly intend to pardon the man for accosting one of your jarls—your brother—and for the murder of another?"

"You have stripped him of his titles and his honor. I intend to grant him the chance to reclaim them on the battlefield."

The cell opened. And Odin strode forward and clasped Tyr's arm. Tyr almost could not suppress the shudder of gratitude that swelled in his chest. His king understood. Believed in him. Odin truly was worthy of Borr's legacy.

"Somewhere out in the mist, the Niflungar watch us," Odin said.

"I have seen them."

The king nodded. "Now we must hunt them down and show them their folly in moving against the Aesir."

Tyr opened his mouth to agree.

And then shrieks of damnation echoed out of the well room. For a bare instant, everyone froze in shock and horror. Turned, even as soaking wet draugar surged out of that room. Axes, swords, shields, all raised.

The closest soldiers turned to engage them. Moved too slow. Three of them dead before anyone else had reacted.

Odin rushed forward to engage the draugar.

"My lord!" someone shouted from atop the stairs. "The dead attack the gate."

Inside and outside. How had they climbed up the icy well shaft? Didn't need to breathe, true. But no one even considered foes could manage that. Well must connect to some underground reservoir.

A draug bore down on Arnbjorn, the jarl still fumbling to draw his blade. Tyr slammed into the dead thing with his shoulder, sent it flying. The draug crashed into a pair of its brethren swarming out of the well room. Beyond, more of the creatures still crawled out of the water.

Tyr snatched up a sword from a fallen soldier. An instant later, a draug raced at him, axe high. Tyr twisted out of the way. The axe buried itself in the soldier's corpse. Tyr swiped the blade across the draug. Just seemed to annoy the creature. This was no runeblade.

"I need Gramr!" he shouted at no one in particular. Another swing of his sword, another useless wound to the draug's chest.

"Go for the necks!" Odin shouted from behind him.

The draug immediately raised his shield to block any such attempt. So Tyr grabbed the shield and shoved, drawing on all his power. Three steps, then three more, he pushed the draug back into the well room. The one he rushed toppled over backward. Its fellows immediately clambered atop it. Their attacks drove Tyr back.

Odin thrust Gungnir over his shoulder, catching a draug in the face. That one crumpled into a heap, a true corpse once more.

Another slashed at him. Tyr dodged away, snatched up a fallen shield. He blocked more blows on that. Finally managed to twist behind the draug and caught hold of it by the mail. He flung it at the wall. The impact barely slowed the creature. But Tyr grabbed it by the skull and smashed that against the icy wall. Repeatedly, until it fell still.

More and more of the draugar had fallen to Odin. Tyr approached behind one and cleaved through the back of its neck. Draug dropped like a stone. Another bore a helm, so Tyr slammed the sword's pommel atop it. Staggered it. Other men tore into it. Arnbjorn drove a blade through its gleaming eye socket, and it stilled.

And then there were no more.

Corpses—many of them fresh Ás corpses—littered the well room and the hall beyond it. Maybe a score of draugar had come up this way. Hard to judge exact numbers. More would be outside, trying to breach the walls.

Arnbjorn clapped him on the arm. "You saved my life."

Tyr nodded. He had. Not long ago he had planned to murder the man, and now he had saved him. Hadn't even thought about it. A mistake? Or maybe Odin was right ... maybe the first step in reclaiming his honor.

"There are more to face outside," Odin said, looking at

Frigg. "Go and bring the runeblade. We need more weapons that can strike these creatures down."

She hesitated, then raced off, taking two men as guards with her.

Gramr. Odin would return Gramr, thanks to all the gods high and low.

§

ATOP THE WALLS, he could see the draugar spread out through the night. Not well. Not through the mist and darkness. They carried no torches and were smaller than trolls. Harder to spot. Sometimes you caught the gleam of their eyes. Sometimes the glint of weapons reflecting fires beyond the gate. Not much else.

Agilaz was up there, shooting arrows with the other archers, but not many. Had to be running low. Besides, arrows rarely slowed a draug.

Gramr would, though. She purred on his back, eager to drink the blood of the dead.

Maybe she could still prove a force for honor. Sating herself on the wretched denizens of the mist, the Niflungar and their vile allies. He need but find a way to control the rage she built in him. Bloodlust that would not be denied.

You need me.

Still couldn't be certain whether the voice was real or a delusion. Gramr was made from a soul, forged into metal. But was she really able to speak in his mind? So hard to say.

"Gungnir talk to you?" he asked Odin.

The king raised an eyebrow. "Gungnir is a spear."

Huh. Suppose that answered that. So the dverg curse on these runeblades was driving Tyr mad. And yet, even could he have given it up, they needed this sword. It could fell trolls and draugar and aught else they might face on the road to Vanaheim. Probably could slay Vanir too. He needed Gramr.

Odin pointed out into the darkness, at the horde of the dead. Opened his mouth to speak. Then wobbled in place. He dropped like his knees had given out. Tyr caught him, eased him down. The king's flesh had turned sallow, almost blue, and felt like ice. Odin trembled in Tyr's arms, shook like a frightened maid.

His eyes seemed glazed over.

Tyr looked up to call for a völva. Dozens more of the men up here had fallen as well. Archers, just dropping at their post.

"Agilaz!" Olrun shrieked, kneeling by her husband's prone form.

What fell sorcery was this? How could so many men take so ill all at once? And Odin, he had eaten the fruit of Yggdrasil. Should have been immune to ordinary ills.

Tyr clasped Odin's face in his hands. "My king? My king, what do we do? Odin?"

The king shivered. Convulsed.

And said naught.

54

*A*midst the chaos of battle, no one paid much attention to a swan alighting in the trees. They ought to have, of course. What swan would fly into such a miasma of death and pain? But most people didn't notice small things, and that gave Sigyn all the advantage she needed. Taking care to make no sound, she crept out to the edge of a branch, then jumped to the next.

From up here she had a clear view of the two sorceresses. The woman she'd seen before, Gudrun, stood watching another woman, this one wearing a bone mask. The masked one stood in the center of a circle drawn with blood—marring the snow in arcane geometric designs—and marked with stones upon which runes were carved. More horrifying, bone-armored draugar guarded the pair, and a troll bound with strange chains. The masked one must be Grimhild, the book she stared down at the grimoire Loki so feared. If she was like those who had eaten the apples, she might still have some powers without it, but her curses and spells would be lost, her power crippled.

As she watched, Grimhild spoke in strange words that left Sigyn queasy, then drew a knife along the troll's throat, spilling black blood onto the snows.

What vileness the sorceress worked, Sigyn could not guess. Pity these women didn't have a fire Sigyn could just cast that book into.

From the way Gudrun stared at the battle, she must be able to see through the mists even more clearly than Sigyn. After all, these Children of the Mist wouldn't be worthy of the name if those same mists hindered them as much as mortal men.

Four draugar and two sorceresses. Even if Sigyn could bring herself to kill someone—and she wasn't certain she could—she couldn't do aught about the undead. She needed to get that book away from the women, render them powerless and put a stop to whatever curses Grimhild now worked. Odin had returned and rallied the troops, yes, and driven off the trolls, but now the draugar seemed apt to break her already beleaguered people. Maybe Loki would return soon, as well, and part of her longed to consult him. But if Sigyn's lover feared that tome, it must truly contain horrors. Now was her chance to help them all, to be the hero to them they had been to her.

Sigyn was so close she could just jump down there and grab it. And then she'd be dead before she got three steps away. Maybe that was the problem—she had already drawn too close. These Niflungar had played the Aesir, counted on the mist to hide them while they sowed chaos and fear among Sigyn's people. Fear of the unknown, fear of what they couldn't see, because fear led people to err.

A slow smile crept over Sigyn's face, and she jumped back to the other tree, as silent as Agilaz had taught her.

True, Sigyn was no warrior, but she was a hunter, and with her enhanced senses, she could prove an uncanny one. As soon as she was far enough out, she pulled the hood of her cloak back up, resuming swan form, and flew out some distance through the woods.

She landed in another tree, far from the Niflungar. Even able to see through the mist, it was too far for the sorceresses to spot. Too far for a human to see at night. But Sigyn could see. Her eyes had grown sharp as a hawk's.

From her perch she nocked an arrow to her bow, then drew it back to her cheek. All the World stilled. The mist vanished and her heartbeat slowed to a crawl. Sighting along the shaft, Sigyn first thought to put an arrow in one of the undead. Then she turned to Grimhild. This woman worried even Loki. She was the true foe the Aesir faced, wasn't she? Grimhild and Gjuki—but there was no sign of the Raven Lord in this battle. With one arrow, one shot to the heart, Sigyn could end all this.

But Grimhild was human, and though she might have been an enemy, she was a woman trying to do what she thought right. Sigyn bit her lip. All she had to do was kill this woman. Her arms shook under the strain of holding the arrow until she had to release the tension, letting the bow ease. Sigyn shut her eyes.

This woman, this sorceress, had brought the trolls and draugar down on the Aesir. She would kill them all, or worse, given the chance. Weighing her life against all the lives of the Aesir ... Sigyn had no choice.

A deep breath and she drew again. "Ullr guide your flight."

Then loosed an arrow at Grimhild. She immediately nocked another, this time sighting the lead draug. She loosed again. Her first shot flew between dozens of branches. An impossible shot through dense woods. Impossible for a human. She loosed another, this one aimed at a draug's throat.

The first arrow hit what appeared to be a solid wall of mist where it embedded. The next clattered off the draug's breastplate. As one, the undead turned in her direction, the movement enough to take the second draug out of position.

"Damn it," Sigyn whispered. At least it would draw them away from the sorceresses. "Come on. Come and get me."

The two women leapt up, shouting at the undead.

A pair of the draugar took off running toward her position. They couldn't see her. At least, she didn't think they could. Could they? "Oh. Troll shit." There was only one way to be certain. Sigyn donned her cloak and flew to another tree at an angle from the undead's approach.

They didn't change directions, kept running for her original location. Perfect.

Except that two sorceresses and two draugar still guarded the damned book, and now the undead stood, blades bared. If they thought they were being ambushed, Grimhild might take the book and run. Sigyn didn't want to buy the Aesir a day—she wanted to buy them victory. And since the sorceress was clearly protected from arrows …

She sighted again at that lead draug, this time aiming for his face. A bone helmet made the shot tricky, but if she could get an arrow into his chin, that might slow the thing down. She loosed.

And the draug moved with inhuman speed, his sword knocking the arrow out of midair.

"Son of a troll," Sigyn mumbled. *That* was different.

The undead creature looked right at her and began advancing on her position.

If she kept this up, sooner or later, one of those things *would* see her. Sigyn flew to another tree, this one closer.

"Protect us," Grimhild commanded the remaining undead. The creature fell into a close posture in front of the two sorceresses, sword ready. If it was as fast as the other one, it'd be able to stop any arrow she directed at them.

So she wouldn't shoot at them.

Sigyn flew around behind the Niflungar camp, close. So close they'd probably have spotted her if they turned, even as she crouched behind a tree. But they were so fixated on where she'd been, they didn't even look.

Not daring to breathe, Sigyn sighted along a shaft, aiming for a tree branch above the Niflung camp. One laden with snow. She had to hit it just right, at the weakest spot. They'd hear the twang of her bow as soon as she loosed. One mistake and she was dead. But she wasn't going to make a mistake. She knew the spot.

Sigyn loosed. Her arrow thunked into the branch. It wobbled for an instant, before the shaking caused it to crack. A pile of snow dumped upon the trio. Gudrun shrieked and covered her head, clearly more shocked than aught else.

Sigyn took off at a dead run. The draug spun on her, immediately shaking off the snow. Sigyn fired a clumsy shot as she ran. The undead creature batted it away, but Sigyn didn't care. She released her bow, dropped into a slide, and wrapped her arm around the book.

Then she yanked up her swan hood and the book melted into her swan form.

The draug's sword sank into the spot where a moment before her human body had been. Sigyn took flight, swooping just over the sorceresses' heads. Predictably, the draug pulled back its next swing rather than risk hitting its mistresses.

Sigyn made as steep a climb as she was able, darting between branches and treetops.

"Hel will have you!" Grimhild shouted after her. "I will feast on your soul, you petty, foolish girl!"

55

*D*espite the heavy fighting beyond the walls, Tyr had not left Odin's side. With the gate breached, the Aesir were forced to head outside the castle. To meet the draugar in a desperate attempt to hold them off until dawn. Tyr ought to be out there with them. Ought to feed Gramr the vile creatures.

But as the king lay chilled to the bone, like to die, Tyr could not pull himself away. "I'm so sorry, my lord."

Frigg too, had not stirred, save to try different remedies. Now she set another runestone by Odin's bedside. "To ward against evil magic."

Odin did not answer either of them. Just turned over and gazed at Tyr with blank eyes.

"I promised your father I'd protect you and your brothers. Now Ve ..." Tyr grunted. Odin wouldn't want the reminder. "And Vili ... I damned nigh killed him myself." Not without cause. "And you—I know not how to fight such a foe."

"Grimhild ..." It was the first Odin had spoken since he fell. Indeed, the barest hint of color had returned to his flesh. Had the king's superhuman constitution allowed him to fight through this? Or had Frigg's runes worked so swiftly?

"My king?"

Frigg too dropped to her knees by his side. Grasped his hand.

"S-sorcery. Kill Grimhild ..."

The Niflung queen. Tyr did not want to leave here. But his king had given him a command. A target.

A feast for Gramr.

Tyr rose. "As you command, my king. Consider the sorceress dead already."

Odin gave no further answer, staring instead at his wife.

§

THE SORCERESS QUEEN did not present herself as a target. So instead, Tyr had cleaved and hewed his way through a legion of the dead. He had lost count of how many draugar had fallen to Gramr. Many dozens, at the least. He had to call on the apple's power just to keep standing.

To keep rushing forward.

Cut a draug's legs out from under it. Cleave through the falling thing's skull.

On and on.

And then, a draug in a bone helm stood before him. Its blade dripped with fresh blood. A wake of Ás corpses behind it.

"Champion ..." the thing rasped. Its voice sounded hollow, echoing through Tyr's head. "Join us ..."

Tyr advanced, Gramr high. "I'm not ready to join the ranks of the dead."

"Nor were we," the draug said, circling Tyr. "No vote was tallied. Still we are ... bound."

"Then allow me to end your suffering."

"There is no ... end ... Eternity is the punishment ... for failure."

Tyr advanced toward this undead. "Difference is, I'm not going to fail."

He attacked, and the thing fell back, giving ground freely, though never allowing Tyr even a small gap to take advantage of.

The bone draug launched a series of attacks so fast Tyr could barely keep up. Blow after blow he parried on Gramr, but one slipped through. Tore a gash along his cheek. He tried to counter, but the draug kicked him in the chest. The force felt apt to cave in his ribs. Sent him stumbling over backward.

"I too ... was once a great man," the draug said. "Prince Álf ... they called me. Even kings ... fall to her sorcery."

Tyr gasped, tried to suck breath through bruised lungs. Gramr gave him strength. "You want me to fail. To excuse your own failure. I have Gramr."

Álf chuckled, the sound so vile it felt like rats gnawing on Tyr's skin. "I too once bore a runeblade. Dainsleif, the great blade ... relic of the Bragnings. Still I fell ... Even as the Niflung blade will turn upon you ..."

Tyr glanced at Gramr. "Maybe you were simply weak."

Álf snarled at him and flew into another bout of lightning fast attacks. If he'd wanted to stop the draug from playing with him, it seemed he'd succeeded. Every effort was directed to parrying the unending assault Álf threw at him. Never had Tyr faced a foe so fast, so precise. In death, the draug had had centuries to perfect his sword craft.

Or else he had lost none of what he'd learned in life.

The draug's blade sheared off Tyr's mail, scraped his knee and drove him to the ground. The reverse stroke should have ended him, but Gramr jerked back into place faster than he'd have thought possible. She had not betrayed him yet.

The draug's blade caught on Gramr, and Tyr surged forward, winding and binding the two blades together rather than let Álf break away. Round and round he went, until the runeblade bit into the edge of the other sword. Tyr jerked away. With Álf's strength, he failed to tear the sword from the draug's hand. He did, however, shear a shard right out of the other blade's edge.

Immediately he lunged in, swinging overhead. Forced Álf to parry. The weakened sword snapped under Gramr's power. Álf hissed, flung the useless broken hilt at Tyr. It happened so fast the pommel caught him in the face. Sent him stumbling backward.

And then Álf tackled him. They both tumbled down into the snow. Tyr lost his grip on Gramr.

She wailed in his mind, enraged. The draug's claw-like fingers strove toward Tyr's eyes. He caught Álf's wrist, but the draug had constant strength, nigh as much as Tyr could call upon. He patted the ground, reaching for Gramr. Beyond his grasp.

Álf's other hand collided with Tyr's cheek. Twice more he beat him, then managed to snare Tyr's mail. Álf rose, pulling Tyr up off his feet, and hurled him. Tyr tumbled end over end before hitting the ground again. Rolled over.

Whole damned World was spinning. Empty stomach heaving.

He barely managed his feet again as the draug closed the

distance in three mighty strides. Álf leapt in the air. Tyr tried to dodge, as though the draug meant to slam its fists down on him. It landed beside him, however. Swept Gramr up in its hand.

No.

No, he couldn't use *her* against him.

He could not do such a thing.

It was impossible.

Álf spun then, swinging the sword to deflect an arrow flying at him out of nowhere. Tyr used the moment to shoulder-slam the draug. Álf flew several feet through the air but did not drop the sword. Damned thing didn't feel pain. Snarling, the draug came up swinging again. This time an arrow caught it in the back.

He turned to look for his attacker.

Zisa was there, nocking another arrow.

Tyr's fist connected with what remained of Álf's jaw, knocking the bone helm clean off. The head beneath was half rotted, revealing bits of skull and gleaming red eyes. Tyr swung again, but Gramr bit through the mail on his upper arm and sliced into his biceps. Everything from his shoulder down went numb, and his blow lost all power.

Not his other hand, though. Álf turned to deflect another arrow. And Tyr caught his sword wrist. Zisa's arrow smacked the draug between the eyes. It staggered backward, losing its grip on Gramr. Tyr caught the runeblade in his left hand and drove it clean through the draug's torso.

The monster fell now.

Zisa stalked over and she stomped on his skull.

She looked to him. And not quite with hatred.

Beyond her, Odin stood, leaning on Gungnir. Tyr had not slain Grimhild, but somehow the king had broken free of her sorcery.

Maybe Álf was right. Maybe Gramr would betray him in the end, maybe Tyr could never be free of her. But for now, she was a blessing.

Tyr jerked the runeblade free of the draug's corpse.

56

*G*udrun could not have fled away from Grimhild's fury fast enough. The Ás bitch had sent the queen of all bitches into an apoplexy certain to end in misery that would have made the torment of the Bone Guard pale in comparison. In her wrath—and with her curse interrupted—Grimhild had sent her entire army of draugar to slaughter the Aesir, giving over any attempt at strategy.

Nor had she seemed to care when Gudrun departed to see to the battle, or so Gudrun had claimed. Grimhild would do aught to get that book back. And why not? If it truly carried all the secrets of Niflheim, its power was perhaps unmatched in Midgard. Enough to unseat Grimhild as queen, that was certain, and perhaps enough to send the woman somewhere from which there would be no return?

Gudrun almost had to laugh. The woman had made a fool of Grimhild, and for that alone she almost wanted to thank the wench. The action would cost the Ás dearly, of course, but for the moment, it meant Grimhild was not thinking clearly. So intent on revenge she could not see the enemy right before her. Nor did Grimhild bother to consider the actual woman who had stolen the book, instead focusing on the horrors she would wrack upon her.

The girl belonged to Loge—she'd seen them together in the ice cave—so she would undoubtedly seek him out. And she, unbelievably, had the cloak of a swan maiden, gifts usually reserved for servants of the vaettir. All Gudrun had to do was scry the mists for a swan flying in the battle—no real bird would ever head into such horrors.

Searching out the swan had required her to call upon Snegurka once again. Her glyph burned on her thigh, a constant reminder of the cost of sorcery. As if feeling Snegurka eating away at her was not reminder enough. The Mist spirit strained against her will, beating at her mind in an attempt to assert control over her body and thus, attain free rein in the Mortal Realm. Gudrun swayed in place, trying to keep the vaettr under control. Sometimes, the price was worth it—sometimes, *any* price was worth victory—at least if it meant she could overcome Grimhild.

The mists before her parted as the spirit revealed the swan's position. As expected, the girl flew about the chaos, probably searching for her lover. Gudrun almost felt sorrow to deny her that reunion.

"Bring her to the ground," she commanded the Mist spirit.

The fool girl had flown low, back into the mists, probably in her desperate hunt for Loge. Grimhild couldn't understand love, and thus had failed to see how clear this girl's course had been. But Gudrun understood, had braved the Penumbra for Odin, and she knew a person would do aught to reach those they loved. Or thought they loved—for Odin was not worthy of her, and his betrayal would cost the Aesir. Gudrun would make certain of that.

Through her Sight, Gudrun watched the spirit thicken the mist around the swan until it choked, crashing to the ground. Gudrun continued forward, eyes locked on the ephemeral image the spirit revealed to her. This woman jerked her hood off, clutching at her throat, desperate for the air Snegurka had stolen from her lungs.

And with the Aesir spread thin, engaging the draugar army, no one even noticed one more body on the ground. Well, no one but Gudrun. She approached the girl and waved off the Mist spirit choking her.

"Try to fly away again and you've breathed your last."

The girl gasped, sucking in lungfuls of oh-so-precious air. Yes. Gudrun knew the feeling. Grimhild had thought it important for her to experience that suffering firsthand, to understand the utter powerlessness one felt without air. You couldn't think, couldn't act, couldn't do aught. Naught else mattered but getting one more breath. Yet another lesson she'd one day have to thank the queen for.

Gudrun knelt beside the Ás woman and yanked the cloak off her shoulders before pulling the tome from her limp arms. "You are a clever one, I grant. Drawing off Álf and the other draugar, even dunking dear Grimhild in snow. That might have been more amusing if you hadn't done the same to me." She slipped the tome into her satchel. There would be time for that later. The important thing now was making sure none of Grimhild's spies knew she had the book, and that meant keeping it from sight and using her own spirits to cover her tracks.

The girl continued coughing, trying to catch her breath.

She slipped a knife from her belt and held it to the Ás's throat. "Tell me, wench. Just who are you to think to match wits against the Niflungar?"

"Sigyn," the girl said, between coughs. Coughs she

seemed to be trying to still, considering the blade so close to her.

"And do you even know who we are? Do you realize your hubris in acting against us?"

"Gods, listen to you." She coughed once more. "Managing to accuse me of hubris while guilty of it yourself in the same breath. Do you practice that arrogance, princess?"

Gudrun frowned. The girl knew who she was. This Sigyn clearly belonged to Loge, but Gudrun didn't much like that the man knew so much of her, either.

"Yes, I know who you are, Gudrun. And, yes, I know who the Niflungar are. Men—and women—who think they're gods. In truth, you are but one more fallen kingdom, just like all the other heirs of Halfdan. Except you just don't seem to know when your time has passed. The Old Kingdoms are dead as your draugar, and like them, you are too stubborn to remain in the grave."

Gudrun's frown deepened. The Ás woman had read the thoughts right off her face. Too clever indeed. And Loge had clearly told this wench far more of the Niflungar than she had expected. Had he told all the Aesir, or just his woman?

"Clever," Gudrun repeated aloud. "But not clever enough to keep your mouth shut when you ought. You play at courage, but I can see the fear in your eyes." Gudrun was an expert in fear, of that, her mother had made damned certain. "So tell me, frightened little girl ... Why shouldn't I just slit your throat and be done with it?"

In truth, she was grateful to Sigyn for her actions. By separating Grimhild from her tome, Sigyn had dealt a blow Gudrun never could have. Embarrassing the queen was an added bonus. Under other circumstances, she might have even liked this Ás wench.

Sigyn pressed back against the tree, a futile attempt to

put more space between herself and the knife. "Well, I could have shot you—twice, in fact. Once in the ice cave and once when I stole the book."

Mercy? Gudrun hadn't even thought of it, but no arrows had targeted her. And back then, in the ruins, Gudrun had been too frightened of Loge to even consider his woman, but reflecting, she had had a bow then, hadn't she? "That just proves you are once again not half so clever as you think yourself." Gudrun shook her head. Sigyn knew far more about her and her people than someone outside their ranks ought. Maybe she was innocent, maybe Sigyn wasn't a killer. Circumstances of birth, however unfortunate, had made her an enemy.

Sigyn smirked. This bitch was reading her face again, and Gudrun didn't like that. "If you think yourself so much cleverer, princess, consider this. I *am* Loge's woman, as you well suspect. If you harm me, he will hunt you to the ends of Midgard and beyond. He and his blood brother, Odin—yes, your precious Odin—will come for you. Do you want that? Is that risk worth what small satisfaction you'd draw from spilling my blood? On the other hand, if you spare me, you win favor from both men."

Gudrun sighed. Put that way, the wench was probably right. Sigyn knew too much, but no doubt less than Loge himself. Odin's blood brother ... Hel, did Odin even know the truth about his ally? She shook her head. A question for another time. Killing this woman carried with it plenty of risk and little possible gain, and yet, Loge and Odin had both made themselves her enemies already. Sigyn had not personally done aught to earn her wrath, and Gudrun didn't believe in killing without purpose.

But neither did she much care for this girl's cocky grin. The bitch thought she could read her, princess of the

Niflungar. Manipulate her? There would be a price for that.

She leaned closer to the Ás woman. "I won't kill you."

"What?"

Gudrun sank her dagger into Sigyn's thigh.

Her shrieks of pain made Gudrun's hair stand on end. The girl fell over, clutching the wound and wailing. Gudrun hadn't ever wanted to hear another woman cry out like that again. She'd seen too much of it, felt too much of it herself. This was her mother—Grimhild! Grimhild was getting inside Gudrun, shaping her in her own image. And Gudrun would not have it. She would be a queen of the Niflungar, but not like Grimhild. Never like that.

She moved to retrieve her dagger. What if Sigyn hadn't had an apple? Gudrun had assumed she had, but ... if she removed the dagger, the woman might bleed to death before help arrived. Had she hit an artery? What in Hel's name was she even thinking?

Damn it. Damn the girl and damn herself and damn Grimhild.

The bitch queen had tried to shape Gudrun and had done so! Grimhild had made Gudrun into something cruel, something like the queen herself.

Gudrun would not be that. Not ever. Her hands trembled as she examined the wound. It didn't seem to have hit the girl's artery. She yanked the dagger free as quickly as she could, then pressed Sigyn's dress against the wound.

"Keep pressure on it."

What was she doing? Helping this Ás wench? It wasn't about Sigyn, though; it was about Gudrun, about not being Grimhild.

Gudrun pulled some herbs from her pouch, then forced them into Sigyn's mouth. "Chew it. It will help with the pain." Gudrun rose and wrapped the mists around herself, eager to be away. The other Aesir couldn't see her, she was certain, but Odin would, as might any völva and most likely Loge.

Hel, Grimhild would have been proud of her. Stabbing a frightened girl just to keep her from following. Of course, Grimhild would probably have killed the girl and then enslaved her soul. Small comfort that Gudrun was a measure better than that.

But then ... No. She had to stop thinking of Odin as a prize she might one day win. He and Loge were foes to over-come, and to face such foes, she needed every edge possible.

Neither Odin nor Loge would dare act against Gudrun while she held Loge's beloved. This pathetic, self-righteous girl might prove the key to undoing the fire priest.

"Fetch a draug," she told the Mist spirit. "Have it bring the girl back to Castle Niflung."

This Sigyn would prove even more useful than she already had.

§

GUDRUN STALKED THROUGH THE WOODS, slipping between the fighting Aesir and the draugar, then out into the deeper forest. She had to get away from here, and not just because of the Aesir. Grimhild's rage would cool, and she'd turn all her vaettir toward finding this book. Gudrun needed some-where where those spirits would not look. Somewhere Grimhild would not think to search, and she needed it in a hurry. If Grimhild even suspected her daughter had stolen the grimoire—well, Gudrun didn't want to think on that.

Where would Grimhild not look? Where would she not send her vaettir? The river? Maybe Gudrun could break through the ice and submerge the book. From stories, the book was indestructible, so it shouldn't harm it. But the current might sweep it away, and Gudrun might never find it again. The mountains perhaps, but she had not time to carry the book so far. She needed an immediate hiding place, somewhere to keep it until she could conceal it at her leisure.

And Grimhild would send her spirits to tear this forest apart looking for it. Looking for Sigyn ... Hel, maybe the girl would have been better off if Gudrun *had* killed her. Assuming Grimhild wouldn't pull her soul back from the Penumbra to torment her for her crimes. No, she'd have to convince Grimhild to spare the girl, convince her of Sigyn's value as a bargaining chip.

Sigyn didn't have the book, but if Grimhild interrogated her ... So Gudrun would need to lie, to tell her Sigyn had already admitted to turning the book over to Odin. Or, better still, to his völva wife. Yes. A völva would be the natural choice for the tome. So Grimhild would search everywhere in the Ás fortress and their camps beyond. Every tree, every rock, every ... fire? Mist spirits would not dig through the ash of a bonfire: even the memory of flame was hateful to them. And why would they? Grimhild would not even imagine her foes might burn her book. To her, it was the most precious thing on all Midgard.

Gudrun slipped into the Ás fortress. Shrouded by mist, none would see her, but the longer she took, the greater the risk. She needed to do this quickly. The Aesir had great bonfires in the courtyard, but once Gudrun approached a fire, her invisibility in the mist would fall away and the Aesir would be able to see her.

Instead, she focused on what she'd seen Grimhild do, shrouding the mist beneath her to solidness and carrying her up, far above the fire. And she let the book fall into the blaze. A few women huddling around it started at the sudden sparks that leapt out, but they wouldn't see.

A blaze of that size would cover the book in ash. Sooner or later, the Aesir would leave this fortress, and then Gudrun could return and claim what lay buried beneath the soot.

And then ... then she would have the power that once belonged to Grimhild.

57

An army of the dead swarmed over the Aesir, breaking down what little remained of their defenses after the constant battles with the trolls. A draug retained the skills of its life, meaning those who were great warriors before had become unstoppable waves of death now.

Even as Odin slew another of the undead, others charged Tyr. No finer warrior graced the Aesir's ranks, so Odin didn't fear for his friend. The bone draug Tyr had fought off not long ago seemed a leader among them, for even the dead now hesitated to face Tyr.

At least until another of the bone-helmed ones closed in on Tyr.

Odin impaled the draug before him and flung it off his spear. Ought to slow that thing down a moment. Not sparing a glance at the fallen undead, he rushed one attacking Tyr. Odin's champion dodged from side to side, barely avoiding the constant slashes, thrusts, and kicks of the undead warriors. Unlike the trolls Odin's people had become accustomed to fighting, this draug fought with controlled savagery—its strength, complemented by skill, precision.

The draug turned at Odin's approach. The thing bore armor of sharpened bone, its face concealed by a bone helm, eyes gleaming red beneath it. Even while looking at Odin, it took another swing at Tyr.

Odin lunged forward, a low strike with Gungnir, forcing the draug to fall back. Or so he expected. Instead, it leapt forward over the spear and slammed its shield into Odin's face and chest. The sudden, violent impact knocked Gungnir from Odin's hands and sent him toppling to the ground.

Dazed, Odin was barely aware of his foe spinning, swinging its sword down at Tyr. The runeblade parried, though Tyr remained on his knees. The draug's foot caught Tyr in the face, sending him sprawling. It immediately twisted and leapt back at Odin, leading with a thrust that ought to have skewered him.

Odin rolled to the side, and the draug's blade whipped around, seamlessly flowing from thrust to a slash that opened Odin's cheek. A roll carried Odin out of its reach, and it spun back to Tyr, who now launched his own series of attacks.

The distraction gave Odin just enough time to scramble over and retrieve Gungnir. Immediately he thrust the dragon spear at the undead warrior. Now the draug was forced into naught but defense, deflecting attacks with its sword, with its shield, always losing ground.

Even it must see the end approach. And yet, what Odin saw of its face revealed only more hatred, not fear. The draug was the antithesis of life, an abomination that ought to be sent back to Hel.

As are we all ...

Odin grimaced at Audr in his mind. The wraith grew ever stronger, every more maddening.

He thrust his spear again, and this time the draug did not parry. Instead, it surged forward into the spear, letting it pierce right through it. The dragon spear punched out the draug's back and, as its momentum carried the creature forward, pierced so far as to become useless in Odin's grasp. Too late Odin realized the thing's intent, as it swung its shield at him and sword at Tyr.

Again the creature's shield caught him in the face, sending him stumbling back to the ground. Everything spun, and Odin's ears were ringing.

Tyr. He had to get to Tyr.

An instant later the shield flew at him. Odin dropped flat on the ground, avoiding the projectile. As he rose, the draug yanked Gungnir free with its open hand and almost immediately brought it to bear against Tyr.

Did this abomination mock them?

Odin rose. He had had more than enough of this *thing*.

Calling upon Audr, Odin stepped in the Penumbra, vanishing from sight. The draug hesitated for a moment, turning to look for him, it's motions slowing as if it moved through a bog. It was all the time Odin needed. He shoulder-slammed into the creature, knocking it to the ground.

Tyr was on the undead in an instant, driving his blade through its face. "My lord ..." Tyr's breath came in pants. "I think I hate draugar."

Odin retrieved Gungnir. "Then what say we kill a few more?"

"What have you done?" a woman shouted.

Odin and Tyr both spun at her voice. The woman wore a form-fitting black dress, slit to leave her thighs bare. With her long golden hair, she might have been intoxicating, if not for the troll-skull mask that obscured most of her face.

"Grimhild," Odin said. Queen of the Niflungar, and the reason for all of this. Once, she had tried to seduce him with flesh and foul Art. Now, she moved to strike them down.

Two more of the bone-armored draugar flanked the woman. They interposed themselves between the Aesir and the sorceress queen.

"Where is it?" Grimhild demanded.

Odin looked at Tyr, who shrugged. "What?" Odin asked. "Your soul? I suspect you traded that long ago."

Tyr advanced on the bone draugar. "I will handle these things, my lord. Finish her."

Two of them? Odin had to admire Tyr's bravado. "No. We do this together."

"Yes," Grimhild said. "Die together!"

The draugar charged forward, one at each of them.

He had no time for this. Odin stepped again into the Penumbra. The draug hesitated an instant, then, through Odin's Sight, snapped into focus once again and began heading right for him.

"Well, damn," Odin mumbled. Apparently draugar could return to the Penumbra or had something along the lines of the Sight.

He stepped back to the Mortal Realm. The uselessness of his ploy did not stop Audr from tightening his grasp around Odin's mind, like a serpent slithering its way up his spine and into his brain. It took all his will to beat the wraith down.

"Kill them!" Grimhild shouted.

Odin felt the air condense, then twisted to the side as an icicle the size of a spear launched from Grimhild at his head.

Fighting both wraith and draug would prove too much —one of them would have him.

And then a wave of heat crashed over Odin at nigh to the same instant a horrendous crash rent the air. The rush of wind threw him and the draug both to the ground. Odin could hear naught but the high-pitched whine now filling his ears. He tried to push himself up, but only managed to roll over.

Had Grimhild ...?

The draug by Tyr was now a pile of smoldering bone. The mist had burned away to steam in a clearing ten paces around the pile, and everyone, Grimhild and the other draug included, was struggling to regain their feet.

Everyone save Loki, who stood with his arms wide, looking over the scene. He held a torch in each hand, though one had gone out.

"B-brother?" Odin mumbled.

Loki spoke, but Odin couldn't make out any words over the whine in his ears. How had Loki done that? Odin had never asked what power the apple had given him. Or was this some fell sorcery? At the moment, it didn't matter.

The draug engaging Odin regained his feet even before him, once again advancing.

Odin grabbed Gungnir, drawing in its strength, using it to help him fight back Audr. His hearing returned with it, albeit slowly.

As the draug advanced on Odin, Loki stepped up beside him, tossing away the extinguished torch. From the other, flames began to spin, then leap and dance up Loki's arm, coalescing into a ball in his opposite hand.

Gods above and below, he looked like some horror born of Muspelheim.

"Go and face her," Loki said. "I will hold off the fallen Bragning champion."

The draug lunged at Loki, but Odin's blood brother spun, whipping flame around in an arc. The creature immediately fell back, clearly frightened by the fires. Flame. Enemy of Mist, as Niflheim and Muspelheim annihilated each other. Lessons Gudrun had taught him swept through the back of Odin's mind.

Loki had bought him time. Time enough to finish Grimhild, and that was what he needed to do.

Tyr was trying to rise, but his strength had failed him. It fell to Odin. Without another look, Odin ran for the sorceress queen. Loki could clearly take care of himself.

Grimhild had regained her feet as well, her gaze drawn by Loki and the final bone draug's standoff. As Odin neared, she turned to him, her hatred magnified. Not a hint of fear. Not yet. "I will finish you myself."

Odin advanced on her. "Surrender now, sorceress. Your army is occupied, and you cannot hope to overcome me alone."

"Fool. How do you think I built an army?" Grimhild vanished, disappearing into the mist.

Odin immediately embraced Sight, revealing her location, and continued his slow advance. "You cannot hide from me."

"I am the chosen of Hel. I need not hide." Grimhild reached a hand toward him.

Odin rolled to the side as another icicle spear launched from Grimhild's hand.

"You think immortality enough, my little king?" Grimhild asked. "You think you know aught of the Art?"

Something slammed into him from behind, knocking him to his knees. He turned and saw the mist itself had coalesced into a club that again swung at him. Odin dove to the side, then roared in pain as an icicle lanced through his side. He scrambled away, trailing blood in the snow, and looked to Loki, still engaged with the draug, though he cast a glance Odin's way.

No. This was Odin's fight. He had to deal with the queen himself.

The Niflungar and their foul goddess had done this, all of it. They had sent Ymir against Borr to test Odin. Because of that, Odin had lost father and brother and more brothers- and sisters-in-arms than he could count. Grimhild had threatened his people and his family and his very soul.

It ended now.

Odin had to protect what was left. What was most precious. His blood.

Thunder rumbled in the sky above. Valkyries, perhaps, keen to finally claim Odin's soul. They would have to return disappointed. He was not done yet.

Odin clutched Gungnir. Handed down from his father and father's father and before. The weapon of his ancestors, the last line of defense for his children.

"You threaten my people! My *family*!" Odin shouted at the sorceress.

"I will tear them from Midgard! I will rend your soul from your body! I will see trolls feast on your children!" She raised her arms, and hundreds of icicles began to swirl about her in a twister.

The sorceress advanced, tree branches shredding as she walked through them.

Odin gritted his teeth. There was no getting through that barrier. There was no fighting such a thing. But if this sorceress thought to threaten his children she would learn there was *naught* that would stop him from killing her. He reversed his grip on Gungnir and flung it right for her.

It hurtled like a bolt of lightning through the air, cutting through Grimhild's twister of death. And Odin charged right in after it. Grimhild leapt to the side, trying to avoid the spear. It flew so fast it slashed open her shoulder. Her barrier slowed for an instant and Odin jumped right through it. Ice blades ripped open a thousand cuts along his body and might have shredded him completely were it not for the mail he wore.

Odin roared through the pain. "My family! My wife! My son!"

He landed on top of Grimhild and slammed her into the ground. Then he pounded his fist into her bone helm again and again, until the troll skull cracked and splintered. Blood seeped from innumerable cuts and gashes covering him. But that was all right. It now poured from Grimhild's broken nose and split lip as well.

"You want a war?" Odin shouted at her. "You want a war!" He pounded a fist into her ribs which snapped with a satisfying crack. The woman gasped, choking on her own blood as Odin hefted her off the ground. "Know who wins a war? The one who won't fucking quit!" He slammed his fist straight down. Her troll skull mask shattered and she fell to the ground in a heap.

Odin kicked her, sending her flying away. This was going to end. He was done looking over his shoulder, done waiting for death to come to those he loved. Father was gone. Ve was gone. Odin would not lose anyone else.

Then, as Odin looked up, he realized he still held the Sight. And it revealed Gudrun, perhaps thinking she was hidden in the mist. Watching, clutching a tree as Odin beat her mother to death with his bare hands.

For a moment he looked at the princess, and she at him. Gudrun started, clearly realizing Odin had spotted her. When he looked back to Grimhild, the sorceress was gone. Odin spun, keeping his Sight up, but all he saw was Gudrun, who looked as shocked as he did, and an unkindness of ravens taking flight.

Odin closed the distance between them at a sprint and grabbed Gudrun, pressing her against a tree. "Where is she?"

"She transformed into ravens," Gudrun said, pointing at a flock of the birds flying away. "I didn't know she could do that ... I have no idea what vaettr she must have bound to ..."

Odin gritted his teeth and pressed the princess harder against the tree until she gasped in pain. Maybe he ought to kill this Niflung, as well. Maybe he ought to kill them all. He'd do aught to protect the family that remained to him.

"You should not have let her escape, Odin," Gudrun said.

"I would not have!" Not if Gudrun had not caught his attention, if only for an instant.

But then, Gudrun had not actually interfered. She had just tried to watch the battle, thinking herself hidden. Had she wanted to see her mother die? What kind of daughter did that make her?

Odin dropped Gudrun, who sank to her knees and rubbed her chest. Gudrun was a sorceress, her mother's daughter, and heir to his enemies. She had come to take Odin away with the draugar, and if Loki and Sigyn had not come to his rescue, he might well be back in that dungeon. But then, he'd only escaped the dungeon in the first place because of Gudrun. The twisted girl loved him, or thought she did. Sick as she was, maybe she *still* imagined some kind of future between them. And despite himself, in his darkest moments, Odin did so as well.

With a sigh, he knelt beside her and placed a hand on her cheek. "You should be gone from this place, Gudrun. Do not pursue me further. If you—or your family—continue to prove a threat to *mine*, you will find out just who the son of Borr truly is. Today was the last of my mercy, Niflung. If I see you again, I'll kill you."

Odin rose, turning his back on Gudrun.

He wanted to look to her, to see her face one more time. To see her safely slink away into the mists.

But he didn't look back. Not once.

PART V

Ninth Moon, Cusp of Summer

58

*A*nother night had passed without sign of troll or draugar. The Aesir had left Idavollir behind, and Odin hoped never to see the jotunn fortress again. With Grimhild fled, he and Tyr had been able to dispatch the remaining draugar.

But no pursuit came.

Nor had he seen sign of either Loki or his woman. Hints of the Sight told him they faced danger, but Odin could not leave the Aesir, not now, not to go chasing after them. Not even after they had done so for him. He was a king, and his people needed him. And so he marched them on, offering the king—emperor as the South Realmer fashioned himself —of Valland plunder from Hunaland in exchange for safe passage.

And after long days and longer nights, they had come at last to what Idunn called the Middle Sea. From here, they followed the coast and passed through more mountains, to Andalus, a country sparsely populated, though torn by war.

And at last they reached the ocean. Nigh to half a moon on the seashore, and though Odin's people remained huddled around their bonfires, he could at last feel the tension begin to seep out of them. Indeed, a full night's sleep had done wonders for them all.

And though dawn had only just broken, already the shipwrights were again at work on the longships that lined the beach. Dozens of them, a fleet unlike any the Aesir had ever built or ever needed. Many of the tribes had built longships for raiding, but never before on this scale. Ships with which to cross the sea and reach the fabled islands of the blessed—Vanaheim. Odin had grown up believing it the home of the gods. He supposed it was, insofar as the Vanir were his people's gods.

Except now, staring over the endless ocean, it had begun to seem ... real. So much of völvur wisdom and legend Odin had dismissed as superstition or stories having naught to do with him. He thought himself a man of the real world. But everything they had been through since his father's murder, that had proved far too real. The World was a wider place than he had credited, and the Otherworlds stranger and more hostile than even völvur imagined. And though watching the fervent passion with which his people built these ships made him proud, it was also a subtle reminder that he didn't really know what else might be real.

Vanaheim. It was an idea, a myth. The islands of spring. What would that even look like? Like the tree Idunn had sent into bloom so long ago, the spark that had started this whole sojourn? The idea seemed ludicrous, nor could Odin's mind even picture an entire land looking like that, save perhaps in dreams. And that was it—they planned to sail toward a dream.

Another moon at most, and the ships would be ready. They would leave the shores of Midgard and with them the mists of Niflheim. And, if Odin had his way, most of his people would never see those cursed vapors again. Vanaheim ought to put them beyond the reach of the Niflungar forever.

Well within reach of the Vanir, unfortunately.

He felt Idunn approach. Perhaps it was his own expanding senses, the apple continuing to interact with the energies he had drawn from Frigg and Gudrun. Or maybe it was Idunn herself, the goddess of spring, of youth. Maybe she had always radiated such energy, and Odin had been too blind to see it until now, with his Sight honed by his trek beyond death, such things were laid plain before him.

"Do they know we are coming?" he asked without looking back at her.

"Hmmm ... doubtful. I mean, most of them don't bother paying much attention to Midgard anymore. But they'll know when we get there. Njord does watch all the harbors and the seas and fancies them his domain. Sometimes he calls up mermaids to sing for him, grand performances. They light up the entire bay for it. My favorite—"

"Idunn."

"Huh. Right. You're not interested in the mer."

Odin rubbed his face. Mermaids? The idea was interesting, but he couldn't afford to get distracted by Idunn's latest fascination. Yesterday the goddess had been teaching his people to train snow rabbits to carry messages around camp. When Odin pointed out that a human runner could do the same task more quickly and accurately, Idunn had only said that messenger bunnies were cuter. And in those words Odin had seen something deeper in her—her mercurial nature was not *all* an act, but it was, in part an affected illusion much like she had used to hide from the varulfur, so long ago.

"I'm interested in keeping my people safe. Will they be, Idunn? Safe in Vanaheim?"

Odin had driven himself nigh to madness trying to reach the Vanir's homeland. He had lost so much himself, and his people, they had lost even more. Fewer than half of their original number remained.

Now, Vanaheim and Yggdrasil were the only hope to save the rest of his people, and to save Odin's children from the World which Odin would have otherwise bequeathed them.

"Oh, yes. It's wonderful, Odin. Blue sea and blue sky, grass so green you just have to dance in it. It's completely safe. Other than the Vanir themselves."

That drew a snort from him. The home of the gods was great—as long as the gods weren't home. Odin shook his head and made his way farther down the beach.

He had slain his own brother. And oft as he looked into the Penumbra, never had he seen Ve's shade. Perhaps Ve had already been drawn on to the Roil, or even beyond, to the unknown Realms. Or worse, maybe Ve was still paying the price for Odin's mistakes, suffering in eternal torment. Life was agony, but now Odin knew, death was even worse.

The valkyrie Svanhit's ring was a hot weight in his pouch. He could call upon her and demand to know his brother's urd, but, even if she knew the answer, it would change naught. And Odin could not afford to sacrifice the one favor the valkyrie might grant him on a single, vain question. Once, he would have done so, yes, but no longer.

Solemn and bitter, he made his way to where Frigg sat on a rock, little Thor propped in her arms, staring out over the sea.

The varulfur twins played in the sand nearby, innocent as ever. Frigg had told him he'd missed their first words. Geri had called Fulla "ma," a scene that had apparently set the redheaded maid into a fit of laughing and tears. Freki, more amusingly, had called Vili "ma," and *that* Odin truly regretted missing. He would not miss Thor's first words. This he swore to himself.

"Our kingdom is out there," she said to the babe, "just waiting for us." Frigg spun at his approach.

Odin held up a placating hand. He hadn't meant to startle her. "It *is* out there."

Frigg nodded at him, then fell silent, rocking Thor. Neither spoke for a long time. Odin couldn't think of the words he wanted to say, couldn't give voice to the feelings so pent up inside him.

At last, he sank down to the sand beside his wife and took Thor from her. "He'll never see him." Odin's voice almost broke. Pain swelled inside his chest, threatening to consume him, until he wanted to weep like a woman. To let break the dam holding back the tide, to not be king, not be the leader the Aesir had to look up to, if only for a moment. But that luxury no longer remained to him, and would never be his again.

Frigg slipped off the rock and sat beside him, clearly sensing Odin's mood. "Who?"

"My father. He'll never hold his grandson."

In answer, Frigg leaned against his shoulder. "Maybe. But he does see him, Odin. You who have looked into the Realms beyond cannot doubt that. Borr—and my father as well—they do see us. Every day."

Odin had seen the Penumbra, had walked there, had fought a valkyrie, and had seen the innumerable ghosts that haunted all the old places of this world. But he had never seen Valhalla. He had not seen his ancestors smiling upon him. He hadn't ever seen his father there. As he did not see Ve.

All he had seen was darkness and hunger.

Fuck, but he wanted to call Svanhit and ask her ... ask her what? To change the nature of reality?

He, a man making himself a god, still could not change that. He could not alter the past, could not bring back the dead, could not have back his father. He would never regain his brother. Even gods were not given all the things they might want. Not everything. Not really.

Buri, Odin's grandfather, had never seen Odin. His son, Odin's father, would never see Thor.

Maybe Loki was right, maybe the visions would consume him. But it was so easy to just ... just escape ...

BORR HELD his newborn son in one arm, the other hand gently rubbing Bestla's forehead. "What shall we name him?"

Bestla laughed weakly. "You're so convinced you can make a better World for him? He's a sign of it, then. Call him Odin—the prophet."

Borr chuckled to himself, staring at his beautiful new son. Odin. Little Odin, prophet of the World that Borr would build in his honor. In Buri's honor. "Look," Borr said. "I think he likes the name."

"Of course he does," Bestla said. "I have a hint of the Sight."

Borr chuckled and ran his thumb over his son's head. His son, a prophet, heir to a grand future.

"He has your father's hair," Bestla said. "And his eyes."

ODIN SHUDDERED, clutching his heart. Was it the apple that had given him over to such introspection? Was it immortality? Or maybe the change was deeper in him, helped along by the transformation wrought by the apple, but not caused by it. How much his life had changed since then. A short time perhaps to grow from being a selfish, arrogant child to a man, a king who must lead an entire people. And a father himself.

And he had never known his grandfather, but ... But he had Buri's eyes? As he saw his own father in Thor, his father had seen Buri in Odin. Circles, patterns of fathers and sons all just trying to do right by one another.

Frigg, gods bless her, made no comment on his emotional display, instead keeping her head on his shoulder, eyes looking out there. As Odin so often did. "I had a vision," she said after a long pause. "The future, I think. The day you and I first met, I saw us there, in Vanaheim, ruling as king and queen. Spring was all around us, and we sat in thrones, looking over a grand city. I didn't understand what any of it meant. Not until you gave me the apple and told me of your plan to take Vanaheim. It was the first time I realized where we were in that vision. And we had taken the islands. We will succeed."

Odin handed her the babe, while she turned to face him more directly. It wouldn't do for anyone else to see him so morose. Odin couldn't afford to be just a man. Probably, while he'd been away, Frigg had felt the same, felt herself forced to be a symbol. Not a mere woman, but a queen. Even now, even in front of him, she didn't show it. But he suspected her time ruling the Aesir had worn on her. Maybe that meant she alone could understand the burdens he bore. His father must have felt those burdens, albeit only as a jarl.

"Did the apple make your visions stronger?"

She shook her head. "I don't think so. I still get the visions, but they're so hard to make sense of. Once, I saw Thor grown. Big redheaded giant of a man, a warrior. I'm sure it was him."

"How?"

"A mother knows."

Odin understood all too well. These days, he too sometimes simply knew things. Indeed, Frigg's instincts might well prove a boon.

"I'm afraid," she said after a moment.

The stark, blatant statement froze Odin. Frigg, who seemed to pride herself on poise and control—Frigg, who seemed ashamed to even hint at her true emotions, she would bluntly confide in him? Maybe that scared him, too.

"Of the future?"

"So many of my visions are dark, violent. Men dying by the thousands. And ... Thor. Thor died in one of my visions —at least I think he did."

"I will *not* let that happen!" Odin slapped his knee. "That is *why* we are taking Vanaheim. I'm going to put an end to the darkness covering our future."

It is our children we must do right by.

And Odin would, at any cost.

Frigg rocked the babe who had begun to bawl at Odin's outburst. She cooed at him, speaking to Odin in a soft whisper. "If we will take Vanaheim, why do my visions show more war, husband? Like destruction follows in our wake."

In their wake? Or in his? Odin was going to ignite a war between the Aesir and Vanir. But it would be the last war.

"I'm going to build something that will last for millennia."

"And to do it, you're going to destroy a kingdom that has lasted for five."

Odin rose, not wanting to hear Frigg's words. She spoke the truth, sure enough. Too much of it, perhaps, or not enough. Maybe he did have to burn down the World around him. Maybe more would die before he could build his paradise. But that was the only way forward.

The only way he could finally save his people, the only way to ensure Frigg's vision for Thor never came to pass. The only way to protect the things that mattered the most.

And what mattered most? People. The people he had left and the memories of those who had gone before.

All of them, born up together in a beautiful mess of dreams and pain and hope. And blood.

Blood binding him back to his ancestors and down into his children. Forever.

59

*I*f Gudrun had not returned to Castle Niflung, Grimhild would have sent Mist spirits to find her, sooner or later. And Gudrun needed time, the chance to peruse the grimoire in privacy. Given her mother's injuries fighting Odin, it hadn't been hard to sneak back to the Ás fortress and retrieve the tome.

Locked in her tower room, Gudrun stared at the mysterious pages once again. Of course, her efforts were as fruitless as always. The book was written in more than one hand, as she had suspected. The problem, however, was that many of the languages were so foreign she couldn't even begin to guess what the symbols meant. Some looked like the runic script of the Old Kingdoms, but others, especially the older writings, featured characters unlike aught she'd known. Diagrams depicted spirit glyphs, those she could recognize. But without understanding the notes surrounding those glyphs, she'd have no way to know what spirit a glyph might call upon, nor how to perfect the spells tied to it.

With a sigh of frustration, she slammed the book closed.

All this effort, and for what? A tome she couldn't read. Grimhild's secrets were still denied to her. Though, watching Odin beat the woman to a pulp had granted Gudrun some small satisfaction—satisfaction she'd been damned sure to keep off her face when she returned and saw Grimhild still bearing the remnants of two black eyes and a broken nose. Healing was not one of the stronger gifts of the Niflungar, after all. Hel took life—she didn't restore it. Grimhild could accelerate her healing by calling upon power from a spirit bound to her, but that became a spiral down toward possession.

Hljod, whom Gudrun had been teaching to read primers, jumped as Gudrun slammed the book. Gudrun waved the girl off. "All is well. How go your studies?"

"It's ... hard."

Gudrun smiled at that. Hljod had wanted power, the power to never be afraid again. Not of trolls or man. Sorcery was a step in that direction, though even Gudrun had things she still feared. Most of all, sorcery itself, she supposed, but she would teach the girl all she could, spare her whatever horrors she might.

A rapid pounding on her door sent Gudrun's heart racing before she could answer the girl. There was no way Grimhild could know she had the book. How could she? How had she found out? Vaettir? Would they search even here? It was impossible. Get a grip, Gudrun. Coincidence. It had to be coincidence.

She stuffed the book behind a pillow and scrambled to open the door.

Her mother stood there, glaring.

Hel, she knew. Gudrun started to glance at the book. Was a corner sticking out behind that pillow? What was she doing? Looking right at the indication of her guilt?

"You took so long I thought you might have another man up here," Grimhild said. Then looked pointedly at Hljod.

"I'm teaching my apprentice to read."

Grimhild rolled her eyes. "Come along." At that she spun and began descending the stairs from the tower.

Gudrun motioned for Hljod to wait in the room and followed her mother out. The farther they got, the more Gudrun's heart calmed. If Grimhild had even suspected Gudrun had the book, her fury would have been immediately apparent. Whatever the queen wanted now, it did not relate to that book.

Grimhild led her toward the dungeons, through long cells to the Pit—a hole in the dungeons, one some claimed had no bottom. Prisoners who sufficiently offended the Niflungar were cast down into that abyss, to fall, some claimed forever.

What was the point, really? Why not just kill the poor bastards with a sword? Oh, but then, she knew the point. It was the fear—fear of the unknown, fear of the darkness, of the drop, probably worked better as a motivator than fear of something so mundane as a sword.

As now, when iron chains suspended Sigyn over the pit. Grimhild had stripped the Ás woman naked and had draugar torture her for days on end, though, as far as Gudrun could tell, the queen had no questions for the girl. She had believed Gudrun's lie that Sigyn had given the book to Frigg, and for it, Grimhild wanted not answers, but revenge. Given time and creativity, even this torment was like to pale before what final end the queen wrought upon Sigyn, unless Gudrun managed to convince her otherwise. Dead, Sigyn offered less way to control Loge and his Ás pets.

Rivulets of blood still ran down the girl's body, occasionally dropping into the abyss. A gag silenced her, though she stared at both Gudrun and Grimhild with loathing. But then, a sorceress was used to being hated by most of those she dealt with, human or otherwise. Still, given how quickly this girl healed, any but the most recent injuries would have sealed themselves.

"What are we doing here?" Gudrun asked. "Are you still torturing this wretch?"

Grimhild frowned, then touched a wall. No markings separated it from the rest of the corridor, but as Grimhild touched it, the wall slid backward, dust tumbling from cracks that must not have opened in years.

The queen took a lantern from the dungeon wall, then descended yet another staircase. Deeper and deeper they climbed until Gudrun thought they must be as far below ground as the castle's towers stretched above it.

"Ever wonder what lies beneath the Pit?" Grimhild asked as the stairs finally ended at an iron-banded door. She took a key from a ring at her belt and unlocked it.

Gudrun frowned and followed her mother. Below the Pit ... Yes, she had wondered and assumed all that lay down here was bodies. Bodies splattered after falling hundreds of feet into a darkened cavern.

The hall wound around a bend and led to yet another iron door, this one a grate, though Gudrun could see naught in the darkness beyond it.

"The Pit," Grimhild said, "is the real dungeon."

"There are more prisoners down here?" Had some survived this fall? It sounded impossible—but then, so had Odin leaping out an eighth-story window and walking away.

"There is one."

Grimhild unlocked the gate and slid it into the wall, then entered a massive cavern beyond. Gudrun hadn't been able to see this because it was simply too large for the light to fill.

The place seemed roughly circular, with an outer ledge surrounding yet another pit. Once again, Gudrun could not see the bottom of it. As Grimhild approached the gap, a bridge of stone grew out of the floor beneath her, forming an archway to an island far distant.

What in Hel's name did Grimhild keep down here that needed such security? Reluctantly, Gudrun followed Grimhild. Fear of what Grimhild would do if she disobeyed outweighed fear of whatever waited beyond, but only just.

The lantern light cast flickering shadows over the stone floor as Grimhild walked forward.

Something moved ahead, with the sound of iron dragging on stone.

Chains, Gudrun realized as she drew nearer: chains of a man with both arms bound to opposite ends of the platform, although both with enough slack he could rise and even walk toward them. In the darkness, she could not make out his features, though she could see he was naked.

"Why keep this man here?"

"Some tools are too valuable to discard, even if they are hard to control. And it is not a man, daughter. This is the first and greatest of the varulfur, progenitor and ultimate ancestor of their bloodline in Midgard. A foe so implacable even the Vanir feared him. This is Fenrir."

Grimhild pulled a tattered shirt from beneath her cloak. A shirt that had once belonged to Odin when he had stayed in this place so long ago. She tossed the shirt at Fenrir's feet. "Come, wolf. Smell your prey."

EPILOGUE

*L*ong had Loki flown in swan form, heading ever back into the far north, back toward Reidgotaland, and toward the island of Samsey the Niflungar called home. He had not thought to return to this place any time soon, but now he had no choice. Odin would be looking for him, Loki knew, and would face hard choices and dangers without his guidance, but Loki could not turn back.

His visions had failed him once, allowing the Niflungar to capture Sigyn and manage to carry her so far off. The had borne her through dark troll tunnels where he could not easily follow in person nor in vision. But now they had reached open ground in their homeland.

He saw them.

The Sight would not fail him again.

Pyromancy, as all divination, could focus the Sight and reveal other times and other places. As now, the visions danced in the bonfire, unfolding images beneath Castle Niflung. Loki knew all too well what monstrosity they kept down there and what havoc the first varulf might wreak upon Midgard. Such things were concerns for another time, carefully hidden away until he could take steps to deal with them.

Some things, however, could not be borne.

The fire surged with his anger, leaping high into the night sky even as Grimhild led her foul daughter into the Pit, as the fires revealed Sigyn suspended there, bloody, frightened, and alone. Deep down, she had thought herself safe, thought Loki could never allow harm to befall her, and, in that confidence, had overstepped her abilities. It only made things worse that through her sacrifice she had, in effect, saved Odin and thus all of the Aesir, all of those for whom Loki himself had taken responsibility.

And now she shivered. And a tear dripped down her cheek as the Niflung queen and princess disappeared into darkness.

Loki roared into the night, unable to contain his rage. And from that unquenchable fury the bonfire expanded, doubled in size, and swept outward in a ring of fire that obliterated mist and darkness.

As Loki himself would soon do.

Gudrun had taken from him the one thing Loki could not live without. And in so doing, the Niflungar had sown the seeds of an inferno that would rise to annihilate all who stood in its way, until at last, the Children of Mist trembled before the rising conflagration.

The flames would soon spread, and, as with the end of all things, naught but ash would remain.

THE CYCLE CONTINUES ...

Next Book: Odin has reached Vanaheim ready to overthrow his gods. But he never expected to find the love of his life among their number.

The Shores of Vanaheim: books2read.com/mlshores

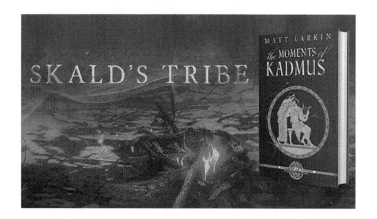

Join the Skalds' Tribe newsletter and get access to exclusive insider information and your FREE copy of *The Moments of Kadmus*.

https://www.mattlarkinbooks.com/skalds/

ABOUT THE AUTHOR

Matt Larkin writes retellings of mythology as dark, gritty fantasy. His passions of myths, philosophy, and history inform his series. He strives to combine gut-wrenching action with thought-provoking ideas and culturally resonant stories.

Matt's mythic fantasy takes place in the Eschaton Cycle universe, a world—as the name implies—of cyclical apocalypses. Each series can be read alone in any order, but they weave together to form a greater tapestry.

Learn more at mattlarkinbooks.com or connect with Matt through his fan group, the Skalds' Tribe:

https://www.mattlarkinbooks.com/skalds/

AUTHOR'S NOTE

Anyone writing historical fiction has to find a balance between historical accuracy and accessibility to modern readers. Writing historical fantasy, this becomes equally true. For example, in earlier versions of the books, I used the measurements "handspans" and "fathoms" instead of feet. Those measurements would have been more historically accurate to Norse cultures, so I *wanted* to use them. The problem was, a reader then had to figure out first, how big a handspan is, and then convert that into feet or meters for it to have any inherent meaning. This extra level of detail actually detracted from the fictional dream by forcing most people to stop and think about things they shouldn't have had to think about.

You also have to carefully balance the use of modern diction—again for accessibility—and period accuracy. Consider: while the word "fuck" has a long history in English, the common usage as an adjective ("fucking huge") is very modern. On the other hand, this usage produces a visceral reaction in modern readers that could never be generated by any substitute. Any attempt to generate this same feeling with another word has to be so close in use and sound ("frakking cylons!") that everyone knows exactly what you mean and you should have just fucking said it ... or forces you substitute in an in-world made up profanity with no emotion attached to it. So you kind of take the stance that the characters are not exactly speaking English anyway, and focus on conveying meaning and emotion, while trying to avoid anachronisms as much as possible.

Adapting mythology comes with its own issues. The original stories don't always fit well within the constraints of any realistic tale, much less the framework of dark fantasy I use throughout my Eschaton stories. A story in which Thor causes the tides by drinking half the ocean stretches verisimilitude way beyond the breaking point.

These very limitations can, in fact, spark creativity. They can force me to reinterpret (or offer simple nods to) the original stories that, I hope, offer additional entertainment to those familiar with the source material (but never require that familiarity).

In Loki we see a prototypical trickster god (and possibly a fire god) with strong parallels to certain deities in other cultures. In later Norse mythology his role changed and become more and more demonized, possibly because of influence from contact with Christians. In *The Ragnarok Era*, I treat Loki as a much more morally ambiguous figure (which I think is true to early Norse sources), and almost as an anti-hero. He is, as in traditional myth, Odin's blood brother—but in his machinations we can see the seeds of mistrust that will one day grow between them.

In *The Mists of Niflheim* we reach the middle of the beginning as Odin attempts his march toward Vanaheim. As I mentioned in *The Apples of Idunn*, this original premise came from the *Prose Edda*. This book also shows a bit more of the early *Volsung Saga* which will play out more over time.

Once again, special thanks to my family, and to Brenda, Clark, and Fred, all of who's input was invaluable in crafting this book. Also, thanks to Clarissa for an awesome reimagined cover.

Thank you for reading,
    Matt

For Robert Lane Larkin. I miss you, Dad.